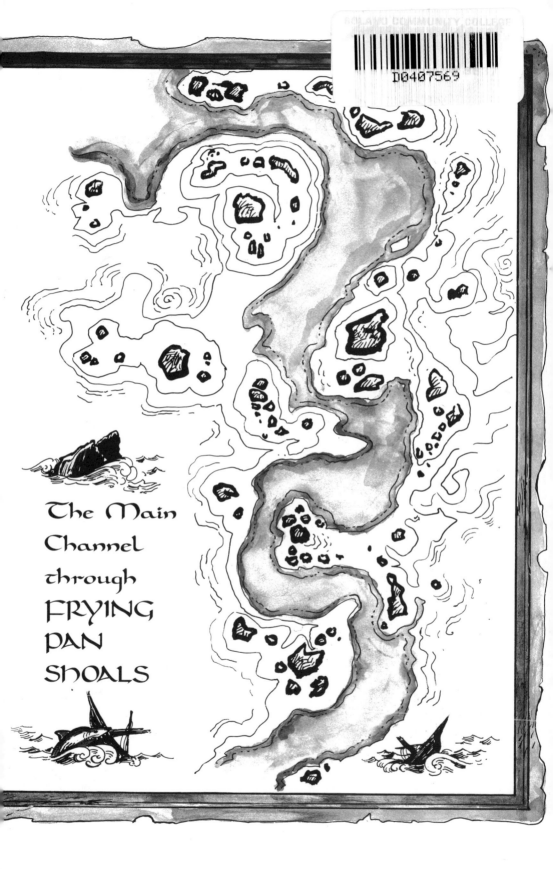

The Main
Channel
through
FRYING
PAN
SHOALS

Among the Many Classic Works by L. Ron Hubbard

★*Dekalogy—a group of ten volumes*

L. RON HUBBARD

BRIDGE PUBLICATIONS, INC., LOS ANGELES

Library of Congress Cataloging in Publication Data
Hubbard, L. Ron (Lafayette Ron), 1911 - 1986
    Slaves of Sleep and The Masters of Sleep
    1. Fiction, American. I. Title
    ISBN 0-88404-655-9

Publisher's Note

This is the first time that L. Ron Hubbard's fantasy novel, *Slaves of Sleep* and its sequel, *The Masters of Sleep*, have been published in a single volume. Though published years apart, both novels chronicle the adventures of Jan Palmer in the parallel worlds of Earth and the Land of the Jinn.

"Slaves of Sleep" was published originally in the July, 1939, issue of *Unknown*—the most celebrated and respected fantasy magazine of its day. The long-awaited follow-up, "The Masters of Sleep" appeared in the October, 1950, issue of *Fantastic Adventures*.

Fantasy was just one of the many genres in which Mr. Hubbard excelled during his long and productive career as a professional writer. During his lifetime, he wrote over 260 novels, novelettes, short stories, screen plays and dramatic works encompassing a wide variety of subjects.

He initially established his reputation as an author of fast-paced adventure, detective and western fiction. Later, he wrote innovative science fiction and fantasy stories that gave new directions to these genres and established him as one of the founders of the Golden Age of Science Fiction.

In 1980, in celebration of his 50th anniversary as a professional writer, L. Ron Hubbard returned to the genre of science fiction and completed one of the biggest and most popular science fiction novels ever written: *Battlefield Earth*. L. Ron Hubbard's masterpiece of comic satire, the 1.2 million word *Mission Earth* dekalogy (a set of 10 books), was published between 1985 and 1987. *Battlefield Earth* and each volume of the *Mission Earth* series became New York Times and international bestsellers and continue to appear on bestseller lists throughout the world.

Bridge Publications has begun a twenty-five year publishing undertaking to rerelease all of L. Ron Hubbard's many classic works of fiction. A number of these, including *Buckskin Brigades, Final Blackout, Fear* and *Ole Doc Methuselah* have already been published, each with a companion audio edition.

Included among the future releases are:

The Adventure of "X"
Arctic Wings
The Automagic Horse
The Baron of Coyote River
Battle of Wizards
Battling Bolto
The Beast
Beyond All Weapons
Brass Keys to Murder
Cargo of Coffins
The Carnival of Death
The Crossroads
Dead Men Kill
Empty Saddles
False Cargo
Flaming Arrows
Forbidden Gold
The Ghoul
Golden Hell
Guns of Mark Jardine
He Didn't Like Cats
Hot Lead Payoff
The Hurricane's Roar
The Invaders
Killer's Law
Loot of the Shanung

The Magic Quirt
Man for Breakfast
A Matter of Matter
Medals for Mahoney
Mr. Tidwell, Gunner
One Was Stubborn
Orders Is Orders
The Planet Makers
Plans for the Boy
The Professor Was a Thief
Raiders of the Beam
Red Death over China
The Room
Sea Fangs
Silent Pards
Six-Gun Caballero
Sleepy McGee
Space Can
Spykiller
Tough Old Man
The Tramp
Twenty Fathoms Down
Vengeance Is Mine!
Yukon Madness
When Shadows Fall
Wind-Gone-Mad

THE PUBLISHERS

Contents

L. RON HUBBARD

Preface

A word . . . to the curious reader:

There are many persons in these skeptical times who affect to deride everything connected with the occult sciences, or black art; who have no faith in the efficacy of conjurations, incantations or divinations; and who stoutly contend that such things never had existence. To such determined unbelievers, the testimony of the past ages is as nothing; they require the evidence of their own senses, and deny that such arts and practices have prevailed in days of yore, simply because they meet with no instances of them in the present day. They cannot perceive that, as the world became versed in the natural sciences, the supernatural became superfluous and fell into disuse; and that the hardy inventions of art superseded the mysteries of man. Still, say the enlightened few, those mystic powers exist, though in a latent state, and untasked by the ingenuity of man. A talisman is still a talisman, possessing all its indwelling and awful properties; though it may have lain dormant for ages at the bottom of the sea, or in the dusty cabinet of the antiquary. The signet of Solomon the Wise, for instance, is well known to have held potent control over genii, demons and enchantments; now who will positively assert that the same mystic signet, wherever it may exist, does not at the present moment possess the same marvellous virtues which distinguished it in olden time? Let those who doubt repair to Salamanca, delve into the cave of San Cyprian, explore its hidden secrets and decide. As to those who will not be at pains to make such investigation, let them substitute faith for incredulity and receive with honest credence the foregoing legend.

So pled Washington Irving for a tale of an enchanted soldier. And in no better words could the case for the following story be presented. As for the Seal of Sulayman, look to Kirker's *Cabala Sarracenica*. As for *genii* (or more properly Jinns, Jinn or Jan) it

1

is the root for our word 'genius', so widely are these spirits recognized. A very imperfect idea of the Jinn is born of the insipid children's translation of "The Arabian Nights Entertainment" but in the original work (which is actually an Arabian history interspersed with legends) the subject is more competently treated. For the ardent researcher, Burton's edition is recommended, though, due to its being a forbidden work in these United States, it is very difficult to find. There is, however, a full set in the New York Public Library where the wise librarians have devoted an entire division to works dealing with the black arts.

Man is a very stubborn creature. He would much rather confound himself with "laws" of his own invention than to fatalistically accept perhaps truer but infinitely simpler explanations as offered by the supernatural—though it is a travesty to so group the omnipresent Jinn!

And so I commend you to your future nightmares.

L. Ron Hubbard
The Pacific Northwest
1939

Chapter 1

THE COPPER JAR

It was with a weary frown that Jan Palmer beheld Thompson standing there on the dock. Thompson, like some evil raven, never made his appearance unless to inform Jan in a somehow accusative way that business, after all, should supersede such silly trivialities as sailing. Jan was half-minded to put the flattie about and scud back across the wind-patterned Puget Sound; but he had already luffed up into the wind to carry in to the dock and Thompson had unbent enough to reach for the painter—more as an effort to detain Jan than to help him land.

Jan let go his jib and main halyards and guided the sail down into a restive bundle. He pretended not to notice Thompson, using near-sightedness as his usual excuse—for although nothing was actually wrong with his eyes, he found that glasses helped him in his uneasy maneuvers with mankind.

"The gentleman from the university is here to see you again, Mr. Palmer." Thompson scowled his reproof for such treatment of a man of learning. Everybody but Jan Palmer impressed Thompson. "He has been waiting for more than two hours."

"I wish," said Jan, "I wish you'd tell such people you don't know when I'll be back." He was taking slides from their truck, though it was not really necessary for him to unbend his sail in such weather. "I haven't anything to say to him."

"He seems to think differently. It is a shame that you can't realize the honor such people do you. If your father . . ."

"Do we have to go into that?" said Jan, fretfully. "I don't like to have to talk to such people. They . . . they make me nervous."

3

"Your father never had any such difficulties. I told him before he died that it was a mistake..."

"I know," sighed Jan. "It was a mistake. But I didn't ask to be his heir."

"A healthy man rarely leaves a will when he is still young. And you, as his son, should at least have the courtesy to see people when they search you out. It has been a week since you were even near the offices..."

"I've been busy," defended Jan.

"Busy!" said Thompson, pulling his long nose as though to keep from laughing. He had found long, long ago, when Jan was hardly big enough to feed himself, that it was no difficult matter to bully the boy since there would never be any redress. "Busy with a sailboat when fifteen Alaska liners are under your control. But you are still keeping the gentleman waiting."

"I'm not going to see him," said Jan in a tone of defiance which already admitted his defeat. "He has no real business with me. It is that model of the Arab dhow. He wants it and I can't part with it and he'll wheedle and fuss and..." He sat down on the coaming and put his face in his palms. "Oh why," he wept, "why can't people leave me alone."

"Your father would turn over in his grave if he heard that," said the remorseless Thompson. "There isn't any use of your sitting there like a spoiled child and wailing about people. This gentleman is a professor at the university and he has already looked for you for two hours. As long as you are a Palmer, people will continue to call on you. Now come along."

Resentfully, well knowing he should slam this ancient bird of a secretary into his proper position, Jan followed up the path from the beach to the huge, garden-entrenched mansion.

Theoretically the place was his, all his. But that was only theoretically. Actually it was overlorded by a whiskered grandaunt whose already sharp temper had been whetted by the recent injustice of the probate court.

4

She was waiting now, inside the door, her dark dress stiff with disapproval, her needle-point eyes sighted down her nose, ready to pick up the faint dampness of Jan's footprints.

"Jan! Don't you dare soak that rug with salt water! Indeed! One would think you had been raised on a tideflat for all the regard you have for my efforts to give you a decent home. JAN! Don't throw your cap on that table! What would a visitor think?"

"Yes, Aunt Ethel," he replied with resignation. He wished he had nerve enough to say that the house was evidently run for no one but visitors. However, he supposed that he never would. He picked up his cap and gave the rug a wide berth and somehow navigated to the hall which led darkly to his study. At the end, at least, was a sanctuary. Whatever might be said to him in the rest of the house, his own apartment was his castle. The place, in the eyes of all but himself, was such a hideous mess that it dismayed the beholder.

In all truth the place was not really disorderly. It contained a very assorted lot of furniture which Jan, with his father's indulgent permission, had salvaged from the turbulent and dusty seas of the attic. The Palmers, until now, had voyaged the world and the flotsam culled from many a strange beach had at last been cast up in these rooms. One donor in particular, a cousin who now rested in the deep off Madagascar, had had an eye for oddity, contributing the greater part of the assembled spears and head-dresses as well as the truly beautiful blackwood desk all inlaid with pearl and ivory.

This was sanctuary and it irritated Jan to find that he had yet to rid himself of a human being before he could again find any peace.

Professor Frobish raised himself from his chair and bowed deferentially. But for his following stretch, it might have been supposed that he had been two whole hours on that cushion. Jan surveyed him without enthusiasm. Indeed there was only one human being in the world whom Jan granted enthusiastic regard and she . . . well . . . that was wholly impossible. The professor was a vital sort of man, the very sort Jan distrusted the most. It would be impossible to talk such a man down.

"Mr. Palmer, I believe?"

Jan winced at the pressure of the hand and quickly recovered his own. Nervously he wandered around the table and began to pack a pipe.

"Mr. Palmer, I am Professor Frobish, the Arabianologist at the University. I hope you will forgive my intrusion. Indeed, it shows doubtlessly great temerity on my part to so take up the time of one of Seattle's most influential men."

He wants something, Jan told himself. They all want something. He lighted the pipe so as to avoid looking straight at the fellow.

"It has come to our ears that you were fortunate enough to have delivered to you a model—if you'll forgive me for coming to the point, but I know how valuable your time is. This model I understand was recovered from a Tunisian ruin and sent to your father . . ."

He went on and on but Jan was not very attentive. Jan paced restively over to the wide windows and stood contemplating the azure waters backed by the rising green of hills and, finally, by the glory of the shining, snow-capped Olympics. He wished he had been sensible enough to stay out there. Next time he would take his cabin sloop and enough food to last a day or two—but at the same time, realizing the wrath this would bring down upon him he knew that he would never do so. He turned, puffing hopelessly at his pipe, to watch the Arabianologist. Suddenly he was struck by the fact that though the man kept talking about and pointing to the model of the ancient dhow which stood upon the great blackwood desk, his interest did not lie there. On entering the room it might have but now Frobish's eye kept straying to the darkest corner of the room. What, Jan wondered, in all these trophies had excited this fervid man's greed? Certainly the professor was having a difficult time staying on his subject and wasn't making a very strong case of why the university should be presented with this valuable model.

Jan's schooling, while not flattering to humanity, was nevertheless thorough. His father, too engrossed in shipping to give much time to raising a son, had failed wholly to notice that the household used the boy to bolster up their respective prides which they perforce must humble before the elder Palmer. And, as a Palmer, it would not be fitting to give the boy a common education, he had even been spared the solace of youthful companionship. And now, at twenty-seven, he was perfectly aware of the fact that men never did anything without thought of personal gain and that when men reacted strangely they would bear much watching. This professor wanted something beside this innocent dhow.

Jan strolled around the room with seeming aimlessness. Finally, by devious routes, he arrived beside the corner which often caught Frobish's eye. But there was no enlightenment here. The only thing present was a rack of Malay swords and a very old copper jar tightly sealed with lead. The krisses were too ordinary, therefore it must be the jar. But what, pray tell, could an Arabianologist discover in such a thing? Jan had to think hard—all the while with placid, even timid countenance, to recall the history of the jar.

"And so," Frobish concluded, "you would be doing science a great favor by at least lending us this model. There is none other like it in existence and it would greatly further our knowledge of the seafaring of the ancient Arab."

It had been in Jan's mind to say no. But the fellow would stay and argue, he knew. Personally he had rather liked that little dhow with its strangely indestructible rigging.

"I guess you can have it," he said.

Frobish had not expected such an easy victory. But even so he was not much elated. He told Jan he was a benefactor of science and put the model into its teak box and then, hesitantly, reached for his hat.

"Thank you so much," he said again. "We'll not be likely to forget this service."

"That's all right," said Jan, wondering why he had given up so easily.

And still the professor lingered on small-talk excuses. At last he ran out of conversation and stood merely fumbling with his hat. Jan scented trouble. He did not know just how or why, but he did.

"This is a very interesting room," said the professor, at last. "Your people must have traveled the Seven Seas a great deal. But then they would have, of course." He gave his hat a hard twist. "Take . . . er . . . take that copper jar, for instance. A very interesting piece of work. Ancient Arab also, I presume."

Jan nodded.

"Might I be out of order to ask you where it came from?"

Jan had been remembering and he had the answer ready. And though he suddenly didn't want to talk about that copper jar he heard himself doing so.

"My father's cousin, Greg Palmer, brought it back from the Mediterranean a long time before I was born. He was always bringing things home."

"Interesting," said Frobish. "Must have been quite a fellow."

"Everybody said he wasn't much good," said Jan. He added ruefully, "I am supposed to be like him, they say. He never held any job for long but they say he could have been a millionaire a lot of times if he had tried. But he claimed money made a man put his roots down. That's one thing he never did. That's his picture on the wall there."

Frobish inspected it out of policy. "Ah, so? Well, well, I must say that he does look a great deal like you—that is, without your glasses, of course."

"He—" Jan almost said, "He's the only friend I ever had," but he swiftly changed it. "He was very good to me."

"Did—ah—did he ever say anything about that copper jar?" Frobish could hardly restrain his eagerness.

"Yes," said Jan flatly. "He did. He said it was given to him by a French seiner on the Tunisian coast."

"Is that all?"

"And when he left it here Aunt Ethel told him it was a heathen thing and that he had to put it in the attic. I used to go up and look at it sometimes and I was pretty curious about it."

"How is that?"

"He made me promise never to open it."

"What? I mean—is that so?" Frobish paced over to it and bent down as though examining it for the first time. "I see that you never did. The seal is still firmly in place."

"I might have if Greg hadn't been killed but . . ."

"Ah, yes, I understand. Sentiment." He stood up and sighed. "Well! I must be going. That's a very fine piece of work and I compliment you on your possession of it. Well, good day." But still he didn't leave. He stood with one hand on the doorknob, looking back at the jar as a bird will return the stare of a snake. "Ah—er—have you ever had any curiosity about what it might contain?"

"Of course," said Jan, "but until now I had almost forgotten about it. Ten years ago it was all I could do to keep from looking in it."

"Perhaps you thought about jewels?"

"No . . . not exactly."

Suddenly they both knew what the other was thinking about. But before they could put it into words there came a sharp rap on the door.

Without waiting for answer, a very officious little man bustled in. He stared hard at Jan and paid no attention whatever to the professor.

"I called three times," he complained.

"I was out on the Sound," said Jan, uneasily.

"There are some papers which have to have your signature," snapped the fellow, throwing a briefcase up on the blackwood desk and pulling the documents out. It was very plain that he resented having to seek Jan out at all.

Jan moved to the desk and picked up a pen. He knew that as general manager of the Bering Steamship Corporation Nathaniel Green had his troubles. And perhaps he had a perfect right to be resentful, having spent all his life in the service of the late Palmer and then having not one share of the stock left to him.

"If I could have your power of attorney I wouldn't have to come all the way out here ten and twenty times a day!" said Green. "I have ten thousand things to do and not half time enough to do them in and yet I have to play messenger boy."

"I'm sorry," said Jan.

"You might at least come down to the office."

Jan shuddered. He had tried that only to have Green browbeat him before clerks and to have dozens and dozens of people foisted off on him for interview.

Green swept the papers back into the briefcase and bustled off without another word as though the entire world of shipping was waiting on his return.

Frobish's face was flushed. He had hardly noticed the character of the interrupter. Now he came to the jar and stood with one hand on it.

"Mr. Palmer, for many years I have been keenly interested in things which . . . well, which are not exactly open to scientific speculation. It is barely possible that here, under my hand, I have a clue to a problem I have long examined—perhaps I have the answer itself. You do not censure my excitement?"

"You have researched demonology?"

"As connected with the ancient Egyptians and Arabs. I see that we understand each other perfectly. If this was found in waters off Tunisia, then it is barely possible that it is one of THE copper jars. You know about them?"

"A little."

"Very few people know much about the Jinn. They seem to have vanished from the face of the earth several centuries ago though there is every reason to suppose that they existed in historical times. Sulayman is said to have converted most of the Jinn tribes to the faith of Mohammed after a considerable war. Sulayman was an actual king and those battles are a part of his court record. This, Mr. Palmer, is not a cupid's bow on this stopper but the Seal of Sulayman!" Frobish was growing very excited. "When several tribes refused to acknowledge Mohammed as the prophet, Sulayman had them thrown into copper jars such as this, stoppered with his seal, and thrown into the sea *off the coast of Tunis!*"

"I know," said Jan, quietly.

"You knew? And yet . . . yet you did not investigate?"

"I gave my word that I would not open that jar."

"Your word. But think, man, what a revelation this would be! Who knows but what this actually contains one of those luckless Ifrits?"

Jan wandered back to his humidor and repacked his pipe. As far as he was concerned the interview was over. He might be bullied into anything but when it came to breaking his word . . . Carefully he lighted his pipe.

Frobish's face was feverish. He was straining forward toward Jan, waiting for the acquiescence he felt certain must come. And when at last he found that his own enthusiasm had failed to kindle a return blaze, he threw out his hands in a despairing gesture and marched ahead, forcing Jan back against a chair into which he slumped. Frobish towered over him.

"You can't be human!" cried Frobish. "Don't you understand the importance of this? Have you no personal curiosity whatever?

Are you made of wax that you can live for years in the company with a jar which might very well contain the final answer to the age-old question of demonology? For centuries men have maundered on the subject of witches and devils. Recently it became fashionable to deny their existence entirely and to answer all strange phenomena with 'scientific facts' actually no more than bad excuses for learning. Men even deny telepathy in face of all evidence. Once whole civilizations were willing to burn their citizens for witchcraft but now the reference to devils and goblins brings forth only laughter. But down deep in our hearts, we *know* there is more than a fair possibility that such things exist. And here, man, you have a possible answer! If all historical records are correct then that jar contains an Ifrit. And if it does, think, man, what the Jinn could tell us! According to history, they were versed in all the black arts. Today we know nothing of those things. All records died with their last possessors. Most of that knowledge was from hand to hand, father to son. What of the magic of ancient Egypt? What of the mysteries of the India of yesterday? What race in particular was schooled in their usages? The Jinn! And here we have one of the Jinn, perhaps, entombed in this very room, waiting to express his gratitude upon being released. Do you think for a moment he would fail to give us anything we wanted in the knowledge of the black arts?"

The fragrant fog from his pipe drifted about Jan's head and through it his glasses momentarily flashed. Then he sank back. "If I had not already thought this out, I would have no answer for you. There is no doubt but what the Ifrit—if he is there—has died. Hundreds or thousands of years . . ."

"Toads have lived in stone longer than that!" cried Frobish. "And toads possess none of the secrets for which science is even now groping. A small matter of suspended animation should create no difficulty for such a being as an Ifrit. You quibble. The point is this. You have here a thing for which I would sell my soul to see and you put me off. Since the first days in college when I first understood that there were more things in this Universe than could be answered by a slide rule and a badly perceived physical principle, I have dreamed of such a chance. I tell you, sir, I won't be balked!"

Jan looked questioningly at Frobish. The fellow had suddenly assumed very terrifying proportions. And it was not that Jan distrusted his physical ability so much as his habitual retreat before the face of bullying which made him swallow now.

"I have given my word," he said doggedly. "I know as well as you that that jar may well contain a demon from other ages. But for ten years I slaved to forget it and put it out of my mind forever. And I do not intend to do otherwise now. The only friend I ever had gave me that jar. And now, with Greg Palmer dead in the deep of nine south and fifty-one east, I have no recourse but to keep the promise I gave him. He was at pains to make me understand that I would do myself great harm by breaking that seal and so I have a double reason to refuse. I could let nothing happen to you in this..."

"My safety is my own responsibility. If you are afraid..."

Jan, carried on by the dogged persistence of which he was occasionally capable—though nearly always against other things than man—looked at the floor between his feet and said, "I can say with truth that I am not afraid. I am not master of my own house nor of my slightest possessions; I may be a feather in the hands of others. But there is one thing which I cannot do. I do not want to speak about it any further."

Frobish, finding resistance where he had not thought it possible, backed off, studying the thin, not unhandsome face of his host as though he could find a break in the defenses. But although Jan Palmer wore an expression very close to apology, there was still a set to his jaw which forbade attack. Frobish gave a despairing look at the jar.

"All my life," he said, "I have searched for such a thing. And now I find it here. Here, under the touch of my hands, ready to be opened with the most indifferent methods! And in that jar there lies the answer to all my speculations. But you balk me. You barricade the road to truth with a promise given to a dead man. You barricade all my endeavors. From here on I shall never be able to think of anything else but that jar." His voice dropped to a pleading tone. "In all the records of old there are constant references to Ifrits, to Marids and ghouls. We have closed our eyes to such things. It is possible that they still exist and it would only be necessary to discover how to find them. And there is the way to discover them, there in that corner. Can't you see, Jan Palmer, that I am pleading with you out of the bottom of my heart? Can't you understand what this means to me? You—you are rich! You have everything you require . . ."

"I have nothing. In all things I am a pauper. But in one thing I can hold my own. I cannot and will not break my word. I am sorry. Had you argued so eloquently for this very house you might have had it because this house is a yoke to me. But you have asked for a thing which it is beyond my power to give. I can say nothing more. Please do not come back."

It was a great deal for Jan Palmer to say. Green and Thompson and Aunt Ethel would have been rocked to their very insteps at such a firm stand had they witnessed it. But Jan Palmer had not been under the thumb of Frobish from the days of his childhood. This concerned nothing but the most private possession a man can have—his honor. And so it was that Frobish ultimately backed out of the door, too agitated even to remember to take the Arab dhow.

Before Jan closed off the entrance, Frobish had one last glimpse of the copper jar, dull green in the light of the sinking sun. He clamped his mouth shut with a click which sounded like a bear trap's springing. He jerked his hat down over his brow. Swiftly he walked away, looking not at all like a fellow who has become reconciled to defeat.

Jan had not missed the attitude. He had lived too long in the wrong not to know the reactions of men. He had seen his mother hounded to death by relatives. He had felt the resentment toward wealth really meant for his father. He had been through a torturous school and had come out far from unscathed. He knew very definitely that he would see Frobish again. Wearily he closed his door and slumped down in a chair to think.

Chapter 2

JINNI GRATITUDE

Each evening, when the household was assembled at the dining table, Jan Palmer had the feeling that the entire table's attention was devoted to seeing whether or not he would choke on his next mouthful. As long as his father had been alive, this had been the one period of the day when he had been certain of himself. His father had occupied the big chair at the head, filling it amply, and treating one and all to a rough jocosity which was very acceptable—until his father had retired to his study for the night. Then it seemed that his rough jests were not at all lightly received. Quite obvious it had been that fawning was a wearying business at best and that those so engaged were apt to revert at the slightest excuse.

Jan didn't come close to filling the big chair. His slight body could have gone three times between the arms of it. And Aunt Ethel and Thompson and, occasionally as tonight, Nathaniel Green, found no reason whatever to do any fawning.

Having very early deserted the bosom of his family for the flinty chest of Socrates, Jan knew quite well that if he had had the dispensing of funds comparable to those of his father in his entire control, smiles and not scowls would now be his lot. But the Bering Steamship Company was not showing much of a profit. Just why he did not know. He had never peeped into the books but he supposed that these continual strikes had something to do with it. The company paid Thompson and most of Jan's lot went directly to Aunt Ethel for household expenses. He had, therefore, no spare dollars to spread around.

The deep, dank silence was marred only by the scraping of silver on china. It was as if they all had secrets which they were fearful of giving away to each other or as if they could say nothing but things so awful that they wouldn't even let Jan hear them. The old house, with its ship models on the mantle and the great timbers across the ceilings and the hurricane lanterns hung along the walls wouldn't have been much quieter had it had no occupants at all.

Jan was glad when the gloomy footman put indifferent coffee before them. If he was careful he could gulp it down and get away without a thing being said to him.

But his luck didn't hold. "Jan," said Nathaniel heavily, "I trust you will be home this evening." The question implied that Jan was never to be found at home but always in some dive somewhere, roistering.

"Yes," said Jan.

"You saw fit to leave today when I needed your signature. When I finally connected with you, I had only time to get the most urgent matters attended to. You are too careless of these serious matters. There are at least twenty letters which only you can write, unfortunately. I am forced to demand that you finish them tonight. If I but had your complete power of attorney you would save me such needless labor. I have so many things to do already that if I were six men with six hands I couldn't get them done in time."

Strangely enough it came as welcome news to Jan. He almost smiled. "I am sorry that I can't be of more help but I'll be glad to do the letters tonight."

Nathaniel grunted as much as to say that Jan better had if he knew what was good for him. And Jan took the grunt as a cue for his departure. Swiftly he made his way to his apartments, fearful that this wouldn't come out the way he hoped it would.

The first thing he did was strip off his clothes and duck under a shower. He came forth in an agony of haste, losing everything

17

and finding it and losing it again as he swiftly assembled himself. His wardrobe was able to offer very little as Aunt Ethel purchased most of his clothing and did little purchasing. But the dark blue suit was neatly pressed and his cravat was nicely tied and he had no more than finished slicking back his blond hair when a knock sounded.

Hurriedly he flung himself into his chair by the desk and scooped up a book. Then he called, "Come in," as indifferently as he could.

Alice Hall stepped firmly into the room. As Nathaniel's stenographer it was her duty, two or three times a week, to call in the evening to let Jan catch up on company correspondence. She was the last of six such stenographers and ever since she had first taken the job four months before, Jan had lain awake nights trying to figure out a way to make certain that she would hold her job. It was not so much that she was beautiful—though she was that—and it wasn't entirely because she was the only one who did not seem to look down upon him. Jan had tried to turn up the answer in vain. She was a lady, there was no denying it, and she was far better educated than most stenographers, evidently having done postgraduate work. She did not make him feel at ease at all but neither did she make him feel uneasy. When he had first beheld her he had had a hard time breathing.

Her large blue eyes were as impersonal as the turquoise orbs of the idol by the wall. She was interested, it seemed, in nothing but doing her immediate job. Still, there was something about her; something unseen but felt as the traveler can sense the violence of a slumbering volcano under his feet. Her age was near Jan's own and she had arrived at that estate without leaving anything unlearned behind her. There was almost something resentful about her, but that too was never displayed.

Now she put down her briefcase and took off her small hat and swagger coat and seated herself at a distance from him, placing her materials on a small table before her. She arranged several letters in order and then stepped over to the blackwood desk and laid them before Jan who, to all signs, was deeply immersed in a treatise on aerodynamics.

Truth told, he was afraid to notice her, not knowing anything to say besides that which had brought her there and not wanting to talk about such matters to her.

She twitched the papers and still he did not look up. Finally she said, "You're holding that book upside down."

"What? Oh . . . oh, yes, of course. These diagrams, you see . . . "

"Shall we begin on the letters? This one on top is from the Steamship Owners Alliance, asking your attendance at a conference in San Francisco. I have noted the reply on the bottom."

"Oh, yes. Thank you." He looked studiously at the letter, his ears very red. "Yes, that is right. I won't be able to attend."

"I didn't think you would," she said unexpectedly.

"Uh?"

"I said I was sure you wouldn't. They asked you but Mr. Green will go instead."

"He wouldn't want me to go," said Jan. "He . . . he knows much more about it than I."

"You're right."

Jan detected, to his intense dismay, something like pity in her voice. Pity or contempt; they were brothers anyway.

"But he really does," said Jan. "He wouldn't like it if I said I would go."

"He'll be the only non-owner there."

"But he has full authority. . . ."

"Does he?" She was barely interested now. Jan thought she looked disappointed about something. "Shall we get on with these letters?"

"Yes, of course."

For the following two hours he stumbled through the correspondence, taking most of his text from Alice Hall's suggestions.

She wrote busily and efficiently and, at last, closed her notebook and put on her hat and coat.

"Do you have to go?" said Jan, surprising himself. "I mean, couldn't I send for some tea and things. It's late."

"I'll be up half the night now, transcribing."

"Oh . . . will you? But don't you finish these at the office in the morning?"

"Along with my regular work? A company can buy a lot for fifteen dollars a week these days."

"Fifteen . . . but I thought our stenographers got twenty-five."

"Oh, do you know that much about it?"

"Why . . . yes." He was suddenly brightened by an idea. "If you have to work tonight perhaps I had better drive you home. It's quite a walk up to the car line. . . . "

"I have my own car outside. It's a fine car when it runs. Good night."

He was still searching for a reply when she closed the door behind her. He got up, suddenly furious with himself. He went over to the fireplace and kicked at the logs, making sparks jump frightenedly up the flue. In the next fifteen minutes he thought up fifteen hundred things to say to her, statements which would swerve her away from believing him a weak mouse, holed up in a cluttered room. And that thought stopped him and sent him into a deep chair to morosely consider the truth of his simile. Time and again he had vowed to tell them all. Time and again something had curled up inside of him to forbid the utterance.

Sunk in morbid reverie, he failed to hear Aunt Ethel enter and indignantly turn out the lights without seeing him in the chair. He failed to see that the fire burned lower and lower until just one log smoldered on the grate. He failed to hear the clock strike two bells and so the night advanced upon him.

With a start he woke without knowing that he had been asleep. He was cold and aching and aware of a wrong somewhere near him. Once again sounded the creepy scratch and Jan stood up, shaking and staring intently into the dark depths of the room. Someone or something was there. He did not want to turn on the light but he knew that he must. He found the lamp beside the chair and pulled its cord. The blinding glare whipped across the room to throw his caller into full relief.

The curtains were blowing inward from the open window and the papers were stirring on the blackwood desk. And in the corner by the copper jar stood Frobish, nervous with haste, a knife peeling back ribbons of lead from the seal. For an instant, so intent was the interloper, he did not come aware of the light. And then he whirled about, facing Jan.

Frobish's eyes were hot and his face drawn. There was danger in his voice. "I had to do this. I've been half crazy for hours thinking about it. I am going to open this copper jar and if you try to stop me . . ." The knife glittered in his fingers.

It was very clear to Jan that he confronted a being whose entire life was concentrated upon one object and who was now driven to a deed which, had conditions been otherwise, would have horrified no one more than Professor Frobish. But, with his goal at hand, it would take more than the strength of one man to stop him.

"You said you promised," cried Frobish. "I have nothing to do with that. You are not opening the jar and you were not commissioned to see that it was never opened by anyone. Your cousin was protecting only you and him. He cared nothing about anyone else. If any harm comes from this, it is not on your head. Stay where you are and be silent." He again attacked the stopper.

Jan, his surprise leaving him, looked anxiously along the wall. But there were no weapons on this side of the room beyond an old pistol which was not loaded and, indeed, was too rusty to even offer a threat.

A sudden spasm of outrage shook him. That this fellow should presume to break in here and meddle with what was his was swelled with years of resentment against all the countless invasions of his privacy and the confiscations of his possessions.

Shaking and white, Jan advanced across the room.

Frobish whirled around to face him. "Stand back! I warn you this is no ordinary case. I won't be balked! This research is bigger than either you or me." His voice was mounting toward hysteria.

Jan did not stop. Watchful of the knife, unable to understand how the professor could go to such lengths as using it, he came within a pace. Frobish backed up against the wall, breathing hard, swinging the weapon up to the level of his shoulders.

"I've dreamed for years of making such a discovery. You cannot stop me now!"

"Be quiet or people will hear you," said Jan, cooled a little by the sight of that knife. "You can leave now and nothing will have happened."

Frobish was quick to sense the change. He reached out and shoved Jan away from him to whirl and again pry at the stopper.

Jan seized hold of his shoulder and spun him about. "You're insane! This is my house and that jar is mine. You have no right, I tell you."

Savagely Frobish struck at him and Jan, catching the blow on the point of his chin, dropped to the floor, turned halfway about. Groggily, he shook his head, still unwilling to believe that Frobish could fail to listen to reason, unable to understand that he was dealing with forces and desires greater than he could ever hope to control.

Once more Frobish flung him away and would have followed up, but behind him there sounded a thing like escaping steam. He forgot Jan and faced the jar to instantly stumble back from it. Jan remained frozen to the floor a dozen feet away.

Black smoke was coiling into the dark shadows of the ceiling, mushrooming slowly outward, rolling into itself with ominous speed. Frobish backed against a chair and stopped, hands flung up before his face, while over him like a shroud, the acrid vapors began to drop down.

Jan coughed from the fumes and blinked the tears which were stung from his eyes. The stopper was not wholly off the jar and stayed on the edge, teetering until the last of the smoke was past, when it dropped with a dull sound to the floor.

The smoke eddied more swiftly against the beams. It became blacker and blacker, more and more solid, drawing in and in again and finally beginning to pulsate as though it breathed.

Something hard flashed at the top of it and then became two spiked horns, swiftly accompanied by two gleaming eyes the size of meat platters. Two long tusks, polished and sharp, squared the awful cavern of a mouth. Swiftly then the smoke became a body girt with a blazing belt, two arms tipped by clawed fingers, two legs like trees ending in hoofs, split-toed and as large across as an elephant's foot. The thing was covered with shaggy hair except for the face and the tail which lashed back and forth now in agitation.

The thing knelt and flung up its hands and cried, "There is no God but Allah, the All Merciful and Compassionate. Spare me!"

Jan was frozen. The fumes were still heavy about him but now there penetrated a wild animal smell which made his man's soul lurch within him in memory of days an eon gone.

Frobish, recovered now and seeing that the thing was wholly on the defensive, straightened up.

"There is no God but Allah. And Sulayman is the lord of the earth!"

"Get up," said Frobish. "We care less than nothing about Allah, and Sulayman has been dead these many centuries. I have loosed you from your prison and in return there are things I desire."

The Ifrit's luminous, yellow eyes played up and down the puny mortal before him. Slowly an evil twist came upon the giant lips. A laugh rumbled deep in him like summer thunder—a laugh wholly of contempt.

"So, it is as I thought it might be. You are a man and you have loosed me. And now you speak of a reward." The Ifrit laughed again. "Sulayman, you say, is dead?"

"Naturally. Sulayman was as mortal as I."

"Yes, yes. As mortal as you. Man who freed me, you behold before you Zongri, king of the Ifrits of the Barbossi Isles. For thousands of years have I been in that jar. And would you like to know what I thought about?"

"Of course," said Frobish.

"Mortal man, the first five hundred years I vowed that the man who let me free would have all the riches in the world. But no man freed me. The next five hundred years I vowed that the man who let me out would have life everlasting even as I. But no man let me out. I waited then for a long, long time and then, at long last, I fell into a fury at my captivity and I vowed—you are sure you wish to know, mortal man?"

"Yes!"

"Then know that I vowed that the one who let me free would meet with instant death!"

Frobish paled. "You are a fool as I have heard that all Ifrits are fools. But for me you would have stayed there the rest of eternity. Tonight I had to break into that man's house to loose you. It is he who has held you captive, who would not let you go."

"A vow is never broken. You have freed me and therefore you shall die!" A thunderous scowl settled upon his face and he edged forward on his knees, unable to stand against the fourteen foot ceiling.

Frobish backed up hastily.

The Ifrit glanced about him. Near at hand were the Malay krisses and upon the largest he fastened, wrenching it from the wall and bringing the rest of the board down with a clatter. The great executioner's blade looked like a toothpick in his fist.

Frobish strove to dash out of the room but the Ifrit raked

out with his claws and snatched him back, holding him a foot from the floor.

"A vow," uttered Zongri, "is a vow." And so saying he released Frobish who again tried to run.

The blade flashed and there was a crunching sound as of a cleaver going through ham. Split from crown to waist, Frobish's corpse dropped to the floor, staining the carpet for a yard about.

Jan winced as something moist splashed against his hand and swiftly he scuttled back. The movement attracted the Ifrit's attention and again the claws raked out and clutched. Jan, assailed by fuming breath and sick with the sight of death, shook like a rag in a hurricane.

The Ifrit regarded him solemnly.

"Let me go," said Jan.

"Why?"

"I did not free you."

"You kept me captive for years. That one said so."

"You cannot," chattered Jan, "you cannot kill a man for letting you free and then kill another for . . . for not letting you free."

"Why not?"

"It . . . it is not logical!"

Zongri regarded him for a long time, shaking him now and then to start him shivering anew. Finally he said, "No, that is so. It is not logical. You did not let me free and I said no vow about you. You are Mohammedan?"

"N . . . n . . . no!"

"Hm." Again Zongri shook him. "You are no friend of Sulayman's?"

"I . . . n-n-no!"

"Then," said the Ifrit, "it would not be right for me to kill you." He dropped him to the floor and looked around. "But," he added, "you held me captive for years. He said you did. That cannot go unpunished."

Jan hugged the moist floor, waiting for doom to blanket him.

"I cannot kill you," said Zongri. "I made no vow. Instead . . . instead I shall lay upon you a sentence. Yes, that is it. A sentence. You, mortal one, I sentence," and laughter shook him for a moment, "to Eternal Wakefulness. And now I am off to Mount Kaf!"

There was a howling sound as of wings. Jan did not dare open his eyes for several seconds but when he did he found that the room was empty.

Unsteadily he got to his feet, stepping gingerly around the dead man and then discovering to his dismay that he himself was now smeared with blood.

The executioner's knife had been dropped across the body and, with some wild thought of trying to bring the man back to life, Jan laid it aside, shaking the already cooling shoulder.

Realizing that that was a fruitless gesture he again got to his feet. He did not want to be alone for the first time in his life. He wanted lights and people about him. Yes, even Green or Thompson.

He laid his hand upon the door but before he could pull, it crashed into his chest and he found himself staring into a crowd in the hall.

Two prowler car men, guns in hand, were in front. A servant stood behind them and after that he could see the strained faces of Aunt Ethel and Thompson and Green.

A flood of gladness went through him but he was too shocked to speak. Mutely he pointed toward Frobish's body and tried to tell them that the Ifrit had gone through the window. But other voices swirled about him.

"Nab him, Mike. It's open and shut," said the sergeant.

Mike nabbed Jan.

"Deader'n a door nail," said Mike, looking at the bisected corpse. "Open and shut." He took out a book and flipped it open. "How long ago did you do it?"

"About five minutes!" said Thompson. "When I first heard the voices in here and sent for you, I didn't expect anything like this to happen. But I heard the sound of the knife and then silence."

"Five minutes, eh?" said the sergeant, wetting the end of his pencil and writing. "And what was this all about, you?"

Jan recovered his voice. "You . . . you think I did this thing?"

"Well?" said Mike. "Didn'tcha?"

"No!" shouted Jan. "You don't understand. That jar . . ."

"Fell on him, I suppose."

"No, no! That jar . . ."

Intelligence flashed in Aunt Ethel's needle-point eyes. She flung herself upon Jan, weeping. "Oh, my poor boy. How could you do such an awful thing?"

Jan, startled, tried to shake her off, urgently protesting to the sergeant all the while. "I told him not to but he broke through the window and pried at the stopper . . ."

"Who?" said Mike.

"I'll handle this," said the sergeant in reproof.

"He means Professor Frobish, his guest," said Thompson. "The professor came to see him about an Arabian ship model this afternoon."

"Huh, murdered his guest, did he? Mike, you hold down here while I send for the homicide squad."

"Don't!" shouted Jan. "You've got it all wrong. Frobish broke in here to let . . ."

"Save it for the sergeant and the boys," said Mike, shaking him to quiet him down.

Jan glared at those around him. Thompson was looking at him in deep sorrow. Aunt Ethel was wiping her eyes with the hem of her dressing gown. And all the while Nathaniel Green was pacing up and down the room, squashing fist into palm and muttering, "A murder. A Palmer, a murderer. Oh, how can such things keep happening to me? The publicity—and just when the government was offering a subsidy. I knew it, I knew it. He was always strange and now, see what he's done. I should have watched him more closely. It's my fault, all my fault."

"No, it's mine," wept Aunt Ethel. "I've tried to be a mother to him and he repays us by killing his guest in our house. Oh, think of the papers!"

It went on and on. It went on for the benefit of the newspapermen which came swarming in on the heels of such a name as Palmer. It went on to the homicide squad. Over and over until Jan was sick and wabbly.

The fingerprint men were swift in their work. The photographers took various views of the corpse.

And then an ambulance backed up beside the Black Maria and while Frobish was basketed into the former, Jan, under heavy guard, was herded into the latter.

And as they drove away, the last thing he heard was Aunt Ethel's wail to a late-coming newsman that here was gratitude after all that she had done for him too, and wasn't it awful, awful, awful? Wasn't it? Wasn't it? Wasn't it?

Chapter 3

ETERNAL WAKEFULNESS

Jan was too stunned by the predicament to protest any further; he went so willingly—or nervelessly—wherever he was shoved that the officers concluded there was no more harm left in him for the moment. Besides, a gang of counterfeiters was occupying the best cells and so a little doubling was in order. Jan found himself thrust into a cubicle, past a pale, snake-eyed fellow, and then the door clanged authoritatively and the guard marched away.

Seeing the cell and the cellmate and believing it was a cell and a cellmate were two entirely different things. Jan sat down on a bunk and looked woodenly straight ahead. He was in that frame of mind where men behold disaster to every side but are so thoroughly drenched with it that they begin to discount it. It was even a somewhat solacing frame of mind. Nothing worse than this could possibly happen. Unlucky Fate had opened the bag and pulled out everything at once and so, by lucid reason, it was impossible for said Unlucky Fate to have any further stock still hidden.

"That's my bunk," snarled the cellmate.

Jan obediently moved to the other berth to discover that it was partly unhinged so that a man had to sleep with his head below his feet. Further, the cellmate had robbed it of blankets to benefit his own couch and so had exposed a questionable mattress.

Jan's deep sigh sucked the smell of disinfectant so deeply into his lungs that he went into a spasm of coughing.

"Lunger?" said the cellmate indifferently.

"Beg pardon?"

"I said have y'got it inna pipes?"

"What?"

"Skiput."

"Really," said Jan, "I don't understand you."

"Oh, a swell, huh? What'd they baste you wit'?"

"Er..."

"How's it read? What's the yarn? What'd they book you for?" said the fellow with great impatience. "Murder? Arson? Bigamy?..."

"Oh," said Jan with relief. "Oh, yes, certainly." And then the enormity of the error came back to him, and he grew agitated. "I'm supposed to have murdered a man but I didn't do it!"

"Sure not. Hammer, lead or steel?" Hastily to clarify himself. "How'd you do it?"

"But I didn't!" said Jan. "It's all a horrible mistake."

"Sure. Was it a big shot?"

"There wasn't any shooting. It was an executioner's sword."

"Exe... Say! You do things with a flare, don'cha?"

"But I didn't do it!"

"Well, hell, who said you did? What was the stiff's name?"

"Stiff? Oh... Professor Frobish of the University."

"Brain wizard, huh? Never liked 'em myself. How come the slash party in the first place. I mean, how'd it happen?"

"That's what's so terrible about it," said Jan, so deep in misery that he did not fully comprehend what he was saying. "I had a copper jar in my room and Frobish insisted upon opening it and when I refused him he returned in the night and pried the stopper out of it because he knew it might contain an Ifrit." Mistaking the pop-eyes for sympathy, Jan went on. "And it *did* contain an Ifrit that Sulayman had bottled up and when the thing came out it took down a sword and killed Frobish and when the police got there they didn't give me a chance to explain. They thought I did it and so, here I am!"

"What," said the cellmate, "is an Igpit? Do you eat it or spend it?"

"An Ifrit? Oh. Why, an Ifrit is a demon of the tribes of the Jinn. Some people call them Jinni or genii. They seem to have vanished from the earth although there is evidence that they were once very numerous."

"What . . . what do they look like?"

"Why, they're about fifteen feet tall and they've got horns and a spiked tail . . ."

"A sniffer."

"What?"

"I said I didn't think you looked like a sniffer when I first seen you."

"I don't understand."

"Sure. Well, go on, don't let me stop you," he said indulgently. "Fifteen feet tall with horns and a spiked tail . . ."

Jan frowned. "You don't believe me."

"Sure I believe you. Hell, who wouldn't believe you? Why I seen worse than that before I finally yanked myself up on the wagon. Once I lamped a whole string of such things. They was hangin' to each other's tails with one hand and carrying purple sedans in the other. And . . ."

"You doubt my word?"

"Hell, no, buddy. Just sit down and be calm. No use frettin' about a little thing like that, see? Sure. I know all about these here . . . what did you say you called 'em?"

"Ifrits!"

"Sure, that's right. You've been done dirt, that's sure. But all you gotta do is tell the truth to the judge and he'll do the rest."

"You think I've got a chance?"

"Listen, pal, I'm in here for shaking down a gent for eight hundred bucks. That's what they say I did. I didn't, of course.

But if I think I've got a story lined up . . . geez, you must be a genius."

The other's volunteered information brought Jan slightly out of himself, enough to realize that his cellmate was also answering to the law. With this in common, Jan took interest in him.

"They arrested you, too?"

"Hell, no, buddy, I use this for a hotel. Look, I don't know where they dug you up or who you are . . ."

"My name is Jan Palmer."

"Okay, your name is Jan Palmer. Fine. But would you please tell me how a gent can live all his life in these United States without finding out a thing or two. Palmer, I hate to say it, but unless you smarten up you ain't got an onion's chance in Spain. Me, I know the ropes. There ain't nobody in the racket that knows more about what's what than Diver Mullins. Now listen to me. You give this cockeyed yarn of yours the bounce and think of somethin' logical. Otherwise, my innercent pal, they'll swing you by the neck until you're most awful dead."

Jan was jolted. He peered nearsightedly at his cellmate, seeing him truly for the first time. There was no mistaking the evil in that face. It was narrow as a ferret's and of an unhealthy pallor. The eyes flicked up and down and around and about in incessant sentinel duty. Shabby and wasted though he was, there was still a certain vitality in the fellow.

"But . . . but," said Jan, "I told you the truth. An Ifrit came out of the jar . . ."

"Look, pal," said Diver Mullins, "I ain't doubtin' your word. I believe every syllable. But I ain't the judge and when you spin that cockeyed story before a jury they'll laugh at you. Now, take me. I ain't in here for the first time. No sir! I know my business. I was located in possession of eight hundred smackers that a sap lost. That's an insult. If I'd have taken it off'n him in a crowd, do you suppose he ever would have knowed about it?"

"You mean you had another fellow's money," decoded Jan.

"Go to the head of the class. Now another gent would say he found it on the sidewalk or someplace and get himself laughed at. But not me. Another fellow would say he didn't know how it got in his pocket. But not me! Them dodges has mildew on 'em. Now I figger . . . "

But Jan had relapsed into his own woes and scarcely heard Diver Mullins' plot to put the entire blame upon another pickpocket and place himself in a savior light. Jan, accountably weary, lay back on the tipsy bunk and gave himself over to dreary speculation.

He retraced the activities of the night and found them to be anything but reassuring. And, to dodge away from their damning possibilities, he dwelt upon the inconsequentialities. He was, for instance, almost certain that Zongri had spoken in Arabic. He, Jan, spoke no Arabic so far as he knew. Of course Frobish would understand the language but how could it be that Jan had come into the sudden possession of such knowledge. Perhaps it wasn't really Arabic. Jan knew not enough to be certain on that score, just as he was too hazy to analyze the Ifrit's "Eternal Wakefulness."

The puzzle was far too much for him and his tired, event-shocked brain gave it up. In a few moments he was falling steeply into exhausted slumber.

The thing which happened immediately thereafter was the turning point in the life of Jan Palmer, for one—even beyond the effect of the murder.

He went to sleep but he didn't go to sleep. He had a sensation of dropping straight down. Heretofore he had been aware, in common with all men, of a delicious period of semi-wakefulness preceding and succeeding slumber. But from that period he had always gone into a deep sleep (so far as he knew) or had come fully awake. Now he felt as though the world had been obscured by a veil which no more than dropped than it was ripped startlingly aside.

A hail rang hysterically in his ears, "Breakers two points off the sta'b'd b-o-o-o-o-w! *B-r-r-reakers* two points off the sta'b'd bow! Captain, for the love of God, we're on the rocks!"

Jan had scarcely lifted his head and felt the spokes of a helm under his fingers and then he was jarred fully awake and almost into sleep again by the most tremendous blow which rocketed him all the way across the quarterdeck, from binnacle to scupper. He brought up against the rail and lifted himself cautiously.

The quiet vessel was suddenly bedlam. The captain's roars seconding the still braying lookout, the crew spilled helter-skelter from the fo'c's'le, rubbing their eyes, scarcely knowing what they were doing but automatically taking their stations.

The masts swooped back and forth across the stars as the captain's savage hands spun the helm. The thunder of breakers could be plainly heard now and, lifting himself a little more, Jan beheld their phosphorescent line which swiftly swung parallel with them.

"Let go the port sheets!" bellowed the captain. "Take in on the sta'b'd main sheet!"

Canvas cannonaded in the fresh wind and then the deck leaped under them as the billowing white cliff tautened in the gloom. On a close port tack the big vessel picked up a bone and scudded back into the safety of the sea.

"Make fast!" roared the captain.

"Lively now," cried a mate somewhere in the waist.

The ship surged ahead anew as the sails were more precisely trimmed and then one by one, the crew made their ways back to the fo'c's'le and more sleep.

When all was in order, the captain turned the wheel over to another man and gave him a course and then, with both hands on his hips, he planted his feet solidly on the deck and glared about him.

"Now! Where's the helmsman?"

Jan shivered and he had every right. The captain loomed into the stars and the gleam of the binnacle which fell upon his face displayed two glittering fangs. From the flame of his eye and the posture Jan knew that once again, in less than four hours, he had run afoul of an Ifrit.

He had no slightest inkling of what he was doing there or why and he had no time to consider it.

Shaking he came upright, holding hard to the rail.

"So you're still here," said the captain, advancing. Suddenly his hand shot out and he gripped Jan by the shirt front and shook him clear of the deck, slamming him back to the planking.

"Asleep! Asleep at the wheel! Why, you ugly pup, I ought to knock every tooth out of your ugly face! I ought to smash your skull like an egg! Do you realize what you did? Has it leaked through your thick skull that you put us miles and miles off our course and almost killed us to a man on the Fraybran shoals? Sleep, will you . . ." And again he lifted Jan up and threw him down. With the biggest boot Jan had ever seen, the captain kicked him down the ladder and into the waist.

"Go get the cat, d'ya hear me? Get it and bring it to me!"

Jan got up and stumbled along the rail. He was stunned by the treatment no less than his strange position. He knew rightly enough what a cat was, but where he could find one aboard this packet he certainly could not tell. He looked fearfully back at the captain who stood like a tree on the quarterdeck, watching him with piercing eyes.

The mate, likewise an Ifrit, started to pass him on his way aft and then recognized him. He flung him back against the rail.

"So!" roared the mate. "It's Tiger, is it?" And he spun Jan about with a blow. "By the Seven Sisters of Circe, if I don't drown you, the crew will! First it's fight, fight, fight. It's rum and women and battle and now, by God, it's shipwreck you're asking for! Run us on a reef, will you!"

Jan spun around the other way and went down with the salty taste of his own blood in his mouth.

"Sleep at the helm, will you?"

And again Jan went down.

"I sent him for the cat!" roared the captain.

"Get it, then," snarled the mate, his upper and lower fangs coming together with a vicious click. "Get it and be damned to you!"

Jan despairingly watched him go. A sailor was nearby and Jan started to appeal to him but the fellow stalked away. Staggering forward, his head roaring and spinning, Jan almost collided with a bosun.

"Wh...where's the cat?" said Jan through cracked lips.

"Get it yourself, you jinx," said the bosun.

"Please, I don't know where it's kept?"

Something in Jan's tone made the bosun look more closely. He could not see very well through the darkness and he swung a lantern out of its niche and held it to peer into Jan's face. He was evidently perplexed.

"What's the matter with you? You sick or something?"

"I...I got to find the cat."

"Never seen a man so anxious to get a flogging. It's in the gunroom where it's supposed to be." He frowned. "Maybe you oughtn't to get it, Tiger. You look awful."

Jan stumbled up the deck toward an indicated passageway. He fumbled through the darkness and found a door which he opened. A guttering lamp showed him bracketed muskets, hung in orderly racks, and glittering cutlasses held fanwise in cleats. The cat had a dozen tails and it was so heavy with the brass on its ends that Jan could scarcely lift it.

Bearing his cross, he made his blind way back to the quarterdeck. The captain was still waiting, a tower of smoldering rage. Jan gave up the whip.

"Peel off your shirt."

Jan fumbled with the unaccustomed buttons and finally removed the garment.

"Lay yourself over the house."

Jan sprawled against the handrail of the sterncastle house.

There was no further ceremony to it. The whip sang with all its twelve hungry tails and then bit so savagely that Jan screamed with agony. He whirled around and dropped to his knees.

"Please God! I don't know why I'm here or even where I am! I didn't go to sleep at the helm. I only woke up there with no knowledge of how I came to be aboard here."

"What?" The captain was plainly perplexed. He too lifted a lantern from its niche and looked closely at Jan's features.

"If I didn't hear it, I wouldn't believe it," said the captain. "Tiger, of all men, beggin' for mercy and lying in the bargain."

"I don't know that name!" wailed Jan. "I don't know anything about it!"

The captain picked off his cap and scratched his pointed head thoughtfully. Then he turned and called, "Mr. Malek!"

The mate came out of a companionway. "Yessir."

"Did you or did you not put Tiger on the helm?"

"Why...ah..."

"Answer me!"

"Yes. I did. But he's never done anything like that before, sir. I didn't have any idea..."

"I'm not blaming you, I'm asking you. Mr. Malek, there's something very wrong here. Either that or Tiger is making a fool of us. He says he doesn't know anything about it. Was he fully awake when he went on watch?"

"Yessir. That is, he seemed so."

The captain again raised the lantern and saw that Jan's head was bleeding. "Maybe it's that crack against the rail that did it. Listen here, Tiger, if this is one of your tricks, I'll make a flogging feel like a picnic in comparison."

"I'm not lying!" wailed Jan. "I don't know anything about any of this, honest to God. I've never seen any of you before in my life."

"Must have been the crack on the head," said the captain. "Go below and I'll look you over."

Jan hastily scooped up his shirt and ducked down the companionway. A room obviously the captain's stood open on his right and he stumbled into it. The height of the ceiling was not as extreme as it really should have been, he thought, and the bed wasn't so much larger than ordinary beds, looking to be only about eight feet long.

The captain was checking up on the ship before he came below and Jan had a moment or two to catch his breath. For the first time he realized the strangeness of his situation. Certainly it was impossible to board a ship in the open sea and he could not otherwise have arrived there. That he had no recollection whatever of arriving had him half convinced that he wasn't there at all.

He saw a mirror across the room from him and, with sudden suspicion, approached it. He was jolted so that he took two steps backwards. He recovered himself and peered more closely at his image.

Yes, now that he made a closer examination, it was himself. But what a difference there was! He, Jan Palmer, was a thin-faced, anemic fellow, but this brute who was staring back at him was bold of visage, brawny of arm, tall and . . . yes, he had to admit it, not bad at all to look upon. But the knife scar which ran from the lobe of his ear diagonally to his jawbone . . . where had that come from? He felt of it and peered more closely at it. He didn't really object to it at all because it didn't mar his looks but, in truth, rather gave him an air.

Puzzled, he looked down at himself. His blue pants encased very muscular and shapely legs. His bare chest was matted with blond hair. He looked back at his image as though it might solve the riddle for him.

"Tiger!" cried a voice in the passageway.

Jan started and saw that the captain was just then entering. The captain looked shocked.

"In here? Well, of all the gall . . . By God, I do believe there's something gone wrong with you. Don't you know enough to wait outside? Come here!"

Jan obeyed. Roughly the captain forced him down to the bed and inspected his skull with great perplexity. It gave Jan a chance to realize that this Ifrit was, seemingly, a lot smaller than Zongri. Either that or . . . or he himself was now bigger than he had been.

"Hell," said the captain, "there isn't even a dent there. Tiger, if you're pulling another one of your tricks . . ."

Jan was frightened at the proximity of that awful, fanged face and he drew back.

The captain once again removed his cap and scratched one of his pointed ears. "And scared, too. I never thought I'd live to see that. Tiger, scared. By God, if this is a game you won't enjoy it."

"It's no trick," said Jan. "I don't know anything about it."

"Hmmmmm. It's just, barely possible . . . See here, give me the straight of this and no lying! What are you up to?"

Jan spread his hands hopelessly. "I'm not up to anything! One minute I am sleeping in a jail and the next I am leaning on the helm of this ship. How I can tell you when I don't know myself . . ."

"Jail? For God's sake, where?"

"Why, in Seattle, of course."

"Where?"

"Seattle, Washington."

"That's one port I never heard of anyway. Go ahead and talk, Tiger, and make it good. I know you've seen plenty of jails but that particular one has escaped me. Go on. What did you do to get in jail?"

"I didn't do anything! They thought I'd killed a Professor Frobish that came to see me but I didn't do it. He wanted to open a copper jar and I wouldn't let him so he came back at night and did it anyway. I was asleep in a chair but I woke up too late to stop him. And when the Ifrit came out..."

"Copper jar? Ifrit? Go on!"

"Well, the Ifrit almost cut him in half with an executioner's sword and then flew away."

"You're talking about Earth!"

"Of course."

"Earth, by all that's... See here, what was the name of this Ifrit?"

"Z... let's see... Zon... Zongri. Yes, that was it, Zongri."

"Zongri! Good God, Tiger, if you're making this up..."

"I'm not!"

"But Zongri was captured and entombed by Sulayman thousands of years ago! I remember hearing about it. He was king of the Barbossi Isles and he refused to change faith with the others." Suddenly he grew very agitated and stalked about the room. Abruptly he again confronted Jan. "See here, did this Zongri say anything to you? Did he do anything...?"

"Yes. He said he was going to sentence me to Eternal Wakefulness..."

"Hush!" said the captain, going swiftly to the port and slamming it shut. He closed the door and then came back to the bed with the air of a conspirator. "Zongri said that?"

"Yes. And then I was arrested and taken to jail because they thought..."

"To Shaitan with that! Oh, the fool, the fool! Eternal Wakefulness!" The captain slammed a fist into his palm with the wish that Zongri was in between. "It's like him. He almost runs my ship on the rocks! He was at the bottom of the war with Sulayman and all our woes since. And now..." He eyed Jan. "Tiger, if you are telling me lies..."

"It's true! I swear it's true."

"Hmmm. Perhaps. If it weren't for the change in you I wouldn't credit any of it. But you speak so well . . . Hmmmmm. You swear to this, you say?"

"Certainly."

"All right. So be it. Mr. Malek!"

The mate clattered down the ladder and thrust his head in the door.

"Mr. Malek, you will take Tiger down to the brig and post a reliable Marid over him. Understand that Tiger is not to talk to anyone, you hear? Absolutely no one! When we get into port we'll find out what to do with him."

Malek took hold of Jan's collar and jerked him to his feet.

"Count on me," said Malek. "He won't see a soul."

"Your head will answer for it if he does."

"That's all right with me," said Malek, jerking Jan down the passageway and into the bowels of the ship.

Chapter 4

SYMPATHY

Jan went round and round his small cell like a white rat spinning about a pole. And his head went faster than he. He shook the bars and yelled at the departing mate, but Malek had no further heed for him. Growing terror caused him to shout at the guard, but the Marid, too, was most indifferent. And so it was that Jan dizzied himself by pacing the walls. He could stand a berating, perhaps, and even face a flogging without really cracking but this situation was the stuff of which madness was made. He had long since ceased to doubt that he was here because, after all, he *was* here. And what in the name of God did they mean to do with him?

Again he besought information from the Marid. The guard was small, with a solitary eye in the middle of his head and a twist to his back, garbed in a single cloak. His lack of shoes was backed by ample reason. He had hoofs.

"Be quiet," said the Marid at last. "Better you sleep." And with that he faced the other way and was wholly deaf.

At long, long last Jan wearied himself to exhaustion. He sank down on the pile of blankets and buried his face in his arms, striving to gather and tie the loose ends of his nerves.

His strange position was bad enough, but not even to be himself...! Who and what was this "Tiger"? True he had some slight resemblance to Jan Palmer, but that was not enough. Tiger was known here, known for a bad actor, it seemed. *But* if Jan Palmer was now Tiger, where was Tiger?

He could not answer that and the weight of it was the proverbial straw. His mind went wholly blank and he lay in apathy.

Once or twice he reasoned that this was still the jail. But each time he lifted his head to prove it, there was the Marid in all his evil dignity. Yes, and in the damp air was the hissing sound of the clean hull carving through the waves, that and the sing of wind through rigging far, far above.

This was a sea, an unknown sea. This was a brig of a ship, the like of which had not sailed the seas for a hundred years and more.

It was too much. And at last Jan dozed, drifting more deeply into slumber.

To no avail.

He had no more than shut his eyes when he was startled by the slam of iron-barred doors and the rattle of dishes which immediately followed. Voices were hollow in the concrete hall and Jan sat up. He looked carefully all around him.

It was no Marid at the door but a blue-coated policeman engaged in shoving a tray of food under the door.

"You gonna sleep forever?" said Diver Mullins, scraping half-heartedly at his lathered face. "Y'rolled and tossed all night long. I hardly got a chance to close m'eyes."

"I . . . I'm sorry," said Jan, blinking at the cell around him and experiencing an uplift of heart. Thankfully he took a deep breath only to choke on the disinfectant in the air. But that hardly lessened his thankfulness.

It was quite plain to him now that the ship and the Ifrits had been of the substance of nightmares. And, more than that, when he looked in the glass and found that Jan Palmer's sickly visage gazed back at him, he wanted to shout for joy.

"Geez, for a gent that's about to be stretched," said Diver Mullins, "you sure can put on the happy act."

"Beg pardon?" said Jan.

"It ain't right," said Diver petulantly. "You commit a moider after supper and you wake up singin' like a canary bird."

"Murder?"

"Don't tell me," said Diver, "that you went and forgot about it."

Jan groaned and sank back on his bunk. He held his face in his hands to steady himself as the black ink of memory drowned him. Murder. He was in here for murder. An Ifrit named Zongri had killed a man named Frobish and now they were going to hang a hopelessly innocent Palmer for the deed.

"Now I done it," said Diver. "I'd rather you'd chirp than beller, my fine-fettered friend. Cheer up. They only hang a man once." So saying he hauled the tray close to him and speared the soggy hotcakes with every evidence of appetite. "C'mon and eat."

Jan, mechanically ready to obey almost anybody, accordingly hitched a stool up to the table and took the offered plate. He even went so far as to butter the dough blankets and convey a forkful to his mouth. And then he found out what he was doing and gagged. He crawled to his bed and sprawled upon it, face down.

"They ain't as bad as that," said Diver. "Course, in lotsa jails they serve lots better belly paddin', but my motto is to take what y'can get your hooks into and don't ask too many questions. Nobody never measured me for a noose or even said they was going to, so I ain't had a lot of experience. But, hell, you hadn't ought to let it get you down like that. You get borned and then you live awhile and then somebody knocks you off or you get pneumonia or something and there you are. Now, take me, I don't have the faintest notion of how I'll meet m'Maker. The information ain't to be had. But you, now, that's different. It's all cut and dried and you ain't got to worry about it anymore. So that's that. C'mon and have some hotcakes before they get cold."

As Jan made no move to answer the invitation, Diver philosophically conveyed the second portion to his own plate and, with the usual appetite of the very thin, put them easily down and finally, having cleared the tray, looked mournfully under the napkins to locate more. His search unavailing, he slid it back into the corridor and fell into a conversation with a counterfeiter across the block. With great leisure, as men do when they know they have lots of time to pass, they discussed the latest inmate with great thoroughness and Diver, after fishing for coaxing, finally laid aside an air of mystery and divulged Jan's story.

"Hophead, huh?" said the counterfeiter.

"Yeah, guess so. He don't eat nothin' and that's another reason. He evidently is feelin' the mornin' after no doubt."

"I know where I can get him some," said the counterfeiter confidentially.

"Yeah? When he gets over his fit I'll ask him if he wants it. He had nightmares last night fit to shake the place down."

"Yes, I heard him."

"Snow's pretty awful stuff."

"Ain't it," said the counterfeiter. "Why oncet I had a sniffer in my outfit—Goo-goo, the boys called'm—and this here Goo-goo . . ."

Jan tried not to listen, even stuffing his ears with the edge of the blanket, but one story led to another and finally they got on the subject of being hanged.

"So they sprung the trap three times on this gent," said the counterfeiter, "and it wouldn't sag with him. They'd take him off and put him back and try her again and still she wouldn't work. Well, the guy fainted finally, but they brought him around and put him on the trap once more. Well, sir, this time she sure worked. He dropped like a rock and the rope snapped his spine like you'd crack walnuts. But how do you like that, huh? Three times and it don't work."

"Leave it to the Law," said Diver. "They can't even hang a man straight."

"Somebody coming," said the counterfeiter.

The block fell silent, watching the approach of the visitors. All but Jan clung to the bars for he was in a state of coma induced by the late conversations.

"Hiyah, Babe," said a jailbird down the row.

"Geez, some looker," said Diver, now that he could see the party.

A series of such comments and calls ran the length of the place and then the party stopped before Jan's door while a jailer, with much important key rattling, got the lock open.

Diver backed up and gave the prostrate Jan a wicked kick to wake him. Resentfully, Jan sat up, about to protest, but all such thought left him when he found that Alice Hall stood before him.

She had carried herself like a sentry through the block just as though the jailbirds did not exist and now, with a tinge of pity upon her lovely face she stood taking off her gloves and studying Jan just as though she were about to begin an operation to change his luck.

"Well, well, well, my boy," said a very, very, very, very hearty voice—one which the owner fondly thought capable of carrying him, someday, to the Senate. "What are they doing to you?"

Jan dragged his eyes away from Alice and woke up to the presence of two others in his cell—Shannon, Bering Steam's legal department head, and Nathaniel Green. Shannon was very plump and so fitted his manner to the recognized one for all plump men. He was very hearty, very well met and very reassuring, though there were those (who had no doubt lost cases to him) who said it was all sham. The fellow's mouth, in its absence of a sufficient chin and nose, looked like nothing if not a shark's. One supposed he had to turn over on his back to eat, so tightly and immobilely did his fat neck sit in his collar.

Jan looked nervous and was not at all sure that he wanted to talk to these two gentlemen. He resented their presence all the more because Alice Hall was there and how badly he wanted to have her sit on that small stool and hear his flood of grief and then give him very sound advice in return. Didn't her brave face have a tinge of pity in it?

"Have you out in no time," said Shannon, sitting down on Diver's bunk so that Diver had to hastily get out of his way.

"Don't mind me," said Diver resentfully.

Shannon twirled his hat and paid no attention to anything save the crown of the bowler. He was getting serious now, evidently opening up a whole weighty library of immense legal tomes in his head. "Yes, my boy, serious as this is, we should have no difficulty in getting you freed, eh, Mr. Green?"

"Of course," said Green swiftly. He hadn't seated himself at all, and looked as though he was about to hurry off on some important errand or other. "Must be done. The company, you understand, is in no such position that it can bear this publicity. Look," and he jerked a sheaf of papers out of his pocket and tossed them to the bunk beside Jan where they fanned out into blazing headlines, "MILLIONAIRE SHIPOWNER SLAYS PROFESSOR" and the like.

Jan shuddered when he saw them and drew back.

"Ha, ha, I don't blame you," said Shannon. "But people forget. Never mind that sort of thing. The point is, we want your version of this...er...crime. Then, we'll demand a bail to be set and take you home." He got serious once more. "Now, to begin, just how did this thing happen?"

It was Alice Hall's cue. She sat down at the rickety table and spread her notebooks to take down the discourse. Jan looked hopelessly at her, hating to have her take his words so cold-bloodedly.

"We haven't much time," said Nathaniel impatiently glancing at his watch.

"I...I don't know how to begin," said Jan.

"Why, at the beginning, of course," said Shannon. "Nothing simpler. When was the first time that you saw this Frobish fellow?"

Jan told them and then, with much prompting, managed to get the story out in its entirety. Very wisely he refrained from following it up with the events of the night just passed. And all

the while he spoke Alice Hall inscribed his words as emotion-
lessly as though she listened to a dictaphone record. Not so the
other two. With increasing frequency Shannon glanced knowingly
at Green, and Green stared impatiently at Jan as though about
to accuse him of lying.

Then, when Jan was through, Shannon's tone was very different from his first. Shannon patted Jan on the knee consolingly
as one will a sick animal or perhaps an angry child. "There, there,
my boy, we'll do what we can. But ... er ... don't you think you
might ... ah ... modify these statements somewhat. After all, if
I wish to have bail set for you, I have to have something I can
tell the judge. It's not that we don't believe you ... but ... well,
courts are strange things and you'll have to trust to my advice
and experience in the matter. I shall enter a plea at my discretion.
Perhaps," he added to Nathaniel, "I can think of something logical."

Green glanced at his watch. "I've got to be getting back to
the office. I've a million things to do before noon."

"Could I speak with you a moment?" said Shannon.

Green irritably acquiesced and they stepped out into the hall
where they spoke in low whispers, looking toward the cell now
and then. Alice Hall kept her eyes on her notes.

"They don't believe me," said Jan.

The girl looked searchingly at him. "You wonder about it?"

"Why ... but what happened, happened. I wouldn't lie!"

The shadow of a smile went across her features. "Of course
not."

"But it *did* happen that way!" wailed Jan. "And I'll tell you
something else. Last night ..." But there he stopped and nothing
could persuade him to finish.

"You shouldn't keep any of it back," said Alice. "Those
gentlemen, presumably, mean to get you out of here and if you
know anything else you should tell them ..."

"I don't know anything else."

She shrugged. "All right, have it your own way."

"Don't be angry."

"I'm not. Why should I be?"

"But you were."

"Maybe I was. What of it?"

"But why should you be angry?"

"No reason at all," she said with sudden bitterness. "You have a story and you'll stick to it. If you're going to act that way I can tell you truthfully, though it's none of my business, that you'll hang. I don't know—and I don't care, I'm sure!—whether you committed this murder or not. But I do know that you'll have to get yourself out of it the best you can."

"What do you mean?"

"I suppose Green hasn't been waiting . . . !" She suddenly cooled her heat and gave her attention to her notes.

"You mean you think they won't help me?"

"I have nothing to say."

"But you were saying something," pleaded Jan. "If you know anything that might help me . . ."

"Help you! Nobody can help you! Nobody will ever be able to solve your problems but yourself. I've worked with your company long enough to know that you know nothing about it and care less. You keep yourself locked up in your room, scared to death by an aunt, a secretary and the head of your father's firm. You let Nathaniel Green do what he pleases with accounts—but why am I talking this way? It can do you no good now. I should have spoken months ago. Maybe I was hoping you'd wake up by yourself and find out that you were a man instead of an infant. But you haven't and now, unless a miracle happens, you'll never have the chance. There! I've said it."

Jan was stunned and scarcely heard Green and Shannon come back until Shannon cleared his throat noisily.

"My boy," said Shannon, "Green and I have talked this thing over. It is quite apparent that you mean to stick to your story."

"It's the truth!"

49

"Of course it's the truth!" cried Shannon. "But the law is a strange thing. Now, my advice is for you to plead self-defense."

"That would be lying," said Jan.

"Yes, perhaps," said Shannon. And then he gave Green a look which plainly said that he had done what he could. "Very well, young fellow, I shall tell the court your story and ask that you be released on bail. Is that according to your wishes?"

"Certainly!" said Jan.

Green almost smiled but checked himself in time. He glanced at his watch. "I must be getting back. Come along, Miss Hall. Jan, if anything can be done, Mr. Shannon will do it. Don't despair. We're with you to the end."

So saying, Green walked out, followed by the lawyer and Alice Hall and the door was locked once more.

Diver came out of the corner and looked at the departing backs and then at Jan. "Geez, fellah, how do you do it?"

"Do what?" said Jan dully.

"The dame," said Diver. "Boy, is she a looker! How do you do it, huh?"

"I don't know what you're talking about."

"Oh boy, are you a deep one. Why man, if I had a gal like that in love with me . . ."

"She's not in love with me!"

"No?" and then Diver laughed. "No, sure not. Innocent, that's you. No, sure she ain't in love with you. Why she was near cryin' when she came in that door and she almost bawled while she was writin' at the table there and you was spielin' that awful lie of yours."

"She despises me, I know she does."

"Sure. Sure she does or she thinks she does. But all you'd have to do, feller, is to square up your spine and act like a man and she'd fall in your lap. I'm telling you."

"I'm sure," said Jan with abrupt heat, "that I'm not interested in what you think of Miss Hall!"

Diver was taken aback, more with surprise than anything else. But presently he began to chuckle. "What a pack of wolves," he said.

"Who?"

"Why that short fellow and that lawyer."

"I don't know what you mean."

"If you don't you're blind as a bat, buddy. Friends of yours?"

"Mr. Green is the head of my . . . that is, the Bering Sea Steamship Corporation."

"Oh boy, I know why those longshoremen go on strike now! Pal, you got three strikes on you and don't know it."

"I fail . . ."

"You're fanned, feller, fanned. How come you ever got yourself into such a spot seein' the way that Green wants to do you in."

"I am sure . . ."

"So am I. I watched him lickin' his chops all the time he was here. What'd you ever do to him?"

"He was my father's best friend."

"And your dearest enemy," said Diver. "Oh, well, what's done is done. But I sure wish I'd had your chance."

"*My* chance!"

"The gal," said Diver with a deep sigh, lying back on his bunk. "Man, I'd almost enjoy bein' accused of murder if I had her feelin' that way about me." And he closed his eyes so languorously that Jan, contrary to all his regular emotions, wanted very badly to kick the guts out of him.

Lunch came and Jan ate a few mouthfuls without any relish. The hours began their slow march down the afternoon and still no word came from Shannon. Dinner time found Diver at the tail end of a long discussion with the counterfeiter over the looks of Alice Hall.

At about seven the cell block was brought to the bars again by an opening door. Ignoring all of them, Alice marched down the concrete to Jan's cell but the jailer did not offer to open the door for her.

Jan stood up, blinking and suddenly tongue-tied.

She was very cool and efficient. "Mr. Green asked me to stop by on my way home and tell you that Shannon was unable to have bail set for you."

"You mean," said the jolted Jan, "that I've got to stay here?"

Slowly she nodded and then found sudden interest in a package she had under her arm. She thrust it through the bars. "It's all right," she told the officer. "They inspected it at the desk. Your Aunt Ethel . . . er . . . sent this to you."

Jan took it mechanically, trying to think of something to say which might detain her a moment. But he thought of nothing and they stood in an awkward silence.

"I hope you aren't too uncomfortable," she said at last.

"I . . . I'm all right."

"Well . . . I had better be going."

"Th-thank you for the package from Aunt Ethel and th-thank you for coming."

"I have to pass the jail to get home anyway," said Alice. "Good night."

She was gone and Jan stood staring at the place where she had been.

"Well!" said Diver. "Open it, you dummy."

"What?"

"The package!"

"It's probably flannel pajamas," said Jan dolefully.

"You don't know, do you? Open it."

Jan opened it and, wonder of wonders, it appeared that Aunt Ethel had broken down for the first time in her life. Here was a box of tea biscuits, a box of candy, three of the latest books, a toothbrush and paste and razor and shaving cream, a new shirt, tobacco, and, at the very bottom, Houdini's textbook.

"Geez, cookies," said Diver.

"Aunt Ethel?" said Jan. "But she would have sent one of my shirts and some of my own books if she sent anything at all."

"The dame!" cried Diver. "She done it but wouldn't admit it. Your Aunt Ethel be damned, buddy. Boy, are these cookies good!"

Jan nibbled on one and looked at the books. For a while he thumbed through Houdini but, at last, gave it up as a bad job.

"If she's just a steno, buddy, she must've spent a week's pay on them things," said Diver, looking at the price marks in the books. "Gosh, you can never tell about dames. A looker like her takin' up for a scared rabbit like you...huh!" And so saying he began to read.

The night grew through its childhood and, suddenly, Jan remembered that there was a chance...the barest, barest chance ...that he might be elsewhere the instant he closed his eyes. He might be deep, down in the brig of a sailing ship plowing through an unknown sea, waiting with terror for what the port might bring. He shuddered as the thought became very real. He was revolted by the thought of becoming Tiger once again.

And yet he was tired. He had had no sleep for an age, it seemed. He was weary until he ached.

But, if the Ifrit had spoken the truth, then...

Then...

And by midnight he lost the fight.

He went down into the abyss of sleep, awakened instantly by the howl of winches and the cannonading of sails and then the grinding roar of chain racing through a hawsepipe. He opened his eyes.

Chapter 5

THE QUEEN!

Jan Palmer was afraid to open his eyes. When Diver had said that he had rolled and tossed the whole night through he had been perfectly willing to believe that it had all been a nightmare brought about by his excessive mental perturbation. But right now it didn't at all appear that he was rolling and tossing upon the sagging bunk in the jail. In fact it was quite plain that he was lying on blankets and that he had no bunk but floor under him.

Cautiously he pried open one eyelid and found that he looked through a grilled window upon the back of a Marid. It was not the same Marid at all, but another one who was much uglier—if such could be possible—than the first. This fellow had a ferocious cast to his single eye and he was girt about with a sword which must have weighed thirty pounds and he leaned upon a pike pole so sharp that it tapered to nothingness rather than a point.

"Now I'm for it," moaned Jan.

And he startled himself.

"Now I'll get the galleys."

He blinked and said it over again. "Now I'll get the galleys."

Well, what galleys? And how did he know that there would be any galleys in the neighborhood? Further, what reason did he have to think that galleys would be in use?

But, just the same he was convinced and he sat up, already experiencing an ache in his back and sinewy arms.

"This is a hell of a note," he uttered. "I'm damned if I'll take it, so help me. Let'm flog. Let'm string me up by the thumbs. But I'll see 'em all in hell before I'll haul an oar."

Plainly, he thought, such a speech showed that he was delirious. But no, his head wasn't hot.

He stood up. "Hey, you one-eyed farmer, where are we?" Certainly, he shouldn't take such a tone with this vicious-looking Marid. He frightened himself.

The Marid's hoofs knocked sharply as he came around and playfully poked the pike straight at Jan's eyes. Jan dodged back from the grill.

"So, what I hear is a lie," said the Marid. "You plenty smart, you Tiger. Lie, lie, lie. All the time lie. You get yours this time."

"I . . . I haven't lied about anything," said Jan.

"We hear. Nobody talks but we hear just the same. Last night you put us on beach or almost which is just as bad. You take too much rum, I think. This time you get the galleys, I think. Now sit down before I shove this through your guts. They'll come for you quick enough."

Jan very tamely seated himself and the pike was withdrawn from the grill. Twice in the next half an hour sailors came by and were fain to linger about the grill but the Marid poked them on their way.

"I do you a favor," said the Marid after a while. "Them men want to cut you up very bad. If you wasn't too drunk last night, I think, you would not have ever tried to put us up on that shoal."

"I wasn't drunk," said Jan.

"Tiger not drunk! I think that's a good one. I tell that one. You know what shoal that was?"

"No."

"See, you drunk. Everybody know that shoal. The Isle of Fire just behind those shoals and you say you not know! Haw!"

"The Isle of Fire? Never heard of it."

"Oh, no, you never heard of it. You never stood off and on in the ship here listening to Admiral Tyronin's flagship people burn up every one. You never on boat that go in to pull off what men left. Haw! You fool, Tiger. Me, I was with you and you still got burns on your leg. Lie to me, I think, and I take pike to you."

Jan thoughtfully lifted up his wide-bottomed pants and stared at his brawny leg. He was startled both by the strength which was obviously in it and by the white burn marks which were there. Then, too, there was a purple scar which ran from knee to ankle and which plainly bespoke a boarding ax. He examined it carefully as though it might vanish under his touch and the Marid, glancing through the grill laughed at what he thought was a joke in pantomime.

"Tiger's memory come back fast enough in galleys," said the Marid. "Good you leave or the crew . . ."

He was interrupted by the clang of a door which opened and closed, admitting a party of men. They came briskly up to the brig and stopped, grounding their muskets with a large gesture. The captain opened the door of the brig and Jan came carefully out, to instantly be thrust between two files of the most evil-looking Marids imaginable.

They faced smartly about, their cloaks swirling, shouldered their arms and marched Jan up a ladder to the deck. The captain made a motion toward the port gangway and the file halted there, tightly ringing Jan.

At some distance a knot of seamen stood, growling among themselves and looking toward the prisoner. But the Marids stood very complacently, hairy hands wrapped about their gun barrels.

Jan blinked in the blazing sunlight which glanced hurtfully back from polished bitts and scoured deck and from the wide harbor. Wonderingly he looked about at the ship itself to find that it was not unlike a cromster of the Middle Ages though considerably larger. The sterncastle deck, however, was cut into by the after house and the helm was a large wheel. A conglomerate rig it was, with a lateen on the mizzen, fore and aft on the main, the peaks held up with sprits, with a large square topsail and a t'g'l'nt above that and with three large staysails forward. A sprits'l was furled under the bowsprit, and long abandoned had such "water sails" been in modern usage. A dozen brass cannon, glittering and ferocious, thrust their snouts out from the quarterdeck rail. Two bow-chasers loomed on the fo'c's'le head. And all along each side, evidently manned from the deck below, were the muzzles of thirty demi-cannon. Aloft there floated from the now naked peak the strangest flag Jan had ever seen. It was a brilliant scarlet and upon it was emblazoned in gold a wheeling bird of prey. Other streamers there were in plenty but he could not make them out, so bright was the greenish sky.

In the harbor about them lay hundreds of other vessels, both large and small, ranging in style from a Greek corbita to a seventy-four. Small shoreboats, not unlike sampans, scudded back and forth on a brisk breeze, carrying all sorts of passengers. Among these, by far, Ifrits predominated, and it was strange indeed to see peaked caps between their pointed ears and massive rings upon their claw-tipped fingers. It was as though the animal kingdom had blended with the human race and that these men-beasts were mocking the ancient history of their human ancestors.

Such, however, could not be the case as Jan well knew. Ifrits were Ifrits. And if the Jinn wished to conquer the sea with ships for war and cargo, eschewing other means of transportation (as far as he could see at the moment) then it was certainly being done.

But about the deck of the vessel on which he stood Jan saw far more human beings than he did Ifrits. In fact only the captain and the mate were of the Jinn. The guard about him was made up of ugly little Marids and there were two or three other one-eyed demons astroll. But the sailors who worked aloft to put harbor furls on the restive canvas were all human beings, seem-ingly not much different from any other men Jan had ever seen beyond their devil-may-care aspect.

"I suppose," muttered Jan to himself, staring intently across the blinding way at a long, gilded vessel, obviously a galley, "that I'll get the *Pinchoti*, damn her. She's the worst puller of the lot."

And again he startled himself by finding that he knew the names of most of these vessels and, indeed, the names of most of the men about the deck. How he came to know them he was not at all sure.

A werewolf, in his human identity, must often feel the beast stirring uneasily within him, threatening to spring forth uncalled. More and more, as time went along, did Jan experience just that sensation, except that, in his case, it was more like that Malay demon, the were-tiger. Scholar that he was, he knew considerable about lycanthropy but never in his life had he thought to experience such a thing, even in a reasonable way, but now, certainly, things were happening to him which he could not begin to discount. Were-Tiger was certainly the only name for it. He was vaguely conscious of latent wells of knowledge within him, of information which he could almost—but not quite—bring to the surface of his brain. It was as though he had always known these things but was suffering, at the moment, a slight lapse of memory.

He gazed critically at the work of a man working on the lateen sail, whom he knew as Lacy. Lacy was bungling the job as usual and it crossed Jan's mind that he bet they could use Tiger's help about the ship just then. Still, he had not the least idea of what he should have been doing.

Further, he found himself in the grip of a very alien impulse. Now nobody in all his life on earth had ever dreamed that there was an ounce of facetiousness in one Jan Palmer. All jokes he had received with funereal mien, startled when others laughed at them. He had always read of pranks with wondering suspicion, puzzled that anyone could get pleasure out of such things. It must be confessed that Jan Palmer had missed much in the way of education due to the thorough isolation of his youth. Never had he felt the slightest desire to understand, much less commit, what might be called a practical joke.

It was with horror, then, that he found himself contemplating the most foolhardy adventure imaginable. Here he was, packed tight by ten well-armed and doubtlessly zealous Marids, all of them wholly humorless. Here he was charged with God knew what crime and faced with devil knew what sentence. And the Tiger in him stirred and laughed silently to see that one of the Marids was carrying his musket on his shoulder, hand well away from the trigger which was, providentially or otherwise, within six inches of Jan's face. And the barrel of that musket was pointed up in the general direction of the cantankerous Lacy, balanced precariously upon the whippy lateen yard.

"Marvelous," chortled Tiger.

"No! My God, no!" gasped the appalled Jan.

There was the trigger and there was Lacy. The shot would go several feet below the seaman, certainly, but it would crack when it passed through the sail.

"Wonderful!" yearned the laughing Tiger.

Jan covered his face with his hands so that he couldn't see the trigger or Lacy. In a moment the Marid would move temptation far away from Tiger. In a moment Lacy would finish his clumsy furl and come scampering thankfully down from the dizzy heights. In a moment all would be well and Jan would have triumphed.

But the joke was too good. Nobody liked Lacy and Lacy was an avowed coward. Jan's finger slipped and his eye fell upon the burnished trigger. It was too much for him.

Out went his finger quick as a blink. The trigger came back softly. Back came Jan's hand to his innocent side. The match fell, the pan flared, the musket roared and leaped upwards to bang the Marid in the head and knock him sprawling.

From aloft, close on the heels of the shot, came the returning crack of the bullet through canvas and, instantly after, the terrified scream of Lacy who stared at the round hole not two feet under his hand. Lacy clung tight to the yard. The yard vibrated enough already in the wind without that; it began to sway and tip and the more it did the more Lacy screamed bloody mayhem.

Malek came streaking down the waist bellowing, "Get him down before the fool shakes out that sail! Get him down, I say, before that canvas catches air and puts weigh on us! GET HIM DOWN!"

A dozen sailors were standing about the deck. Lacy was in no trouble at all, though swaying back and forth fifty feet from the quarterdeck straight down must have been very uncomfortable. The sailors began to laugh happily. Lacy screamed curses, almost fell off to the right and clutched so hard that he overdid his adjustment and almost went off to port. The yard wove great circles against the greenish sky. Lacy screamed in terror. The sailors doubled up on the deck, holding their sides with glee.

"GET HIM DOWN, DAMN YOU!" screamed Malek as canvas began to shake loose and fill. Uneasily, the ship pushed ahead against her anchor cables, pointing toward another vessel not a hundred yards dead ahead. And now the unstayed lateen billowed with a crack which almost boosted Lacy all the way off.

Malek despaired of getting anything done for him. He seized the halyards and, braking them on the pins, swiftly slacked them off. Lateen yard, Lacy and a mass of disorderly canvas came billowing down to the quarterdeck. Lacy climbed off and weakly sought the wall where his shoulders hitched convulsively. Malek blew sourly upon his rope-scorched hands. The sailors, to the best of their ability, stilled their mirth.

Malek hitched at his belt to get his exposed pistols around into reach. With grim visage and glittering fangs, he stalked down toward Tiger. But Tiger was gone again and Jan cowered in his soul.

"So, you are a different man, are you?" scowled Malek most awfully. "So, you know nothing, do you?" His fingers wrapped around the butt of a gun and he brought it forth, tossing it up so that it came down with the muzzle in his fist. With this for a club Malek stepped so close to Jan that Jan could count the crumbs in his beard. The guard, especially the victimized Marid, pressed close about and seized Jan's arms from behind.

"Let him alone," said the bosun, coming over from the starboard rail. His thick, rolling body was belligerent and his heavy face was dark. He was a very tough human being. "I seen it with me own peepers, Mr. Malek. This here Marid, like the dummy he is, was monkeying with his trigger. I seen it, I tell you."

Malek looked doubtfully at the bosun. "You expect me to believe you?"

"We seen it too!" chimed some of the other sailors, coming up. "This here Marid was the one. It wasn't Tiger. Nosir!"

"Captain Tombo!" shouted Malek as the captain appeared in a hatch. "Tiger is at it again. I . . . "

"He isn't either!" yelped the crew. "This here Marid . . ."

"Stow it," said Captain Tombo. "What's the odds? Leave him alone, Mr. Malek. He's out of our hands now. The port captain is taking charge."

Behind Tombo came a portly and foppish Ifrit who fanned the air before him with a perfumed handkerchief to fend off the odor of sailors. He handed a signed release to Tombo.

"Thank you, Boli," said the captain. "There's your man. I wouldn't be too extreme if I were you. After all, Tiger's got some little reputation."

"For brawling, theft and rapine," sniffed Boli, gazing with disgust at Jan. "But the matter isn't in my hands either. This is a case for the crown. Yes, indeed, the crown. Hail my boat," he added to Malek.

Malek shouted to a barge which had been drifting under the quarter and now it was pulled forward to the gangway. It was crammed from gunwale to gunwale with armed men, but they were port sailors and rather given to fat and softness.

"Down with you," said Boli, punching Jan in the back with his sword scabbard as though appalled at the thought of touching him with a hand and so soiling it.

Jan started down the ladder. Along the rail thronged the fickle ship's company, wholly won again by the incident of Lacy.

"S'long, Tiger."

"Give'm hell, Tiger."

"Mess 'em up, Tiger."

"Give Her Majesty m'love, will yuh?"

Jan suddenly found that he was grinning up at the faces above him and swaggering down the steps. The boat was bobbing in the slight swell and, loaded as it was, the gunwale was none too far above the water. The guard sailors were ready with their weapons as though expecting anything to happen and rather surprised that Tiger took it so mildly. Evidently he knew some of them, thought Jan.

Suddenly he remembered his manners and stepped back so that Boli, fat and awkward, could enter the boat first. And, seeing that the guard was quite on the alert and that the boat was, after all, bobbing rather badly even in this glassy sea, Boli was nothing loth to have a hand all of a sudden, even from a criminal.

Jan felt things stirring inside him and was too frightened to think the matter through, afraid lest he discover another awful plot within him. He took hold of the bowman's boat pike and helped him hold the barge in to the landing stage.

Boli, striving to see over his chest ruffles, watched the barge drop four feet below the stage and then bounce four feet above it. In truth, the condition was very ordinary, seeing that there had to be some manner of swell about a vessel anchored in the roads, but Boli had had one or two in the captain's cabin and he well knew that his reputation only wanted a ridiculous incident to throw down much of his carefully built authority.

"Here, you," said Jan (or rather Tiger) to the gunwale guards. "Give M'Lord the port captain a hand before I knock you about. Look alive, swabs!"

The two moved hastily, getting up on thwarts to reach for Boli's hands and steady him. They were going through a usual routine but the presence of Tiger had rather shattered their composure. Boli wished ardently that the vessel weren't so far to sea.

"Easy, now, M'Lord," said Tiger, looming above Boli as a church steeple rears above its alms house. "When she starts down, step aboard and lively. And you, y'landlubbers, don't muss'm up or I'll break your skulls like they was eggs. Now!"

He eased Boli ahead. The barge swooped down from the height of the port captain's head. Boli, aided by Tiger's left hand, stepped to the gunwale as it flew downward. His men eased him quickly aboard while the barge kept on going down to four feet below the stage.

Tiger, still holding the bowman's pike in his right hand to help the bowman hold the barge in, suddenly yelped, "Don't pull her in, you fools!" And pulled her in with a jerk which almost hauled the bowman out of the boat.

The next instant an awful thing happened. The barge, four feet under the stage, started instantly on its upward surge. But this time it didn't miss the underside of the protruding stage. With a rending jar, the gunwale caught under the stage itself and the wave did the rest.

With a swoop, the barge capsized! One instant it was a normal enough boat, full of sleek and flawlessly uniformed sailors and the next the only thing which could be seen was the keel, all dripping and bobbing on the waves. From tumblehome to tumblehome, the boat displayed its bottom.

"Help!" bellowed Tiger, safe and dry on the landing stage.

But before help could even start, sailors out of the barge were rocketing into sight all about it, having ducked out of the terrifying but perfectly safe air pocket under the boat.

Tiger waited to see no more. He went overboard in a long dive. The green water fled past him. The dark barge was over him. And just ahead was a pair of very fat legs kicking desperately. Tiger encircled them deftly and hauled hard. Down into the sea went Boli!

Tiger came up by the stage an instant later to let a wave boost him to a hold. Boli was floundering like a grounded whale but still Tiger did not let him be. Up he came and up went Boli to his brawny back. Swiftly Tiger made the deck, surging past the ship sailors who were fishing up the boat guard, man by man.

Laying the port captain out on a hatch cover, Tiger pumped him thoroughly dry, taking the weak but strengthening protests as unworthy of notice. Artificial respiration seemed to work wonderfully upon Boli and in no time at all the man Tiger had rescued from a watery grave was sitting up turning the air scarlet and azure all about him.

The barge men were hauled up, every man of them, to be dumped in all postures by the ship sailors. There was no great love lost between seamen and this spying patrol which policed the port.

All the while Jan was shuddering in horror. If he was in trouble now, what would he be in, in a few moments. But he was utterly powerless to do anything about it and he was aghast to hear himself say, upon Boli's running out of breath, "By God, M'Lord, it's lucky I was there. If you'll take a sailor's advice, M'Lord, I'd jail that bowman for a month, so I would. Why, by God, sir, even when I yelled at him to desist he insisted upon hooking his pike into the stage itself and pulling you under it! Beggin' M'Lord's pardon, but you'd better get some sailors in that crew of yours that know their business. Damned if not."

Boli glowered and had dark suspicions. Tombo and Malek tried to keep scowling and be severe. The sailors attempted to stifle their merriment until a more appropriate moment.

"Is your breath all right now, M'Lord?" said Tiger with earnest interest. "Captain, perhaps he'd better be let to rest in a cabin, if I might suggest it. That was a very trying thing and though he came out of it like a hero..."

"Tiger!" said Tombo.

"Sir?" said Tiger.

Captain Tombo tried to scowl more ferociously. But it happened that he had, on many occasions, suffered great delay because of the effeminate whims of this gross port captain and, for the life of him, he couldn't carry that much sail at the moment.

"Tiger," said the captain with a glance at Boli. And he was about to go on when he saw the bedraggled silk which hung in bags all about the Lord. He changed his mind.

"Sir?"

"Give them a hand in righting that boat."

"Yessir."

Tiger sped down the gangway once more where the ship's mirth-convulsed seamen were working. They said nothing. They couldn't and still keep their laughter inside where it would not offend Boli's ears above. But their eyes were full of great affection.

They righted the boat and, shortly, Boli's guard came down, leaving a river of water to run behind them on the steps. Gingerly they got into the barge. Nervously they prodded Tiger into the sternsheets. Fearfully they aided the port captain to his seat of state amidships.

They shoved off and all along the rail above, sailors waved farewell. Even Captain Tombo smiled and Mr. Malek put a rope-scorched hand to his cap and raised it slightly to call, "So long, Tiger. We'll all be in to see you."

Boli rolled around and glared at his prisoner. Now that the port captain was on, so to speak, his own deck, he was quite recovered (save that his ribs ached from respiration treatment).

"You are very clever, my fine bucko. Everywhere you set your foot, things happen. I have heard it. Well! Do not think for one moment that your saving of Admiral Tyronin from the Isle of Fire, that your timely bombs at the Battle of Barankeet, that all your other mad deeds will stand a bit in your favor. You have flown too high! Whatever these charges are," and he fished a sealed packet from his soggy shirt, "and I don't doubt that they are severe enough, you will be tried for the crime at hand, not for deeds of questionable character long past. You have been recommended for trial by the queen herself and if she doesn't sentence you to swing, it'll not be the fault of mine."

There was so much hatred in Boli's voice that Jan shivered. Out of him, like a dying fire, went the reckless madness which had brought him to that deed just done. He could not reason that Boli's hatred was not only born of that deed but of another, more delicate thing. Boli was badly built, ugly beyond description, and before him sat a tall, handsome fellow of a rare kind, calculated to stir the most frigid of feminine hearts. But Jan could not see himself. Jan was just Jan now. He recognized no ships, he recalled nothing. He even fumbled for his glasses to wipe them in his confusion and was mighty startled to find that he wore none—indeed, did not seem to need any.

"The queen?" he gulped.

"The queen," said Boli, satisfied now that he could feel the uneasiness in his prisoner. "Not four days past she put five heads on pikes outside her palace and that for mere thievery on the highroad. I am given to understand that you have some dread stigma attached to you. Ah, yes, my fine prankster, it seems that your lighthearted days are done. Before you there is nothing but doom and death."

Boli enjoyed himself for the moment and almost forgot how wet he was. For the remainder of the voyage across the harbor, he piled up torments and watched his victim squirm. But, when he reached the quay, a number of loafers, beholding M'Lord the port captain as soggy as a drowned rat, burst into braying mirth.

Boli swept an imperious eye across the rank on the dock and roared, "Sergeant, arrest them! Up, I say! I'll show you the price of laughter, that I will!"

And though his guard tumbled swiftly up the gangway, when they got to the dock, not a man was left. Only laughter's echoes were there.

Snorting, Boli stamped to the wharf while four men carried Jan along at the point of their swords.

Jan, bewildered, stared up at the buildings of the town. They stretched back across the plain for miles. They reached around the harbor for leagues. What an immense town it was! Commerce jammed the wharves. Men sweated and swore, hauling cargoes about. Horses stamped and neighed as they strained at rumbling trucks. A bewildering array of signs spread out in every direction and the odd part of it was that one moment they were so many chicken scratches to Jan and the next their meaning was quite plain. Taverns and brokers' offices, sailors' hotels and shipping firms, trucking barns and chandler shops. Immediately beside them reared the customs, a building some four stories in height and of a queer architecture which was prominent in its immense scrolls and swoops and towers. All the buildings were like that, presenting a baffling line of distorted curves and garish, mismatched colors.

Along the docks bobbed fishing boats, small beside the towering castles of the ocean-going ships. From the scaly decks of the little craft a variety of weird seafood was being hoisted so that Jan knew it was still very early in the day.

Boli stamped away up the stairs to his quarters where he could get a consoling nip and a change of clothes. His guard, forgotten, stood about, damply keeping an eye on their prisoner and very careful not to get within arm's length of him. Jan found quite accidentally that when he wandered along he carried the whole company with him and so, benighted as he was with woe, he strolled restlessly back and forth, the men moving with him but well away from him and all about him.

Jan stared down at a pile of flapping fish just tossed from a tubby little vessel's hold. He had never before seen any such denizens of the sea as these. Their eyes were lidded and winked and winked. They were as wide as they were long and their heads were as big as their bodies. For all the world they resembled sheep and Jan wondered distractedly if they tasted like mutton. Some of this catch was being laid on a miserable peddler's cart, the wheels of which spread out very wide at the top and very narrow at the bottom, giving it a bow-legged appearance. Presently the two who had been loading it were accosted by the master of the fishing vessel who held out his palm for his pay.

One of the pair was a woman. Her hair was snarled beyond belief and a filthy, scaly neckerchief was swathed about her scrawny neck. Her dress glittered with dried scales which showed up very brightly against the black dirt which smeared the whole, shapeless garment. Her pipestem legs shot up out of hopelessly warped shoes and got no thicker when they became a body. She could have passed through a knothole with ease and, doubtless, such an operation would have taken a lot of the dirt from her. She chose to be niggardly about the price.

"You soul-stealing lobster!" she shrieked in a cracked ruin of a voice. "You . . ." Jan wanted to stop his ears. "Last time you charge two damins the feesh! This time you charge t'ree damins. We don't have to buy! We don't have to deal with the slimy likes of you! We'll take our trade elsewhere!" Her companion, an incredibly diseased fellow, tried to calm her. The fisherman tried to break in with the explanation—quite obvious—that these fish were especially fine, big ones. She would have nothing of it. Her rage mounted higher and higher, in direct ratio to the humoring it got from the two men. Finally this virago seized one of the fish by the tail and began to lay about her with all her might, screaming the foulest of language the while. Her rage made her blind and she lambasted several of the guards who could not get out of the way fast enough.

Jan was successful in ducking a swing but he tripped over a bitt and fell to stare up and get a full view of this termagant's ugly face. He recoiled, frozen with revulsion.

This shrew, this harridan, this screaming unholy catamaran, resembled no one if not his Aunt Ethel!

He recovered and scrambled back. At a safe distance he peered wonderingly at the woman. The voice tone, now that he listened for it, had a certain timbre; the eyes, the nose, the very ears carried the resemblance. Her build, the way she stood now that she was calming down in the wreckage of her victory, was also similar. And finally, though he could not understand how it could be, he was forced to grant this revolting creature the identity of his aunt. Aunt Ethel, wife to a diseased fish peddler! Aunt Ethel, brawling like a harlot upon the common dock!

But how on earth did she get there?

Now that hostilities had ceased and a lower price had been paid, the woman signaled to the man to be off and the two pushed the cart along toward the shoreward end.

"My darling Daphne," said the fish peddler, "the price we saved won't cover the cost of bandages for my head. By swith, how it rings!"

"Be quiet, you wretched apology of a man. I'll deal with you later when we get home."

But Jan had to know! He stepped forward beside the cart. "Aunt Ethel," he said, "how . . . ?"

She stared at him angrily and brushed on by just as his guards leaped up to take him again and keep him from communicating with others. She glanced back in high disdain and snorted.

"Y'see? Y'see, you worm-eaten miscreant? I'm sunk so low that convicts talk to me! Ohhh, you wretch, if you think your head rings now . . ." And so they passed out of sight just as Boli, much fortified, hove like a barge into view.

Boli had a fresh company of Marids with him who swiftly and efficiently took Jan in hand.

"Take care," said Boli. "Your heads answer for it if he gets away."

A sedan chair was borne to them by four humans and into its cushioned depths sank Boli. He raised his handkerchief and flourished it and the party moved off.

Dread began to settle heavily over Jan. What had possessed him to first frighten the wits out of a sailor and then upset a whole boatload of guard sailors, to say nothing of almost drowning the port captain, M'Lord Boli? What unplumbed possibilities did this swaggering, brawny body of his contain that he had never before felt? And would he do something the very next minute to make his doom absolutely certain—if it weren't already so?

He was almost treading on the heels of the last two chair bearers. And suddenly it occurred to him that all he had to do was take a slightly longer step and into the street M'Lord Boli would go, perfumed handkerchief and all. Ah, yes, and just ahead there was a lovely, wide mud puddle where horses had been tethered not long before. What a bed for M'Lord Boli that hoof-churned muck would be! Just a slightly longer step and . . .

"I won't!" yelled Jan.

M'Lord turned around in astonishment. "What was that?"

"Nothing," said the miserable Jan.

On they marched and finally negotiated the mud puddle. Jan sighed with relief when they got to the far side and on dry pavement once more. He took courage at that. It seemed that a sharp exertion of will power would cause this Tiger to fade away. And God knew that one more misstep would put M'Lord Boli into an even higher howl for his head.

He took an interest in the town and found that the mixed lot of the population was very, very unbalanced where wealth and position was concerned. Ifrits were to be seen at rare intervals and each time they were being borne in splendid carriages which were invariably driven by humans in livery.

Too, the silken-robed proprietors of these great stores, when seen standing outside, were all of the Jinn. Although human beings were not without some small finery here and there, not one actually wealthy one was to be found. The police were all Marids, resplendent in green cloaks and towering, conical white hats. Marids did not seem to be servants but monopolized all the minor positions of responsibility.

Here and there men turned to gaze after the marching guard with curiosity. Sometimes men saluted the port captain and he daintily waved his handkerchief back. Sometimes Marids held up traffic to let the procession through and then glowered ferociously upon the prisoner as he slogged past.

Once or twice people yelped, "It's Tiger!" And gaped helplessly until the company was out of sight. Jan recognized them but didn't recognize them. One he knew for sure was a tavern keeper on the waterfront. The other, a buxom female, he knew not at all. He was afraid there were tears in her eyes.

Far ahead, shimmering in the heat, Jan could see a large square opening out. It was easily a mile on the side and parklike trees enclosed a great lake. Too, there were barracks and a parade ground and, set far back, was a low, domed edifice which was deceptive. It appeared to be a normal building at first, done with the usual swoops and curves. But the closer one got, the bigger it got until, from across the huge square, it had the proportions of a mountain. The dome was seemingly solid gold and the sun on it made a man's eyes sting. The balconies were evidently masses of precious stones—or else they were all on fire. The fountains which geysered so brightly before it went a full hundred feet into the air and even then did not reach a height as great as the top of the steps in front—steps down which a cavalry division could have charged with ease.

Humans began to be less and less in evidence. This park was evidently the haunt of military men, all of them Marids except the officers who were Ifrits. Their gaudy uniforms fitted them loosely, held close only by sword belts. The men were in scarlet and the officers too, except that the Ifrits had a great, golden bird of prey awing across their breasts and three golden spikes upon their shining helmets.

Coming away from the palace was a small party of men in azure. They too had golden birds upon their tunics, but from the roll of their walk and the curve of the swords at their sides it was plain that here was a party of naval officers on its way back to the harbor.

71

Coming abreast of the group, Jan glanced wonderingly at them. He had not yet gotten used to seeing fangs glittering in each Jinn's face and those fellows looked especially ferocious. It almost startled him out of his wits when one, more fearsome than the rest, cried out in a voice which bespoke a mortal wound.

"Tiger!" cried this Ifrit. And then, tearing his luminous orbs away from the man, he held up an imperious hand. "Stop, I'd speak to your prisoner."

"Come along!" M'Lord roared at his guard. "Commander, you speak to a royal prisoner. Have a care!"

But the guard couldn't very well walk straight over a commander in the navy and as the commander had stepped in close to Jan, they had to stop. Boli raged.

"What's this?" said the naval officer. "By the Seven Swirls of the Seven Saffron Devils, Tiger, what are you into now?"

"Come along!" roared Boli. And to the officer, "Sir, I'll have your sword for this! I tell you he's a royal prisoner and not to be spoken with by anyone. Answer him, prisoner, and I'll rip out your tongue with my bare hands!"

"Tauten your foul face, lover of slime," said the officer. And to Jan, "Tiger, I told you that if you got into trouble to come to see me. This confounded law which makes it impossible for you to have rank of any kind has got to be changed! You wouldn't revolt if you had any status. What's up?"

"Damn it, sir!" cried Boli, leaping out of his sedan chair and waving the handkerchief like a battle flag, "get back before I'm forced to order a stronger means!"

The officer, knowing well he was out of bounds, fell back slowly, looking the while at Jan. "Don't forget, Tiger. If they don't let you go send the word and I'll be up here for you with my bullies if necessary. We haven't forgotten what you did for us on the Isle of Fire."

But the guard was moving off and Jan was pushed along with them. He was dazed by being known by men he did not know.

And suddenly it came to him that now was the time to trip those bearers. Out went his foot but in the nick of time he tripped himself instead of sending Boli hurtling down those steep steps.

"Come along," snarled M'Lord, all unwitting of his close squeak.

Jan, breathing hard and thankfully, made haste to pick himself up and follow after.

They went through two immense doors, guarded on either side by silver beasts which towered fifty feet above them. Like ants they crawled along the polished floor of a hall which could have berthed a frigate with ease.

Ahead, two doors, so tall that the neck cracked before eyes could see the top of them, barred the way with their black bulk and before them stood a crimson line of Marids, larger than most, and leaning now upon silver pikes.

The chair bearers stopped. The guard stopped. Boli raised himself importantly. "M'Lord Boli, captain of the port, with a prisoner to be thrown upon royal clemency!"

"M'Lord Boli," said the major of the guard, "enter."

The great doors swung back without, it seemed, any hand touching them, and between them stalked the company.

Ahead Jan saw a white throne rearing up thirty feet from the floor, hung with tassels of gold and set with diamonds. Behind it, full fifty feet across, hung the great scarlet flag with its golden bird spread upon it.

The hall, which would have housed the biggest building in the town, was peopled scatteringly by brightly clothed courtiers and officers.

The blaze of the throne was such, under the onslaught of the sun which poured through the wall-sized, stained glass windows, that Jan could not see the person in it. But as the procession drew near he was startled to find two lions chained with silver at its base, lions as large as camels who eyed the approaching Boli with wet chops and licked their lips over the prisoner as an afterthought.

Above them reared the throne itself and Jan, blinking in the blaze, beheld the queen.

She was taller than these other Ifrits. Taller and uglier. Her arms were matted with black hair which set strangely against the soft silk of her white robe. Her hairy face was a horror, her lips spread apart by upper and lower fangs like tusks. On either side of her jeweled crown were black, pointed ears like funnels. Her nose was mostly nostril. Her eyes were as big as stewpans and in them held a flickering, leaping flame which scorched Jan to his very soul.

He looked down, unable to stand the blaze. He looked down as he marched nearer behind M'Lord Boli. He looked down as the last two sedan bearers topped the double step which surrounded the throne. He looked down and saw their *heels.*

Suddenly there was nothing he could do about it. As he mounted himself he lurched a trifle. With horror he found that he deliberately caught at the scabbard of the guard on his right and—oh, quite accidentally—lifted it between the legs of the carrier.

The bearer lurched. His comrade, thrown out of step and balance, lurched. The two men forward, feeling the chair go back, surged ahead just as the two in the rear also strove to stop the sudden motion.

CRASH! And down went M'Lord Boli in a heap of howling guards. Shot he was like a catapulted rock straight out of his chair and directly between the huge lions!

There sounded a concerted scream in the hall. The guards, falling this way and that, had no time to see the horrible death which was even now bending dually to scoop up their fat morsel of a master.

But Tiger!

He leaped over the sprawling men. He charged up the second double step which put anyone in reach of the giant beasts. And the very instant the mouth of the first opened to gulp Boli's trunk down raw, the mouth of the second was gaping to finish the other half.

But Tiger!

He leaped astraddle the port captain and let out a mighty roar. With his left he smacked the left-hand lion resoundingly upon the nose. With his right he almost pulled the long tongue out of the mouth of the right-hand lion. And when they jerked back in astonishment at such audacity, back leaped Tiger, hauling Boli swiftly by the baggy seat of His Lordship's pants.

Tiger lifted Boli to his jellied legs and made a great show of dusting him off, though the crack of the dusting was unseemly loud.

"Your Royal Majesty!" cried Tiger. "You'll please forgive this man's clumsy antics. He feeds his bearers on very bad rum to make them trot the faster and it's the quality not the quantity of the fare which made them stumble. I swear, Your Royal Highness, if the smugglers in your Royal Realm don't stop paying off our lordship the port captain in such filthy bellywash, they'll be the death of him as you can very well see! Are you all right, sir?" he said solicitously to Boli. "Ah, yes, not a drop of grease on the outside and so no fang struck home. By the way, Your Royal Highness, I happen to be a prisoner of the port captain here, and I think he is very anxious to get on with his business of having my head and so, pray give him leave to speak. There, M'Lord, talk up, talk up and don't keep the noble Jinni waiting!"

Boli had up enough pressure in him to splatter himself all over the hall. But such was his terror of the queen that he suddenly lost his rage, vowing that Tiger's death would be none too quick to suit him. He took a grip on his vocal chords and though, when he tried them out they squeaked alarmingly, he strove to hold forth.

"Your Royal Highness, I know not the crime of . . . of . . . this . . . this . . ."

"It's the lions," said Tiger helpfully. "They breathed too much gas into him. Go ahead, M'Lord, pray cough up the letter my captain gave you."

A slaying scowl swept over M'Lord's fat face but forthwith he dug out the sea-worn message and, via a courtier whom the lions considered indigestible, gave it to the queen.

Her black-haired hands wrapped about it so that their curved talons clicked against one another. She looked for some time at Tiger and then broke the seals. She read with great attention and then with growing alarm. She had been, when Tiger tripped Boli, on the point of uproarious laughter but now thunderclouds settled over her visage and her great round eyes flashed lightning.

"Has he spoken to anyone, you bumbling clown?"

Boli shivered so that waves went through him like a shaken pudding. "N-n-no, Your Royal Highness. Only . . . only a fish peddler's wife."

"What's this? What's this? Find her. Find her at once and throw her into the dungeon for observation. Oh, woe take you, miserable milksop! A goat could run my port the better! Did not his captain charge you with the seriousness of his detention? Had you no idea of the enormity of the trust given into your hands? Doddering imbecile! Go wave your stinking perfume in the faces of the waterfront harlots and take the stain of your filthy boots from my polished halls! Begone!"

At the voice which made the whole gigantic room shake, Boli shook as a tree in a gale. He backed hastily, tripping over the double step, falling against some of his men and then, more swiftly, backed at express speed with his guard clear across the hall until the great black doors clanged shut in his face to blank him from view.

"I ought to have his head," snarled the queen. "I, Ramus the Magnificent, to be served in such a chuckleheaded fashion!" She fixed her eyes then upon Jan who, quite empty of any Tiger now and only aware that he was asking for death if he so much as blinked, stood with bowed head before her. She grunted like a pig and then made a motion toward her guard with her heavy gold sceptre.

"Take him away! Put him in the strongroom in the left wing and let no man speak to him, human or Jinn. And you, general, as fast as horses can travel, as fast as ships can sail, bring me that vile troublemaker Zongri!"

"Zongri?" ejaculated the general. "You mean Zongri of the Barbossi Isles? But how is this? Thousands of years ago..."

"Silence!" roared Ramus the Magnificent. "Bring him to *me!*"

"Your Royal Highness," said an espionage agent, stepping slyly forward, "this Zongri but yesterday arrived here in Tarbutón. I know where he is to be found."

"You serve me well. Go with the general and show him the way. I must have that fool!"

"Your wish is our law, Your Royal Highness," said the general, backing out.

"Commander, you know the ship of Captain Tombo?"

"Yes, Your Royal Highness," said the officer.

"Take him a suitable present for service so discreet. A fine present. See the treasurer."

"Yes, Your Royal Highness."

She sank back on her throne with a worried scowl and then, glancing after the guard which escorted Tiger away, growled something to herself and burned the message in the incense cup at her elbow.

Jan, backing perforce, did not miss the gesture. God, he groaned, it's as bad as that. Damn the day I first set eyes upon that copper jar.

Chapter 6

ZONGRI

The strongroom depended mainly for its strength upon its extreme height from the ground. It was no more or less than the topmost room in a turret so lofty that it was not unusual for clouds to obscure the earth of a morning. But Jan had seen too much of late to be so very amazed with the furnishings of the place or at the fact that it was very strange to be imprisoned in such splendor.

Money was no fitting measure for the furnishings. On the floor, to soften the alabaster, lay great white rugs of wool, thick as soup tureens. The walls were covered with shimmering cloth of gold into which amazing battles had been deftly worked. A sergeant could have drilled a squad on the bed and a bosun could have bent a mains'l on the posts. This last occupied the center of the room and a circular series of steps surrounded it, making it into a sort of fort of its own. All around the walls ran a ledge so softly cushioned that a man could quite easily have drowned in it and, instead of chairs, chaise lounges of a graceful pattern stood face to face and yet side by side, so as to offer easy means of conversation.

The scarlet-cloaked Marids posted themselves on the landing outside and bolted the door with twelve bars of iron, flattering even the strength of Tiger's brawny body. Disconsolately Jan wandered through the room. At one side a silver staircase spiraled steeply up through the roof and, thinking he might find a way out, Jan mounted it and thrust back the trap at the top. A gale almost blew his hair off but he went on through to find that he stood upon the highest level of the palace except for the golden dome and he was almost even with that. The platform itself was hardly like an ordinary turret top. The floor was mosaic and the parapet was all green tile. Seats were handy at every side but Jan was interested more in escape than scenery.

Going to the edge, he leaned hopefully over. He recoiled at the height. Below, a squad of men were red ink dots on the pave. But he did not give up. Around he went, examining all sides of the hexagonal structure, but nowhere did he find the slightest semblance of a ladder, nor did he think he could have navigated it if he had. He sighed and walked back toward the trap but, now that he knew escape to be impossible, he was willing to give some small attention to his prison roof and he was somewhat startled to find, all about him, mounted astrological instruments of a pattern extinct these thousands of years. They were all in gold and silver and pivoted on glittering diamonds and so delicately balanced that the slightest touch on the mother of pearl handles swung them swiftly, and yet a slight turn of the same handle fixed them instantly.

Jan was instantly taken with the beauty of an astrolabe on which were engraved fanciful representations of the Zodiac. The *rete*, he noticed with a start, gave a very creditable star map, not at all antiquated for it showed Polaris as the North Star. Until that instant he had supposed himself dropped back a few hundred years, but no! Polaris was its modern one and one-fourth degrees from true north! From a very pretty object this astrolabe became a vital part of his life. He thought hard for a moment, recalling the sun's position for the date and as he paced about he beheld a large chronometer under glass. He had all the data he needed. He swung eagerly back to the astrolabe and measured the altitude of the sun. He then observed the sun's place in the Zodiac and turned the *rete* until the position matched the circle on the plate's observed altitude. Quickly he made a line from that point to the circle of hours on the outer edge, holding his breath lest the answer be wrong.

What madness was this? It was his own Today, the Today of the earth! There was the sun and here was the time. He was bewildered and wandered to the parapet again to gaze out across the square miles of roofs to the bay where corbitas rubbed fenders with seventy-fours. He looked down at the patrol walks where soldiers marched with ornate, inaccurate old muskets. It seemed that all the bric-a-brac of antiquity had come home to Tarbutón like driftwood in the tide or like the mysterious tale of the Sargasso Sea. This place was heir to the glories of yesterday and yet was astoundingly very much in today!

Again he eyed the astronomical instruments as though they might have lied to him. Their glitter had originally been such that he had overlooked a perfectly good eight-inch telescope which stood regally in their midst. Before it was a small platform, cushioned with weatherproofed cloth wherein the observer could take his ease and his science simultaneously.

Jan got into the seat, determined to inspect the town and possibly ferret out any modern touches. Evidently the instrument was used for this at times as it was not fixed focus. He wheeled it down at an angle and trained it on the streets to wander the thoroughfares in comfort. Frenchman, Irishman, Jew and Hindu. Englishman, Russian, Chinaman and Greek. Nubian, Indian, Carib and Spaniard. White man, brown man, yellow man, black man. Every nationality was there, strangely clothed but unmistakable of face. Pulling carts, sorting bales, buying food and running errands. Loafing and sweating and gossiping and weeping. Laughing and drinking and swearing and dancing. Millions of them! Women sunbathing upon flat roofs. Thieves dividing their loot in dark alleyways. An Ifrit beating his insolent slave. A moneylender wailing outside his shop while the robber scurried unhalted down the amused avenue.

What a wild panorama it was! All the vices and pleasures and bigoted zeal, all the love and hate and sophistry and hunger. All the hundred odd emotions could be seen ranging up and down those broad thoroughfares or upon those wide roofs, in the shanties and the ships and the tavern yards, in the stores and courts and funeral parlors, and there was but one constant in it all. Emotion! Things were happening and life was fast and violent.

Strange were the mosques and with their crescents rising up between a crossed steeple to the right and a pagoda tower to the left. Strange to see an idol with a dozen hands serenely surveying a court while just over the wall lay the dome of a synagogue.

Jan swung the telescope slowly across the garish scene and found himself gazing upon a towering hill, all alone in the plain. A temple, massive and plain, was sturdily square against the sky and the broad, steep steps were blazing with the robes of the worshippers, going and coming. Jan discovered that they were all Ifrits, served by Marids, and that not one human being accompanied them further than the lowest step. But wait, there were humans atop that hill. He focused the telescope better.

A long procession was just then starting out from the great entrance. A huge gold coffin all draped in white was being borne by human slaves, each one clothed in the livery of mourning. Before went a priest of the Jinn bearing a golden bird awing at the top of a tall pole. Behind came a naval ensign and a personal flag. This was the funeral of some officer, it seemed, for here came the uniformed sailors with weapons all reversed. And following them were men in blue with golden birds upon their breasts and shining swords at their sides, the hilts turned away from their hands.

Then, from the balustrade, Jan saw a hundred human girls step forth, each one with a basket of petals to strew them under the marching feet as though the dead came as a conqueror and not a corpse. Humans, then, were servants of the temple, for all these girls were clothed in white robes, the hoods of which were thrown back to display a dozen different shades of hair. Jan ran the telescope along the line of them idly. Suddenly he stopped and swiftly adjusted it again. His eyes grew large and his face paled. For there in the midst of those beauties was Alice Hall!

He could not mistake her, though she was more lovely than ever and without any care at all about her. Her robe, like the others, was slit from hem to knee and her graceful feet arched as she walked down with the procession.

"Alice!" shouted Jan, leaving the telescope. But, instantly, the temple drew back three miles across the plain and not even the glittering coffin could be made out with the eye. When he looked again he had lost her.

"You called?" said a voice behind him.

Jan whirled as though to defend himself but he relaxed on the sight of the very old Jinn who stood there in the trap. The fellow had gentle, mystified eyes and his fangs were long departed. His claws were cracked and yellow and his hair was silver gray. Upon his head he wore a very castle of a hat which was wound around and around with cloth which bore astrological symbols.

"You have taken an observation, I see," he sighed. "I trust that the fate you found was not too unkind."

"The fate?" said Jan, climbing swiftly and guiltily down. "Oh . . . yes . . . no. I was checking your time." And he motioned toward the chronometer.

"It loses a second every day," sighed the ancient astrologer. "But tomorrow is a great event. It returns exactly to its accuracy and my computations will be the easier therefor." He looked and sounded too tired to live, as perhaps he was. "So many, many computations. Every morning for the queen. Every evening for the lord chamberlain. And fifty times a day when questions come up. If . . ." he hesitated, "if you've already cast up your fate you know, you might save me some calculations. I dislike prying into a man's birthday. It's so very personal, you see."

"I must confess," said Jan, "that I didn't, really. I only checked the time."

The ancient one sighed dolefully. Finally he got out a pad and began to request the data he needed. Jan gave it to him and the modern dates and hours did not at all startle the old fellow. At length he shuffled over to his instruments and bent his watery gaze upon the star tables which were engraved on silver. For a long time he leaned on the tablet, scribbling now and then but sighing more than he scribbled. He advanced to the astrolabe to check his Zodiac from force of habit and then, sinking down upon a bench beside a desk, pulled forth a volume half as big as he was. Jan helped him open it and for a long time the old fellow pored over magic writing.

Until then he had been weary unto death but now, of a sudden, he started to take an interest in life. He read faster and faster, turning pages as leaves dash about in a hurricane. He leaped to his feet and sped to the star charts anew. He faced Jan and fired a very musketry of questions. Yes, the dates were right but what on earth was wrong? But the ancient one, bobbing about now like a heron after fish, threw himself down upon the book and ate it up all over again.

Finally, sweating and almost crying, he leaned back, dabbing his forehead with a handkerchief all embroidered with suns and moons. He looked wonderingly at Jan and Jan grew very uncomfortable. The astrologer's glance became more and more accusing and slowly the weariness seeped into him once more.

"What is wrong?"

"She'll laugh at me," he mourned. "More and more they laugh at me ever since the day I said Zongri would make trouble within a year. They said he was dead these long centuries. But no. He is not. An hour ago he was hauled into the audience chamber by the battered guard which took him in the town. They laugh at me just the same. It was a terrible error for me to guess that

Lord Shelfri would be kind to the princess. It is that which makes them laugh. Yes, it is that. He killed her, you know, and then hanged himself just last month and so now they laugh. And they'll not believe me now. It is not possible. No human being could do such awful things in a land of the Jinn. It is impossible and yet I must tell them."

"What must you tell them?" cried Jan.

"It is for her ears alone. And if she laughs and refuses to execute you while she has the chance, then it is Ramus who must suffer the consequences. It is all the same to me. I am old. I have seen the Universe turning, turning, turning for a hundred thousand years. I weary of it, human. I weary of it. You, lucky child, will probably never live to see the sun roll across the heavens more than a dozen times more."

"You mean . . . you've read my death there?"

"No," he sighed. "No, not that. There is no certainty. I shall not alarm you. You may die. You might not die. But what does it matter. If you do, it is you who will lose. If you do not, the lives of many Jinn will pay the toll. But I am old. Why should I care about these things. Ahhhhhhh, dear," he sighed, rising. "And now I must go down all those stairs again and give my report to the queen."

Jan followed him down to the room below, helping him on the steep stairs. But before the old man departed he looked all around and shrugged as if seeing all the folly of the Universe at once.

"It is not often this happens, you they call Tiger. While you yet breathe, rejoice. This you may or may not know is the strong-room and it is strong not to detain the visitor but to protect the queen."

"You mean . . . it's her room?"

"At times when the nights are hot she comes here to have me read the fortunes of her people and her reign. That, you they call Tiger, is the bed on which Tadmus was murdered, in which

Loru the Clown was stabbed to death by his chamberlain, in which lovely Dulon died in giving birth to Laccari, Scourge of Two Worlds. Ah, yes, you they call Tiger, the whim of a queen has placed you upon an historic bed. Why—I have read in the stars. God save us all!"

And so he was let out and wandered down the steps sadly shaking his grotesquely hatted head, his mutters lingering long after he was gone.

Jan looked with horror at the great bed. And then, despite everything he could do to hold himself back, he leaped up the steps and landed squarely in the middle. He bounced up and down.

"Not bad," said Tiger.

"Stop!" cried Jan.

"Oh, boy. All we need is some dancing girls and a keg and what a time we'd have!"

"How can I think of such a thing at a time like this?"

"Hell's bells, why not? A short life and a hot one and let the devil have a break. It's not every day he gets such a recruit as Tiger."

"Blasphemy from *me*?"

"And why not? Why not, I say? Where's the idol tall and mighty enough to be revered? Where's the god or ruler strong enough and good enough and clever enough to get more than a passing glance from such a fellow as I? Not that I am worth a hiss in hell, but that all these other pedestaled fools rate but little more. Show me a good god, a true king, a mighty man and all my faith is his for the asking—nay, not even for the asking. Who am I to be bowed by anything? Not Tiger!"

"But the queen and the God that made you . . ."

"The queen is a filthy harridan and I have yet to meet the God that made me. I am Tiger! I am Tiger, son of the sea, brother to the trade winds, lover of strength and worshipper of mirth! I am Tiger and I know all the vices of every land! I am Tiger and with my eyes I have seen such sights as few men so much as dream about. Dancing girls, honey-sweet wine, music enough to tear the soul from a man. Aye, women to blind you with their golden eyes and flowing bodies. Aye, rum which mellows the throat and roars in the guts. Aye! Violins and drums, trombones and harps and feet so swift and so sure that the head whirls to follow them. Dancing girls! Aye! Such a one as graced the last steps of Captain Bayro with fresh roses this very day. Ah, for her I would crush this kingdom with my fingers and give it to her upon a diamond dish. Where has she been that I have not seen her? Where has she kept that sweet ankle and those silken curls? Where has she hidden that mouth made for kisses and laughter and songs? Ah, yes, the Temple of Rani. The Temple! Where no human dare tread except as a Temple slave; where all Tarbutón's mighty go to babble their sins and kiss golden feet and win support for their hellish endeavors. The Temple! Where the great horns bellow like bulls and the flying feet of the dancing girls sweep the worshipers into drunken stupor. The finest beauties of the realm to beguile the Jinn with dancing. And that one, ah, the finest of them all! S'death to enter that Temple. Death! But for the likes of that sweet mouth, but for the slimness of that ankle . . ."

"Stop!" cried Jan. "She is sacred!"

"Sacred? Why not? All things of the Temple are sacred. But though death might wait upon such a venture, if ever I get out of this mad palace, sure as the west wind blows, I shall kiss that mouth . . ."

"She's sacred to me! To me! Her name is Alice Hall, the only woman I ever looked at. She is Alice Hall, the only woman who ever looked upon me with other than contempt. Seal your mouth and speak of her no more!"

"Sacred, you say? And why should a woman be so sacred as to never be touched. Surely now there's no reason in that at all! Love? For love I would lay down my split second of life. Love? Certainly I could love her, perhaps already I do love her. Yes, there's no use to deny it. Of all I've ever seen she is the *only* one. And what could be more sacred than to worship at that shrine? What could be more sacred than to burn the joss of desire before that cupid's bow of a mouth? Yes, that's given only to the strong. That's given only to the man-devil with courage enough to take it. Yes, she's sacred. Sacred to me! And as she is a Temple girl, a dancing girl, raised out of sight of all humans *I* shall be the first to plead with her. *I* shall be the last for she will be mine! Now, puny and halting weakling, try and stop me!"

Jan leaped up from the bed, whirling as though to face an adversary. But no one was to be seen. And deep inside him he felt the Tiger stirring, heard the Tiger laughing. More and more as the hours passed he had experienced it. He had given it some slight leash on the ship and the musket had been fired. It had taken more and the boat had overturned. And more and more to send Boli hurtling between two lions. And now, like the camel that stuck his head in the tent, slow degree by slow degree, presaging an end which might well be whole weeks away, he who contained the Tiger would be contained *by* the Tiger. And at such a prospect of being ruled by the lawless, pleasure mad, irreverent sailor Jan recoiled with his own part of his soul. And even when he did it he heard the Tiger, far off, deep down, veiled and showing himself like the sharp fangs of a reef in the restless, heaving sea, laughing at him.

The body first and then . . . then the heart? Who had the Tiger been? How had be become submerged at all?

And Jan in a spasm of terror would have thrown himself down on the bed anew if the door had not been flung back by a captain of the guard.

"Her Royal Highness, Ramus the Magnificent, now demands your presence in the audience chamber for trial!"

Jan stared dully at the pompous fellow and then obediently crawled off the bed and placed himself between the waiting files. They marched down the winding steps and through half a mile of halls and, with the greater part of him shaking at the prospect of the judgment, he could not help thinking that it would be a priceless joke if the Marid on his right should accidentally knock against the one in front. He was sure they would all go down like dominoes, so stiff were they in their garish capes.

But the joke never came off for the instant they entered the chamber Jan came up with a paralyzed gasp to behold Zongri, all in chains, standing on the steps which led to the throne. And Zongri was looking at him with eyes which were shot through and through with flashing fires of rage.

Chapter 7

THE MAGIC RING

The audience chamber was clear of all except three com-
panies of guards. The queen sat immobilely regarding Zongri's
back. Up before the throne the files marched Jan and then fell
back to leave him isolated between two poker-stiff Marids.

The lions yawned hopefully, the sound of it gruesome in the
echoing hall. As though that were a signal to begin, Ramus, the
Jinni queen, pointed her sceptre at Jan.

"Speak, renegade Ifrit!" she ordered Zongri. "Is this the man
upon whom you pronounced so untimely a sentence?"

Zongri shifted his weight. He was a tower of scorn and anger
and his chains clinked viciously. "That one?" And he stared hard
at Jan, a little of the resentment fading out of him. Jan held his
breath, suddenly realizing that, in Tiger's form, he was not likely
to be recognized by a Jinn who had seen him but fleetingly and
in bad light at that.

"That one?" said Zongri. "You mock!"

"Look well, jackal filth," roared the queen. "If he is not the
one, you shall be detained until that one is found. And this one
came to his captain with a strange tale indeed."

Zongri came down the steps a pace. He was above the reach
of the great lions just as Jan was below them. And, framed between
those tawny heads, Zongri looked more terrifying than ever, even
though he did not seem quite so large as he had upon the first
night. Even so he was bigger than any one of the guards, bigger
even than Ramus and certainly half again the size of Tiger.

Zongri's fangs clicked together as he worked his jaw in thought. Then he again faced Ramus. "You bait me! You try to trick me into lies! A trap worthy of you. The one I sentenced was a puny fellow, one these lions would have scorned to eat. A weakling with panes of glass over his eyes to protect them. A very owl of a scarecrow with his head stuffed with books and his heart so much sawdust. Try again, ruler of apes, for Zongri will not this time be led into untruth."

Jan's spirits began to pick up and he even straightened his spine and Tiger almost let out a merry whistle.

"Look again!" roared Ramus. "I tell you that this one brought such a tale to his captain and though he is known as Tiger and though he is not unknown for certain brawling deeds, it is possible that he is not wholly the one you describe in form. Witless one, have you no eyes at all?"

"I," said Zongri in a voice like a file through brass, "happen to be wearing your chains, Ramus. But my patience is great. For thousands of years I waited for my release. It taught me how to bide my time . . ."

"It taught you little else!" roared Ramus.

"But it *did* teach me that," said Zongri, looking as though he wanted to fly at her throat. "And I can wait until you visit me in my own realm, the Barbossi Isles, where I would have been even now if your cursed ships were not so glutted with cargoes for the weaklings I find here. How am I to know what has transpired in the ages since I left? How was I to know that the jest of Eternal Wakefulness, once so marvelous, would bring any danger here? How was I to know that soft living and slaves had reduced my race to the point of putty? My magic beyond my power? And if I have done this thing, what of that?"

"What of that?" bellowed Ramus in a fury. "You witless son of chattering monkeys, can you not see the desolation which would spread if all humans in our world would come to know the

TRUTH? Quick now, stop blabbing your ignorance and closely look upon the prisoner. We must *know*!"

Again Zongri fixed his raging eyes upon Jan until Jan could feel them lifting off his scalp and tearing his clothes to ribbons. Suddenly Zongri tensed and took an involuntary step downward. Then, so swiftly that all his chains clanked as one, he faced the queen.

"If I can truthfully identify this man, you free me?"

"Of course."

"And allow me to depart?"

"With our most heartfelt relief!"

"Then, Ramus the Maggoty, know that the human before you is Jan Palmer, victim of the Eternal Wakefulness and long may he roast in hell!"

Jan almost fell forward on his face but staggered upright again.

"Ah," said Ramus, "I see that the prisoner admits it too. Very well, Zongri, we bear you no great malice . . ."

"I would that I could also say it," growled the giant Ifrit.

". . . and will suitably see you away to your home."

"And no thanks earned," snarled Zongri.

"*IF* you take away the sentence from this man!" snapped Ramus.

"Bah, why bother with that? Kill him and have it over!"

"Aye, that *would* be your solution, witless one. How like your sons you are, to choose the last resort first. This may be Jan Palmer but it is also one they call Tiger, a man who earned a better fate by feats of daring in a dozen battles and who once saved the life of Admiral Tyronin, one of my finest officers. Certainly if it must be done, 'twill be done, but stay awhile. How, pray tell, were you able to put such a sentence upon him?"

"You said you would release me."

"I said I would to be sure but I had not stated all my conditions."

"You harpy!" screamed Zongri, leaping straight at the queen. Only the swift action of the officers on the steps kept him from reaching her. She had not so much as blinked and only smiled when Zongri was thrown back to his original position.

"We might forget to wend you home at all, Zongri," she reminded him. "We have deep graves here for those who do not please us. Now, to business. We ask you to spare us the necessity of murdering this man, for, while your line has never done us anything but wrong, his at least has done us some slight good. To be very truthful, Zongri, we would much rather destroy you than this common sailor here."

Zongri was so angry he could not even speak. He cast the guards away from him and stood there, his ripped shirt showing a vast expanse of heaving, hairy chest. The other Ifrits averted their eyes from him but not inexorable Ramus. She was almost laughing to see such a powerful man so completely entangled at her whim.

"Come, speak up," said Ramus. "By what magic power did you bring this down upon Tiger? Speak! I would as soon execute you as not—in fact I have no compunction whatever in the matter."

"I speak not from terror of your threats," growled Zongri, "but to avoid having to longer stay in such a treacherous place, gazing upon such ugly faces. Very well. You seem in this age to know nothing of the yesterdays. You know nothing or have completely forgotten the day when Sulayman brought us all to account by the magic which was his by virtue of his seal." He seemed to doubt the wisdom of going on but Ramus motioned for the executioner to step nearer and Zongri swept on like a rolling storm, his temper rising to white heat but telling his tale just the same. "Know that the seal was lost to him some years after..."

"Come to the point. We have heard all that," said Ramus.

"It was lost to him and so was his power lost. You have heard of that seal?"

"If you speak of the triangles laid so as to form a six-pointed star surrounded by a circle, we know the Seal of Sulayman." She chuckled to herself to see her guards wince at the mention of the potent thing.

"Aye," said Zongri, "such was the seal. Such was the Seal of Sulayman and even a replica of it upon a leaden stopper carried sufficient force to entomb me all those bitter years, worn though it had become." He stopped again and stubbornly decided he would not continue. But once more the executioner stepped forward and once more Zongri blazed with the fury of impotence. "You have no right!"

"And you'll have no life," said Ramus. "It's all one to me whether to cheer you on your way or bury you."

"To Shaitan with your threats. I speak to save myself further defilement."

"Then speak."

"When I was released I touched the stopper as I said those words and, because the seal was made by Sulayman himself and with that ring, there was enough power there to do it."

"You are not telling us the whole truth," said Ramus.

"Robbers, thieves!" shrieked Zongri.

"And what is that upon your hand?" said Ramus.

"Very well!" he screamed at her. "You'll have it all! I have shown great patience. I have tried to leave you as I found you. I have tried not to destroy this city until I myself could occupy it with my own men, for conquest is my lot. But, abortively, my hand is called. Look!" And he thrust it forward.

She leaped back.

He jerked the ring from his finger. "Look! I searched but a day to find it. Sulayman got it back and I knew how to find his tomb. It lay in the miserable dust which remained to him and I took it up and put it on and all the secrets of the two worlds will be mine! All the land will yield to me. Earth will disgorge all her buried treasures, walls will fall at my bidding! Look well and be as stone!"

But nothing happened. Baffled, Zongri whirled around to face his guards. Again he howled the decree and still nothing happened though he held the ring high over his head.

Ramus was the first to laugh aloud. "Oh, vain fool, in its life the ring gave all its wisdom to Sulayman the Wise. But because it was worn by human, it lost its power over humans. And now, think not that I know little of magic. *You*, an Ifrit have worn that ring and so have destroyed its power there. Between you and Sulayman," she chortled, "you'll have it as powerful as a doorknob!"

"Beware!" howled Zongri. "Stand back. If it lacks that power, it still has many more. Stand back, I say!" And it seemed that only the lions would fail to obey as they strained toward him hungrily.

The Marids were so hypnotized by the strength of the man that they did as he ordered and, for the moment, Jan was standing quite alone, close beside the plate and iron which fastened the leash of the right-hand lion. Jan was sweating and then, suddenly, felt lightheaded. Tiger grinned a wicked grin.

Down dropped Tiger to the floor and out of Zongri's wrath-blinded sight. It was the work of an instant to jerk out the confining pin. The chain had all the slack out. The lions were maddened by Zongri's loud roars, completely intent upon his dervishlike movements.

"See! I strike off my own chains!" shouted Zongri. And with a clank the enormous fetters dropped into a rusty coil about his feet. "And now, treacherous clowns..."

But the chain gave way in that instant and two thousand pounds of lion sprang straight up at Zongri's hairy throat!

Zongri flung up his arms to meet the shock and staggered back. But Tiger was not at all idle. He went up over the beast's back like it was a ratline and before two roars had gone shatteringly down the hall he was astride the brute's head and twisting his tender ears until they creaked like cabbage leaves.

It was a mad tumble of Ifrit and human and jungle king and so ferocious were the bellows coming out of the melee that the other lion, seeing them all hurtle down toward him, did not attack at all but leaped back in terror.

A dozen stouthearted Jinn officers flung themselves upon the chain and yanked some slack from it. Two more sent the pin clanging home where it belonged. A stouthearted major dived into the mess and flung Zongri out of it and across the pave. He grabbed again but the sailor had already leaped free, the lion lunging after. The chain pulled the brute back on his haunches and Tiger, seeing instantly that the devil was again chained, gave him a resounding cuff across his tender nose and snapped his fingers so hard that the beast started.

Complacently, Tiger stepped back between the two Marids who were still frozen in place.

Other guards picked up Zongri and lugged him forward to again stand him up before the throne, this time well clear of the lions.

"Hoho!" said Ramus. "Were you going to leave us so soon, Zongri? Stay yet awhile. Don't you enjoy the company? Major, take the ring away from him!"

That officer leaped up to do her bidding and yanked Zongri's hands toward him to remove the seal. But, in a moment, the major gave a yelp.

"What have you done with it?" he cried.

But Zongri was obviously jarred by the discovery for he jerked loose from the officers and scurried about the floor on all fours, searching. In an instant all the guards followed suit. Ramus watched them with a worried frown as though half-minded to do some looking herself. But soon every inch of even that huge hall had been thoroughly searched without any result.

Zongri was the first to give up. "Your thieving guards have stolen it!"

95

"Sir, they are my personal, household troops. Not one man of them would stop at laying down his life for me. Besides," she added, "my officers here have been watching them like hawks and I have been watching the officers. There were not so many."

"I demand that you search them all!" screamed Zongri.

"It shall be done," said Ramus. "Major, tell off three officers to do the searching. The seal is too big to hide."

The searching was quickly done by the process of patting the capes of all Marids without result.

"And now the officers!" yelled Zongri.

"Even that insult I shall permit," said Ramus, "though I beg their forgiveness at such an affront. Major, search them."

The major, by the same process, did so and when he had finished, still without result, the voracious Zongri bellowed, "And now search the major!"

That officer disdainfully stepped up to Zongri and let himself be mauled, though his face had an expression as though he smelled something very bad.

"Are you satisfied?" said Ramus, troubled into mildness.

Zongri stared all about him, bewildered and growing angry to the point of insanity. Everyone in the room had been searched and the floor had practically been torn up and yet— With a sudden growl, Zongri leaped at Jan.

"You, you sniveling wretch!" cried Zongri. "You, the cause of all this! What have you done with that ring?"

Two officers started to intervene but Tiger swept them back by throwing out his arms. "Search!"

Zongri would have ripped the clothes from him shred by shred but the executioner was thoughtfully swinging his blade back and forth from the hilt and the glint of it slowed Zongri down. He searched Jan by the patting process employed before, but used now with such force that it almost broke Jan's ribs.

"This," said Tiger, "in payment for saving the ingrate from being lion beef. Search and be damned!"

Zongri ran out of pockets and patience at the same time and dealt Jan such a blow that he sent him skidding a full thirty feet across the glittering floor.

"Boor!" cried Ramus. "Haven't you done enough already?"

"It's a pretty show!" cried Tiger as Jan scrambled up. "I never saw a man work so hard to cover up a thing."

"What?" said Ramus on high.

"Why, 'tis plain as your horns, Your Royal Highness. The fellow dropped it into that well he calls a mouth and gulped it down like pastry. Wasn't I within an inch of him when he did it?"

"What's this?" cried Ramus. "What's this? What's this?"

"You lying fiend!" yelled Zongri, making ready to leap at Jan anew. "You filthy-tongued . . ."

"Stop him!" ordered Ramus. "Ah, so that's the way it is, putting my most trusted troops to abuse to pull a shabby trick. You'll learn my might yet, you snake-tailed donkey! Guards, put those irons on him, I say, and throw him into the darkest dungeon we have to offer until he sees fit to give us back that ring."

Zongri was swiftly overpowered despite his struggles and the irons rasped back into place.

"What about me?" said Tiger truculently.

"You!" roared Zongri. "Plenty about you! I'll hunt you down and rip out your throat if it takes me a thousand years to find you! You, you're doomed! Break your sentence, bah! It can't be done. Who including God can destroy knowledge once given or separate personalities once fused. You, root of all my misery, will meet me in the realm of Shaitan if not upon this land. Take me away!" he cried. "Take me away where I won't have to *look* at him!"

The guard was most obliging and Tiger laughed gleefully to see him go. And when Zongri had vanished, Tiger faced the throne once more. "But that, Your Royal Highness, still solves nothing. I, begging your pardon, am a man of action. Do I live or do I die? It's all the same so long as it's definite!"

Ramus leaned forward and spoke in a troubled voice. "Slave, your problem is not to be solved in a day. For the safety of my people I cannot let you free. For your service unto us I cannot have you killed unless you make it necessary. For the present until your fate can be decided, I must hold you in the tower. Guards, escort the gentleman to his quarters."

A few minutes later the great metal door swung shut behind him and once more he was alone in the great room. But whereas before, Tiger had always died out instantly after action and Jan had shivered and shrunk from the next event, there was now a difference.

It had grown dark long ago and someone had lighted an array of tapers in the diamond pendant candelabra. By their flickering lights Jan made a quick but thorough examination of the whole room, scouting all places where observers might be posted. Finally he yawned very elaborately, somewhat amazed at his histrionic powers. He pulled off his merchant sailor shirt and stepped out of his pants and then, clad only in his floppy-topped seaboots he stepped over to the candles and snuffed them out one by one, yawning the while.

At last the room was dark except for the subdued light which rose up from the starry-lighted port. Jan crawled in between the silken sheets of the great bed, boots and all.

And then, secure, he reached into the floppy top of the right one and pulled forth a thing which weighed at least a pound. Even in the darkness the Seal of Sulayman blazed and crackled.

Chapter 8

TIGER?

When the doze of an instant faded him from one scene to another, Jan, not yet used to the thing, failed to realize what had happened to him. Strangely enough he had the sleepy sensation of one who has spent a night of snoring. And so, without opening his eyes, he contentedly fumbled under his pillow for the blazing Seal.

It wasn't there.

In an instant he was on the floor turning his bed covers seven ways at once, making dust and oddments of clothes, books and cockroaches fly as from a bomb explosion. He got down on his knees and frantically fumbled with no more result than losing some skin from his knuckles. Up he leaped and plunged into the bed anew, ripping and rending it until it flapped like a flag on its hinges.

"What the hell's goin' on?" complained Diver. "You nuts or something?"

That brought Jan into a realization of his whereabouts. He stopped stock still and then, like a cloud, the odor of disinfectant and unwashed feet and halitosis settled over him. Like a hum of bees the sounds of restless men came into his ears. Like a judgment he heard a bell tolling somewhere over the city, calling people to church.

It was jail and it was Sunday.

And the mighty Seal of Sulayman was somewhere far away, in another bed, clutched in quite another hand.

Hopelessly Jan sank down upon the bunk.

"Geez, I thought you was goin' nuts for a minute," said Diver. "Not that you ain't already," he added with a sniff. "Now pick up that junk and make the place look decent or I'll give you something to think about."

Jan glowered at his cellmate.

"G'wan, snap into it," said Diver.

For a moment more Jan stayed where he was and then a queer thing happened. With sudden alacrity he got up and made a great show of putting the cell in order. He had thrown things so far and so fast that they were now carpeting the place, scant though their number was. And Jan went at it with such a will that Diver was forced to stand up against the bars to get out of the way.

It was done in an instant and Jan stood back. "How's that?"

"Huh," said Diver, ambling back to his bunk and sitting down upon it.

CRASH!

The astounded pickpocket was jolted through and through as his bunk gave completely away and slammed him down on the floor. He bounced up and gave the iron a resounding kick which instantly brought a yelp of pain out of him. Holding his toe he went hopping around like a heron and swearing like a pirate. Presently he subsided and frowning terribly picked up his few belongings and then, kicking Jan's things out of the one remaining bunk, dropped his own upon it and took his seat there. He gave a growl as though daring Jan to do something about the theft but Jan quite cheerfully picked up his own goods from the floor and put them on the wrecked bed and then, to Diver's suspicious amazement, reconnected the chain hooks, making the "wreck" quite as good as new.

"You done that on purpose," snarled Diver.

"Me?" said Jan innocently. "Why, you took my bunk and that leaves yours, so now yours is mine."

"Yeah, but this thing here isn't fit for a hog to sleep in!"

"Then why should you object?" said Jan complacently.

Diver eyed him doubtfully and seemed about to make a fight for it when breakfast appeared. Diver was much too interested in his stomach to put fighting before eating and so he snatched the tray under the door and put it on the table and, placing his arms guardingly about it, appeared on the verge of devouring it all himself.

Jan sat watching him for several seconds and Diver began to relax, throwing a scornful grunt in Jan's direction. Diver got his muscles in working order, snapped his teeth a couple times experimentally and fell to.

Jan still watched him. Two eggs vanished and the remaining two were about to follow the example of the first pair when Jan let out a startled exclamation.

"Look out!"

"What's wrong?" snarled Diver.

"Why, good golly, you wouldn't want to eat *that*, would you?" And he advanced, placing his hand close to the plate to indicate something.

Diver took his eyes off Jan and looked at the plate and there, squarely between the two eggs was the biggest cockroach he had ever seen! And not only that but only *half* of him was present.

Diver clapped one hand over his mouth and the other over his stomach and his snaky eyes got big as dollars.

"Quick!" said Jan. "I've heard they're poison as arsenic. Guard! Guard!"

The officer, having distributed the last tray, came speeding back. "What's the matter with you two guys now?"

"It's Diver!" said Jan urgently. "He's poisoned! Hurry, he may die even before you get him to the infirmary! Don't stand there gawping like an idiot! DO something!"

Jan swiftly aided Diver to the now open door and the guard led the staggering pickpocket away. Diver still had his hands where he had first put them but now looked as green as a shark's belly.

"What's up?" said the counterfeiter urgently.

Jan yawned and watched Diver out of sight. Then he grinned. "It's something he thought he ate." And so saying he calmly sat down at the tray, chose clean tools and ate the ham and the toast and drank the coffee with very great relish. Tiger purred with contentment and the luxurious feeling which always followed a job well done.

The feeling of well-being, however, did not last very long. Jan, recalling Alice's present, stripped down and prepared for a shave. All went well until he confronted himself in the glass. With a shock he beheld nobody but Jan Palmer.

Chapter 9

THE SECRET OF SLEEP

He passed through the veil as one who pushes cobwebs from his face in an old deserted corridor, sleeping hardly at all, so great was his anxiety to discover if his treasure was still there. Though he knew he could never bring it into his land of waking, there were still many things to be done in his other world. And if he understood imperfectly how it was that he found himself a man within a man, he could nevertheless make the best of it.

He stirred restively upon the great white silk expanse, strangely conscious of having been there all the night and of resting very poorly. But he was not greatly concerned and his strong body was not one to demand more than the scantest rest.

His fingers shot under the pillow and he gripped a weighty circle of metal so hard that if his hands had not been those of a sailor, he could have cut himself severely upon the worn edge and the rough-cut stones.

Anxiously he stared all about him, making certain that the room was untenanted save for himself. And then, to make sure because he was half afraid it wasn't true, he lifted the cover and eagerly inspected the ring anew.

The Seal of Sulayman! The crossed triangles and the magic circle about them seemed to vibrate with a mighty power. Solomon the Wise, ruler of his world, mightiest monarch of all time! And he had worn this ring upon his hand and had thereby been wise and great and omnipotent. And what if he had destroyed its power for evil over humans? What if Zongri had made it powerless in turn against Ifrits? Was it not enough that it still brought all wisdom, that it struck away all locks and that, among other things, would reveal the hiding places of all the treasures of earth?

And as he gloated over it a rattling at the door struck terror to his heart. The face of Tiger hardened and grew grim and his quick, clear eyes swept about him for a hiding place. But he had no time for that. He could only throw himself out of the bed and drop a white silk robe over him, concealing the seal in his sash.

It took several seconds to remove the bolts from without and he had dropped back upon the bed and was just in the act of stretching when the door swung inward. Three Marid sentries stepped back and stared fixedly into space and then there came into view a woman who made Jan's every muscle grow taut with wonder.

She paused on the threshold, looking up at him at his seat on the lofty bed. And, in turn, he looked down, unable to tear his gaze away from her.

She was robed in the sheerest of golden silk which showed every curve of her voluptuous body. Her only jewels were a girdle and a cap of pearls which lay like a moon against the midnight of her hair. Her eyes were fathomless seas of jet, making the pallor of her lovely, somehow bold face all the more exquisite. She appeared as one sculped in alabaster and given, by some enchantment, the breath of life.

It seemed to please her that he stared. With a small, amused smile she broke the spell by walking slowly forward with an ease not unlike flowing silk.

Jan stood up as she mounted the steps and mechanically gave her a hand to help her over the last. She nodded her thanks and gracefully sat upon the edge of the bed, signifying that he too could be seated.

He wondered wildly who she was and what she had to do with him. And he was not at all insensible to the hypnotic power of her eyes, which jangled with the hotness of the Seal of Sulayman, lying like a coal in his sash.

"You wonder who I am," she said.

He nodded.

"And why I have come here?"

Again he nodded.

She laughed and indicated the Marids who were now closing and bolting the door again. "Those fools. I wonder that as little happens as there does in this palace. It is so very simple to order them about and pass them by . . ."

"But they have orders that I am to speak to no one."

She laughed musically. "Do they? How funny. And yet I, who have no earthly business here, can walk airily through their ranks and into your presence as if they were so many dolls." The chamber awakened at her renewed mirth and the small glasses on the shelf above the bed hummed in gay sympathy. "Ah, now, but I am not mocking you. One would hardly mock Tiger, would they? You wish to know why I came?"

"Indeed I would, M'Lady."

"How gruff! And, I might add, handsomely gruff. Mark it all to curiosity, my Tiger. All to that and nothing more—except perhaps a fear that you were very lonely shut up here in this awful place and everyone ordered not to speak to you at all. You *were* lonely, weren't you?"

"Why . . . yes. Why shouldn't I be?"

She reached out her hand and took down two crystal goblets and a tall-necked bottle of amber wine. She poured them full and then held them up to the light to give him the one which contained the most.

"To the cheer of company," she toasted.

He was very acutely aware of the danger here for she was the first human being he had seen about the palace and he well knew that a human would not be permitted to come here so easily, no matter her beauty. But when he saw that she drank, he politely sipped his answer to her toast. His caution was prompted more by Jan than Tiger for the wine was innocent compared to suddenly remembered beverages which went down with great authority.

"I am here," she said finally, "with a good reason. Now am I more welcome?"

"Welcome!" said Tiger abruptly. "If you've ever studied your lovely self in the most indifferent mirror, I wonder that you can still see. And you talk about being welcome." He clinked his glass against hers and drank it down.

With great difficulty Jan fought for the upper hand and again the Seal burned horribly against his side.

"I am here," she said, "to counsel you for I am sure that in all the time you've found yourself in such a strange predicament not one of these thoughtless, witless Jinn have thought to ease your mind about it. Ifrits," she added, "are really very stupid people."

"I have not found them so," said Jan.

"No? But you have not talked to them so very much, then. For they truly are stupid. You have no idea!"

"And what, may I ask, is your counsel?"

"Anxious to be rid of me? How can that be? But I had heard on great authority that Tiger was a gallant fellow, not to be denied. But, then, I forget, you may be mixed now with some strange personality from outside our crude world and perhaps you have an icicle or two on your ears." She looked and only found the ring holes in the lobes.

"Ah, a sailor indeed," she cried joyfully. "And what have you done with your gold hoops?"

"I pawned them," said Tiger suddenly. "Pawned them to buy a dancing girl a veil. I didn't want it but she did. And how was I to know that she belonged by rights to a captain of infantry and that he would enter the hall just as I was presenting it? You have no idea," he laughed, mimicking her.

"Gold hoops for a dancing girl?" she said, prettily shocked. "How horribly wicked. And now you have neither dancing girl nor rings."

At the mention of rings, Jan fought to the surface. But the lady had jumped up and was detaching two hoops of gold from her girdle which she instantly spread and fixed in his ears!

"Now!" she cried. "Now you look like a true sailor."

"I feel like a very stupid one," said Jan, discovering cunning in his being. "How is it that I am here, shut up in an observatory tower when reason dictates that I should be in the deepest dungeon or else hanging on the highest gibbet in Tarbutón."

"Must we have to do with reason?"

"Yes."

"Ah, you sound like the Tiger I have heard about. Never satisfied with anything. Here you are shut up in the queen's very own room, waited on by the finest of her servants, feasting upon the most palatable of food and with nothing to do but enjoy yourself. And you wonder about it!"

"Rather!"

"After all," she said, "I hear you once saved the life of Admiral Tyronin, among other things. And though your numerous escapades may make it impossible for you to be kept always on silk, the state owes you something."

"The state saw fit to put me on a stinking merchant tub."

"So?"

"With a stupid, flogging fool for a captain."

"Ah, that is sad. Perhaps the state feels you have been punished enough and wishes now to make amends."

"I am here," said Jan, "because of some strange information I might communicate to others. Information of which I confess myself wholly ignorant. If I am dangerous why doesn't the royal might do away with me and have done with it. I know very little about anything. I am a raw mass of questions. I know not even where this land is, though more and more I know my own deeds and misdeeds in it—as even now I recall certain other things I have done which might or might not have endeared me to the state. But I who was one am now two and I heartily dislike it."

"Two, indeed. Brawling, laughing, drunken Tiger could never have taken a sight with an astrolabe."

"You know about that?"

"I am a very dear friend of old Zeno. Ah, yes, you are a strange blend now. I detect a scholar and philosopher in you, Tiger, things which go strangely with your clear brow and handsome strength."

"A scholar, perhaps. And little good it's ever done me," quoth Jan. "To do cube root in the head avails a man little against prison bars."

"Scholars are scholars because they must fall back upon books to supply their lack in the strife of living. Scholaring, I am told, is a very dread disease. The more one knows the more one knows he knows nothing. And the more he knows that he knows nothing, the more ardently he desires to really know something and so, more study. And more study, the more he knows he knows nothing, the more . . ."

"M'Lady, I beg of you, desist!"

"I am growing dizzy, too. But tell me, which of you has the upper hand? Scholar or warrior?"

Jan suddenly wanted to answer both at once and was strangely aware of some alchemy within him, by which he was losing none of the knowledge and memory of Jan but was gaining the heart and courage as well as the knowledge and memory of Tiger. The nearness of this heart-quickening woman was completing the weld. He felt drunk.

"The question's a hard one," he said. "And perhaps I'd be able to answer it better if I knew what I was talking about. To begin, where am I?"

"Why, in the Kingdom of Tarbutón, of course."

"Oh, I know that well enough and I seem to know every alley and wall crack in the land as well. But I speak of geography. Am I fifty south and forty west? Is that sea the Mediterranean? And where is the United States of America in regard to this place?"

"Such weird names, my sailor. But certainly one who has sailed the world would know more about it than I. Not one of those places or numbers do I know." She brightened. "Why, can't you tell with old Zeno's instruments up there?"

"The astrolabe tells only of time and latitude. Zeno's time gives me no longitude and though I suppose my reading of fifteen south might be correct, I doubted it very much because, you see that places us in the Amazon jungle or the Belgian Congo or among the headhunters of New Guinea or . . ."

"How many places there are that I have never heard the least bit about! Tell me of those places—especially about the headhunters. Are they like ghouls, pray tell?"

"You've avoided my question."

"What an inexorable fellow! But how can I answer if I do not know?"

"You mean . . . you mean you've never heard of the United States or . . . or Africa . . . or Arabia . . . ?"

"Ah, yes, I know that one from ancient history. Arabia! But that is far away and the route to it is wholly forgotten. Why I dare say even one of our elders would find it difficult to discover Mount Kaf in that world, much less the names you spiel so glibly."

"You're mocking me. Tell me the truth. Where am I?"

"Sweet sailor, in terms of your land I can speak nothing. I know them not. But lest I displease you I shall leave off this teasing and give you truth—truth as I have heard Zeno tell it. Here we call your world—your *other* world—the Land of Sleep. And perhaps your world calls this world the same . . ."

"Calls it nothing. They do not even know about it. The Land of Sleep, you say?"

"Why, yes, that should be fairly plain. At least that is how Zeno tells it. There are two worlds of sleep or two worlds of wakefulness, whichever you will have. That is, so far as human beings are concerned. Human beings are weird people. Long ago we found that they had souls."

Every hair on Jan's head was standing up straight. What was she doing, speaking of humans as *other than herself?* But, outside of knowing the pitfall which gaped to trap him, he made no further recognition, so badly did he wish to know more of his condition.

"I think I know something of this," said Jan. "The American Indian had some such insight. In sleep his soul walked from his body and visited another land."

"Yes, that is true. Long, long ago we found the Indian had to be very closely watched because of just that consciousness. Here and there others, or so says Zeno, have been vaguely aware of leaving their bodies when they slept, but it has become apparent—or was until you came here—that, so far as actual realization was concerned, these humans here know nothing of their other world—that other world of yours which contains all the strange names. And in their other world they know nothing of this world so that when they rest and sleep in either, they resume their second life in the other. Zeno says this leads to all sorts of silly dissemblances among the brighter humans here. They go about talking of 'double personalities' and 'split egos' and such."

"But . . . but how is it that the same man is so different in the two worlds?"

"That is pulling me in rather deep, my sailor, and you really should talk it over with Zeno. He could tell you all sorts of odd things about it and, truly, he is somewhat obsessed with his theories of it—perhaps because he never dares talk about them. Yes, you should talk to Zeno." She poured more wine and sipped at hers and then artfully changed glasses and drank of his.

"Don't you really know?"

"I hate to appear so stupid and you are a scholar and might pick a flaw in what I say. I do not know that I speak aright. I can give you Zeno's theories but even those I know imperfectly. You see, your question is wrong. There really isn't just one man or one soul or one human. People, even the Jinn—who are considerably less nebulously built and far less destructible, I assure you—consist mainly of a certain kind of energy. Some philosophers say that all energy is the same energy but that argument is pricked by asking the question, 'Even if all energy is convertible into other kinds of energy, does it follow therefore that life is convertible into other kinds of life?' And of course it isn't in the same way that a tree stores heat and then, when burned, gives off the heat again. We had a fakir here—quite a mad fellow by the way—who had somehow reached an ecstatic state whereby he merged both his souls into one..."

"Yoga! The Veda! The goal of the greatest cult in India! The attainment of complete Unity! And they say their souls go elsewhere and..."

"Well! Dear me, if you're going to become so excited and so disgustingly philosophic about it, I shan't allow another word to be pried out of me, I assure you!"

"I didn't mean to offend," said Jan contritely. "But you see, all this explains the great Mysteries of psychology and philosophy. And after all..."

"Oh, I suppose a man would be quite excited rightly enough. It is, after all, rather personal to him."

"You see, there is such a thing as dual personality, you know," said Jan more calmly. "A man may be a perfect saint and a perfect beast all in one body at different times."

"That's not so strange from what I've seen of men!" She drank and made him drink with her, and then, setting down her glass did not seem to find any further interest in the subject of dualism. Rather, the sailor himself had her eye.

"But don't leave me there," begged Jan. "You say a man's soul wanders between these two worlds..."

She sighed. "You have answered my question. The scholar has the upper hand. Oh well," and she shrugged. "If I quiet the scholar perhaps the sailor will come back. A man doesn't have just one soul—or so Zeno says. He has two souls and these work interconnectedly somehow. His life force, as different from plain energy, is capable of only one focusing. He is either here or there and as the world in which he lives forms the body which he has, and so, when one is awake the other is asleep. Brothers, you might say, across the Universe. It's a thing very difficult to achieve, this uniting of both in one body at the same time. And I dare say old Zeno might be interested in knowing whether you carry Tiger back with you to your other world."

"Tell me," said Jan. "How is it that you are so frightened here that humans might learn of this double world?"

"Sailor—please be a sailor, will you, and not a graybeard?—there was once this fakir and there have been others. They were quite enough. Here all humans are slaves. This world is ruled by the Jinn; it belongs to the Jinn and always did and always will be. Once human souls did not effect this change from world to world but merely wandered. There may be other worlds, too. How am I to know that? But, I say, human sleep souls wandered . . . Where was I?"

The sailor was telling in him now. He pressed another drink upon her, himself not in the least blurry.

"Human souls wandered," prompted Jan.

"Oh yes. And we were torn apart by the cursed wars of Sulayman against us. The Jinn may live forever if they are not accidentally killed—though very few have ever escaped that and Zeno is the only one I can call to mind who can remember things of a hundred thousand years ago—before humans were more than apes, it seems, or so he says. The Jinn, I say, were torn by wars. There were not many and this land was large and bountiful and the Jinn were unable to even maintain themselves upon it. Besides, neither Jinn nor Marid enjoys manual work. And so, to ease the burden, several wise ones decided to carefully nurture a plan. It was easy, quite easy, to make bodies. But souls were quite another thing . . . Where was I?"

He poured her still another drink and drank one with her. "The Jinn made bodies...."

"Well ... not exactly made them. To be frank, they stole them out of cemeteries in that world of yours. By enchantment they strove to bring them to life but it could not be done. And then some very bright fellows among us—I assure you they were very, very great magicians—snared these wandering sleep souls and made them come here. And as the days are of disproportionate length, though all is on the same ratio, the sleep soul was sixteen hours here and sixteen hours in its own world. It was no great trick to breed the trait into the race or to breed those revived bodies, made whole again by clever Jinn surgeons. And so, there you have it. The Jinns needed slaves and they got slaves and we've had some trouble because some fellows here get very important and try to incite others with their discoveries. Usually we kill them, for when the sleep soul is trapped here, both bodies die and so we are spared. And so we have slaves. Lots of slaves. And we do them a great favor, too. Eh, sailor? Is this not a fine land? Is it not beauteous? And is it not a great, great pity that we cannot allow humans in their own world to know about it and, perchance, do something to stop it? What is so bad about slavery? We are generous. Right generous, I think. The soul here is the true soul. Just as yours is the soul of a sailor, how unhappy you must have been as a scholar in your other world? I ... uh ... where was I?"

He poured her yet another drink and drank another himself.

Languorously she stretched. "Ah, but you're a handsome devil, Tiger." She smiled and moved closer to him.

Tiger smiled and reached out to put his arm about her. But, suddenly, there was a terrible clamor outside and footsteps raced up the stairs and all the palace reverberated with terrified shouts.

The woman came up straight and the door burst inward.

Old Zeno, his towering hat askew and his robe all tangled in his rickety legs, stumbled to a halt.

"Your Royal Highness!" he cried. "Zongri..."

"You fool!" shouted Ramus, leaping to her feet. "You thick-witted jackal! What do you mean by this?"

Jan recoiled from her, for out of that comely shape rose the terrifying body of the queen, glittering fangs, matted black hair, split hoofs and ugly, scowling visage.

"Your Royal Highness!" quavered Zeno, not to be stopped. "This morning it was found that the pigeons of the royal Barbossi post had been missing for a day! And we have just found the dungeon guards all dead even to Captain Lorco! It's Zongri! He is gone and a swift lugger is missing in the harbor! Your Royal Highness! Forgive me, but the pigeons have long arrived in the Barbossi Isles and those cutthroat pirates will even now have crossed half of the channel. When Zongri meets them they will come back and we have but four ships of war ready for battle while they must have forty! Your Royal Highness, we're doomed!"

Ramus shivered. She hurried down the steps, hoofs clicking, to step to the seaward window and look to the horizon.

"Since morning?"

"Or since night!" cried Zeno. "It is the end of everything! My charts told you! I read them to..."

"Quiet, wreck of a Jinn!" She rushed out of the room and as she charged down the steps, Jan could hear her bellowing, "Get me Admiral Tyronin! Withdraw the cavalry from their outposts! Officers! Guards..."

Jan dabbed at a very moist brow and Zeno looked fixedly at him.

"Well?" said Tiger. "You ought to be happy to have been so very right. It will put you up a mile or two around here."

"Laugh," said Zeno sadly. "Laugh, light-headed sailor. You have caused this. And Zongri is not returning to level this kingdom half so much as he is to find you and put you to the stake.

God help you, blundering mortal, for that is all the help you'll ever get. I know."

And, so saying, he walked away and the Marids barred and bolted the door behind him.

"Zongri," said Jan, going to the place the queen had stood. "Coming here . . . for me!" And a cold chill of horror went up and down his spine. But suddenly he straightened and marched back to the bed where he tossed off two drinks neat.

He threw the empty bottle aside and ripped off the white silk robe. Placing the ring upon his wrist—so large it was—he addressed himself to the task of getting on boots and pants and shirt.

"Zongri will take care of me in time. But before that, by Allah and Baal and Confucius, I've still a dancing girl to see!" And who knew, he thought, hauling on a boot, but what this same dancing girl, who might be Alice Hall, would prove his salvation at least in the other world?

Chapter 10

THE TEMPLE DANCERS

He stood squarely before the door and Jan took a deep breath as though for a plunge into cold water, and Tiger fingered the great seal upon his wrist and chuckled. The ring had struck Zongri's fetters from him and now, now he would investigate its efficacy on other types of locks.

"By the Seal of Sulayman! Open wide!"

Jan almost leaped out of his wits at the resulting crash, so certain was he that it would be heard by every Jinn in the palace. On the instant of command every bar, inside and out, leaped upward from its bracket and fell down with a clang. The great lock was rended as though a bolt of lightning had struck it. The portal smashed back against the wall and Jan stood facing three astounded Marids.

But he was braced to go and they were too startled to properly receive him until he was almost upon them. And then their swords sang from the scabbards and the first lunged with his pike.

Tiger took a step of the hornpipe and the pike passed him by. He ducked and a saber clanged into steel just over his head. He skipped back away from the slash of the third and instantly drove into him like a battle ram.

They left the top step like an explosion, the Marid's scarlet cloak wrapping them all about and billowing as they fell down the flight.

Tiger, like his name, came up standing at the bottom—standing on the chest of a very battered Marid. Scooping up the guard's saber and pistols and hurtling back to jeer at the howling pair who charged down from the top, he raced to the next flight and took it in three jumps. He was in a corridor and for a moment he had to think out the palace's plan. Then, knowing that it was inevitable to avoid going through most of it, and with the yells of the Marids banging his eardrums, he again raced forward and down another flight.

Around the next landing he heard voices but so great was his speed that he could not check himself. Like a catapulted stone he shot toward five officers who instantly faced about, recognized him and snatched at their swords.

Jan knocked them sprawling in five directions and, though a little stunned himself, did not consider it necessary to pause and help any of them up. He soared like an eagle down the next flight, hope burning in him that he could find a way around the great audience chamber. But so great was his speed, with proportionately little time for scouting, that before he could check himself he was thirty feet into the enormous hall and charging straight at the throne.

Ramus had been giving irate instructions for the city's defense and when she thought she beheld a rambunctious page she started to roar out at him.

The floor was so slippery that it was almost like skating. Jan curved away and though still two hundred feet from the throne, he was stamped by his blues as well as his human form and, instead of an angry shout, the queen cried, "TIGER!"

He was already diving toward the immense black doors, already estimating the guard across it. So far they were faced the other way and if they would only stay so he had a chance of getting through them.

"TIGER!" roared Ramus and when again he disregarded her she shouted, "Take him! Captain of the Guard, STOP THAT MAN!"

As one, the cordon before the doors whirled around, pikes up. It was like a picket fence leaning over and every point glittered hungrily to receive him. He could not stop because of his speed and the floor. And though (who knows?) Ramus might have had it otherwise, the order stood and the instinct of the pike soldier is to spear whatever he sees.

"TIGER, YOU FOOL! YOU'LL BE KILLED!"

But he was even then on the pikes—or rather, *almost* on them, there being quite a difference. For Tiger, with all a sailor's agility, slashed sideways with his saber, engaging two pikes at once and feinting them aside, to plunge instantly through the gap. The Marids saw steel flash before their faces and, astounded by the maneuver, ducked back. And by the time they had recovered to again level their weighty weapons for the kill, Tiger was fifty feet away from them and multiplying the distance with alacrity.

Ahead was yet another cordon, that which guarded the outside doors. And these, hearing the clash of steel on steel, were alert and waiting, soon astonished to find that a human being was racing out of the palace toward them. These men had ample warning and Tiger saw in the instant that they could not miss stopping him.

To his right and left were other great doors, leading into the depths of the palace again. He did not think twice. He roared, "By the Seal of Sulayman! Open wide!"

The right-hand door crashed open, its lock so much iron junk. Beyond, a large room yawned. But already the guards were advancing from the front entrance and Tiger waited not at all but plunged in.

He was over the threshold before he saw that he had come to the last place in Tarbutón that he wanted to be—the office of Ramus' chief of staff!

The soldiers in the place stiffened in their chairs and along the wall to see a sailor dash in without any more ceremony than a bloodthirsty flourish of a saber. Instantly they perceived that an assassination was in order.

The general fired point-blank with the pistol he always kept on his desk. But the ball buried itself a good foot above Tiger's damp head. Steel flashed as men made for him.

Tiger had no time to think about it. Battle was battle to him. But Jan cried out, "By the Seal of Sulayman! Down with the wall!"

With a thunder of cracking stone, the front of the room fell outward, obscuring everything in a white cloud of mortar. The flash and roar which had followed the order and the sunlight which abruptly poured in upon them held the soldiers for a terrified instant.

Jan leaped through the fog in the opening and clutched at a vine which grew down the building's face. He let it through his hands so fast that it smoked. Earth smote the soles of his boots and he raced off on the rebound, diving into the protection of shrubbery and running bent over while branches sought to flog him.

The uproar he left behind him was spreading like the waves of a rock dropped into a pool. He saw an outpost dashing in toward the palace and ducked low, halting for a moment. The scarlet cloaks streamed by and an instant later he leaped into their dust and sped toward their unprotected section. The sentry boxes fled by on his right and he dashed through the deep dust of a road to gain the less pretentious and more welcome rank of stores which faced the square.

Citizenry gawped at him. A Marid in green instantly suspected the worst and scudded in pursuit, his long green cape pouring after him and the whistle in his mouth trilling hysterically.

Jan sprang into an alleyway and pressed himself against the wall. The policeman rounded the turn an instant later. Tiger stuck out a foot and the officer went down with two hundred pounds of sailor to pin him to earth and still the whistle. Tiger trussed the Marid with the green cape and then, waiting not to see if the alarm had been answered, surveyed the scene about him and decided upon a drainpipe which led to a two-story building above.

Like the sailor he was, he dug in his toes and hand over hand rocketed up the sheer face. He flung himself over the parapet at the top and looked down. Two policemen had answered the call promptly but they were just now arriving beside their squirming, swearing brother at law and their immediate attention was for him and not a possible quarry.

Jan drew back his head. Before him, side by side, stretched a long avenue of roofs, inviting him to try his broadjumping proclivities. He took the dare but he traveled at a slightly slower pace for he was feeling his exertions a little.

An hour later, having startled three separate sunbathing parties out of their respective wits but without having met with any further misadventure, he came to the base of the hill toward which he had stubbornly worked. He let himself to earth and sought a clump of trees and there, sprawled at length, he got his breath and gazed admiringly at the architecture of his goal. Before very long, however, his admiration turned to something very near dismay. The priests who had caused this place to be constructed had kept a watchful eye upon their own security.

The great, varicolored cube which, like the head of some monster, swallowed and disgorged thousands of Jinn, was high and aloof upon its hill. And though grass grew upon those precipitous slopes it definitely ended the landscaping. This place was a fort! And the canny high lords of it gave no intruder a single tree for cover. It was the crowning insult to see priest sentries on a parapet which ran the circuit of the roof. Tiger fumed. One had to ascend those steps or wait for night and he was not fatuous enough to suppose that he could pass his brawny humanity for an Ifrit.

Night, he decided disconsolately, it would have to be.

Though he well apprehended the danger of entering the town again, he was aware of thirst and hunger and suddenly bethought himself of a certain deep dive where the proprietor was indebted to him through said proprietor's undue faith in dice. Jan smiled as he very vividly remembered a night when Tiger had won the place, tables, hostesses and kegs and had magnanimously loaned it all back forever. It was weird to recollect such a thing because Jan had never experienced it himself, just as Tiger couldn't have told one end of an astrolabe from another. But now Tiger could work an astrolabe and, no doubt, Jan could shoot dice with maddening precision.

By alleyways in which his feet were trained, he flitted through the dusky shadows and came, at last, to the rear entrance of the dive. Cautiously he edged in and peered at the occupants of the taproom.

Several human beings, persons who were very much in keeping with the dingy furtiveness of the place, sat at the scarred tables along the wall, drinking questionable beverages. As long as they were human Tiger knew he had nothing to fear from them and so boldly entered, marching up to the bar and casually greeting the keeper.

He was a man of rotund build, placid and usually cheerful, and because of those attributes and his obvious docility, he was allowed to operate his tavern, though it was a favor rarely accorded humans.

His mild little eyes turned to Tiger, started to move away and then came back with a crack and pop. "Good God! YOU!"

"And what's the matter with that?" said Tiger.

"Listen," said the proprietor in an excited whisper, "you've got to get out of here. They know you come here! The alarm is out for you and not ten seconds ago there was a squad of Marids here looking for you!"

"Then they won't be back very soon. Lazy fellows, Marids.

Would you mind digging into the larder and setting forth fare fit for a gentleman? I'm famished!"

The tavern keeper eyed him wonderingly. "You ain't scared. I know you wouldn't be scared. But you ought to have pity on me. Just think what'll they do if they find you here? Geez, Tiger, I don't know what you done, but the patrol was the Queen's Desert Troopers and they looked upset as hell."

"The queen objects to my leaving her tea party. If they come back I'll swear you didn't recognize me. How is that?"

The man was very doubtful but he was not able to withstand Tiger. He stuck his head through a square hole and spoke to his wife in the kitchen. Then he looked at Tiger again and dabbed at his forehead with his apron.

"Hot, ain't it?" he said weakly.

"Can't say as I've noticed," said Tiger with a grin.

The proprietor puttered with glasses and his hands shook so that he almost dropped three in a batch. He gave it up. "Look, Tiger. Like a good guy, would you go over to that table agin the wall and make yourself as small as possible?"

Tiger shrugged. "It's all the same as long as the food is good and there's lots of it." He wandered to the designated spot and began to seat himself. Suddenly he started.

At the table next to his were two men he was certain he knew and yet for the life of him he could not place them. One was hook-nosed and spidery-handed and possessed two liabilities in the form of evil, bloodshot eyes. The other was obese and as slick as though he had been freshly lubricated—though with somewhat rancid oil. They were quite obviously of a certain class of slaves whose masters specialized in the lower orders of crime and had a kicked cur look about them which filled a beholder with disgust.

Tiger lowered himself slowly into his chair. He was very puzzled. He usually remembered faces very easily and the names as well and though he told himself that he would not ordinarily notice such vermin and that he had seen them here on other occasions, he was not at all convinced. Who, he demanded of himself, were they?

Presently the proprietor came with a ham and a chicken and three bottles of different wines. His cargo sounded like castanets and he almost missed the table with it, so intent was he upon the door. Hurriedly he made a second trip for bread and then withdrew to morosely seat himself at the end of his bar and keep an eye upon the place from which he was certain doom would soon enter in the form of the Queen's Desert Troopers.

Tiger ate slowly, pondering his problem and somewhat annoyed that he would bother to dwell upon two such scurvy beings. There was a certain familiarity about them which was incongruous and then Jan's fund of knowledge took a hand.

I'm changed, Jan told himself. Why couldn't it be possible for these two to be known to me in the other world?

And with that as a starting point he carefully surveyed their features until he was as exasperated as though he had a word on the end of his tongue and couldn't say it.

At last the two gentlemen in question, being two to Jan's one, took exception to his scrutiny. They muttered about it in low voices and evidently decided that it wasn't to be tolerated. The one with the bloodshot eyes came ominously to his feet and stalked over to Jan's table.

"If you got something to spill, out with it, pal."

The obese member of the duet waddled over to back his partner up. Jan looked from one to the other of them and they mistook his attitude for apology.

"All right," said the fat one. "But don't git so nosey, see?"

And they would have walked back had not a bolt of lightning struck in the center of Jan's brain. "Wait a minute. I know you fellows."

"Yeah, well we don't know you and don't want to neither. So if..."

"You," said Jan, seeing the almost indefinable line of features at last and pointing to the fat one, "are Shannon!"

"Huh?" said the indicated one.

"And you," said Jan in sudden excitement, "are Nathaniel Green! That's it! That's it! I could feel it! Look, sit down. I've got a matter to talk over with you."

"He's cockroachy," said the indicated Green.

"Look, buddy," said the greasy caricature of Shannon, "we're minding our own business and if you want to pick daisies from the under side, you'll forget to mind your own."

But Jan was laughing, looking from one to the other of them. "Green! Poor old Nathaniel Green. Where's your watch? And you! Shannon! A tub of lard with a coating of dirt and as surly as a kicked pariah!" His laugh grew louder.

The pair were uneasy on more than one count. They were quite aware of the pistols in Tiger's belt and of the size of Tiger's shoulders and were somewhat intimidated by the correct language springing from a sailor's mouth. It looked like a magic spy trap to them and they weren't having any. They shuffled, growling, back to their table, got their hats, haggled over the reckoning and left.

"Who are those men?" asked Jan when the keeper came over to find out the cause of the argument.

"Them? Gutter pickin's. Dauda's jackals. They eat his leavin's. What's the idea gettin' me in trouble with a guy like Dauda? Ain't you got no sense, Tiger? You come back here with the troopers on your trail, talkin' like a swell and lookin' . . . well, lookin' different. I wouldn't knowed you at first. But listen, Tiger, will you finish up and get out of here. You know you're welcome to anything I got but they'll be comin' back pretty soon and it's as much as my life is worth. After all, the Queen's Desert Troopers don't go pokin' around unless a man's assassinated a duke or something."

"All right. To save your nerves I'll finish and go," said Tiger. "Besides, I don't think much of your trade anyway. They stink."

Dusk found him again at the foot of the temple hill. The enormous cube stood out against angry clouds and from every entrance there streamed the light of flaming braziers. Torches flanked the avenue of steps and their fitful flare fell weirdly upon the throng of Jinn. Evidently some great rite was to be held for all the crowd marched upwards and none marched down and it was plain from the fanfare of flashing jewels that the worshippers were dressed for some state occasion. Perhaps, thought Jan, the word had gone about that Zongri comes with a fleet from the Barbossis. But whatever it was, his chances of entering that place undiscovered were very remote indeed.

He was almost on the verge of turning back when there again came to him the vision of the dancing girl upon the steps and, simultaneously, the memory of the girl who had shown him the only kindness he had ever received. She was there, a dancing slave to the Jinn and who knew but what the morrow would find him dead in this world and, consequently, the other as well. Certainly he owed it to her to try, if he could, to free her and give her into the keeping of one who would repay favor with favor—Admiral Tyronin, whose influence was great enough to protect her and who, even in the event of defeat, would very probably be suffered to retire to his island estate on parole. High officers, remembered Tiger, seldom suffered greatly in these wars.

No, he could not leave her there to be ultimately thieved by some persuasive Jinn—as was the fate of these dancing girls. And besides, every atom of him demanded to confront her and speak to her.

Tiger strode forward, skirting the mound until he came to the rear. As on a cliff the temple blazed above him, Marids in silhouette upon the walls. He loosened his saber in its sheath and looked to the priming of his pistols and then began the ascent.

Of all mortals, only dancing girls had come here in the
history of the place except those few who had dared it to end upon
a pike at the foot of the steps, grinning at awed beholders. There
was treasure in this place to tempt even honest men and in the
town it was sometimes said of a thief that he was bold enough
to "scale the heights of Rani."

Tiger, scaling the heights, was not thinking about being bold
but only of discovering an entrance and making his way through
the place to the quarters of the dancers. The long grass caught
at his boots and strove to hold him back, but he made it pay by
grasping handfuls of it and so hoisting himself upward. It was
no great trick to ascend the slope but Tiger had been giving his
attention to the ground and did not see the next barrier until he
had almost fallen into it. The dark hole gaped and he held hard
to the edge, one foot already in. Hastily he drew back, eyeing
the trap in the flare of the torches above. Here, dug so as to be
unseen from the plain below, was a moat about thirty feet wide
and as deep. But no water was here, only a hiss and rattle as things
moved on the floor.

"Snakes!" said Tiger, feeling the hair rise on the back of his
neck. He took a hitch on his nerve and felt with his foot over
the edge. But the drop was sheer and the slimy things at the bottom rustled as they moved to the foot of the drop, waiting.

He cursed impatiently at such Jinn hellishness. But he wasted
very little time mourning about it. He had only one recourse—to
ascend by the stairs through the main entrance!

He made the decision and put it into action at once, striding
along the outer edge of the moat, watchful for other traps but
well informed by the lights above.

Shortly he had come again to the front of the building and,
dropping on his face, crept toward the great balustrades, toward
stronger light and toward guards.

Marids were posted at the end of every wide step, their steel
helmets as bright as their single eyes and their pikes bearing

streamers which did not in the least impair their usefulness. But so stately was their bearing and so bright the torches in their eyes that Jan was able to come within touching distance of one's back without being seen. He lay in the protection of the balustrade's shadow and pondered his next move. More and more, as obstacles arose, he determined to put his plan into action and now he was certain that his salvation, at least on Earth, depended upon his reaching Alice Hall in this world.

He was very sorely tempted to steal the sentry's cloak but he well knew the folly of trying to pass off his brawn for a Marid's stumpy ugliness and so he began to work himself up toward the temple by keeping in the shadow of the steps where the Jinn thronged not ten feet away. He wondered a little just what method of killing him they would use if they caught him, for now, regardless of how the queen might want him treated, the priests of Rani would do—as they rightfully did—whatever they pleased. As an ex-captive of the throne, sought by troopers, perhaps a lash would be the most he merited. But he well knew that if he invaded Rani, the long arm of that goddess would find him in whatever state or abode he sought refuge. But he wasn't caught yet.

Again he almost tripped into the moat and was angered to find that it butted against this pavement's edge. Had he gone to all this trouble only to be balked by the same barrier? He raised his head a little and stared at the crowd whose brilliant robes almost brushed his face. He again eyed the moat. And then, bethinking himself of the urgency of his mission, gripped the edge of the pavement and swung himself over the darkly tenanted space.

He swung himself along, holding to the slippery edge of the steps, trusting that his hands would escape being seen. But the torches were bright and his luck was in at the moment and he came to safety on the other side. Again he examined the ground about him. The temple's foundation was about eight feet high and on it stood columns whose backs were against the stone walls. He sprang up to the ledge. Somewhere there must be a postern.

Above him on the roof, guards paced mechanically back and forth like great black dolls. To his left spread the colorful panorama of the steps and behind him, far below, sparkled the lights of harbor and city.

His questing fingers examined the wall ahead of him and then, with relief, they touched the cold iron of a small door. It was locked but that worried him not at all.

"By the Seal of Sulayman," he whispered, "open wide."

Softly, the door swung inward as though pulled by an unseen hand. Jan slipped through the opening and silently closed the portal. He was in a long hall, momentarily deserted. Through the archways which flanked it he could see the limitless expanse of the temple's main room where torches flared smokily and sent gigantic shadows to chasing each other along the walls and ceiling.

At the far end was a gargantuan idol, gleaming with precious stones, all of gold and silver and ivory. The hands rested upon the hilt of a sword some fifty feet long and the feet were spread apart in an attitude of battle. This was Rani, Rani, goddess of the Jinn, terrible of eye, lovely of form, lustful and mystic, beauteous and murderous. Other humans—and few they had been— had paid for such a sight with their lives.

Jan tore his eyes away from the terrifying figure and cast about him for further ways. But he dared go neither up nor down this hall for at each end he could see temple guards and passing crowds. And certainly he could not walk forward into the place of worship. Sailorlike he looked aloft and took heart. The wall was built in gradually narrowing stones and each one offered a ledge, four feet above the last. And the columns which supported the roof were interconnected by beams.

He heard someone close a door near at hand and the mutter of voices approaching and he lost no time swinging up and leaping from ledge to ledge. A moment later he looked down upon the horned heads of priests. They paused, talking together, before they entered the great chamber.

"Then it is settled," said the oldest of the lot, one dressed all in yellow silk. "He cannot injure us for he is one of the believers and so also are his very warriors. What, then, say you to the prophecy of defeat for Ramus?"

They held up their clawed right hands in the Ifrit gesture of the affirmative.

"It is time," said another, "that we were accorded greater freedom here. A plague on Ramus. Let the prophecy ring loud enough to take the hearts out of the officers here. He will repay it handsomely with greater freedom."

"Very well," said the old one. "Let the rites begin."

They moved out of the shadows and while some of them went furtively down through a trap in the floor, the others, including the ancient one, walked boldly out into the chamber itself.

Jan pondered their words. Certainly, by "he" could they mean Zongri? And Tiger, of a sudden, remembered vague rumors of dissatisfaction among the priesthood for Ramus' refusal to take part in their rites and her placing such great reliance upon the soothsayer Zeno and his stars. Zeno had broken the monopoly of Rani on prophecy when the queen had elevated him to his high place.

Now that the hall below was deserted, Jan dropped swiftly down to it again with a new idea. He opened the trap in the floor and found a steep stairway leading through gloom. He closed the trap over him and made his way along a tunnel which seemed to lead for miles beneath the earth. But, wiping cobwebs from his face and pausing constantly to listen and look for possible guards, he finally reached the end of it. Here was another stairway, going up.

Somewhere far off he heard a hundred mighty horns bellow hoarsely for silence. And as he mounted, the single voice of a speaker came to him with increasing distinctness. Then he came to a parting of the stairs. One continued up but the other led off on the level. Jan chose the ascent rather than run a chance of losing himself in a labyrinth.

By the number of steps he knew that he was well above the floor of the great chamber and that he must now be within one of the walls. Again the way became level and he found that he had entered upon an observation gallery.

He was not much amazed, being well versed in such obtuse subjects as ordinary necromancy, to find that sets of eyeholes were bored through the stone so as to match with the eyes of figures with which the chamber was decorated. He wondered that the Jinn permitted such an obvious trick and his opinion of their wits fell accordingly.

The chamber was spread out before him in all its shadowy splendor. Full ten thousand Jinn and Jinnia, resplendent in sparkling jewels and shimmering silk, stood upon the gradually raised floor. They faced Rani but between them and the idol intervened a semicircle where a mass of priests were now undergoing some sort of ritual. Their bowed heads were all inclined toward Rani and over them rolled the sepulchral tones of the temple master, he who had been in the hall near Jan.

What he was saying Jan neither knew or cared. All his attention was concentrated upon the ringing rank of temple dancers who were intermingled with Marids in rite regalia. One by one he studied the girls but in those hundreds and at his height above them, he found it very difficult to find Alice Hall. His spine tingled as he thought of her there, a part of that savage splendor, hypnotized by the intoning music which now began to flow from an unseen recess in the chamber. At this signal the girls stood up, throwing back their white capes and stepping ahead of the Marids, their diamond-decked bodies rose in the guttering torchlight.

Suddenly he found her. She was a pace or two ahead of all the rest and seemed to be a key to their movements. He hardly knew what the others did, though he was conscious of their forming geometric patterns in slow, easy grace to the increasing tempo of the horns and drums.

With difficulty he bethought himself of Rani and turned his attention to the idol. The enormous figure was supported by heavy chains so placed as to be invisible from the front. And so it was not with as great a shock as the others below that he saw the goddess begin to move slowly from side to side.

Puerile, he thought to himself. Probably the thing was hinged like a marionette and, without doubt, it had speaking tubes connected with it so that priests could simulate its voice.

The music became faster, louder and he found that he had been unconsciously beating to it. The wild strains, guttural and hoarse, brought the hot blood pulsing to his face and it was with difficulty that he tore his eyes away from the idol.

He knew quite well what he intended to do just as he completely understood the horrible consequences which might follow. But Tiger was bold and Jan was cunning and in a moment he strode down the runway, searching for yet another passageway which might admit him to the chamber itself when the occasion came. But his only chance lay in the one branch he had found and now he paced down it, watching ahead of each turn, certain that he would run into priests.

Finally he found another branch but this one led straight up and that he did not need. Ahead he saw two spots of light which came up against a short ladder. By mounting it he again discovered that he could see out and that, also, he could get out when that occasion came.

It did not take him long to find that he was inside the idol's base for, by looking straight up he could see the gigantic wings which sprouted stiffly from the goddess's shoulders and swooped earthward toward him.

He was slightly puzzled to see that during his change the goddess had taken her hand from the sword and now held her arms out straight above the heads of the dancers. From this angle the goddess had a staring look which was awful to see.

The dancers swayed and dipped and the music quickened. Soon they were in a semicircle, spinning like tops, their hair flying out from their heads and their supple bodies weaving. With a crash the music stopped. In the deep stillness the dancers fled back until they were again in their original places. Throwing themselves down in an attitude of supplication, they waited.

The priests sped away, leaving only their ancient blackguard of a master. The venerable one spread out his hands to the goddess. Somewhere a drum beat hysterically for an instant and then was still. From his cassock the master took a long, shining whip and let it curl like a snake along the pavement. Again the drums shattered the stillness and deepened it by their ceasing. The master's whip cracked like a musket.

"Rani!" cried the ancient one. "Rani! By the symbol of this whip with which we hold you, we demand that you answer."

The goddess was not swinging now. The feet moved until they were together. The head, full a dozen yards in diameter, bent so that the glowing eyes stared down at the master.

"Rani! Behold! We have offered you music and dancing. We offer you worship! Answer and answer well!"

Again the whip cracked and Rani moved a trifle while a flutter of awe ran back through the crowd.

Jan thought to himself that the Jinn were a witless lot to be fooled by a hundred and fifty-foot marionette.

"Who," cried the master, "shall be the victor in tomorrow's battle? Zongri or Ramus the Magnificent?"

A deep, unintelligible rumble came from the goddess.

And then, from the sides of the hall, on two platforms near to Rani's head, the priests Jan had seen before took station. In their hands they held long poles which had glowing coals on their ends. With these they thrust at the goddess's shoulder.

A tremor shot through the idol which Jan thought very well done. Again the master cried out.

"Rani! Who shall be the victor? ANSWER!"

A snarl of pain and rage followed. The stare in those glassy eyes changed to a waking expression of wrath. Rani moved and the chains rattled savagely.

"ANSWER!" howled the master.

A flood of strange words poured from the moving lips, to hurl across the chamber and rebound like a cannonade.

"Be still!" cried the master. He whirled about. "Rani has spoken! Woe to Tarbutón. The fate of the battle will fall upon the banners of Zongri and Ramus will be vanquished forever!"

A gasp ran through the chamber, a sound which expressed shock and growing terror.

Again the goddess spoke, unbidden, in those rolling accents. But the men on the platform beside her head stabbed out with the coals and Rani was still.

"Now," thought Jan, "while their wits are paralyzed, I'll show them how their goddess lies—in fragments at their feet!"

He raised the ring and cried, "By the Seal of Sulayman! Part the chains!"

Mortar flew from the walls in great, angry puffs. Iron clanked in falling and then crashed resoundingly to the floor. The ancient one whirled and stared with disbelief at the monstrous figure which teetered forward toward him.

Jan ducked, waiting for the concussion of the fall. It came before he expected it—so violently that the stone cracked wide before him and the whole temple rocked!

He heard a scream of terror from the Jinn and then the rush of twenty thousand feet seeking exit through the dust-choked gloom.

Tiger sprang out of his observation post and raced across the floor. Because the dancing girls were farthest from the entrance, they huddled against the jam, staring with terrified eyes at the fallen goddess, half of them probably convinced of its former power.

Tiger waded through broken granite and chips of gold. Under his feet rolled the diamonds which had bedecked the headdress.

He had eyes only for one jewel, the dancing girl nearest to him. So stunned was she that she remarked not at all that it was a human being who came racing out of that fog of dust. Her lovely eyes were round with horror and did not even turn to him when he scooped her up into his arms.

The priests were as mad as the rest to get away from there, failing to understand that nothing else could happen. The death of their master had unnerved them and two rushed by Tiger within a foot without paying the slightest attention to him. Tiger disliked being ignored. When the largest priest struck the jam, Tiger snatched him by the shoulder, tearing away the flowing yellow cloak which had covered him from crown to toe. The Ifrit scarcely noticed the loss.

Throwing the color of protection about them, Jan bore the girl through the packed masses, bullying a way out of the entrance and down the long stairs. Unnoticed, he reached the avenue at the bottom and dodged into a side street as soon as one presented itself. The weight of the dancing girl was slight and impeded him but little.

Already terror was beginning to spread through the city and far off bells were ringing and horns blowing. Jan cared nothing about them. By alley and dark thoroughfare he sped swiftly to the waterfront, hardly pausing at all to leap down off a dock into a small fishing smack.

The fisherman leaped up from his dozing on a pile of nets and his two sailors came up standing a moment later. They were still asleep so far as their wits went for Tiger had only to let the dock lights glitter on the saber and cry, "To the *Morin,* flagship of Admiral Tyronin!"

The sailors mechanically cast off, seeing in Tiger an espionage officer or some other in whom they would not dare take any great interest. The lateen sail dropped from its yard and filled, and in the fresh night wind they scudded between anchored vessels whose lights made yellow sea serpents upon the water.

The girl had been staring at Tiger for some time and, seeing him smile at her, she spoke. "Who . . . who are you?"

"Tiger."

"*You* are *Tiger?*"

"Does notoriety reach even to a Jinn temple?"

"I have heard naval officers ask a blessing for you . . . But . . . how is it that you entered the temple? That is death to a human!"

"For once it wasn't. Not yet, anyway."

"But why . . ." she hesitated in sudden fear. "Why have you taken me away?"

"Did you like that place?"

"Oh! No, no! I am glad to be stolen. But . . ."

"You have no need to be afraid." It seemed so strange to see Alice Hall here and yet not be known to her. "You have never seen me before?"

"Why . . . of course not. I have seen no human being other than my dancers since I was a child!"

"Have you ever heard the name, Alice Hall?"

She repeated it slowly after him, a puzzled look upon her face. "Al . . . ice. Alice Hall. I seem to have heard it somewhere before."

"Of course you have. You *are* Alice Hall."

"I?" She shook her head. "But no, I have no name but Wanna. You are making fun of me."

"No indeed."

"You are a very strange fellow. Why did you come to the temple?"

"To get you."

"Me?"

"I saw you once before—here. In a telescope."

She looked unwinkingly at him and drew the yellow cloak more tightly about her against the cold wind. She ventured a smile and clutched at his hand as he turned to watch the side of the flagship come up to them.

135

The fishermen brailed their sail and the boat drifted in to the landing stage. Jan took a hoop out of his ear and handed it to the captain who stared at it in amazement, changing his opinion about espionage instantly.

Tiger took up the girl again and trotted up the ladder to the deck where a Jinn officer stood with threatening mien.

"I wish to be taken to Admiral Tyronin immediately," said Tiger.

The officer scowled.

"My name is Tiger."

It was as though he had stuck a pin in the lieutenant. The Ifrit whirled to his lounging guard. "Take this man into custody immediately."

"I demand to see the admiral!" cried Jan.

A voice from the quarterdeck of the seventy-four smote them. "What is this?" And boots thumped on a ladder and over the planks and so into the light of the guard lantern.

With relief Jan recognized Commander Bakon who had stopped him before the palace.

"Tiger!" cried the commander. "Good god, man, what are you doing here? Get back ashore. Lieutenant, call that boat . . ."

"I'm here to see Admiral Tyronin," said Tiger. "And see him I shall."

"But what is this you have here?" And Bakon saw the yellow robe. "The cloak of . . . of a priest!" And he saw the girl's flashing jewels. "And . . . and a temple dancer! Tiger, have you gone mad? Was it you who caused that commotion up at the temple which we have been hearing and watching for half an hour?"

"That's neither here nor there," said Tiger. "I asked a favor."

"On your head be it," said the commander. "His Lordship is just about out of his head, what with expecting to meet forty ships with four and then all that uproar over on the beach. What was it about?"

"Rani fell over on her face."

"What?"

"Because she lied," said the dancing girl swiftly. "She said that Zongri would win and a greater god smote her."

Bakon blanched.

"The admiral," reminded Tiger.

"Well, remember that you asked for it," said Bakon dispiritedly. He led the way aft and to the quarterdeck. They descended a short ladder and found themselves in the admiral's quarters. The door of the inner room was open and Tiger could see the ugly and now worried Tyronin bent over a chart, pencil poised. The light of the lantern increased the lines on his hairy face.

"Your Lordship," said Bakon, bowing slightly.

"Yes? Yes, what is it now?"

"You perhaps recall a sailor called Tiger who once brought us the line which pulled us off the beach on the Isle of Fire when . . ."

"Tiger? Yes, what about him now?" Tyronin saw the man and stood up. The group moved into the room and His Lordship started at both yellow cloak and dancing girl. "What's this?" he thundered.

"Sir," said Tiger, "tomorrow you are to meet Zongri in battle. I am the chief cause of his coming attack and for that reason I . . ."

"Bah! I only know that you are trying to play upon my generosity and make trouble for me with the queen. Did you know that the town is being combed for you? No, I suppose not! Did you know that you are to be arrested on sight? Oh no, of course not! And you thought I would blind myself to my duty to Her Majesty and take you in like some stray cur! And you come with a Rani dancing girl with probably the blood of a priest upon your hands as well as his cloak and expect me . . . ! God! GUARD!"

"Wait," pleaded Tiger. "I . . ."

"SILENCE! Guard, place this man under arrest. Put the dancing girl in Malin's cabin and make certain she does not escape.

This man is Tiger. You may have heard of him. He is not to be trusted for an instant and you are to make certain that a sentry with a primed pistol stands outside his cell with the muzzle of that weapon trained upon him whether he is waking or sleeping. There!" He faced Tiger. "At midnight we weigh anchor to meet Zongri's fleet. It is too late to put you ashore now. But if fortune favors us you'll be surrendered to the queen on our return."

The sentry took Tiger's pistols and saber and at pistol point escorted him back to the deck. Tiger was conscious of the girl's despairing eyes upon his back—and conscious too of the short-lived gratitude of man.

Chapter 11

THE HEARING

Jan awoke to the uneasy realization that elsewhere he was asleep with a cocked pistol pointing at him and as the body, alive but without vital force, might roll and turn, he hoped that Tiger would offer no offense.

He swung his feet down to the concrete floor and found that Diver had been restored to him. But Diver was still snoring and Jan wondered where Diver was and what Diver was doing. Someday he would find out, perhaps, though he was not very interested. And the counterfeiters, where were they and what were they doing while their earth bodies snored so resoundingly? Not, of course, that it mattered much.

He sighed deeply and stuffed the pipe Alice had brought him and got it going. Thoughtfully he reviewed Tiger's deeds and misdeeds. He was almost dispassionate about it—for a little while. With the theft of the dancing girl, Tiger had stamped his death warrant. While nobody could prove that he had had any connection with the destruction of Rani, merely the touching of a sacred member of that temple would doom him. And the queen? What would she say when she found how he had duped her about that seal?

Soon he began to sweat. Certain he was that that night he would sleep himself into death. Tyronin's foolhardy resistance to Zongri's great fleet would probably doom the ship. If, somehow, it didn't, Zongri would find him. Whether Ramus or Zongri held forth for victory, Tiger's puckish pranks were over. As it was early he laid back upon his bunk and tried to dispose himself for further slumber. But he was too nervous for that and though he interspersed visions of a pointed cocked pistol framed in a door with a pair of cockroaches climbing sturdily, being half in and half out of each world, he found no rest in either.

He was almost glad when the jail began to stir about but he was far too worried to enjoy his food. He listened to Diver's jibes and heard them not at all. And as the morning progressed he found he could not sit still but must walk up and down along the bars.

Finally, at eleven, they came for him, Shannon and a guard. Shannon's false heartiness sought to cheer him up.

"Now you just do what I tell you, Jan, and this'll all be okay. We'll let you tell your story just as it happened and then I'll throw what weight I can behind it and pretty soon we'll have you out of here slick as grease."

Jan didn't answer and Shannon kept it up until they came to an antechamber to the judge's office where a thin, skeleton-faced fellow sat thumping the table with his pince-nez.

"This's Doc Harrington," said Shannon. "This's Jan Palmer, doc."

"Ah," said Harrington, looking professionally at Jan. "Let us get down to business." He put forth pencil and paper and invited Jan to sit and write the answers to certain questions and, when that was done, to put down the first word which came into his mind after another word was given. That too was over shortly.

The psychiatrist examined the result and his brows went up, up, up until they almost vanished in his sparse hair. He pursed his lips and pulled his beard. He adjusted his pince-nez and took them off. He scowled at Jan and then read the paper once more.

"Okay?" said Shannon.

"Ah . . . yes. Splendid."

"Then, let's go."

They entered the judge's office where batteries of legal books stood ready to fire opinions on any sort of case imaginable and where nervous feet had worn out the rug by the desk.

The judge was a well-fed, rather dull person who carried his dignity of office very easily—never having been bothered with any original thoughts and so injure it.

"Sit down," said the judge.

Jan sat down and looked around him. Aunt Ethel was there, dabbing at her eyes—which were quite dry—and muttering, "Oh, the poor boy, the poor boy."

Thompson sat against the other wall, gnawing on a bowler. Nathaniel Green paced back and forth, looking at his watch and complaining about the delay.

For an instant Jan was frightened and then became flooded with relief when he saw Alice Hall sitting at a small desk ready to take down the proceedings for Green's edification. She looked wonderingly at Jan but beyond that made no sign.

"Now, let's get down to it," said the judge. "In brief, young man, sketch your story of how Professor Frobish came to be murdered. We're all your friends here so you need have no fear."

Jan looked them over and experienced a desire to laugh in the judge's face. With the exception of Alice there wasn't a person in the room who had the least desire to find him innocent. Indeed, Aunt Ethel and Thompson, Shannon and, last but not least, Green, stood to profit enormously by his bad luck.

"Just say I'm crazy and have done with it," said Jan truculently. "No matter what I say, that will be the verdict."

"Why, my poor boy," whimpered Aunt Ethel, "you're among your own . . ."

"I'd rather be in a hyena's den," said Jan. He noted how they all started at his tone. "Well, with nothing to gain or lose, I may as well give you the truth." And, so saying, he very briefly sketched the facts of the case.

When he had done with his terse statements, the psychiatrist unobtrusively placed his penciled findings upon the judge's desk and the judge bent over it for some time. Then he sat back, making a steeple out of his fingers and nodding. Just when everyone thought he had gone to sleep, he rang for his clerk and sent out for a form. When it came, he filled in a few blanks and then turned to Green.

"You will have to sign this. You and two others."

Shannon almost leaped for the pen when Green was done. And Thompson and Aunt Ethel had quite a lively race for it. But Aunt Ethel won and placed down her name with vague murmurs about what a terrible shame it was and how insanity would have to run in the Palmer family that way. She didn't see how she could ever live it down.

The formalities over, the judge reached toward a buzzer.

"Wait a minute," said Jan, getting up.

The judge sat back and then again, more hurriedly this time, bent a finger toward the button.

"If this is justice," said Jan, "I'm going to work for the anarchists. You've heard nothing sufficient to convince you that my story is or is not true. These people," and he took them in with a wave of his hand, "are only too anxious to have me put away."

There were murmurs which showed that the company demurred heartily.

"You have not even called," said Jan, "for exhibit A."

"Er . . . exhibit A?" said the judge. "But my dear fellow, calm yourself. This is all very regular . . ."

"There is the matter of looking at the copper jar," said Jan.

"But I see no necessity . . ." began Green impatiently.

"You mean there really is a copper jar?" said the judge.

"Indeed there is," said Jan. "How about it, Alice?"

"Why certainly there is," she said swiftly, though to tell the truth she had never so much as noticed it in all her visits there.

"And an examination of that jar," said Jan, "will prove my story perfectly."

"How is this?" said the judge. "My dear fellow, this form is signed. And besides, it is almost time for lunch."

"I demand that you have that jar brought here," said Jan.

"Now, now," said Shannon soothingly. "He's a little violent at times, judge, and . . ."

"I know," said the judge, nodding. Again he reached toward the button which would call a guard to take Jan away. It seemed that even then the sanitarium ambulance was waiting.

There was the sound as of a chair being shoved determinedly back. Alice Hall eyed the judge with disapproval. "Your Honor, the papers would like to print a story to the effect that you might have received money to put a millionaire in jail."

It was a terrible chance she was taking, Jan knew. And while he feared for her, his heart warmed toward her more than ever before.

"What's this?" cried the judge at the wholly unjust charge. "Are you mad?"

"Not at all," said Alice. "And I wonder if he is, either. His mistake lies in having been meek to a crowd of wolves. The papers, I think, would enjoy such a story, true or not. If it is even whispered about that Jan Palmer, heir to the Palmer interests, was railroaded to an insane asylum to cover up the thefts of his manager, Nathaniel Green . . ."

"What's this?" shouted Green. "Young lady, you are fired! Leave this office instantly."

"I may be fired but I shall not leave. Your Honor," said Alice, crisply. "If Jan Palmer wants a copper jar brought here, perhaps it would be wise to bring that copper jar."

"I . . . uh . . . see your point," said the judge. "*O'Hoolihan!*"

In an hour the morosely lunchless judge was sitting in sad contemplation of the copper jar while Green walked in circles and said, "Nonsense, nonsense, nonsense! I'm due at the office this minute!"

"And so," said the judge, "this is the jar out of which the Ifrit came."

"Yes," said Jan, stepping up to it and lifting the leaden stopper.

"And how tall is an Ifrit?" said the judge.

"Fifteen feet," said Jan promptly. "But in another world they do not seem so tall—either that or we are larger."

"Fifteen feet?" said the judge. "And the jar is but four feet. My dear young man, I fail to see . . ."

The psychiatrist tittered and the judge was suddenly pleased with himself.

"Well!" said the judge, "that is that. It proves nothing except the charges already brought. The justness of them is plain to see."

Alice's face fell. She had wagered her job and lost, but her sympathy and attention was all for Jan.

In a very quiet voice, Jan said, "Your Honor, if I were you I would think twice before I call proof disproof. I might go as far as to say that it is dangerous for you to do so."

"A threat?"

"Now, now, Jan," said Aunt Ethel. "He is *so* violent at times, Your Honor . . ."

"Aye, proof!" said Jan. "And a threat as well. A threat which I am quite capable of carrying out. There is one phase of this story which I have yet to mention. It is the answer to the ancient problem of the wandering sleep soul. And so, one and all . . ." He took a firm grip upon the leaden stopper, his palm pressing hard against the anciently imprinted Seal. "And so you are brought to this.

"By the Seal of Sulayman and by the token of all the deeds already done by its mighty power, I invoke upon all of you, the sentence of Eternal Wakefulness!"

The psychiatrist tittered in the quiet room and the others gathered heart. As nothing had happened they were sure nothing would happen.

"The ambulance is waiting," said the judge. "O'Hoolihan, escort the young man out."

Jan stopped beside Alice. "Don't worry. Things may yet turn out well." He did not miss the moistness in her eyes and he knew then that even though he might be mad, she loved him.

Chapter 12

BATTLE!

At dawn the sound of ten thousand kettle drums struck violently at once shook the seventy-four from stem to taff!

Directly under the starboard gun deck, Jan leaped up, not yet awake but already aching from the concussion.

"Sit down!" barked the third sentry of the night, gesturing with the pistol.

Jan stared at the muzzle and then at the seaman's pale face and obediently seated himself upon the edge of the berth.

There came the groan of shifting yards and the pop of fluttering canvas as the seventy-four came about to bring her port batteries to bear. She heeled under the buffeting wind and began to pitch as she picked up speed. Pipes shrilled and bare feet slapped over planking and then the whole vessel leaped as the demi-cannon blasted away.

"What time is it?" said Jan.

"About six-thirty. Now pipe down. I'm sorry but I'm not supposed to talk to you."

"That's fine by me," said Jan.

A shriek of hurtling round shot pierced the air and a series of muffled thuds reported that the seventy-four had been hulled. But again yards creaked and canvas thundered. Again she came about and heeled. The re-charged starboard batteries brayed flame and shot.

The sentry glanced up at the deck above and nervously wet his lips. Screaming grape slapped like giant hailstones in the rigging and he flinched.

"You're lucky," said Jan. "If we're sunk you get a nice clean burial. All in one piece."

"Shut up!"

"Well, isn't that better than being drowned *and* lacking arms and maybe legs? Listen to that musketry. We must be closing in on Zongri's fleet."

A broadside of their own was instantly answered by the roar of another close by. The seventy-four reeled, hesitated and then picked up speed again.

"Is that water I hear?" said Jan.

"Water? *Where?*"

"Hulled, probably. Many more like that and we'll get it before the rest of them up there. Still, I don't mind it. If a man is going to die, he might as well have some privacy."

"Stop it!"

"Why, that doesn't bother you, does it? Maybe you'd rather be blown up than merely sunk. And the sharks won't be able to get at you in here."

There is nothing worse than a dark hold when a battle rages, listening to the broadsides thunder and feeling the seventy-four trip and wallow as round shot took its count, hearing wounded scream and weep, sensing the rising levels in the bilges and having no idea whatever of how the battle goes. Men prefer dying where they can see the sun.

For an hour the din was incessant and for an hour Jan remarked upon each expert broadside which was poured into them.

"The way she's listing now," said Jan, "we've probably lost a mast and they're too busy to cut it away. That cuts down the speed, you know, and makes it very easy for us to be boarded. Wasn't your relief supposed to be here by now?"

"Never mind me relief!"

"Ah, there'll be much weeping in Tarbutón this night for our brave lads. And weeping too in another world where men are nervous beyond account as they slumber. And how many will be the obituaries in the morning paper? Accidents, heart failure, murder. By the way, you haven't any people, I trust."

"I have my mother!"

"And a girl, too, I suppose. She's probably down at the wharves now, straining her eyes to sea in the hope of seeing the red banner returning. But, from the way that water rushes under us, I think she looks in vain. Personally, it's nothing to me. Returned, I'd be executed. It matters very little how a man dies just so long as he is in one piece. This is a nice place now. The water is coming up under us at a very fast rate. We're hulled between wind and water and higher too, I'll wager. And as she lowers herself in the sea, more water will pour in . . ."

Round shot splintered a timber over their heads and the guard ducked to rise an instant later and steady his pistol, looking ashamed.

"Stop it!" grated the sentry. "When water comes over this deck, there's time enough to worry about that."

"Ah, but I was just about to tell you that water is already seeping over it from under this bunk. See?" And he pointed to a trail of oozing slime, the scum of the bilges carried seven feet above their safe level. "We're sinking," he said quietly.

But the sentry stood firm. The fury of the fight was deafening and the sound of activity on their own decks gave him heart. He twitched as spars crashed down over them, one end protruding through the gun deck. It had dropped through the hatch.

"Do you smell smoke?" said Jan.

"How could there help but be smoke?" challenged the sentry.

"Wood smoke, I mean. And what is that crackle?"

"Muskets, you fool."

"But you're testing the air. We're on fire and that means we'll have to come to grips with another ship and the toss of grapnels aboard. And they're enough for yet another to grapple from the other side and sweep our decks as we have . . . There! You heard that? Irons! There they go again! We're locked to another ship!"

The sentry heard hull grating against hull and the savage yells of sailors as they swept over the rails. Cutlasses clashed and pistols barked.

The sentry was uneasy. If they were swept from their own decks the ship would be deserted, abandoned to burn and sink. But he steadied the pistol in his hand and watched Tiger.

The tide of the hand fighting crashed back and forth over their heads, now in the stern, now in the waist. The smell of smoke thickened even in the double bottoms.

"Hear that rattle? We're locked port and starboard to Barbossi vessels now. That's the end of us."

And indeed the yells did redouble and the decks sagged under the crushing weight of men. The violence of this finishing fight ate into the sentry's nerves. The water was almost to his knees now and the rush of it back and forth as they rolled in the trough made it hard for him to stand.

A blasting smash close at hand almost knocked the sentry down.

"Hulled!" cried Jan. "Hulled from a range of a foot!"

The water was roaring into the ship now and the sentry could not stand at all. Suddenly his nerves gave way. He wheeled, forgetting his prisoner, and vaulted up the ladder to the open air.

Jan shouted with relief. He slapped his hand over the seal and cried, "Open wide!"

The brig door was shattered on its hinges. He rushed through it and dashed up the ladder which led to the gundeck. The planking was slippery with blood and he had to leap to clear piles of dead and dying behind the gun carriages. A square of blue showed over his head and he swarmed up the ladder to the quarterdeck.

Two sailors wearing the badge of the clenched talons were at the top. They faced him and their stained cutlasses swept back. Jan saw an officer stretched in death across the companionway mat. He ducked and snatched up the sword, flashing it erect to parry the downcoming slashes. He pressed back their steel and gained the deck.

All was carnage about him and the once trim vessel was but a sinking hull, held up now only by the grapnels of the two Barbossi vessels on either side. But Jan had no time to consider the situation. A third sailor had joined the two and the three cut at him from as many sides. He skipped backwards to put his shoulders against the taffrail. He caught a glimpse of the last of the seventy-four's sailors fighting against the house and thought he saw the glint of blue there, showing that one or two officers were yet alive.

The officer's sword, a rapier half again as long as a cutlass, flicked like the tongue of a snake and kept them at bay, no matter how hard they strove to smash it down and so, breaking it, close in to the kill.

A flag was caught by Jan's eye. The vessel on their starboard was a flagship! Zongri's vessel! And that towering Ifrit who waded forward to help finish off the last of the seventy-four's crew was Zongri!

Jan redoubled his efforts and, leaving off mere guarding, began to attack on his own. The long steel flashed and laid open a sailor from shoulder to belt but the pain of it only brought the man on with fury.

Slowly, Jan was working himself along the rail, approaching the ratlines of the mizzen. His swift wrist worked tirelessly and finally, ripping under a cutlass, dashed in and came out dripping.

"Two!" exulted Tiger. "Come on! You can't live forever! Come on, I say! I want you!"

The rapier licked over one of the sailor's hilts.

"One!" cried Jan. "One! Come on!"

But the fellow had enough and rushed away. Jan flung himself up into the rigging, swarming to the crosstrees. So great was the vessel's list that he was out over the deck of the Barbossi flagship.

Before him spread the battle, covering half a dozen square miles of blue water. White smoke drifted like scud clouds everywhere but the cannonading was done. Somehow Tarbutón had gotten eight ships into commission and had reinforced these with merchant vessels. But now the superior number of the Barbossi— pirates they were at best—had locked all but three Tarbutón men-o-war in iron grips. The three were far off, already hull down, fleeing for their lives with a score of Barbossis in pursuit.

Jan took a deep breath, not knowing whether he would meet with success or not.

He wrapped an arm about a halyard and gripped the ring. "By the Seal of Sulayman!" he roared, "I command the sundering of every bolt and lock in these two Barbossi ships below!"

He reeled from the jerk he received. The grapnels which held so tight to the railing went abruptly limp, their splicing unwound. And then, slowly, the two Barbossi men-o-war began to fall apart! Plank by plank they disintegrated, but all at once so that, within a minute or two they were nothing but floating wood upon the water, all snarled in hemp and canvas through which struggled hundreds of men, screaming with terror as they fought toward the maimed seventy-four.

The knot of fighters on the quarterdeck below drew back, staring at the wreckage. For a moment friend and foe were side by side without offering a single blow.

Already, four Barbossi men, two on each ratline and others waiting to step up, were intent upon Jan in the rigging.

Jan looked down, seeing cutlasses flashing in their teeth as they paused to wonder and shudder at the wreckage of their own.

Zongri had leaped back from the fray, his massive torso red with blood, his face blacker than ever with the grime of smoke. And now he seemed to raise two feet in stature.

"The Seal!" he bellowed. "Who . . . ?"

He looked aloft. The seal's flashing in the sunlight was not easy to miss. And Zongri saw something more. He sprang to the ratlines, knocking his own men aside and raced up, roaring, "YOU! By RANI, today you die!"

"Rani is dead!" Tiger mocked him from above, tightening his hold on the rapier. "Last night she died in a heap of rubbish just as I shall kill you!"

Zongri was losing no time. His fangs were agleam and his eyes had lightning in them. His red hands shook the rigging and the very mizzen mast.

"By the Seal of Sulayman!" cried Jan. "I demand that every bolt in every Barbossi..."

SLASH! Zongri's great saber passed within an inch of Jan's feet.

Jan's rapier licked out and stung the Ifrit and then Jan raced up the mizzen topmast.

"I command!" he roared, "that every Barbossi vessel be treated as these two."

He had no time to witness the caving in of the fleet. Zongri was reaching for his boots but far off he heard the terrified screams of the Barbossi pirates and the splash of masts dropping into the sea.

"Are you satisfied!" cried Jan. "Down or I'll burst this very ship apart under us!"

"I'll have your heart!" roared Zongri. And the topmast quivered underneath their climbing weights.

Jan got to the t'g'l'nt and paused for an instant. "You fool! You're done! Your fleet is gone and you've lost!"

"I'll have your life!" screamed Zongri, mounting still.

The wind had drifted the Tarbutón seventy-four away from the floating wreckage. The list was so bad that no man could have climbed the down side of the shrouds.

Jan took one last look at Zongri and then at the sea. He had to dive, there was nothing for it. But a hundred feet down made him wince.

"By the Seal of Sulayman!" he shouted, kicking off Zongri's reaching grasp. And then, in a long dive, Jan left the mast. Even before he started to go he had begun it and it was scarcely out of his mouth before he hit the water. "Out with the mast!"

Green raced by him and he struggled to stop his descent. He fought his way upward again, swimming hard all the while to get as far from the ship as possible. Concussion hit him before he reached the top again and when he came spluttering and blowing to the surface he saw that the seventy-four had no mizzen.

He tried to raise himself in the sea but a wave did that for him and he saw the mast, all tangled, floating some distance away.

Zongri, naturally, had been unable to clear himself of the rigging and, with it looped all around him, he fought hard to stay up, stunned and bleeding from the concussion.

Jan struck out swiftly for the seventy-four. There were halyards trailing now that the mizzen had dropped and he snatched one and pulled himself up it.

Almost against his head a serpentine thundered. He ducked and then bobbed up again to leap over the rail.

A strange sight met his eyes. Wounded and beaten into hiding, the seventy-four's crew, a full three-quarters of which remained, were massed upon the quarterdeck and still they came out of the hatchways. In the waist of the ship, Barbossis, weaponless now except for what they could pick up on the frigate, were trying to organize for a rush.

The three stern chasers and the serpentines were being loaded again in great haste and others were being lifted up through the afterdeck to reinforce the battery.

Flame and thunder and smoke rolled down like a blanket over the attackers in the waist and when it cleared there were furrows plowed through them. But the Barbossi men had not given in. They were finding muskets and cutlasses and hurriedly forming, their front ranks already beating at the men on the raised quarterdeck.

"By the Seal of Sulayman!" cried Jan, "I order that every weapon in Barbossi hands fall apart!"

Astounded, the seventy-four's gunners stopped at their loading to stare down into the waist where equally astounded sailors were hastily trying to fit blades to hilts and barrels to stocks. And even when they picked up whole ones from the deck, *they* came apart.

"Surrender!" roared Jan, "or be shot down where you stand!"

It did not take them long, confronted with the battery and small arms on the quarterdeck, to make up their minds. They threw down the useless segments of weapons and a deafening cheer resounded from the quarterdeck.

Jan turned to see two hairy, clawed hands wrapped about the rail. Zongri, bleeding and soggy, mounted. But he had no more than set his foot on the deck than twenty muskets were at his breast.

"Chain him," said Jan. "We'll take him as a trophy to Tarbutón!"

A growling voice beat upon Jan's ears. "What's this? What's this?" said Tyronin. "Who issues orders here? TIGER! Why you . . ."

"Aye, Tiger!" said Jan, "and I'll be issuing orders for many a day to come. Get those decks cleared of prisoners. Put them under hatches and pick up those afloat on wreckage. Assemble your fleet and with all speed make way for Tarbutón!"

The audacity of it made Tyronin reel. He was about to bluster but Jan cut him impatiently short.

"I want no trouble from you. This is the last time I'll remind you, but I've no use for an ingrate. Get busy!"

The men, beginning to understand now what had happened, their eyes fixed upon the flashing seal on Jan's wrist but also appreciating how he stood there, battle grimed and terrifying, raised another cheer.

Tyronin was stupefied by it. He looked slowly all about him and then, seeing light, nodded briskly and set to work.

Bakon, severely cut up, had energy enough to touch Jan's hand and smile from Jan toward the abruptly busy admiral.

"I knew, Tiger. Someday this had to happen. God bless you, my friend."

Tiger smiled back at him and then strode toward the companionway in search of Alice.

Late that afternoon, the huge black doors of the palace were thrown wide to admit the triumphal procession which now left the city hoarse with cheering behind them.

The officers of the shattered fleet were bunched together, sullen or hopeless or defiant, and many of their looks were reserved for Zongri who marched quite alone, almost sinking under the weight of his irons—Zongri who had come back to again take up his rule and lead them swiftly to appalling defeat.

Behind the captives were borne several figureheads salvaged from the vanquished ships; gaudy things of frightful mien which glowered now all in vain.

The hall resounded to the echoes of the marching feet and the assembled army officers, half of them glad and the other half sad about the navy's victory, sent up a great shout when roaring drums and screaming horns heralded the approach of the victors. No news as yet had reached the palace beyond the tidings that the fleet returned victorious and so it was that Ramus sat up like a giant poker in her throne and wiped her disc eyes and blinked very hard. And so did every courtier and secretary and officer blink.

For in the van was a great chair of gold—Tyronin's personal chair, reserved always for the Lord High Admiral—and in that chair sat two human beings! It was so great a shock that the queen was heard to gasp. A slave, no, two slaves and one robed as a temple dancer! riding in such state?

And what was this? Behind them trooped Tyronin and all his captains, perfectly willing, even anxious, to cheer their leader onward!

"By the blood of Baal!" croaked the queen. "What insanity is this? TIGER!"

The chair stopped before the throne with all the horde of high officials grouped about and Jan stepped down. He was grimed and tattered but the radiance of his handsome face made up for all the rest of it. He helped the dancing girl to the floor.

Alice, told time and again on the voyage in, that such was such and this was that, still could not realize it. Later the dancing girl would gradually take a part of her personality and so brighten it. But now she was dazzled by the jewels and silks and still unable to believe that this handsome devil, who was but yet was not Jan Palmer, had the upper hand amidst these frightful people.

"TIGER!" cried Ramus again. "By the death of the devil, man, what's this?"

"Your Majesty," said Tiger, bowing perfunctorily, "I give you Zongri again and I give you the prisoners of a shattered fleet. The pirate might of Barbossi is no more."

"Admiral Tyronin!" thundered Ramus. "However this miracle came about is less amazing than why you allow a human—albeit Tiger—to occupy your place..."

But Tyronin indicated Tiger and said no more.

"Your Majesty, last night I thieved a dancing girl from the Temple of Rani..." there was a sharp gasp, "and unfortunately caused a goddess of granite to be destroyed. I see there on your right a high priest. He has business with me?"

The high priest stepped angrily forward, purple at the confession. "Chattering ape of a human, you have the face to confess that you..."

"Hush," said Jan. "Commander Bakon, have the fool removed."

The high priest was removed and half a dozen other priests took heed and made a great show of getting out of the hall. The army, knowing not which side to take, took none for the moment.

"Your rule has not been onerous to this land," said Jan. "Pray retain the throne. I care not for its worries."

"You...uh...what?" cried Ramus.

"Unless of course," said Jan, "you want every human being in this world to awake this instant and so swarm over you and put you down. I dislike threats." But he touched the glittering seal upon his hand and all saw it and recognized it. In that instant the army set up a great shout for Tiger and almost brought the roof down on their heads.

"Your Majesty," said Tyronin, "have no fear of this man. Single-handed he routed the enemy and he has convinced me that he intends no ill."

Indeed she could have done nothing about it. Alice felt the shock of her eyes and moved nearer to Jan, holding his arm tightly. He touched her hand reassuringly.

"You . . . you leave me the throne?" said Ramus.

"Aye," said Jan. "It is yours."

Ramus covered up by instantly getting busy. She roared out for the guards to take the Barbossi prisoners and strike off their heads. But Jan, marching up boldly between the two lions from which Alice dodged, shook his head.

"They'll cause no more trouble," he said. "In them you have the nucleus of your new fleet." He had come up to her right and leaned against the arm of her throne. "Zongri, now, that is a different matter."

"You said I was to rule."

"But not against my wishes," said Jan gently. "I advise that you sentence Zongri to ten thousand years of very hard labor and so have done with him."

Ramus sighed quiveringly and did as she was ordered.

Zongri was led beaten away and he had no more than gone when a squad of men in naval uniform dashed in at the door, saw Jan up beside the throne and approached. In their midst they had two of Dauda's jackals and they were a very astonished pair. They quaked with terror as they gazed all about them at this unknown population.

They saw Alice and recognized her with a start. They looked closely at the tall man beside her and, after a moment, recognized a man who might have been Jan Palmer, but wasn't the Jan Palmer they had known.

An instant later another naval patrol came in from another way, dragging a fishmonger's wife who was all covered with dungeon straw. The young Ifrit lieutenant came to a smart stop and addressed Jan. "Sir, we found this one and yet another who was arrested but this morning by the orders of the queen. They both profess to know nothing of this world and so we presume they are the people you require."

"Ah, yes," said Ramus, "I did have brought to me such another one. By Baal, Tiger, have you sentenced all these people? But what's to be done if they scatter about?"

"I myself can keep the secret. This lady with me has hers safe enough. And as for these others . . ." He paused and eyed their sorrowful lot. Shannon, Nathaniel Green and the judge of the court which had passed judgment upon him.

"Spare us!" wept Shannon. "We meant no harm to you! We are almost mad with finding ourselves where we are. What insanity . . ."

"Speak not of insanity," said Jan, wincing. "You find yourselves in the land where your soul goes in sleep. Later you will remember that you have been a fishmonger's wife and thieves. Just now you are brought before Ramus who holds over you the power of death."

Ramus looked at Tiger and there was a certain shine in her eye which Alice did not at all like.

"Her Majesty," said Tiger, "might be persuaded to spare your lives and merely imprison you if you undo a great wrong in another world."

Aunt Ethel wept and wrung her filthy hands. Green shivered like a tree in a hurricane. And the sweat rolled from Shannon like lard.

"Your Honor the judge," said Tiger, "these men and this woman have lied to you and so, in that other world, have done away with me. You can expect execution here if restitution is not made there. Am I making myself clear?"

"Oh, indeed, indeed!" wailed the judge.

"Very well," said Tiger. "Then you will be imprisoned here and not killed. Clear them out, lieutenant, and post reliable Marids over them. I have done."

Ramus looked at him and sighed. "You . . . you vanquished them single-handed, Tiger? Ah, God, but I always knew you had it in you. Pity me for having to so abuse you for what I thought was the good of my realm." She touched his hand and then faced her chamberlain. "You oaf, have the entire apartments of the left wing burnished for His Lordship, Baron Tiger!" She looked at Alice and smiled sweetly. "My dear, have no fear of us. So long as you hold your secret, no Jinn will ever raise his hand against you. Lord Boli, you fat fool! Get into town and buy a hundred serving wenches for her Ladyship. Swiftly now and get rid of some of your fat!"

Tiger marched his bride-to-be down the steps. There was no ill will anywhere about him now. It had been spread about what the high priests of Rani had meant to do and how Rani herself had gotten her just deserts. And but for Tiger the town would even now be sacked and raped and in flames at the hands of Zongri's pirates. And so two army majors instantly elected themselves as escort and pushed others courteously aside and with the blue of the royal navy preceding them, the party marched toward the apartments in preparation.

Alice was beginning to lose some of her fear. She looked searchingly at Jan's face and then squeezed his arm.

"Then it's true," she whispered. "It's true, it's true, it's true!"

And Jan gave her Tiger's swaggering smile and, content, she walked proudly beside him, returning the bows of the multitude through which they passed.

• • •

Back on Earth, a few days later, an item ran in a Seattle paper.

EMBEZZLER COMMITS SUICIDE

Millionaire Heir Finds Losses

Nathaniel Green Leaves Confession
Note on Deathbed

Seattle, Wash._____ Nathaniel Green, long known in local shipping circles as manager for Bering Sea Steamship committed suicide last night at his home on Queen Anne Hill. . . .

Jan Palmer, recently absolved from the slaying of Professor Frobish, told police that even after he had noted the missing amounts he had not seen fit to bring charges, but, rather, had been on the point of discharging Green.

"It is not from any merciful intent," said Palmer at his home last night, "for the company was almost ruined. But I did not wish to mar my honeymoon or worry my bride."

This aftermath of the strange case of Professor Frobish climaxed the most publicized affair of the year. Green, who was mainly responsible for Palmer's false imprisonment in a local asylum, had evidently sought to cover up his embezzled funds by murdering Professor Frobish and thereby throwing the stigma of the crime upon the young millionaire. Though Judge Dougherty says that this is probably the case, no post mortem action is to be taken against Green and so the matter has been closed.

L. RON HUBBARD

Foreword

The unhappy advent of an Ifrit, one of the Jinn so ably described in the Arabian Nights, into the workaday world of Seattle, Washington, some time since, gave more adventure to Jan Palmer than his scholarly stomach could quite tolerate. The Jinn, Zongri, had been imprisoned in a copper jar by Sulayman in ancient times and the jar had come into Jan's hands. As the harassed president of Bering Steamship Corporation, young Jan did not need the further curse which was laid upon him by Zongri as a "reward" for being let out. The Curse of Eternal Wakefulness thrust Jan into the discovery that man, when he sleeps, wanders in far and unknown lands. Jan's sleep-self proved to be a redoubtable, brave but unconservative sailor named Tiger in the land of the Jinn where Ifrits were masters and the sleep-souls of humans were the slaves. Tiger, the other self of Jan, thrived on mischief and punishment and made news in a world where sudden death was commonplace. The dismayed Jan found that Tiger was much too much for him.

Incarcerated for murder because of Zongri and greedy relatives while "awake" in Seattle, doomed by the mischief of Tiger while "awake" in the land of the Jinn, Jan was in serious trouble in both worlds. His only solace was Alice, his secretary who, when she "slept" was actually Wanna, a temple dancer in the world of the Jinn.

At last, mastering the problem of his duality and solving, in a sea action in the world of the Jinn, the Curse of Eternal Wakefulness, Jan became, as himself, truly the head of Bering Steam, for in Seattle he was now partly Tiger and in the world of the Jinn, as Tiger, became a Baron of the Realm because he was partly the brainy Jan.

So matters stood for some time. But Tiger's nature was unruly and, in the world of the Jinn, little by little began to outweigh the good sense of Jan. Escapade after escapade brought Tiger and Wanna, his dancing girl, down the ladder in the favor of the Jinn. Humans in the world of sleep were, after all, slaves. At length, after nearly oversetting the government itself, Tiger, as punishment, was returned to the fleet as a common sailor. As Jan in this world, he became more and more immersed in scholarly concerns and became less and less Tiger. Wanna, too, began to separate her natures as time went on and became less the dancing girl of the Jinn and more the authoritarian housewife in Seattle.

At the time our story opens, Tiger had managed promotion up to the rank of gunner's mate in a man-o-war in the world of the Jinn. His "awake" self Jan had become more and more timid and desirous of escape from his responsibilities with Bering Steam. The gulf had widened until each part of the dual nature was less and less aware of the other each time the border between the worlds was crossed.

Ramus, ruler of Tarbutón, the principal nation of the Jinn, had become old. She dispatched an expedition to the land of Arif-Emir who owned a strange gem called the Two-World Diamond. Arif-Emir refused to part with his stone, though Jinn custom seemed to indicate that it should be lent. A war was declared and Admiral Tombo with a fleet of twenty sail was sent to beat Arif-Emir into submission. Aboard Tombo's flagship was Tiger. And while Jan slept in Seattle—

Chapter 1

AHOY BELOW!

Tiger, for some time, had been trying to attract the attention of Admiral Tombo. Fifteen enemy ships of the line, under the command of Arif-Emir, had ceased to swing restively to their anchors in Balou Bay and, in a fluttering burst of sails, had begun to turn toward the harbor mouth, obviously bent on sailing out and giving battle to the twenty men-o-war which so long had dared them.

In the fighting top of the *Graceful Jinnia,* Tiger had long since spotted the turbulence on the decks of the enemy in Balou Bay and had long since begun to make said intelligence clear to the quarterdeck below. He had begun in a very naval manner, saying, "Ahoy, the quarterdeck! Enemy standing by to get under weigh!" He had progressed through "Ahoy below! Enemy vessels slipping cables!" And now he cried, "Hey, you fatheads! Arif-Emir is comin' out to eat us alive!"

Admiral Tombo looked like a fat scarlet doll, mostly hat, from Tiger's height of a hundred and thirty feet of mast. He was in a fevered discussion with his staff and the captains of his ships, here assembled in the bright morning. The rage in their voices rose and fell, the click of their fangs punctuating their angry speech. Ifrits, when angry, can cause a considerable stir. There was no penetrating their din; three duels had been challenged in a hot ten minutes and one face had been slapped loudly enough for the sound to reach the fighting top where Tiger stood the watch.

Tiger, big, brawny and human, sprawled against the lip of the basket and looked around at the waiting fleet. The ships of

165

Ramus the Magnificent, Ruler of the Jinn, stood to hand, few sails set, sun flashes on their brass cannon, fresh spray upon their gilt scrolling. It was a brisk morning and a chop sea was running in a fifteen-knot wind. Every man-o-war present had spotted the sudden activity of the bottled enemy and a laundry bag of signal flags stood stiffly and urgently quivering from the halyards of each.

Landward the cream-sailed ships of Arif-Emir were falling into battle station behind their pennoned leader, making an increasing line of battle. The flagship, probably with Arif-Emir on her quarterdeck, was opposite Gallows Point already and her bow was beginning to lift to the chop sea which extended just within the harbor mouth. There they came, fifteen ships, five first-raters of eighty guns and ten frigates of twenty-four.

Tiger looked down at the wrangling captains and their angry admiral. Bored, Tiger put a brass trumpet to his mouth and tried again, "Hey, fatso! Your pal Arif is going to dine on you for dinner."

Still none looked up from below. Tiger had his orders. He was a gunner's mate, sent up here to take a lookout because of some words he had had with the gunnery officer the day before, gunner's mates not ordinarily being required to perform such duties. A lookout was supposed to stick to his post. But following orders was no long habit with Tiger. He put the trumpet in its clips, swung over the side of the basket, wrapped his cap around the topping lift which led down to the quarterdeck and, with this to protect his hands, swung his heels into space and swooped down like a meteorite to the quarterdeck. He dropped to the planking, knocked out a spark which had generated with the friction of the passage downward, and put his cap on the back of his head. He advanced toward Tombo.

"I won't have it! I won't have it!" Admiral Tombo was screaming. "My orders are to stay on station here! I'll not go away without the diamond! I won't leave until the transports come with marines! I won't!"

"Condemn you!" howled a big Ifrit, "*Your* ship isn't out of food! *You* don't have a mutinous crew! We can't maintain this blockade and we won't! Ramus is dead! You heard the dispatch. How do we know what's going on at home? Who'll fight for our preference at court? She's dead and that cancels her orders! Arif-Emir is never going to come out. I say sail for home and Ahriman take the diamond!"

Tiger shouldered through them. He was a human, they were Ifrits. He could not become an officer in this land, being human, but he couldn't be severely punished either, being valuable. He tapped Admiral Tombo on the shoulder.

"If you're going to sail for home, you better get under weigh. Arif-Emir is standing out of the harbor with all sails drawing."

One captain had been about to thrust him aside but his news struck them into motionless statues for an instant. Then they scrambled for the landward shrouds and the first one who reached twenty feet from the deck sung out: "It's Arif-Emir!"

The captains below him were confused but still ugly. They turned back on Tombo. "Your commission is from Ramus. She's dead! I don't recognize your commission. Whatever the value of the diamond, I'm sailing for home!" He dropped over the rail, balanced his eight feet of bulk on the boat boom and then slid down into his gig. With mutters and glares, the other captains followed him. The Marid boat crews one by one presented oars, took aboard each one his captain, let fall and swept away across the choppy brilliant sea.

Tombo was at the rail. All the while they were leaving he was shaking his fist. "Damn you! By the Seven Sheiks, come back here! You'll stand to and fight! *I'll* fight. I'll whip them with one ship! You're mutineers!"

Tiger watched it passionlessly. Finally, he tapped Tombo on the shoulder again. "Sir, if you're going to make good that promise, we better be getting some sails set and some guns run out. Arif's last frigate has cleared Gallows Point."

The admiral took one last look at the departing gigs and then spat into the sea. He turned around, hitched up his pants, pushed his cocked hat into a more solid position and ran his eye along the maindeck battery.

"Mr. Malek," he said to his waiting lieutenant. "Beat to quarters!"

Tombo looked at Tiger. "What are you doing with your hat on the quarterdeck?"

Tiger shrugged and compromised. He took himself off the quarterdeck, dropped down to the port battery and began to tally off his gun crews as his men poured up to the frantic roll of drums.

Sailing commands rang out from the sailing master and topmen dropped billows of canvas down into the sunlight. With thunderings to match the drums the sails were sheeted home. The helm came up, the braces sang and creaked to the strain, the buck of the vessel grew short and businesslike. The *Graceful Jinnia* stood up to meet the enemy, one ship against fifteen.

Two hours later she was a bloodied and shuddering ruin, her every spar gone, her sheets trailing in the sea, her sodden hulk lifting less and less to the running sea. More and more her castle lifted, less and less of her bow was shown and then she plunged with a bubbling sigh into the littered water. The tangled flag of Ramus, twisted about a staff, was black against the frothing maelstrom for an instant and then the ship was gone.

Admiral Tombo, the sailing master, Tiger and twenty men, the remainder of her crew, were prisoners aboard the *Tong-Malou*, flagship of Arif.

Chapter 2

FOG

Jan Palmer awoke with an aching head and gazed out of his windows at a fog-whitened Seattle. All and he were distinctly not well.

He felt his temples and confusedly looked at his hands. But they were not covered with blood as he had supposed, oddly enough, they would be. Here he was in his own bedroom; there was his wife Alice sleeping prettily with tousled hair flowing across the pillow; there was the harbor and the low tufted fog from out of which came the snores of perturbed shipping—perhaps one or two of his own ships, since he was the sole owner of the Bering Steamship Corporation. He was sure he should not be here and yet he was here. He was certain he should be half dead and yet he was alive. What had happened?

Dimly, he felt memories slipping away from him. Gropingly he tried to capture them and examine them. For an instant he recalled a long gone time when he had been present at the opening of a strange and ancient copper jar of Arabian design. For a moment he heard and felt the breath of a Jinn which had flowed swiftly from the jar, snarling threats and growing hugely. For a moment he saw the man who had opened that mysterious jar and saw the man fall dead and heard himself being cursed with the "Curse of Eternal Wakefulness." Then there were blurred recollections of never sleeping, of passing from this land to a land of sleep, a land where Jinns ruled and all humans were slaves and where all humans went when they slept. And he recalled himself as Tiger, a redoubtable and mischievous sailor in that strange land

169

of sleep and how, as Tiger, he had become strong and how, as himself, Tiger had become wise. But the recall of that meeting of self in the Land of Awake and self in the Land of Sleep faded and grew tangled like some nightmare one cannot quite grasp. He felt like a man whose vitality was ebbing from him. He felt as though some necessary portion of him were slipping away and he could not tell how or why.

For many years now he had not slept but, transferring from the Land of Awake where he was Jan Palmer into the Land of Sleep where he was Tiger, he had lived a dual and highly fascinating life. In the Land of Awake he ruled Bering Steamship Corporation with a vigor which had never manifested itself before the opening of that jar and the subsequent adventures had made him Tiger. Asleep, he was awake again in the land of the Jinn where, as Tiger, he carried out an amusing role. It had been a highly satisfactory continuance of a beginning which had seemed harshly adventurous. The Jinn ruled humanity when humanity slept, for the soul wandered far in sleep. But Jan was suddenly unaware that his soul had ever wandered anywhere. One last datum tried to penetrate his wits: The soul of Alice, his wife, was Wanna in the land of the Jinn and Wanna was waiting for Tiger somewhere in the world of sleep. And then that fact too was gone.

Suddenly his headache vanished. He looked at the fog, he listened to the hoots and snarls of vessels in the harbor, he thought of his duties in running Bering Steam and he was suddenly afraid.

Of what was he afraid? He tried to answer that. He could not. He thought of the desks and the vice-presidents and then he knew. He thought with a shudder of their spectacled eyes, of the orders and forms they thrust at him, of the decisions they required him to make. He thought of the toil and monotony and he shivered. Something had slipped from him. He could not tell what it was, he could only sense for a moment that part of him, a vital and terribly important part of him, the part that was all nerve and laughter, had gone. And then he didn't remember that he had remembered that anything had been taken from him. He stood, shallow-chested, pale and afraid and watched the fog deepen over the water.

Alice got up and slipped into a robe. She smiled at him sleepily and then looked again. She gazed around her as though sensing some change and stared back at Jan.

"Funny," she said, "I must have had a dream. I could swear I could have told you about it a moment ago." She frowned a moment and then shook her head. "No. It slipped away from me." Then she looked at him. "Are you well?"

"I feel all right," said Jan shakily.

"Well! I've got to get you downtown for the board meeting," she said. And she began to dress.

He did not realize she had changed, that something was gone from her as well, for all memory of it was gone in him. He saw a businesslike wife, concerned with her husband's affairs, married too long to have any romance left about him. He thought about the board meeting and he saw with a shiver of fear the spectacled faces. And then he began to dress. It was a dull and terrible day.

"I think I'll go sailing," he said suddenly.

"You'll get to that board meeting!" said Alice. "Sailing indeed! With all that fog. Not a breath of air and every ferry boat apt to run you down!"

Miserably he laid aside the sneakers he had picked up and grasped his business shoes.

"Yes, Alice," he said meekly.

Chapter 3

THE TWO-WORLD DIAMOND

There was no tragedy in Balou; it was a holiday. Here in the land of the Jinn, where human souls were captive to the Ifrits, their masters, there were few enough occasions for gala displays. But today there was one. All that morning there had been the thundering of broadsides beyond the breakwaters and great billows of white smoke had hidden the extent of the action there. And the crowds had gathered and watched from Gallows Point. But now the entire town of Balou was filled with ringing bells and waving banners. It had watched in anxiety, for its food came from across wide seas and the blockade had placed roasted rat as the highest item on a bill o' fare. And it cheered now because the blockade was broken and Arif-Emir had thrown wide the granaries where had been stored the military rations he had saved. And the crowd cheered as well out of an enthusiasm for any victory, even one tallied to the credit of Arif-Emir.

It was afternoon and the shadows were long when the parade came up from the wharves. First there were Marids, dull and stupid servants of the Jinn, blowing long and brassy horns. Then there were humans pulling chariots full of Arif's officers. And then there came Arif, solitary and tremendous in a golden sedan chair, high on human backs. And behind him came the captives.

The crowd cheered dutifully when the officers went by—to have done otherwise would have been to bring Marids down upon it swinging their long whips. It waved small flags and tossed caps for Arif, for he had sent ahead the order about the food. And then it began to scream and huzzah in earnest for the captives.

The Masters of Sleep

Admiral Tombo, sea-stained and powder-scorched, disdained the chains which gripped him and pulled him on and bowed from right to left. His yellow fangs were gleaming as he grinned. Eight and a half feet tall—tall even for an Ifrit in the World of Sleep—he made a very impressive sight. But after he had gone a few blocks it began to be impressed upon his rather pompous mind that these cheers were being volleyed at a target slightly behind him. Tombo glared around to see who was usurping some of the glory of being a captive, hard won from the sea. But it was not Mr. Malek the sailing master, for Mr. Malek walked in sad dejection, having calculated that the only end to this would be an execution. So it was not Mr. Malek. Tombo looked further back. Then, with a shock of horror, he looked ahead of him.

Just before the captives went the golden sedan of Arif-Emir. With a wand, Arif was waving blessings at his people. With the enormous pomposity of which only an Ifrit is capable, Arif was grandly making magic signs, pieces of gold, crosses and stars and other things, shedding his glorious light upon the multitude. And from his turban light was also shed, the somewhat more pure glory of the fabulous Two-World Diamond.

Tombo looked anxiously behind him again and gone was his rancor and in its place was solid fear. For six of the captive sailors of the *Graceful Jinnia* had taken upon their shoulders one Tiger and Tiger, with a pomposity of which Arif was never guilty, was shedding his clowning light upon the multitude and with a stick he had picked up in the street, was making somewhat altered signs in the air. And the crowd of human slaves who lined the walks, each time that Tiger moved that stick, screamed in convulsions of laughter.

The Admiral tried to yank back on his chains and get to the human gunner's mate who so dangerously mimicked Arif. But the chains were tightly fixed to the rear of Arif's sedan chair. Tombo tried to shout but he could not be heard. There was anxiety in

173

his drowned voice for here clearly went all hope of Arif's mercy. Tombo had hopes of that mercy. Perhaps Arif would not have heard that Ramus was dead, perhaps Arif would make Tombo an emissary for peace terms back to his own land. And there, confound it, was Tiger, brawny and irrepressible, making a fool out of Arif in the Emir's own town!

Tiger met Tombo's glare with a pompous condescension. And made another magic sweep of the ragged stick to bless the admiral too.

The Marids who brought up the rear were too stupid to see either impropriety or humor. They planted their hoofs solidly upon the pave and marched with a wonderful drill. They would have speared a captive had he tried to escape but beyond that their orders did not go. And so went Arif-Emir, all the way to his palace, wonderfully conceited at the enthusiasm of his citizens and slaves.

The palace guard, however, was commanded by an Ifrit named Au-Abdullah, a young fellow who wanted his way made in the world and Au-Abdullah had seen it all from afar. He rushed now from his post at the command of the palace guard, drawn up in formal ranks, and leaped to the step of Arif's sedan chair and pointed urgently backwards. The last of the crowd was cheering and shrieking at Tiger and Tiger benignly waved his symbols back.

Arif turned three shades bluer than indigo. He lurched up in his chair so abruptly that he overset it. He landed in the street in a tumble of cushions and bearers.

Tiger and the sailors were up instantly to dust him off. They had been chained, but all together and so could move at will. And chains or no chains, Tiger made a thorough job of rescuing Arif. He rescued Arif so well that Arif fell down three more times, got his green cloak over his head so that he could not see, got his sword between his legs so that he fell down again, stepped on his cloak so hard and with so much rage while it covered him that he almost broke his own neck. Anyone in the realm of Ramus could have told him that being rescued by Tiger was equivalent to being fed into a corn grinder and boiled in oil in the bargain.

There was a terrible furor, a surge of citizens and slaves, a rush and tangle of the palace guard and officers, blundering effort from Marids, crossed-up orders, fallen down soldiers and turmoil enough to make a small-sized battle.

And then, at last, out of the crowd came enough sensible orders from Arif to clear him from his helpers. His sword sang as it swished from its sheath, his voice cracked with rage as he bawled for the offender to come forth. The air split with the volley of his oaths and flared along the paths of his glance. He was angry. He wanted to kill a human named Tiger.

But Tiger was not there.

Tiger, with three bully-boys from the late *Graceful Jinnia,* was very thoroughly missing. Tombo was there, shivering with fear for once in his life, for he was sure he would be a substitute target for that sword. Malek was there. Seventeen humans were there. But four of the captives were gone. Their chains lay, neatly unlocked, in the pile of upset Ifrits and Marids which were just now untangling themselves. The pocket of the officer in charge of the prisoners had not only been picked of keys but also of heavy coin.

Arif-Emir, his rage not abating, had no thought of slaying the captives at hand. He wanted the very special blood of Tiger.

"Who was the man?" howled Arif in a voice which made mortar fly out in chips from the palace wall.

"His name is Tiger," said Tombo, thrusting forward, seeing a course to be steered. "Our worst human. I'll identify him for you the moment you catch him. He's a disgrace! The indignity upon the Jinn must be avenged!"

"Produce him!" screamed Arif. "All right! Produce and identify him. We have means! There are things that can be done to repay it! We know of things! Produce him!"

Taking swift advantage of this insanity, Tombo grabbed at Malek and the two yanked loose the staples which held their chains. They promptly shouted out that they saw their quarry and went plunging off down a sidestreet which was quickly filled by a rushing torrent of Marids, curious humans and a few officers.

Twenty minutes later, Tombo and Malek, who had somehow gotten lost from the main stream of pursuit, lay panting in the bottom of a lugger, covered with the empty sacks which, on the return journey from another land, would contain meal. They had boarded unnoticed by anyone on the wharves, since the crew seemed to have gone to join the welcoming and stayed to behold an execution.

Two hours later a still raging Arif, beard stiff with flecks of foam, anger whipped now by an account of his "triumphal procession," was doubling and trebling rewards for the return of his captives. He paced furiously back and forth in his black throne room from which he ruled the independent principality of Balou, long-time rebel against the major state of Tarbutón.

A Jinn officer, shaking a trifle at the necessity of facing Arif, drew up and saluted. "Sire—Sire, I have bad news—"

Arif faced about, eyes searing the messenger.

"Your kerchief, sire, lest you be provoked," said Au-Abdullah.

Arif flung the kerchief into the officer's face, thus giving him the right to speak without being beheaded for what he said.

"Sire," said the officer, gripping the kerchief firmly and even then backing off a trifle, out of the road of a sudden swish of Arif's blade, "I have to report that the two Ifrits saved from the *Graceful Jinnia* are also missing."

Had it not been for the kerchief, Arif would have struck but it was held before him the instant he drew back the blade. Au-Abdullah retreated a pace or two.

Arif's clenched hand trembled upon the sword grip.

"And sire," said Au-Abdullah with a rush, "I have more news."

"Speak!" roared Arif.

"The Two-World Diamond, sire!"

Arif reached to his turban but reached in vain. The fabulous gem was not there. He grew gray. He shook. He staggered back and looked at the apprehensive faces of his officers.

"You know what this means," he said in a hoarse voice. "If it comes into the hands of a human slave and he knows its use—"

They had known about it longer than he but they had not dared say. And they knew what would happen if that diamond went astray. It was for the purpose of safeguarding the Two-World Diamond that Ramus had gone to war with him. In his hands she had considered it unsafe and she had felt it would be too dangerous for Arif-Emir to continue in possession of it.

He rallied. His anger was gone in the face of this necessity. He looked around at the tense faces of the Ifrits.

"Ransack the town. Tear it to pieces if you will. That diamond must be found! You, Au-Abdullah, close the harbor to all outgoing ships. You, Hribreh, begin to tally all slaves, examining each and all his possessions with your regiment. At all costs we must find these people! They have the diamond!" He steadied his towering bulk against a pillar for he was shaking now but with fear, not rage. "What did you remark the names of these people to be?"

"Admiral Tombo, a certain Malek and the human sailors," said an Ifrit naval officer. "There was some mention of the man named Tiger, the one who mocked you, sire."

Arif, unstable at best, began to anger again. "Have them in. If they are not in the town they are in the port. If they are not in the port and manage to escape to seaward, we will sail them down. Of Tombo, the fool, I have no qualms. He would never betray the secret of the diamond. But that Tiger—" He was beginning to work himself up again, his hands clenching and unclenching sadistically. "He'll be taught, when we get him, he'll be taught!" He flung an arm to them. "After him!"

But far out to sea in a certain trading craft, four human sailors stood and gazed off where a gun had flashed red as a signal to close the port.

"Think they're shootin' at us?" said Muddy McCoy.

Tiger, his big skull aching beneath the stained bandage which covered a cutlass wound received in the fight, grunted a negative. "Closin' the port," he said. "Steer small, Walleye, we want what speed this hooker'll make."

Tiger sat down, finding himself a little dizzy after all the activity of the day and a loss of some blood. He took out the content of his pocket and looked at it.

"Fifty in silver and a piece of glass," he said. "I hope it's the goods."

The vessel was half-decked for the protection of cargo and to all appearances the cargo space was empty save for sacks. There had been just one lugger ready to get under weigh along the docks. And there were two very large eyes peering now from just under the aftermost sacks. They were very large, very cruel and extremely purposeful eyes. Whatever might have been said about Admiral Tombo, he seldom stopped short of any appointed goal.

"Malek!" he whispered hoarsely. The two eyes were joined by another pair, all yellow from corner to corner. "Malek, look!"

"Hweeoo," said Malek. He was an extremely pessimistic Ifrit, Malek, but now and then he thought he saw hope. In such moments he did rash and stupid things. Now he had almost spoken aloud but that was remedied by Tombo's seamanlike hand across Malek's mouth. "Butsh juz Tiger," squirmed Malek.

"It's Tiger, all right," whispered Tombo. "But look!"

Malek peered around the restraining fingers, and the rays of the sunset just that moment struck splinters of light from the Two-World Diamond. Malek jumped and quivered. If Tombo's hand had not remained there he would have given forth a string of startled oaths. Tombo let him quiet down and then, with a stern glare, released him.

"How'd he get it?" whispered Malek.

"However he got it is not important, you fishbrain. That he's got it is obvious. There's only one diamond on earth that big and that bright. And he didn't have one on the *Graceful Jinnia*."

"He got it when he jumped Arif-Emir!" decided Malek brightly. "He took it right out of his turban. Hah! Now we can take it home—" He would have struggled up if Tombo had not slapped him down again.

"One thing you forget," said Tombo. "Tiger's human. If he always seems to land on his feet, he's still *human*. He's a slave. He doesn't care a rap what happens to any of us important beings." Tombo thought for a moment.

"What you scowling about?" said Malek.

"I just remembered that I gave him a taste of the cat not two days ago. He's got no reason to love any Ifrit. They scaled him down from a barony when he made trouble once too often and he's going to stay a slave if I have anything to do with it."

"Let's just move up and jump them," said Malek. "I'd probably get hurt but it's all we can do."

"Jump them!" said Tombo hoarsely. "Take a look, Mr. Malek. You see that man at the wheel?" Malek did. "Well," continued Tombo, "that is Walleye, sentenced to sea service for three murders. He's a fast man with a cutlass and he's got a cutlass." Malek observed this. He had been a trifle confused by the fact that all four men on the poop were wearing white djellabas, cloaks used by merchant seamen in these parts to keep off the sun.

Tombo saw that Malek had collected this data. Then he continued. "The man cutting bread is Stagger Ryan, one of our strongest topmen. A man who can hand-over-hand up a hundred and sixty foot lift is apt to be in condition. And you observe the knife, Mr. Malek?" Malek did, on close peering, observe the bread knife.

Tombo then pointed to the seaman who was coiling sheets beyond Tiger. "And that one, if you'll recall, is Muddy McCoy who, for all his short size, was the slipperiest rough and tumble man aboard. There we have three: a murderer who was fleet champion with a cutlass, a professional strongman still agile enough to jig on a royal yard, and a dirty-fighting ex-pickpocket who was feared by every crewman on the *Graceful Jinnia*. Now observe you, Mr. Malek—you're strong enough and bigger than they but you're stupid." Malek agreed despondently. "And observe me," said Admiral Tombo. "I have seen more active days. Any two of them could be overcome by either of us, perhaps. But you will note, Mr. Malek, that they have armed themselves and we do not so much as own a toothpick."

Mr. Malek grew very despondent when he realized this. Then he rallied. "But there's the diamond!"

"True," said Tombo. "They do not know anything about the diamond or exactly what a man can do who possesses it. They do not know, probably, that it was the goal of our entire expedition and they certainly would not know what havoc they could effect with it if they wished. But I wish to call one more thing to your attention, Mr. Malek."

Malek blinked expectantly.

"The man who has the diamond is Tiger," said Tombo.

Mr. Malek heaved a very dismal sigh, wriggled backwards and gave up. "It's impossible," he agreed.

"Not entirely," said Tombo grimly. "Tiger does not know the power of that diamond. Not even I know all its power or behavior. But I know far more than he. Sooner or later they will sleep."

"We may not have a sooner or later," said Malek. "Arif-Emir will find out this vessel is gone, that it was the last one to clear port. He'll be after us fast enough and winds don't hold forever."

"That's our risk," said Tombo doggedly. And he fixed his eye on the quartet on the poop while they ate, bathed in the red light of sunset, an effect which Tombo greatly admired.

"What's the glass?" said Walleye, hanging on to the tiller with one hand and eating bread and cheese with the other.

"Steady, I guess," said Tiger absently.

"I mean the rock," said Walleye. "If it's genuine ice, we could buy us half a kingdom, anyway."

Muddy McCoy wriggled. He had serpentine movements he had to make before he could talk about anything and he made them now. There was always a sly, conspirator air about him even when he was asking for the bread to be passed. "Let me see, Tiger."

Tiger carelessly tossed him the diamond and continued to eat. Muddy looked at it critically in what daylight was left and then he reached up and put a sharp edge of it on the binnacle glass and drew down.

"Hey!" said Walleye. "Whatcha wanna do? Ruin things? Look at the scratch. Now I got to dodge it to read the course!"

Muddy chuckled and burbled over the diamond. "It's real, all right. Feels like five or six hundred carats. If we ever get away without being caught, we can have a good time."

"Give it back to Tiger!" said Ryan, catching Muddy's wrist as the little pickpocket tried to put the gem in his pocket.

Muddy chuckled uncertainly. Tiger put it absently in his pocket and went on eating bread and cheese.

"You sure are thoughtful-like," said Ryan. "What's the matter?"

Tiger shrugged and then grinned. He was not an extremely handsome man but when he grinned he lit up the surroundings. He yawned and lay back in the coiled sheet and looked up at the first stars. "I was just trying to think of something I felt I could remember, but that's no matter. You interested in this diamond?" He pulled it out and looked at it. His inspection was casual, then abruptly intense. He looked at it very closely.

It was a limpid stone and its many facets were almost blinding when the light struck fair upon it. But he had seen something else. Down deep in its depths, etched there by some necromancy he could not understand, he saw the *three*-dimensional Seal of Sulayman, three triangles made with only six lines. He blinked and looked again and then sat back. Tiger was not unacquainted

181

with the two interlaced triangles which was Sulayman's ordinary seal and which had itself vast powers. He had seen the original seal knock every bolt and fastening aside which it met. But here, here was a greater mystery.

He sat up, uncoiling himself. There was a small ditty box on the deck. By rights, this seal should knock all the fastenings out of the ditty box.

"By the Seal of Sulayman," said Tiger experimentally, "I demand that every nail in this box fly out!"

Nothing happened.

Tiger looked at the diamond, shrugged and put it in his pocket again. He sank back into the sheet coil.

"What did you think would happen?" said Muddy, always a little pleased at the failures of other men.

"He's got a right," said Ryan.

"I'm just wondering," said Tiger. "Somebody was awful anxious to get this diamond, namely Ramus. Now that she's dead—"

"Ramus dead?" gaped Ryan. "Gosh, how'd you find that out?"

"He's always spoonin' up the Ifrits," said Muddy.

"If she's dead," said Tiger, unperturbed, "that means that there's a throne vacant."

"Hey!" said Ryan. "You mean you think maybe this diamond is a talisman, huh? Maybe it's got power. Hey, Tiger! You'd make a swell emperor. Hey, how about it, you jokers. Wouldn't he make a swell emperor?"

"He'd get us all in trouble in five minutes," said Muddy.

"You shut up!" said Ryan. "I say he'd make a swell emperor!"

"He may have been quiet enough the last year or two but he always gets in trouble," said Muddy. "I say he'd get us all killed!"

"Come on, come on," said Walleye. "The sun's down and that's the end of my trick. Is somebody goin' to take this wheel or do I just let it go."

"Your watch, Muddy," said Tiger.

Muddy growled, wriggled, whined something under his breath and took the wheel.

Tiger shrugged down into the coiled sheet. "Steer small. And call me for breakfast."

Walleye and Stagger grinned and stretched out on the planks. Muddy's beady eye roamed between the luffing of the mainsail head, against the brilliant stars, the compass and, now and then, over Tiger's sleeping form. The glitter of greed was strong in his gaze.

It grew darker as the twilight faded out. The wind held. The night slid through. Tombo, when the watches had changed twice, slid aft toward the poop. Walleye was once more at the wheel and his sight, at best, was poor. Tombo slid a cautious hand over Tiger's form, gently feeling for the diamond. He examined him well and then, baffled, drew away. None had approached Tiger, he knew that, for he had watched the night through. And yet the diamond was not on Tiger's person, that he knew.

Baffled, Tombo withdrew to the cargo space and covered himself with sacks. He whispered the news to Malek.

"I knew we'd fail," said Malek.

"You may know that," said Tombo, "but I don't. All I know is that the diamond has never before been in human hands. It becomes part of the soul, you know."

Malek blinked.

"It's gone now for Tiger sleeps," said Malek. "It will be here when he wakes. We'll have to plan for that. Go to sleep."

Chapter 4

A Christening

In Seattle, Washington, Jan Palmer wended his timorous way through traffic, enroute to a ship christening. He did not like the idea. He did not like the crowds which would be there. He did not like the directors of Bering Steamship with whom he would have to talk. And he did not, in short, like anything faintly approximating a ship christening if it caused him to consort with humanity.

Dimly, as he drove, feelings like false recollections seemed to tell him that his return to utter self-consciousness was a new thing, a thing which would pass as it had before. But he was not sure how it had passed before. He was sure, from the way the people addressed him, that they were quite surprised to discover him shy. He felt that, even recently, he had been very bold. But he had no proof of it. He was, in short, in something of a muddle. And he had no idea of how serious that muddle could become.

With no recollection of his dual nature, with no distinct awareness that he was elsewhere one Tiger, a redoubtable opponent for any man, Jan could only run on the computation now that he was just Jan, a shy if unwillingly powerful shipping magnate, as they say in *Time*.

The skeletalized world which was Dodd Shipyards, where crane and scaffold and beam presented a disorderly hodgepodge to all who did not understand the intricacies of assembling vessels, at length enfolded him and his roadster and he alighted into the inevitable shipyard mud to the tune of the inevitable riveters and the flash of the burning torches.

184

His disorganized condition of mind at the thought of meeting people caused him to park on the wrong side of the administration building whereas a goodly assemblage was especially congregated at the front entrance to meet him.

There was some confusion in the ensuing half hour wherein Jan joined the crowd to wait for himself to arrive, and waited very patiently until he discovered that it was his arrival which was expected when patience fled and anxiety came on him in floods. Conversing with so many people was entirely beyond him, he felt, and the realization, suddenly, that he was expected to make a speech at the christening entirely unbolted him.

Somehow, despite such minor affairs as Mrs. Chewenson's getting paint on her gown—it was she who was to break the champagne bottle, the loss of the bottle itself, the points of etiquette which a retired naval commander insisted upon or corrected and a small boy—one of the Chewenson children—almost falling a hundred feet down into the dock from the dedication platform, the christening proceeded. The ship was Bering Steam's newest fleet unit, an especially constructed vessel for the northernmost runs for which was needed an icebreaker bow. She was being named after Zachariah P. Palmer, one of Jan's more respectable ancestors whose shrewd cheating on the China coast in old clipper days had earned him a name as a great man and had laid the foundations of the Palmer fortune. Another small hitch almost occurred when the ribbons of the champagne bottle became tangled up in Mrs. Chewenson's bracelets but it was solved when the retired naval commander, with some presence of mind, wrenched it free and sent it after the vessel, already sliding down the ways. The ice-breaker bow and the champagne bottle connected with a satisfactory smack and then the ribbon-wound bottle, swinging back on the line which suspended it above the platform showered everyone with apple cider and carbonation. The Chewenson boy was again saved from falling off the platform into the dock, the *Zachariah P. Palmer* missed a ferry boat which had uppishly cruised astern of her ways and the party retired. It was, all in all, a highly satisfactory, extraordinarily average christening. None marked that Mrs. Chewenson had utterly forgotten to say that she christened the ship anything, no slightest originality was to be found in any of the speeches made and the whole thing, in short, was strictly in the tradition.

Everyone went off to make a party of it and Jan found himself, at length, alone on the platform, somewhat stained with apple cider but at least feeling able to breathe. But the whole thing had unnerved him and his fingers, as he put a cigarette in his mouth, visibly shook. He reached into his trousers pocket for a lighter and for some seconds stood there running his thumb across what he supposed was a lighter wheel but which was, in fact, a diamond of many score carats. When he discovered that his cigarette wasn't getting lighted he looked to see why. The flash of the stone nearly blinded him. Even in this murky sunlight it was comparable to the *zzzzt* of a welding rod.

He hurriedly put the stone back, sure that somebody would think he had stolen it. But the riggers were far away and he was alone on a high platform above the vacant ways. He sneaked another look at the stone. It flashed as bright as before. A thing as close as this to pure light seemed to howl aloud its presence. He stabbed the stone back into his pocket and stood there, looking blankly at the splinters of bottle on the platform. He thought this thing out from several different directions. Each time he arrived at the fact that he could not possibly have come by this stone. But there it lay, cool in his hot, pocketed hand. Then he considered the matter from another angle. The stone was not a diamond but paste. He knelt, took up a piece of champagne bottle, wiped some of the cider from it and then, looking about to see that he did not appear to be observed, ran the edge of the diamond across the glass. The splinter of bottle fell into two halves.

Hastily, Jan put the diamond back into his pocket. He felt chilly. Suddenly he realized that the value of the stone must range into the hundreds of thousands, perhaps millions. And anything as valuable as that must have been missed. Further, when one was known to possess such a stone, he was not entirely safe from being blackjacked, knifed, drugged, beaten or just plain murdered. The shot of this realization received instant reaction from Jan.

"Good lord! I wish I was somebody else!"

There was a strange, swishing feeling. The world spun giddily. And Jan Palmer, who thought he was high enough off ground when standing on the platform, found himself clinging to a boom tower, his hands engaged in cable splicing.

He ran a piece of cable in his finger, slipped on the tower, sagged against his safety belt and looked down two hundred feet at the pygmies in the yard. The wind of high altitude fanned him. The *Zachariah P. Palmer* was a toy being towed by a toy tug into a slip. A loneliness came to him. And acrophobia nauseated him.

He ripped his eyes from the earth below. He looked at the ledge on the tower and saw that his hands were big, broad tools built for skilled but hard labor. He glanced at his clothing. The glance also took in some ground and he hastily looked up. But he had observed that he was dressed in leather and olive drab wool, not in a business suit.

Thoroughly dazed now by the realization that he did not look like and was not dressed like Jan Palmer, he again almost let go, the safety strap alone supporting him. Empty air was under his feet, two hundred feet thick.

For some time he remained where he was, afraid to stir, but when he found that he did not instantly fall, he discovered courage enough to look below again. And he saw the platform under him, a hundred feet below. Murky Seattle sunlight glinted from the chips of broken bottle. Coils of smoke came off the timbers where the *Zachariah P. Palmer* had slid down. And on the platform stood a man who, even from this height, was unmistakably Jan Palmer. He wore Jan Palmer's business suit, his hat and his shoes; he had the build and, as far as one could tell, the height of Jan Palmer. But it was obviously not Jan Palmer, as Jan up the pole hurriedly assured himself, because Jan Palmer was up *here* dressed in leather and olive drab, belted and kitted like a high rigger; yes, and with the hands and muscles of a high rigger even if he did not have a high rigger's insolence about altitude.

The man on the platform below, evidently, was not without his own qualms. He looked up the boom tower and frowned. He looked down at the ground and the ways, still undecided. He looked at his hands and felt the texture of the expensive suit and then, rummaging through his pockets, drew out the diamond and stared at it.

Instantly Jan was alert, immediately some of his fright vanished. He had considerable wit and he knew considerable lore. He had studied something of Arabianology, he had some inklings about magic and demonology. And the instant the murky sunlight flashed from that diamond he became entirely certain that it had a vital role in this sudden shift of identity. It was not a difficult line of reasoning for the diamond, appearing so suddenly in his life, was the only strange factor in the equation. Just what it had to do with this, Jan did not know or stop to compute at this time. Instead he hastily grabbed for his safety belt and—with some amazement as to his strength—swung himself down the spikes toward the ground. Two or three times he almost missed a step but somehow this unusual body of his knew better than to miss and with an automatic gesture he each time saved himself.

In a short space of time he was on the ground. Clanking because of the tools belted around him, he started for the launching platform. A bulk abruptly loomed before him.

"Murphy! What the hell are you doing off the job? Get back up there!"

Jan looked at the foreman. He started to say, "I beg your pardon, sir, but—" and he said, "Dry up, Donovan! You want a spanner around your neck?"

Donovan stepped back and Jan, much amazed at his own tone of voice, hastened on.

The man dressed in Jan's clothes was coming down the steps as Jan reached the bottom. Jan looked up, the man looked down.

"I'll trouble you for that piece of ice," said Jan truculently.

"I beg pardon?" said the man who looked like Jan.

"The rock," said Jan. He was making an effort to be polite and proper but the wrong words kept coming out. "The glass, dummy. Fork it over before I beat your skull in!"

The man hastily backed up the steps. He seemed confused. In his turn he was trying to be tough and he was getting, "I beg pardon. Excuse me, I didn't understand you."

"You'll understand, all right," snarled Jan, swarming up the steps.

The man turned and fled to the top. Jan was one jump behind him. He grabbed the fellow by the collar and shook him so hard he lifted him clean off the boards. Thus dazing his captive, Jan thrust his hand into the fellow's pocket and grasped the diamond. The second he had it, he shoved the man aside. Jan looked at the stone. He tried to think back. He knew this must have to do with some incantation. He tried to think of incantations.

He peered more closely into the diamond, thinking hard. The fellow grabbed at him and he knocked him back again. Jan cast his wits back across the moments he had last been Jan. What had he said?

The foreman was coming to the bottom of the steps. Jan looked at him down there, thinking the while. The fellow in Jan's clothes made another attack and Jan grabbed him automatically by the collar and held him up in the air where he struggled and wheezed.

"Hey, drop that!" bawled the foreman. "Hey, Murphy, you ape! That's Palmer of Bering Steam! Let him go!"

At that instant, gazing abstractedly at the foreman, Jan recalled what he had said. "Good lord," he whispered, "I wish I was somebody else!"

There was a blur and a swish, a feeling of emptiness and then solidity. And he was at the bottom of the steps looking up at a high rigger shaking a man who looked like Jan Palmer.

It took him a moment to recover himself. Then he understood what had happened. He had said the right words all right. But he had been looking at the wrong man. The foreman had become the high rigger, the high rigger was Jan and Jan was the foreman! And here he was down at the bottom of the steps, rigged out in a burly body, chewing tobacco and wearing stained suspenders, looking up while, evidently, a high rigger wondered why he was holding the head of Bering Steam by the collar.

In a fright for fear he would lose his own identity utterly with this shuffling, Jan started up the steps on the run. And then he felt calmer, tougher than was his wont. In fact, he felt like he could lick this high rigger Murphy without any trouble whatever. And with that feeling returned some of his wits. It was strange to feel bossy and competent, very strange. But he did. And he felt coldly calculating and somehow knew that as the foreman he could play a very hard game of poker.

He arrived at the top of the steps. The man who looked like the high rigger was trying to focus his eyes on the man who looked like the foreman—the real Jan.

With an abrupt insight, Jan saw it would not do to wish himself back into himself and leave, thereby, the rigger in the foreman's form and the foreman in the rigger's form. This cold calculation was something new. But he could use it.

"See here, Murphy," said Jan. "You can't do this! What's that you've got in your hand?"

The foreman as the high rigger looked stupidly at the diamond.

Jan reached out and took it. "Stand back now," he said. "Leave Mr. Palmer alone."

Jan extended the diamond back toward the "high rigger." "Here, take it!"

The high rigger reached toward the diamond, agape with amazement, for he had not yet divined how he, a foreman, came to be Murphy, a high rigger. "Good lord," said Jan, "I wish I was Murphy."

There was a whir, a nothingness, a blur and solidity. He found himself back being Murphy. He had his hand outstretched and was just then grasping the diamond. He took it.

"What the hell!" shrieked the foreman, now again himself. "What's going on?"

The man who looked like Jan, actually the high rigger Murphy, was ready to bust somebody in the eye. Jan extended the stone toward him. "I think this is yours, sir," he said. Dully, Murphy made a grab at the bright stone, his outrage gathering momentum. "Good lord," said Jan hastily, "I wish I was Palmer!"

A whir, a whirl, solidity. As himself, Jan Palmer, he hastily grasped the diamond. He pocketed it.

"What the devil!" screamed the foreman. "I must be drunk! I could have swore—"

"You could have swore!" said Murphy. "One minute I'm up a pole. The next I'm somebody else! What—"

"Gentlemen, gentlemen," said Jan, marshaling up all his nerve for the occasion. "I am sure there has been some mistake."

"Mistake!" howled Murphy. "I—"

"Shut up!" said the foreman. "Are you all right, Mr. Palmer?"

"Quite all right," said Jan feebly. And gripping the diamond hard in his pocket he made his way past the foreman, who was trying to dust him off, went down the steps and took his way past riveters and over mud to his car.

He sat behind the wheel for some time, nervously disorganized. He had the odd sensation of not quite fitting in himself as though he had somehow been stretched like a sweater tried on by too big a man.

At length, seeing that he was in an L of the building and could not be observed, he took out the diamond and looked at it. Vague memories were trying to stir within him, a feeling that he had been lately otherwise than he was. The nearest he came to anything was when he closed his eyes and had a picture of a tiger before him but it meant nothing. Of the world of sleep he now had no clue and, having none, he had only his knowledge of Arabianology bequeathed to him by his father's cousin, Greg Palmer, the only relative for whom he had ever had any respect.

He peered cautiously at the diamond with the air of one who has no confidence that what he handles is not a hand grenade. He looked carefully around him and gazed once more at the diamond. And then he saw it, the three-dimensional seal deep within its depths.

Instantly he recalled the two-dimensional Seal of Sulayman and the copper jar. He recalled the death of one Frobish at the hands of the Jinn which had escaped from that jar after Frobish had opened it. He recalled his own incarceration, the swindles of Green—

What a curious blank! he told himself. The Jinn, the jail, his nearness to being executed for Frobish's death because Green wanted Bering Steam for his own, the help of Alice, his wife, then his secretary. But what had happened in between? Ah, now it was coming back to him a trifle. He had experienced a period of great strength and power in this world, a joy of life and a self-confidence which had never before been his. Ah, yes. There was something else, somebody else. He had gone somewhere when he slept. Or had he only dreamed? But no, he had changed. He was somebody else somewhere else, that he knew. And something had been but lately struck from his life. Wait, it was almost on his tongue. A curse—the Jinn from the bottle—The Curse of Eternal Wakefulness! Now he was getting somewhere. A curse had kept him awake somewhere, somehow. The Jinn had cursed him to eternal wakefulness and being cursed he had then, when he slept, awakened— But here he was stuck again. Where had he awakened? Only day before yesterday he had felt powerful. Now he felt weak. Something had happened.

Whatever might have been Jan's drawbacks in the field of action, he at least could think. And he was thinking now with swiftness and accuracy. Something had happened to him day before yesterday, today he woke up without any feeling of power but with a diamond.

When he had occupied the body of the high rigger he had felt strong. When he had been in the body of the foreman he had felt cold and calculating and possessed of much brass. Now, as Jan again, he felt self-conscious— This definitely had something to do with being asleep and awake and it had much to do with this diamond.

Who was he where? He was somebody else somewhere, that was certain.

Again he looked at the diamond, pocketed it and drove toward home. He wanted no taste of the office. He wanted to sit down in his study and ponder this thing out. But as he drove his wits kept turning.

Obviously this diamond was an other-world item. There was another world. Where it was and why it was had something to do with sleep. This diamond might or might not have something to do with sleep. But it certainly had something to do with throwing identity.

Carefully he plotted it. One could desire or command himself into another body whenever he possessed this diamond and the owner of the other body transferred into his. By expressed desires, one could possibly go on chain fashion through the whole human race, scrambling up the identity of everyone with whom he transferred. *But* it was vital to keep the diamond. The diamond stayed in the hands of the person one was quitting. What changed? he asked himself. Evidently, the soul.

He scarcely realized that he was home, so abstracted was he when he drove into the drive of the old Palmer mansion. Although it was now his, he followed his boyhood habits about it. He let himself in the back and went down into his study where the bric-a-brac collected by generations of seafaring Palmers gathered dust and the criticism of Alice.

He set himself at the desk, placed the diamond before him and prepared to study it further. But an unaccountable drowsiness stole over him. The copper jar, source of so much dismay earlier in his life, stood empty in the corner, its lead stopper fallen to one side.

Alice, his wife, entered. She had heard his car enter the garage and she knew she might find him here. She intended to make him go over the household accounts with her and demand an increase in her expense allowance for, romantic as she might have been as a secretary, she was, after all, a woman. He was too preoccupied to answer her, she thought. She was about to become impatient when her eye caught the glint of the diamond. She gasped.

Jan was leaning back, eyes closed. She supposed he slept. She came closer and peered at the diamond. Gingerly she pushed it with her finger. Gathering courage she picked it up.

She softened. Dear, dear Jan. Always so thoughtful. But this stone was far, far too expensive for her birthday next week. But he was a dear to think of it. It was too showy, besides.

There was the ringing of a bell upstairs and she suddenly recalled that Amy Farlan was coming over that afternoon for tea and a chat about the girls. Alice took a look at Jan. He was either asleep or too deep in thought to notice. It would not do any harm to go up and show Amy. Of course Jan would have to take it back for a less expensive gift but still, it would give the girls quite a twitter.

She took it upstairs and showed Amy who cattily agreed that it was far too showy, who became class (synonym for money) conscious and began to talk about her ancestors and the Mayflower and one thing led to another and the diamond, thrust into Alice's pocket, was soon forgotten in the more interesting details of Gertrude's wearing last year's hat to church last Sunday.

Jan, unaware either of this fascinatingly intelligent conversation in progress upstairs or the absence of the diamond, dozed on, not asleep, not awake. Alice, who had a theater appointment with some friends, had Jan's dinner sent down and took herself away. And at length came home to bed. In his study, Jan slept deeply, sprawled out on his desk. The diamond lay in the pocket of Alice's frock tossed carelessly across the foot of Alice's bed.

Chapter 5

OLD THUNDERGUTS

The sea was blue and the waves were white and the little lugger plunged through the brightness of the morning sun, heading outward from the coasts of Balou.

"What's on your mind, Tiger?" said Walleye. "You been sittin' there lookin' stunned for about twenty minutes."

Tiger didn't answer. He sat on the rail. He had been going through his pockets from time to time and he was convinced at last that the diamond was gone. He had now fixed an eye upon Muddy McCoy and the eye was not pleasant to encounter.

Walleye gave her a couple of spokes down and glanced back at Tiger. Then Walleye followed Tiger's gaze and, being a man much accomplished in looting, suddenly read the tale. His face grew very stiff.

Muddy McCoy was whetting his knife, oblivious of these gazes. He was humming an obscene and serpentine ditty and wriggling to the tune of it. Ryan, who had been setting all taut forward, drifted aft at this moment, saw the tension in Walleye's face, glanced to see what Tiger was looking at and then regarded Muddy McCoy.

Ryan stopped as he reached the poop deck. "The diamond or the money or both?" said Ryan.

"The diamond," said Tiger and moved quietly toward Muddy.

Walleye gave his attention to the wheel. Ryan drew a cutlass from the stand at the rail and tested its edge. Muddy, suddenly aware, looked up, took all in with a glance, sprang back and writhed into a defensive posture, his knife juggled in his palm, shifty gaze flicking from Tiger to Ryan but giving Tiger most of the attention.

"I didn't do nothing!" cried Muddy, a thousand guilts twisting in him.

Walleye spared a glance from his steering, looked at Muddy. Everyone hated Muddy because Muddy hated everyone. Walleye wondered disinterestedly if the sharks would get a bellyache if they ate the corpse after Ryan and Tiger had finished. He was about to decide that the sharks wouldn't because they would not be able to stomach Muddy's unwashedness when he spotted something which, in this byplay, had gone unnoticed. There were three sail to windward and they had their courses set for the lugger. They might be coming to get them or they might merely be on course for Balou Bay now twelve hours sail astern.

Muddy went up on the rail, shivering with fright. "I'll jump!" he screamed, his knife hand shaking.

Tiger reached out. Muddy's knife flicked, missed and went sailing amidships as Tiger's huge hand knocked his wrist. Tiger swept Muddy down to the deck and held him easily, going over him with care.

Ryan repeated the search.

"Must've swallowed it," said Ryan.

"Would've choked him," said Tiger.

"I'll kill myself! I'll kill myself!" shrieked Muddy irrationally.

"Ought to cut him open for precaution," said Ryan practically, raising his cutlass.

"I'll save you the trouble, lads," said a calm voice from the deck below.

Tiger and Ryan whipped to stare in that direction. Unseen by Walleye, Tombo stood, legs braced against the lift of the lugger. He had a pistol in each hand and the pistols, Ifrit size, were cocked. Behind Tombo stood Malek, armed with two more cocked pistols, the remaining store of firearms on the lugger.

"Drop your knives to the deck," said Tombo.

Tiger and Ryan dropped their knives and stood up.

"Hey!" said Walleye. "What's goin' on? You better look at them sails out there. They ain't goin' to Balou. They just changed course for us!"

"Now," said Tombo, his big fangs shining brightly, "you can give me the Two-World Diamond. If we have no trouble, you will be permitted to live to sail us home."

Tiger raised an eyebrow. All Ifrits, if powerful, were not quite bright at times. The entire proceedings about Muddy had been entirely misunderstood by Tombo or not understood at all. As humans the sailors had not needed to communicate as bluntly as Tombo's mind would have required.

"My dear admiral," said Tiger, "I have just searched our shipmate here for the stone and he doesn't have it. Walleye may have it, Ryan may have it, but I confounded well don't. It was in my pocket last night when I slept. It's not there now."

"Do I change course?" said Walleye anxiously, eyes all for the three sails which were now bearing down so close that the bones in their teeth were visible.

Tiger looked up, saw the three vessels for the first time, read them and turned to the sheets. "Stand by. Let her off the starboard six points! Watch yourself, admiral." Tiger let the sheet run, the ship turning and the wind drawing aft. When he and Ryan had slacked off and secured both sails and they were picking up speed with the wind on their port quarter, Tiger looked fixedly at the ships. A gun in the bow of the foremost spoke and a ball skipped through the waves and plunked short of them. The report was dull against them.

Tombo looked to this new concern. He glanced at his guns. He was still holding them on his quarry but he had been ignored with such purpose that he could find no grounds to complain of it. He was not an overly bright individual, even amongst Ifrits, a fact attested by his having risen to the rank of admiral. But bright or not, even Tombo could not miss the flag which fluttered from the truck of the foremost ship. It was blood red—it meant "No quarter" and it meant piracy. Things were happening a trifle too fast for him.

The course change had slowed them but now they were picking up knots. But they were not picking up enough of them. They were square-rigged, the three oncoming ships, and although a lugger points better and sails faster into the wind, it cannot match the sailing qualities of square rig, designed to reach and run.

Malek sighed. The sun had been behind these oncoming ships and so they had gained upon them unseen. But Malek was confirmed in his pessimism. "I knew we'd never make it," he said mournfully, and shoved his pistols, uncocked, in his sash.

Tiger watched a second shot bounce toward them. He puckered his brow. He looked at their wake. He looked at the foremost vessel.

"Starboard your helm," said Tiger. "Bring her up into the wind." He and Ryan slacked off the sheets and the lugger, thus headed, was soon slatting her way to a halt.

The strangers came around in a wide sweep and with slacked braces idled in to trumpet distance.

A huge human in a red shirt stepped into the rigging of the largest ship and aimed a brass trumpet at them.

"Come aboard!"

"Send a boat!" Tiger yelled back.

The human in the red shirt played an eye over the lugger, discovered that it did lack a boat and so, with a volley of orders, got a cutter into the sea. Manned by humans, the cutter was soon under the counter of the lugger which, slopping off, now lay in the trough; booms trembled as the canvas thundered.

Tiger gave them a ladder and shortly a bow-legged, toothless, sun-stained man dropped over the rail, glared around and then confronted Tiger.

"What's your cargo?"

"Empty sacks and two Ifrits," said Tiger. "We're just out of Balou Bay and I wouldn't be surprised if men-o-war weren't far behind."

"You steal this?" said the boarding officer.

Tiger grinned.

"Well, that's one point in your favor!" He went to the rail and yelled down and the boat's crew, all but one, swarmed up.

The bow-legged one's grin grew wry when he looked at the two Ifrits. "Over you go." He turned to Tiger. "I'm prize crew. You'll join Old Thunderguts on the flag. Can't say what he'll do with you. Wouldn't advise trying to escape by rowing. The bows been achin' for some target work. On your way now. Lively. Now lads, step lively." And he ignored the captives and began to assign his prize crew to watches and stations aboard the lugger.

Tiger and the rest dropped into the boat and were soon along-side the flagship which was proclaimed to be, by smeary letters across the stern, obliterating an old name, *Terror*. They swarmed up the Jacob's ladder and stood in the waist, giving a hand while the cutter was swung aboard, all but Tombo and Malek who stood apart, disdainful.

The ship was entirely a hurraw's nest. Refuse filthied her waterways, grease and dirt bestained her decks. Crowded by a ver-minous rabble who showed every sign of debauchery, the *Terror* might better have been named the *Horror* for so she would have appeared to any seamanlike eye. Her rigging was askew so that her masts raked differently. Her halyards were chafed. Her blocks were rusted. She was a seagoing spitkit and would have been a disgrace to an army transport service.

The cutter stowed Tiger and company, surrounded by the idly curious crowd, and were thrust aft to the quarterdeck.

Tiger had supposed that he would be greeted by the red-shirted man who had hailed him from the shrouds. And he was not at all prepared to find a man in a gold crown, blowzy drunk, swathed in a silk robe and seated on an improvised throne.

A sailor went up and bowed before this creature. "Your Majesty, prisoners await your will."

Tiger blinked. There was a guard of men here on the quarter-deck which had cocked pistols in their sashes and carried drawn cutlasses in their hands. They were not neat and they were not sober but they looked businesslike. These were different than the crew at large. They seemed to be a guard around this preposterous throne.

The man in the red shirt was giving orders to get under weigh again and seemed to have nothing to do with the enthroned individual.

The man on the throne looked up, fixed a sullen and vengeful eye upon his captives and said, "I, the Thunderbolt, pronounce the sentence of death."

The guard moved forward toward the captives.

"That," said Tiger, "would be a waste of good money. We can furnish a ransom of three hundred thousand pieces of gold!"

Tombo, Malek, Muddy and Walleye looked with amazement at Tiger. But Tiger stayed very cool. Ryan grinned.

The guard stopped its forward motion. It drew back.

"Three hundred thousand pieces of gold for the lot of us," said Tiger, more loudly.

"There's two Ifrits," muttered somebody in the crowd behind them.

"Ought to be killed," said somebody else.

"Damned navy sons," said somebody else.

"How much?" said the red-shirted man, orders to the ship forgotten and facing Tiger now.

"Three hundred thousand pieces of gold," said Tiger, even more loudly.

"You heard my orders," said the Thunderbolt on his throne and took a swig from a gin bottle.

But the guard turned back to him. There was a great deal of whispered argument. The man in the red shirt finally detached himself and came over to Tiger.

"How do we collect this?" he said.

"By holding us on the beach near Tarbutón," said Tiger. "One messenger, the gold back in one hour."

"How does a human come to have gold?" said the red-shirted man.

"Because these two Ifrits are my captives," said Tiger. "One is very rich." He laid a seemingly affectionate hand on Tombo's lofty shoulder. "He owes me his life. He will pay."

Tombo was too stunned to object. He did not have three hundred pieces of gold that he knew about.

There was further conference.

"Kill the sailors and save the Ifrits," announced the Thunderbolt.

"Wouldn't do," said Tiger boldly. A knife had appeared in his hand as though by materialization and the knife had its point at Tombo's throat. "Put us all in the same hold or your golden goose ceases to exist."

Tombo was very upset. He was becoming extremely confused. Malek sighed pessimistically.

There was another conference. There were gestures. Thunderbolt finally laid about him with the gin bottle and rose up. "All right, you swabs. Put him in the brig. Put them all in the brig!"

And as Tiger and the rest were thrust down the ladder into the dark hold, the Thunderbolt was heard to hiccough, "You never do what I tell you. Never. But I get the next captives and I get to do it like I want!"

Tiger and his companions were locked into a space much too small and without sufficient height. The water was running along the outer skin of the ship again as the vessel gathered weigh. The water gurgled noisily in the bilge just under their feet.

Tombo sank down against the wall, a very bewildered Ifrit. "But I haven't got three hundred thousand pieces of gold, Tiger. Why did you tell them that?"

"Save your brains for admiraling, Tombo," said Tiger.

"But he'll kill us," said Malek. "These are escaped slaves turned pirate. That's Old Thunderguts himself, the most infamous rogue afloat. We're dead men."

"I'm still breathing," said Tiger and placidly pulled out a piece of cheese and a chunk of bread snatched from the lugger's stores, passed them around and began to eat lunch.

At two o'clock that afternoon, the inmates of that crowded cell were confounded to find their number increased. It was very dark. The cell door had not opened. And yet there was sobbing in the cell. Whatever might have been the dispositions of these hard cases, the ability to sob was not included amongst their accomplishments. Accordingly they took a hasty census.

With many grunts and mutters, they discovered that they were now Tiger, Walleye, Muddy, Tombo, Malek, Ryan and one who sobbed. An inquiry was undertaken by all but Tiger silenced them and conducted his own.

He very swiftly located the source of the grief as coming from the one corner left vacant on their first admission to this place. He then discovered that the weeping came from a girl. He fished through his pockets and discovered flint and steel and in a moment, by a flow of sparks, beheld her. Tiger sank back on his haunches, the breath coming out of him as if he had been struck.

They had all seen the girl by the sparks. But Tiger had seen more. Her delicate and lovely face, seen through her veil, discovered her to be Wanna, one-time temple dancer, the fragile beauty who had become by his conquest, Tiger's consort!

Tiger got his breath back. She should have been waiting for him in Tarbutón, many a league away, safe in what remained of the baronial possessions which he had mostly squandered. But here she was, aboard this shabby ship, a desirable woman just a few yards away from a thoroughly blackguard crew.

"How in Baal's name did you get here?" demanded Tiger hoarsely.

Her weeping stilled. She seemed to be listening, hopefully but fearfully, "Is—is it really you?"

"Yes," said Tiger practically. "It's me!" His male wrath was rising. "What did you do to get yourself here?"

"I don't know, I don't know," she said and began to weep again. Tiger dried her tears with a corner of his headsilk and sat down, his arm around her.

"It's my girl," he whispered menacingly to the others in the cell. "Somehow she got here from Tarbutón. Stand clear or I'll bust a skull!"

Muddy and Walleye scuttled back. Ryan braced up to help Tiger if there was a fight. Tombo's breathing, if anyone had noticed, had stopped on Tiger's first announcement and began again, excitement in it. Tombo scented something he could use.

"Stand and deliver," whispered Tiger to Wanna. "What happened. And stow the weeps. You'll have the guards down on us."

"Where are we?" said Wanna between sniffles.

"Aboard a scummy buckaroon," said Tiger. "Old Thunderguts."

"The Thunderbolt?" gasped Wanna. "The pirate emperor?" And she really began to cry.

"Hush it!" said Tiger fiercely. "How'd you get here?"

He managed to return to her some of her self-possession and at last she began a connected explanation.

"When I woke up this morning (sniffle) I didn't mean any harm (dabs with Tiger's headsilk) and I put on my bathing gown and started to go to the baths (two sniffles) when I felt in my pocket and there was something there (more dabs with the headsilk) and I took it out and oh! I almost went blind! (Swift recovery with no sniffles whatever.) It was a diamond as big as my hand! What a stone! I almost fainted with surprise. And I looked at it and then I realized (on the verge of weeping now) that you were not there to protect me (sobs) and I ran back to our rooms and I locked myself in and almost died with fright for fear somebody had seen me look at it. It's enough (deep sobs) to get murdered to have a diamond like that. And I didn't know what to do (sniffles) and I worried and worried and I didn't know when you would be home or even where you were sailed to and I thought maybe I'd just have to stay in and starve to death (loud sniffles and a sob) for if I went out I'd get robbed and so I wanted you to come home because the diamond would have bought back our estates and then I got more and more scared for fear somebody had seen me so I hid the diamond under the mattress and all of a sudden here I was! Oh, Tiger, even if we're going to die, I'm so glad to see you!"

Tiger patted her. He was much puzzled. "Wait. You must have said something when you were hiding it."

"Oh yes. But only that I wished I was with you."

There was a slither of leather and claws. Hoarsely Tombo said, "I'll take that diamond now."

But Tiger was already aware that it was not on her person. He confirmed his belief with a short whisper to her and her answer after a brief search about her.

"Get out of here," said Tiger to Tombo. "She don't have it. What's the matter with you, you damned Ifrit? What's so valuable about this diamond?"

Tombo weighed the situation slowly. He thought slowly, Tombo. He vocalized all his thoughts in his head. And he supposed he must be very wise to be able to think so slowly and take so long to reach conclusions. In short, he was a fool. But he had brawn and determination to put foolish conclusions into solid actions and power to spare.

Tombo was assured that the diamond was not then present. He permitted himself to be pushed back. He and Malek could easily overcome these unarmed humans, such was the disproportion of size. But Tiger might inflict damage.

"I'll wait," said Tombo. "But if the diamond comes here, it is mine."

Chapter 6

THE WRIGGLING MAN

Jan Palmer awoke to find himself none too well-oiled after a night's slumber across a desk. Some servant had brought in a tray of dinner and it was thirteen hours cold. Nevertheless he took the slab of roast beef in his hand and chewed it, poured out a cup of coffee and sipped it. The cold coffee told him that this was not evening, the slanting beams of sunlight confirmed it since his seaman's eye detected that they came from the eastern windows. He stood up and rang a bell. Fumbling around in his studio bathroom he located and applied the materials necessary to make his cheeks smooth, like in the ads. The Swede girl made the coffee hot and presently, seated again at his desk and much refreshed by the brew, he thought about the diamond.

So certain was he that it was lying there, right in front of him, where its glitter had mesmerized him yesterday, that it took him several minutes to digest the fact that it was *not* present. He immediately began a scramble through the stacks of papers and sail plans and when nothing resulted from this, looked under and around the desk, into the waste basket and around the office.

He summoned the Swede girl. Yes, she vas brought his supper to him the night before. No she vas not seeing a diamond. And if he vas accusing her of being a thief he vas going to get a notice and soon right away. He mollified her and was about to start his search all over again when Alice appeared.

Alice was a very businesslike girl. She had no traffic with idleness. A man, particularly the head of Bering Steam, should toe the mark, measure up, bear down and generally comport himself. Neither he nor she was aware of the fact that she had had no complaints a very few days ago. Something poetic had vanished from her nature, something strong from his. She was a hard-eyed ex-businesswoman who had gotten her man and, having gotten him, was making very sure that he did all the business necessary, not only for the money involved but also because she had a life-time habit of keeping a man at his job.

"You aren't at the office," she said. "It's nine."

"Yes, dear," said Jan, meekly.

"The moment you take your hands off the reins your board of directors is liable to take a slice of Bering for themselves."

"Yes, dear."

"Now that we have that settled, I'll run you down. I'm going shopping for the tea party this afternoon."

"Alice," said Jan, stopping her as she turned toward the door, "have you seen anything of—well, of a diamond?"

"Oh, yes, of course, you silly boy. It is a nice present but it is simply too expensive, what with the government and its silly taxes and all. You'll have barely enough cash to pay your income tax as it is, despite the fact that they are letting you keep one half of one percent of your own money this year and only telling you how to spend two-thirds of that. So you just trot right back to the jewelry store and tell them that a much less showy present will be quite adequate."

Jan blinked at this, got it straight and with husbandly wit decided not to disabuse her of this fable she had erected. "Very well, my dear. Give me the diamond and I'll do what is right."

She looked around as though expecting to find it in the room, then poised a finger against her lower lip, looked at the ceiling and thought. Jan watched her in suspense.

"I showed it to one of the girls—let me see— Did I put it down in the drawing room? No—"

"Think, dear," said Jan, hiding his agony.

She went up to the drawing room to make sure and Jan anxiously followed her. Then she remembered that she had been wearing a gown with pockets and ran up to her bedroom. Jan swiftly sped after her. She asked her maid what had happened to the gown and the maid wanted to know what gown and Alice had to recall the specific gown and the maid wondered if it were the pink gown and Alice didn't think it was and the maid wanted to know if it had been placed right here and being possessed of the unnecessary information that it had been in that exact place said no she hadn't seen the gown and Jan in desperation went to the closet where they should have gone in the first place and it was discovered by sudden brilliant recollection on the part of the maid that it had gone to the cleaners and oh if she'd known it had been the gown on the foot of the bed she would have known right away.

This intellectual exercise was not much appreciated by Jan. He grabbed a phone and called the cleaning establishment and was told that the gown must still be on the truck which was not due back until five.

Jan raced out of the house, deaf now to the female brand of rationality, and wrapped his hands around the wheel of the roadster. He did not realize, until he had begun to drive, an occupation which stirred thought processes with him, that he was most terribly concerned about something which had appeared without warning and had disappeared in the same way. He knew there was a very good reason why he was urgent about it. He did not know the source of the nightmares he had had the night before and he did not know what would happen to him if he did not find this diamond. But he had a churning anxiety about it and he drove madly back and forth, looking for a truck bearing the sign and seal of the Frazall Cleaners.

About eleven, after several calls back to the plant, he located his quarry and ransacked the truck for the dress. But search as he might through the pockets of all the gowns present, he could not find the diamond and with a sagging mind, drove wearily homeward.

Alice, bright and happy, met him at the door with the diamond in her hand. "We found it when we turned the mattress on my bed!" she announced.

Jan sighed with relief and asked for it.

"Not until you give me a kiss," said Alice. "There, that's a good boy." But she didn't give up the diamond. "If I were you," she said, "I—"

Whirr! Zzzt!

Jan found himself in a coy position, holding the diamond, looking at his body on the other side of the doorsill. The face which belonged with his proper self blanked in astonishment and started to look down. Jan whipped a quantity of female sleeve aside from his hand, looked at the diamond and said, "Good lord, I wish I were Jan."

Zzzt! Whirr!

He was back in his own body again. Hurriedly he snatched the diamond away from Alice.

"Wha—what happened. I—I—" gasped Alice. "I—I'm sure I was you for a minute! I felt just as though—"

"Nonsense," said Jan hastily. "Delusions, delusions. Why don't you go see your Dianeticist. Something restimulated, no doubt." And he rushed past her and down the steps to his study. He barred the door, he locked the windows and then he laid the diamond carefully on his blotter.

He took off his coat and threw it on the sofa. And then he squared up to his library and began to haul down armloads of books on Arabianology. Shy as he might be with men and business, Jan Palmer was very much at home with tomes. His telephone rang and he threw it in the wastebasket and stuffed a sofa pillow in on top of it and, seating himself, began to run through catalogues of talismans.

• • •

By four o'clock he had found it. He scanned the Arabian script with his muscles gradually relaxing. In the ancient copy of Ibn Mahmud's *Magical Stones and Jewels of the Eastern Kingdoms*, on page 872, he read:

"TWO-WORLD DIAMOND. This miraculous stone, said to have been found in a meteorite near Thebes, despite its blue-white quality, was etched by magical means in the workshops of Sulayman with the seal commanding the air elements, a tetrahedron which appears well within its depths. Weighing two hundred and ninety-six carats, it is reputed to be without flaw. Its mysterious qualities are remarked in a manuscript of Abdullah Sid who states that it becomes the soul companion of its possessor but attaches itself to the material being. By its means it is possible to escape from the confines of earthly flesh and wander at will but the stone remains in the possession of the body quitted. It has the power, as well, of translating itself from the world of the Jinn to the human kingdom when in the possession of a human. It was used by Sulayman himself for this purpose to expedite his government of the Jinn. In the hands of the Jinn much of its power fails since it was designed for human use. It has many additional powers as described by Abdullah Sid but is primarily used by the Jinn, by whom it is said to be possessed at this time, to achieve immortality since it permits them to leave behind their dying selves and transmigrate to a younger body, the soul of which is then cast into the Infernal regions. It is supposed to have been stolen by one Arif, an Emir of the Jinn, from the treasury of Sulayman on the death of that monarch and has not since come to human knowledge."

Jan read it twice. The reference to the world of the Jinn stirred a definite unease in him. Confident, then, that amongst his collected books he would either find the manuscript of Abdullah Sid or that he would find where it could be procured, he began once more to ransack the library.

The Swede girl came with his dinner, since madame was dining out, and setting down the tray after Jan had let her in, eyed the diamond. She was somewhat huffy now that her innocence had been proven so utterly and so interested she was in that innocence that her interest in the diamond did not take form, for itself, until she was in the kitchen again. There the sly-eyed lumberjack who was her professed fiance and who had been lately kicked out of a logging camp up on the Skykomish or Snohomish or Snoqualimie or some equally Seattlesque name listened with some fascination to her tale of a diamond that was as big as her fist and down in the boss's study. The sly-eyed lumberjack, who did a quantity of wriggling not only from the lice one picks up in logging camps but from a natural disinclination to stay straight or sit still, recalled that he had an appointment down at the Friends of Russia Communist International Objectors Social Hall Lumberjacks Local No. 261 and, explaining that as Chairman of the Committee for Making Dissatisfied Minorities Dissatisfied he had much propagandizing to do, took an early leave. Kissing his sweetheart, Chan Davies, the lumberjack, went wriggling down the drive, writhed out of sight and then quickly hitched himself behind the shrubs and wriggled back again.

Meanwhile Jan had located the whereabouts of the manuscript. In a list of rare and lost works he had found this line:

"Abdullah Sid, manuscripts of. Deposited in the library of Alexandria and lost when the library was burned by Julius Caesar. No other copies known to be in existence."

However Jan might swear, or vent his contempt upon the Roman upstart, as many another scholar had, the manuscripts of Abdullah Sid were lost. Ibn Mahmud, not being prophetic enough to know that anyone would be so thoroughly unlettered as to destroy at a whim the works of the ages, had not listed all the properties of the diamond in his description.

Jan laid the tumbled tomes aside. Baffled, he looked at the diamond. What properties did it have? The suddenness of his first discoveries had unnerved him to be very experimental. He knew how thoroughly dangerous it would be to make random tests. One might wind up in the Infernal regions with no succor or he might find himself an elephant or he might, who knew, discover himself consorting—God forbid—with Ifrits!

His puzzling was so intense that he did not hear the slip of a window catch, expertly undone with a wire. He felt a small breath of air and then he turned to discover a man with the chief Communist political argument, the lead pipe, upraised in his hand. He dodged and struck out. Jan was slight of build and stature. The lead pipe came on through his defense, slammed at his head, connected and connected again. Jan fell beside his desk. Sweeping the Two-World Diamond into his pocket, the lumberjack, who was against wealth only so long as he had none, rushed off in quivering glee, writhing all over himself at the thought of how many servants he could now keep.

Jan, inert beside the desk, groaned faintly and was still.

Chapter 7

TURNABOUT

It was dawn on the *Terror* but the only intelligence of it that the people in the brig had was activity in the decks above them. Tiger, stiff with having cradled Wanna's head on his arm all night, flexed himself like a big cat. In so doing he disturbed the others who still slept and they started to object until they found that it was Tiger who had done the disturbing, at which they relapsed into sufferance.

Tombo and Malek, at the other end of the cell, eventually began to awaken and with many growls and grunts prepared to take up the day.

No guards appeared, no food appeared. In this shabby and unregulated vessel, one could not expect such a humanity as food and water. But food and water did not engross the inmates' thoughts very long. Tombo grunted into an erect posture.

"Now we'll see," he said, "if the diamond has come back." And he came forward through them toward Tiger.

In the open, Tiger might have proven a physical match for an Ifrit but not here where the Jinn's arms could so quickly encircle and crush. Accordingly, Tiger let his pockets be patted. He raised objections at any handling of Wanna for he had already assured himself that she did not possess it. Tombo decided she had no pockets in her filmy garments anyway and satisfied himself by examining where she had slept. He then bumbled on to a search of the others in the cell, very watchful lest any quick passing be done by these humans.

There was a sudden yelp of amazement and the crunch of Tombo's clawed fist striking a blow. Muddy squeaked in pain and writhed back. As little light as there was, the diamond caught it and glittered as it lay in Tombo's palm.

"So you decided to try to swindle me, did you! If you foolish humans only knew the power of this stone! But I leave you to rot and die. Malek! Take my arm!"

Tombo, bending beneath the overhead, saw that Malek was in place. Then he juggled the stone around, peering at it and throwing sparks off a flint with his knuckles so that he could see the sign within the stone. Finally he was satisfied.

"To Ramus City both! Fly!" cried Tombo.

There was a gust and a spin of air, a blurred spot where they had been and a rush from Tiger.

There was a thunk upon the floor and Tiger was grasping emptiness.

Tombo and Malek were gone!

Stupefied by this vanishment, accustomed as they were to the activity and powers of the Jinn, the five humans remained motionless for some seconds. And then Tiger scrambled around on the floor and finally came up holding the diamond he had struck from Tombo's hand at the instant of departure.

"Huh!" said Tiger. "A magic stone!"

His companions pressed around him. Wanna wept disconsolately in the corner. Tiger struck flint and steel again and again, looking thoroughly at the stone.

"That sign in there has something to do with it. The way it's held!" said Tiger. "Here, everybody grab hold of everybody. Come on, Wanna. If they can do it, we can!"

They formed a circle, each holding the next. Then Tiger, holding the stone, cried, "To Ramus City all five! Fly!"

Nothing happened. Resolutely, Tiger turned the stone with another side up. Again he pronounced the command. Again nothing happened.

• • •

For two hours and more they worked at it and always without success, trying different commands, trying different positions of the gem, facing it to various points of the compass.

Finally, with one last try wherein Tiger said, "Anywhere, let's GO!" They gave it up and sank back.

"Must work for Jinns and not for humans," said Tiger. "How'd you get this stone, Muddy?"

"I didn't steal it! I didn't do nothin' wrong. I just woke up and there it was, and I didn't do nothin' about it and I didn't know it was even on me until the admiral shook me out. Honest, I—"

"Pipe down," said Tiger. "Wanna leaves it in Tarbutón and it turns up back here again. Don't know why it tried Muddy! By the way, Wanna, what happened when the old lady kicked off?"

"You mean Ramus the Magnificent?" said Wanna, dutiful subject that she had been.

"I mean Ramus of the Triple Chin," said Tiger.

"She died."

"I know," said Tiger patiently.

"That was some time back," said Wanna.

"Whatever time it was, what happened?" said Tiger.

"They kept it secret," said Wanna and then evidently decided that it was still a secret for she said nothing more.

"How'd she die?" prompted Tiger.

"Old age, some said. They kept it awfully quiet for days. And then Zongri—"

"Who?" said four voices at once in startled alarm.

"Zongri, King of the Ifrits of Barbossi Isles. The cousin of Ramus. He was at the palace when the news came and he took charge of the kingdom. And some said it was terribly lucky he was, too, because there might have been a revolution or something and people killed. So he took command of the government and had himself crowned king and recalled all the navy ships that

216

had been sent against Arif-Emir, and the last morning I was there he was supposed to be making plans for a full-scale attack on Arif because of some silly jewel. So it is fortunate that Zongri—"

"But Zongri!" said Ryan. "He's Tiger's worst enemy! He swore he'd see Tiger dead. He escaped from the slave camps only last March! He'll murder Tiger on sight and kill the rest of us for the fun of it!"

"That's so," said Wanna whose education was, after all, only that of a temple dancing girl. And then she began to weep.

"Not only that," said Ryan remorselessly, "but Arif-Emir will stretch us in the sun, every one and let us dance a jig on air. We just escaped him! That leaves us without a haven anywhere in the world! Whew! Am I glad we didn't take that voyage to Ramus City like Tombo! This is *safe* compared to Tarbutón or Balou!"

"And the item over which Zongri and Arif will fight," said Tiger, not without mirth, "is right here in my hand."

"Oh, Tiger! Throw it away!" pleaded Wanna. "It's too dangerous!"

Tiger, following the Arabian adage of always listening carefully to the advice of women and then doing the exact opposite, chucked her under the chin. "Honey, if I were Old Thunderguts up on deck—"

Whirrrrrrr! Zzzzzzt!

Startled and jolted and much agog even for himself, Tiger found his eyes looking forward the length of the *Terror!* He tensed up to fight for his life. The guards with their naked weapons were strolling about the quarterdeck, enjoying the morning sunlight. The makeshift throne creaked to the roll of the vessel in the smooth swell. Yellow sunlight, blue water and a dirty ship were all before his gaze. And none attacked him! He raised his hand and found out that it held a gin bottle, half empty. Come to think of it, he felt a little drunk. He glanced at himself and discovered that he was clothed in ermine which had raised many generations of moths. Further, he was flabby and ancient and he didn't smell good.

• • •

He digested this. He was Old Thunderguts! He took a swig at the bottle to brace himself. Then, surrounded by enemies as he was, he made his wits work swiftly—which is to say, he made Old Thunderguts' wits work as well as his own soul's. He came up with the realization that the diamond was at the bottom of this change. He recalled his last words. He looked into his hands and pockets. But the diamond was not there. Abruptly he understood that Old Thunderguts must be down in the brig possessed of Tiger's body and Tiger's strength and that Wanna was down there, too!

Tiger as Thunderbolt steadied himself and thought fast. The diamond must still be down there. By some accident this thing might get upset at any instant. Therefore he had to act swiftly.

"Guard!" he roared.

"Your Majesty!" said a buckaroon officer.

"Why are we cruising here?"

"By Your Majesty's orders, sire. We are standing on and off out of sight of land off Tarbutón to pick up any stray cargoes which might show and to seek opportunity to transfer our prisoners to shore for ransom. No sails in sight, sire. Your fleet is ready to hand." The officer bowed.

"I am bored!" said Tiger as Thunderbolt. "Have up the prisoners!"

The guards wandered away to do his orders and Tiger as Thunderbolt waited a little nervously for fear that something might have happened down there or that this affair might not go off. That he was nervous upset him because Tiger as Tiger was never nervous. Besides, Thunderbolt's body had lice.

In time the guards came back dragging their captives with them. The young officer in charge was much discomfited by the disappearance of the two Ifrits for he feared it would be visited upon him. But he was not at all dismayed by the bawlings of the big sailor in the yellow headsilk.

"Damn your peepers! I tell you I'm emperor!" howled Thunderguts as Tiger. "I'll roll heads for this! I'll maim and brain men for this! Leave me go!"

Tiger as Thunderbolt sat calm and bored, waiting for their nearer approach. They came at last, despite much wrestling on the part of Thunderguts as Tiger, to the foot of the throne.

"You look," said Tiger as Thunderbolt, "to be a lad of too much sense and balance to go mad. You say you're the emperor of the buckaroons?"

"Aye, blast you! I'll rip you apart! What magic is this?"

"What's that you have in your hand, guard?" said Tiger as Thunderbolt.

"A diamond I took off him, sire. I mind your rule of share alike or lose a head and here it is."

Tiger as Thunderbolt gasped a little with relief to have his hands upon it again. And he was amazed that he would feel nervous at all.

"You're Tiger," said Tiger as Thunderbolt.

"I'm the emperor of the buckaroons!" shouted Thunderguts as Tiger.

"I am bored," said Tiger as Thunderbolt. "There are those aboard who suppose I am getting old. There are those aboard who would conspire and reduce me that keeps them full of rum and heavy with money. Well, I'll tell you what I'll do. I'll take you on, one knife apiece. You're a likely, brawny lad and I've every reason to suppose you're a good fighter. If I win, I'll have proved it. If you win, you can have my crown, understood?"

An amazed crew was gathering aft to hear this. They had, in fact, lately listened to conspiracies to unseat the aging old ruffian whose desire for blood was often satisfied at their expense and without profit.

"Your name's Tiger," said Tiger as Thunderbolt. "I've heard

of you. One-time baron of the realm of Ramus, a hard man in a fight."

"I'm Thunderbolt!" cried Thunderbolt as Tiger.

"So you contest my throne. So we'll have at it. Lads and subjects. Do you consider Tiger a good leader? You'll have heard of him. He says he's runner-up for the title. Do you agree to accept him if he wins?"

The crew was ready for any amusement, particularly a fight, particularly a way which would unsaddle them of Old Thunderguts. If the big sailor won, the guards could always finish him off if he didn't work out. The chief virtue of Old Thunderguts was that he had made such a reputation in his earlier days that he was a byword which caused fear in merchantmen and navies. So be it.

"Yeah! Hurrah!" said the crew.

"Then clear the quarterdeck," said Tiger as Thunderbolt. "Lash the helm and pass up two knives."

Wanna, much unsettled, was weeping over Tiger's being so far out of his head as to believe himself to be a buckaroon monarch and she clung to Thunderbolt as Tiger pitifully until swept back by the guards.

"All off the quarterdeck!" said Tiger as Thunderbolt.

"Wait!" said Thunderbolt as Tiger, for his rage had cooled to a point where he realized that he would be stabbing his own body and was, in short, in a considerable mess against unknown magic.

Tiger as Thunderbolt threw his opponent a knife. The quarterdeck was cleared. And then Tiger gripped the stone and whispered, "If I was you—"

Whirrrr! Zzzzt!

Whirrr! Zzzzt!

Tiger steadied himself as Tiger and plunged ten inches of good steel into the heart of Old Thunderguts. There was no need to strike again. The buckaroon emperor pitched to the deck, the steel still in him, quivering with his death spasms. Tiger swooped over him, swept up the diamond and whisked from its sheath the overlength rapier the emperor had worn.

There was a shudder of pleasure amongst the buckaroons. But the guards had long had their own selections of who was to be the next ruler—the officer in the red shirt. With Red Shirt at their head, the guards sprang forward.

A sailor who is used to a cutlass does not much apprehend the dangers he runs against a rapier. This was one reason Old Thunderguts had so long maintained his sadistic reign. And Tiger, who had studied the rapier as something a baron had to wear, knew how to use it.

He used the rapier so quickly and with so much efficiency that Red Shirt's followers, the remaining two, fell away, leaving five men very dead on the planking before Tiger. Red Shirt, however, with his rule in sight, was heedless of death and desertion. Fighting with more strength and skill, he fended with a knife in his left hand and struck hard blows with his right-hand weapon, a vicious boarding pike some two feet longer than the rapier.

Tiger skipped up to the top of the after house, nimbly avoiding the thrusts of the pike. He tripped over a coiled sheet as he fell back. Red Shirt came up over the edge of the house. Tiger scooped up the coiled line and threw it expertly. Red Shirt, tangled pike and knife, went backwards like a clawing cat. But a bigger cat slashed through. Tiger, with two quick punctures, let out Red Shirt's sinful life.

Tiger did not stay to watch the throes. He spun about and from the house looked down at the mass of buckaroons in the waist.

"Cheerily now, lads. Step up with your steel, any of you who think my orders are not worth obedience! Step up, I say."

They looked at him, already tall above them by virtue of the quarterdeck's raise and the house and tall again in his own right. His headsilk was yellow in the sun, his face was calm and determined, his seaboots were planted like they belonged there.

A naked rapier was red to the hilt in his hand and the red ran. And from headsilk to boots and boots to headsilk he looked to one and all very, very much like the new emperor of the buckaroons.

They cheered him again and again, not because they had to but because they appreciated a deliverance and a victory.

The other ships swung in to find out what was happening and each of the three was told of the victory. One ship was doubtful until Old Thunderguts' head was thrown aboard it and its skipper invited to a contest. Then it too flew signal flags in celebration.

"And now," said Tiger to a crew which thought it would get a new rum issue, "you'll holystone these decks, you swabs, mend these sails, reverse these halyards and set the ordinance to rights. You're a lot of stinking pigs but I've got a strange notion to make men of you yet!"

And with Ryan and Walleye as his new officers and Wanna installed in the emperor's cabin, Tiger prowled the ship, ended disputes with a quick knock-out of disputants, cruised his fleet and ended all disputes there by trouncing one captain and smashing the head of one would-be mutineer, and generally, at a minimal cost in blood and sweat, began the building of a fighting organization. On the *Terror*, with the throne jettisoned, Tiger ate a peaceful evening meal.

"I think Tombo will be back," he said.

"Sure," said Ryan, scooping up a knifeful of split peas and then, eating them, gesturing toward the unseen land, "and I'm thinking he'll be back with twenty sail or more."

"It isn't Tombo I'm worrying about," said Tiger. "Arif-Emir may come down on us. And he'll be twice as mad. It's his diamond."

"It ain't either," said Walleye. "It's ours. Possession is ten points of the law on the high seas. I wonder if we'll ever live to make liberty on its value."

"I dunno," said Tiger. "Pass the salt horse."

Chapter 8

THE WILLIWAW

The doctor finished binding Jan's head up. "You might have died," he said cheerfully. "An inch to the right and you'd have had a fracture of the skull. The cranium, however, is a most remarkable structure. It has inherent design, according to some engineer up at M.I.T., which resists such injuries to the maximum extent. The skull, he says, is stress-analyzed on the principle of arch supports so that there are at least seven primary arches resisting destruction in the face alone. I believe—"

Jan groaned. He was sitting in the living room where the servants had carried him and the morning sunlight which streamed in was entirely too cheerful to fit his mood. A canary was twittering handsomely beside the yellow drapes and a jay in the branches of a tree outside was making critical comments about the canary's tone truth. The Swede girl was getting in people's way, weeping and apologizing for Jan, and in describing his assailant to the police, had discovered her liaison with the criminal to her own astonishment.

The doctor went on with his lively discussion of the resistances of the skull, completing his bandaging. Alice sat at a secretary desk writing notes of invitation to a tea party and commenting sideways now and then on her amazement that Jan would lie down in his study all night without calling anyone and on her concern that he might miss out on a board meeting scheduled for that afternoon.

Jan, unable to follow anyone's discourse fully and being dazed in the bargain, followed none. Instead he gloomed about his diamond. Lately, he realized, there had been a change. Alice had changed, he had changed. There was something missing but he could not know what it was. There was the matter of the diamond. Somehow, when that had appeared, life had altered. But it had not altered because of the diamond, possibly. The diamond was part of a picture. Jan wanted to know the whole picture. The diamond, he had felt, would have changed things again and for the better. But now it was gone, never, he felt, to be regained.

Alice remarked for the severalth time that after all, he did have a board meeting and he took this fact between thoughts and used it as his excuse to get away from these people.

He tottered upstairs, the Swede girl following after, wringing her fingers and hoping she was not going to be blamed. Jan closed the door to his bathroom and so separated himself from her wailing.

He shaved gingerly, nicking himself several times. The act tired him and when he came out he was unable to face the additional task of changing his pants. Besides, the Swede girl was still there. He put on a clean shirt, for the old one was stained with his blood, and squirmed into a sport coat. He staggered down the stairs, the Swede girl following him. Alice was at the bottom.

"Dear, I hope you feel better," she said. But before he had a chance to warm to this, she added: "And please mail these letters on your way to the office. It will take a load off me. I am so busy."

Jan took the letters. He was about to reply submissively when he astonished himself. "Mail your own damned letters!" he said. "What the Great Horn Spoon's the idea trying to make me run your errands? What am I, an errand boy? And as for you," he roared, turning on the Swede girl, "go down to your galley and stay there and shut up that confounded yapping! And if I ever catch you haying around with another condemned Commie I'll give you exactly what you deserve, a taste of the cat! Now!" he barked, dropping the letters and thrusting Alice aside, "get out of my way and stay out of my way."

He left and the two women promptly collapsed into one another's arms in an orgy of tears.

Jan reached his car and recollected himself. He was somewhat startled now that he looked back on his own conduct. He was almost remorseful when he thought of the stricken look on Alice's face. After all, she had done nothing—she had so often said so and was oh so very right. But a sterner gleam came into his eye and he drove workwards at great speed and with considerable recklessness.

He entered the Palmer Building, conscious of a headache but caring nothing about it. He swept through the outer offices of Bering Steam like an Alaskan williwaw, leaving papers to spin and settle in his wake. He entered his office, shot all the correspondence off his desk which, of old, he slavishly signed and began to push buttons.

The board had decided the name of the lately launched ship. He himself had considered Zachariah Palmer an avaricious, selfish disgrace to the race, who knew no interest that was not dollar marked. The board had blandly overridden his objections just as they had been overriding everything he said lately. He was conscious that he had known for days now that three members were jockeying Bering stock to get an advantage. With that advantage they would monopolize certain portions of Alaskan trade in such a way that freight rates would soar. In capitalistic short-termism this same group had overridden the Alaskan Highway, thinking it would injure Bering's trade traffic, overlooking the fact that you need a population to have trade and that you need fast highway transport to have a population. Jan wanted that ship named *Greg Palmer* after the only Palmer he had ever respected. And he wanted Bering to throw its weight behind an Alaskan Highway that was a highway, not a military miscarriage designed to favor Canadian mining interests. And he punched the buttons loud and long.

But he didn't get members of the board or vice presidents right off. He got instead a squat, square, self-assured, bad-mannered example of the underprivileged called a Union Delegate. This individual happened to be a member of the Friends of Russia Communist International Objectors Seaman's Union Local No. 530 and he dwelt under the remarkable assumption that anyone who belonged to a democracy or indulged in trade was a capitalist and that only Communists were free and he believed besides that the only way Communism could make the world free was to enslave it and the only way to do that was to set up a super-capitalism called Sovietism. But however confused might be this character's ideologies, his manner was forthright. He had just finished intimidating two Bering captains into thinking that the crew really commanded the ship through the Union Delegate and, having heard that young Palmer had "gone soft in the head lately" was commenced upon a course of persuading him that the crews really commanded the company as well. This individual, by name, Simon Lucar, came in, picking his teeth, his hat on the back of his head.

Knowing well that the best defense is an attack, Lucar sought to unsettle his opponent by beginning, "We've had a lot of charges lately about racial discrimination, Palmer. People with no other nationality than 'United States' have been permitted to hold jobs on your ships! This discriminates against all the minorities! I want it stopped! I want to inform you here and now that by the terms of our contracts, our hiring hall gets to appoint all the jobs on every ship whether the men can do the work or not. You have let two men be hired as oilers just because they knew their work. Did you inquire if they were minority members? No! Did you pay them the same wages as the downtrodden minority members like the Bulgarians? Yes! This is intolerable! I—"

Jan had measured him up and down. "Who the hell are you?"

Lucar drew himself up. "I am the Union Delegate from the Seaman's Local No. 530. I—"

"We deal with American unions only and you know it!" said
Jan. "We use you only when your dirty tactics make us short on
crews. Get out!"

"You can't bully me, you—you capitalist!"

"You get out or I'll throw you out!"

"Racist!" jeered Lucar, measuring up Jan's slightness in-
accurately.

There was a crash. It was Lucar going backwards through
the glass door. There was another crash. That was Lucar being
picked up and launched battering-ram fashion across the hall to
bring up against the men's room. "I'll get you!" whined Lucar,
struggling up.

"Go to hell!" said Jan.

Lucar instantly collapsed. He collapsed in a very peculiar way.
He collapsed as does a man when he is dead.

Jan started to grab his collar but the pallor on the man's face
told him something. His rage cooled. His timidity returned. He
bent and felt for a heartbeat. There was none!

Jan began to tremble a little. The man was dead. He was not
cut or badly bruised. But he was dead. Peering stenographers
gathered. Somebody sent for a doctor. Somebody else sent for the
police.

Jan pushed through the crowd and staggered back to his office,
broken glass crunching underfoot. He leaned against the wall and
reached into his pocket with a quivering hand to get his handkerchief and mop his face. But he did not contact a handkerchief.
He contacted a cool something. He grabbed and hauled it forth.

The diamond!

Dizzily he went over the morning's events and the events of
the night before. The diamond had been stolen. But here it was
in his pocket! It must have been in his pocket all morning! Big
as it was he had not realized it!

The diamond. He had not done enough to this Commie to
kill him. Besides, it is impossible to kill Commies with a tap on

the head. This diamond swapped souls. What had happened? He was not the Commie and he wasn't transferred anywhere. What had occurred?

Suddenly Jan flashed brightly. He had said something right there at the last. Something— Ah! He had said "Go to hell!" Had the Commie actually gone?

Hurriedly Jan thrust his way through the crowd. He could hear the elevators bringing up people. He knew police would be there in an instant. He held the diamond close to the Commie. "Come back from hell!"

The Commie did not stir.

This added a frantic note to Jan's voice. Something was wrong. He looked at the diamond. Suddenly he saw the tetrahedron within it. Banishing and conjuring signs were well known to Jan. The diamond was flat. The tetrahedron was pointed toward one flat surface. To conjure, or invoke, the point would have to be upwards.

"I conjure you to return from hell!" said Jan.

The Commie stirred! Jan's breathing became a little less irregular. The stenographers drew back. Two police officers shouldered in. The Commie sat up, eyes caught for an instant by the flash of the diamond. Then he looked up and saw Jan. He let out a scream and wriggled back. He saw the police.

"Arrest that man!" said the Commie with that opportunism which has spread the ideology so far amongst morons. "He attacked me with a deadly weapon!"

"Who attacked who?" said one of the police.

"He attacked me!" yelped the Commie. "He suddenly went crazy! Insane!"

"Did you?" said the officer.

"Yes," said Jan. "I—"

"Have to come along with us," said the officer. "You too if you want to prefer charges," he added to Lucar.

"But this is Mr. Palmer, president of Bering Steam," said a clerk.

"Don't care who he is," said the officer. "Law is law."

Unappreciative of this point in the mechanics of democracy and probably never realizing that if he had been up against a *commissar*, not a mere corporation head, he would, by now, have been riddled in his tracks, the Commie tailed triumphantly along. "He suddenly went insane," he informed all who asked. And "went crazy and attacked me" became the statement on the blotter.

At the station Jan was booked, fingerprinted, photographed and stripped of possessions. The diamond, as the dangerous weapon, had been taken from him immediately after arrest, before it could be used by Jan's dazed wits. The diamond was placed, with Jan's wallet, rings and tiepin, in a box and the box was put in the safe. Jan was herded into a cell.

He was confident that his attorney would have him bailed out of there in a matter of a few hours. In that confidence he was mistaken. The board of directors, intent upon blocking a highway, managed to dissuade the company lawyer from posting bail, and, in view of the fact that Jan had once been accused of murder, bought further delay by sending a psychiatrist down to see Jan in the jail, meanwhile informing Alice that her husband had been taken ill. These little tasks attended to, the board went on quietly with its meeting, hopeful that it could have another session tomorrow and the next day and the next and so settle things very much its own way throughout the concerns of Bering Steam. Palmer had been too definite lately, they agreed, forgetting the last few days of relapse.

The psychiatrist was a very learned man if not quite bright. He examined the idea that the blow on the head might have unsettled Jan's wits but being a rather backward individual the psychiatrist had neglected to read anything about Dianetics, though it was well known to his fellow psychiatrists.

Dr. Dyhard looked fixedly at Jan and tapped his pince-nez on his thumb.

"My boy," said Dr. Dyhard, "I see definite indications here of a classic schizophrenia with paranoid delusions. You maintained this diamond was stolen from you last night by a Communist lumberjack. You committed mayhem on a Communist union leader today. The diamond was still in your possession this morning, therefore you must have merely fallen and bumped your head. I believe you consider yourself to be persecuted. As a capitalist you doubtlessly believe that your persecution comes from Communists. My boy, Communism is merely an ideology. It is just an idea. There is no danger from Communism. Communists were our firm allies in the last war. They are not persecuting anybody.

"Now I tell you what I propose to do. You once were accused of murder. You were jailed for it. Oh, I know, I know. You were acquitted. But here you are trying to murder somebody again. This is a dangerous situation. You must learn to control yourself. There is a new operation called the transorbital leukotomy which is just what you need."

Jan hitched himself further back on the bed. "I don't need any operation."

"It is my belief you have delusions, my boy. We can cure you of anything with neurosurgery. It will adjust you. It will make it so that you don't become angry. It will make you much more tractable."

"A what?" said Jan.

"A transorbital leukotomy. It is a very simple operation. The patient is given an electric shock which burns out some of his troublesome brain. Then a long thin instrument is inserted into the skull just above the left eyeball. The instrument is then delicately swept from left to right so that it tears up the neurones in the frontal lobes. Then the patient is given another electric shock, a mere 110 volts AC from temple to temple. The long thin piece of steel is then inserted above the right eyeball, thrust in several inches as before and gently swept from right to left which tears up the rest of the neurones in his frontal lobes. Then he is given another electric shock. A few days later he may recover. After that his delusions do not worry him. Nothing worries him. He is adjusted—"

"This is not a real operation!" cried Jan.

"Oh, but it is!" said the psychiatrist. "And that is exactly how it is done. We neurosurgeons have the answer to sanity, all right. People never give any trouble when we're through with them. You'll be adjusted, able to perform simple tasks like feeding yourself and you'll have no further anger toward people—"

"Stop it!" cried Jan. "You're giving me the creeps! This doesn't really happen in this modern society! It sounds like the Dark Ages or Aztec sacrifices or—or—"

"Ah, but it is what is being used everywhere," said the psychiatrist persuasively. "We have many, many techniques. First, there's electric shock. That cures most people. Thirty or forty shocks and they aren't much concerned about thinking anymore. Then there's insulin shock—"

"What's the difference between such treatments and Bedlam?" cried Jan.

"Oh, a world of difference," said the psychiatrist. "We are scientific about it. Then we have the prefrontal lobotomy. In the old days people used to recover from one—the neurones would grow back and they have been known to think again. But we have fixed that. Now we cut out a big piece of skull and take out a wide section of the frontal lobes—"

"But the frontal lobes are what make man a thinking animal!"

"Precisely. And insanity comes from thinking. Men think and men go insane, therefore thinking is insanity. We have worked it all out perfectly. Then we have the topectomy. This instrument is like an apple-corer. It takes long, cylindrical sections out of the brain—"

"That's vivisection! You're experimenting on human beings!"

"Ah, but they are all crazy human beings," said the psychiatrist. "That is the difference. Everybody knows there will never be any cure for thinking. Freud has failed. Everyone has failed. And our patients are tractable, very tractable, most of them."

"*Most* of them?"

"Well," hedged the psychiatrist, "less than half of them get much worse after the operations but we can always keep them in institutions and out of sight."

"People must get killed with these things!" cried Jan.

"Mortality rate is very, very low," said the psychiatrist. "You'd be surprised. Less than a quarter of the people die on the table. My boy, we psychiatrists are scientists. We have said so. We do these operations on people in every institution in the land. Why it is an automatic procedure. Once people are sent to an institution they come into our hands and what we say is right is right because we say it is right. And," said the psychiatrist, getting angry at this rebuttal against authority, "if you think you or anybody else can question our right to do these things you are mistaken. Now I have tried to use persuasion. I will have to use force! You need treatment because I have said so. And you're going to get treatment!"

"I won't sign any paper!" cried Jan.

"I am afraid," said the psychiatrist, "that it is out of your hands."

"My wife won't sign any paper!"

"I phoned your wife before I came to call on you. Your company asked me to look you over. I told your wife strong means, maybe an operation was in order. And she wept and said it was too bad but if a psychiatrist said so, it must be so. There is only one cure for these rages you indulge yourself in. And that is a transorbital leukotomy!" He was getting quite purple.

"Do you mean to tell me I have no civil rights left?" cried Jan.

"Look at your rage! You think you are being persecuted right this minute!" said the psychiatrist. "You think people are against you. You think I am against you! That's insanity! Who supposes anyone has any civil rights when he is insane! Who has any say-so about insanity but a psychiatrist. You claim that is a denial of democracy and an invasion of private liberty. That proves you are a paranoid! You think you are being persecuted! That proves it! You think I am against you! You'll see who has the say now!" And he ground his teeth. He reached out to grab Jan and Jan, humanly, struck back.

The psychiatrist fell against the bars.

"Guard!" he screamed. "Guard!" and Dr. Dyhard's knees were shaking in terror. "Let me out of here! Let me out! I'm caught! I'm trapped! Let me out! He's a maniac!"

The guard hastily let Dr. Dyhard out. Dyhard, safe on the other side of the bars, straightened himself up with vicious jerks. He glared at Jan with eyes bloodstained with anger. "I'll call an ambulance from the state hospital!" said Dyhard. "This man is hopelessly insane. A classic paranoid schizophrenic."

Down at the Friends of Russia Communist International Objectors Social Hall where the conservatives of Moscow met, Lucar told his story several times. It is not often that a Communist can succeed in getting a capitalist in jail and all were interested. A couple of fellow travelers, men who spread the word without getting paid in rubles for doing it like Lucar and Davies, heard the embroidered tale and, being employed on newspapers, saw that the word was spread on page one of the evening dailies.

But though all Seattle may have read about it, only one pair of eyes, scanning that bit of gratuitous propaganda, leaped and shifted with interest. Chan Davies, who had been hiding in terror all day, certain that the diamond had been stolen from him in sleep, sure that somebody knew, writhed and wriggled happily at this news and came out from under a culvert near Redmond and hooked a ride into town.

He went boldly, if crabwise, up to the back door of the Palmer mansion and coaxed the Swede girl out into the dark. Just as he had originally convinced her that the Swedes were discriminated against as a minority in America and thus that all Swedes should invest savings with Communist organizations because only Communism could protect them, now he convinced her that he had been the victim of Jan's racism rages.

After all, it said right in the story that Jan was frothing about Communism and had attacked every Communist in sight and it also mentioned a diamond which he had in his possession. It became obvious that the diamond was something Jan had tried to pin on Davies just to persecute Communism.

He was soon explaining all over again to Alice what had happened. Alice, weeping, assured him that if any charges existed they would be dropped. She was very upset by Jan's suddenly going mad and this strange persecution complex he had. She had just now signed commitment papers and a slip giving Dr. Dyhard the right to do all within his power to make Jan tractable. And she was now on her way down to the jail to pick up Jan's possessions.

Chan Davies writhed and wriggled and said he would be happy to go along and act as bodyguard. Alice accepted his offer with thanks.

But law, when they had arrived at the station house, forestalled any plot Davies might have had afoot. The sergeant in charge of prisoners' possessions was courteous but to the point.

"I am sorry, Mrs. Palmer," he said, "but it so happens that your husband's possessions were, if I may say so, a little funny. He had a diamond on him as big as my palm."

"Yes, of course," said Alice. "And he bought it, I suppose, for a present for me. I have come for whatever he left here."

"Well, as a matter of fact, Mrs. Palmer," said the sergeant, "unless you've got a bill of sale for that diamond or can tell me where it was bought, I'm afraid we're going to have to hold it."

"What?" said Alice.

"You see, when it comes to a stone that big being in the hands of a nut—excuse me—of a prisoner, we can't take too many precautions. Do you know where he bought it?"

"Why no. Can't you contact him?"

"Ma'am, he's out of reach now. They took him up to the spin-bin."

"But surely you can't hold property just on suspicion!"

"I'm sorry, ma'am, maybe we can't but we're doing it. The United Jewelers of America list a flock of big stones as stolen and we're checking with them. It'll take a few days. If we can't find out if it *was* stolen, then we'll have to return it, of course. But as long as we've got it, we're checking."

"That's illegal," said Alice.

"That's good sense," said the sergeant. And as far as he was concerned the interview was over.

Alice shrugged, put the wallet and small possessions in her purse and guarded by a tragically disappointed Davies, drove back home again.

Chapter 9

*B*UCKAROONS

For nearly the entire day Tiger was too busy with ships to worry about diamonds. Once upon a time these renegades had had a purpose. Escaped slaves, all, they had sought to form a revolution against the rule of the Jinn. With headquarters on a small island called Denaise, they had for many years recruited and plotted. But the Jinn were many and the temptations were great and they had slipped away from their original plan, misguided by the ease with which they gained loot and blunted by the tenacity of the Jinn to control the world.

Their original emperor had been named Lenny. A dreamer and an organizer, he had yet lacked the ability to execute his plans when execution was due. Lenny had had on his staff several talented and worthwhile officers but he had also had one Stahlbein. Stahlbein had made himself extremely useful; he seemed to be much in sympathy with all plans as drawn. He attended to all correspondence and legal work and gradually, since he was efficient, details became more and more left in his hands. One day he could suddenly carry out his own plans. Seeing the folly of the idealism of Lenny and sharing none of the human sympathies of the initial planners, Stahlbein knew no remorse for what he did. Lenny and his closest officers were taken ill suddenly and as suddenly they died. Announcing the fact as an act of Jinn, Stahlbein, all innocence, stepped into command, a command he had long organized and shaped to his own designs, which had nothing to do with idealism. Stahlbein had seen that he had a powerful and rapacious group in these escaped slaves. He had chosen piracy, masking it under the name of vengeance and assuming the vain-glorious name of the Thunderbolt, had sailed forth on expeditions of avarice and rapine. He had murdered and ravaged when Lenny would have saved. He had enslaved when Lenny would have freed. He had used Lenny's doctrines to pervert and blind his crews. And, degenerated at last into mere buckaroons, they had abandoned themselves to slaughter for the sake of slaughter.

Tiger knew some of this. He learned more. He found that there were still able people in these crews and these he promoted to proper station. He rid the ships, by launching them in a cutter to make their way home, of eighteen malcontents with the new order. And likewise he rid the vessels, but with vinegar and sulphur, of other vermin.

There was a furious energy about Tiger when he had a job to do. True, when his talents were insufficiently occupied and when life was apparently a joke, he could waste himself gloriously. But with a purpose and a need, so long as they lasted, there was no better man than Tiger for any job. In another world he had stability and constancy but no strength or direction. But with the strength and direction in this one, he could and did on occasion work miracles.

By the first dogwatch he had wrought marvels. The maga-zines had been overhauled. Powder had been repackaged into new cartridges. Stores had been sorted, and fouled or spoiled items had been jettisoned. And two general drills had been held.

He had spoken aboard each ship, giving them in tough sailor language, sentiments which might have been couched in much more flowery terms.

"You wanted freedom, you swabs," he had said. "You wanted to master the Jinn. You scrubbed the dog and lined your bellies and forgot your goals. Well, I'm here to remind you. Anybody that's against doing what you originally set out to do, over the side and homeward bound in whatever boats we can spare. The rest of you, if you've got the guts, may be standing up to a

Jinn-officered fleet in a day or two and outnumbered a dozen to one. There's a chance the human crews will sit down on the job for the Jinns. But there's a chance they'll fight. You've monkeyed the deal for years. Now's the time to sling hot pitch. You're for it or agin it. What's it to be? Mastery of the world or a boozing den on Denaise and sometime dancing on Gallows Key? Which is it?"

They cheered him and worked with a will for the most of them were sick of idleness. And they began to shape up ships where wrecks had floated before.

Back aboard the *Terror*, Tiger sat down to dinner in the cabin. Wanna, big-eyed and wondering, sat cross-legged on a cushion and watched him eat. She several times seemed to be on the verge of asking a momentous question and several times held her words. At last when Tiger had finished his food she ventured to speak.

"Tiger—" and there was honey in it. "Tiger, when we're home again, will you—"

"Well?"

"Will you let me wear the diamond?"

Tiger grinned. He reached into his sash. He fumbled for a moment. Then he reached again and searched further. He looked around him on the deck and then, shooting out an arm, grabbed Muddy. But with a very few pats he ascertained that Muddy, who stood the while wailing and slopping soup from the serving tureen he had carried toward the door, was innocent.

With a frown Tiger sank back. He pulled off his headsilk and let his tawny locks into his eyes. He thought. Now and then he pointed a finger in one direction or another as though tallying up his thoughts by cracks in the planking.

"Huh," he said at last. "That's a funny thing. The diamond's playin' games. It's gone, then it's here."

"Maybe it has a spirit that carries it," said Wanna thoughtfully. "In the temple we had three talismans that had spirits which took them around. I remember one of the girls had the office of feeding one of the spirits."

"Probably it was a priest," said Tiger, who cared little for superstitions of the Jinn.

"No, they were real spirits. One of them sang awfully cute."

"I'll bet he did," said Tiger. "But that isn't solving where that diamond goes."

All day long he had had a headache. When they sank the *Graceful Jinnia* he had taken quite a drubbing but afterwards he had never felt quite so carefree. Today he had been far more thoughtful and cautious. Dim recollections of things he felt he had never seen or done were stirring in him. Blast this headache! That wound should have ceased troubling him some time back.

Absently he felt in his sash again. The problem of the diamond weighed upon him. He was sure that anything that valuable, with the three-dimensional Seal of Sulayman in it, had marvelous powers. He had counted on those powers more than he had realized but now, with the diamond missing, he began to understand some of his bravado anent the fleets of Zongri and Arif-Emir. He had planned on the morrow to make a few simple tests. He was sure that it had unexploited possibilities as witness the way it seemed to have transported Wanna to this ship and Tombo and Malek away from it. There was no lack of evidence that the diamond had abilities. Probably it had latent abilities he did not even suspect.

Suppose it did not come back. That struck home. A sense of anxiety, quite foreign to Tiger, was upon him. He felt as though there was a part of him which had come back to him after an absence and he felt also that that part was in trouble. And he felt, suddenly, that he might lose in this contest with Zongri or Arif or both, a thing which had not before entered his head. How much he had counted upon that diamond. He had not known it until this instant when, thinking upon the shoddy ships he now commanded, he realized how much he needed the aid the diamond might have given.

• • •

He stepped out through the stern ports to the small walkway and from this gallery looked down upon the purling white and blue of the wake. He was very thoughtful, a strange thing for Tiger.

He looked toward the even and unmarred horizon. That way lay Tarbutón. He changed his gaze. At a further distance lay Balou. From Tarbutón or Balou a fleet would come forth. Left to join, the fleets of Tarbutón and Balou would soon decide where their mutual interest lay.

Denaise, the stronghold of the buckaroons, lay a hundred leagues to the south, a palm and pine island with a landlocked harbor. Any reduction of it would be expensive to a fleet. Its surrounding cliffs were too high to admit scaling parties; the only attack point was through the harbor mouth. A few guns there could stop an enemy with ease. But when it came to a booty such as this diamond must be, when it came to Tarbutón and Balou joining forces, that attack might be dared and, further, might well succeed. The buckaroons of Denaise had, until now, been a matter of small moment to the Jinn who looked on piracy as no great crime considering the crimes to which they lent themselves in their ordinary courses of action. No, Denaise attacked by thirty-five or forty ships of the line, would fall. Besides, a fort was a kind of trap. He could not retire to Denaise.

From where they stood, reaching idly back and forth, the r'yals of any ship putting out from Tarbutón would be visible. And any vessel approaching Tarbutón from Balou would also be in sight. It had been Tiger's audacious intention to plunge down on either fleet, the moment it showed, and disorganize it. He had hoped to learn to make the diamond help him. If he could master a few ships he was sure that their human crews, advised of the nature of the plans, would desert to the buckaroons. With these ships he might conquer the remainder. With a fleet thus taken and redirected, he had hoped to attack the remaining fleet and so come into command of the sea lanes of the Jinn world. Command of those lanes meant command of the Jinn whose traffic was all by sea.

He sighed. His head ached. He felt unnatural, as though he was also somewhere else. He reached in his sash again for the diamond on the chance that it might have come back. But it had not. Moodily he stared at the wake.

For several days Tiger repeated that gesture, for several days he paced the gallery across the *Terror*'s stern and watched for the coming of the fleets. Each morning he searched Muddy and Wall-eye in case the diamond had come to them. Each morning he made Wanna look through her flimsy clothes to make sure she did not have it. But the diamond stayed away. Time passed. Soon, all too soon for the state of these vessels and the undrilled condition of the gun crews, a fleet would appear. And then, diamond or no diamond, he had no choice but to attack.

Idly the buckaroons stood on and off the coast of Tarbutón, reaching, waring, reaching, watching for the fleets.

Chapter 10

A FASHIONABLE OPERATION

"**H**ow many fingers do you see?" And Dr. Dyhard held up one.

With a dismal sigh, Jan said, "One."

This was an obvious source of aggravation to Dr. Dyhard. He had been conducting these tests for two and one-half hours and he had been getting right answers.

He had had Jan transferred to Balmy Springs up toward Bellingham for Alice had pleaded with him, when she understood how serious the case was, to take every possible step and spare no expense. The last phrase had its own particular appeal to Dr. Dyhard. All his reputable colleagues had adopted Dianetics sometime since and were prospering. Dyhard had never prospered. Too thoroughly bad a surgeon to remain in the A.M.A., he had taken up neurosurgery and from this had degenerated into county work and was almost outlawed for his belief that socialized medicine should be adopted by all his brethren. They, feeling that Dyhard's type could not support a personal practice and must therefore lean on the state, spoke to Dyhard on professional occasions only. But Dyhard was somehow not averse to maintaining his own side practice whenever he could get a patient and had therefore short-circuited Jan from the state institution to Balmy Springs, where, with skill, he could run up a considerable bill. The Palmers, everyone knew, were rich. Mrs. Palmer, Dyhard had found out, was credulous where medicine was concerned. Jan Palmer, Dyhard knew very well, was going to get a ten-thousand dollar neurosurgical operation if it killed him.

"What do the hands of my watch say?" said Dr. Dyhard grimly.

"Three-thirteen," said Jan with patience. He sighed. The room was small, barred and padded. The guard did not appear to be bribable, not that he was honest but only that he was stupid.

Jan raised himself a trifle on the bed, the better to look at Dyhard—and a strange thing happened. Jan's elbow slipped and he bumped his head on the bed upright. Since arriving here some days before he had been remarkably docile aside from some vague stirrings of rebellion. His head hurt furiously for a moment, for the wound was still tender. But instead of seeing stars he saw, strangely, a swinging hurricane lantern, turned low and suspended from an overhead beam. For an instant after the blow he could definitely feel the lift of a ship under him and hear the purl of a wake and the creak of spars in a light window. The odor of pitch and salt lingered with him a moment, then the image faded. The room, the bars and Dyhard steadied into reality and three dimensions. But something had changed. The feeling that he was somewhere else was strong in Jan, the feeling that he was strong was stronger.

For a little while, out of his usually mild eyes, came the solemn but mischievous glance of another self, Tiger.

"Now how many fingers?" said Dyhard, raising two.

"Six," said Jan.

Dyhard blinked and came alive. There was a quiver of eagerness to him now. "What time is it?"

"Twenty-six bells!" said Jan. "Beat it, doc. You're wasting county time."

"Aha!" said Dyhard. "You're beginning to feel persecuted! I can tell! Your auto-erotic libido is converting! Now how many fingers!"

"You better stow it and scram," said Jan, "or I might decide to gnaw them off. Where's the guard? I'm hungry!"

"Hah!" said Dyhard. "Definite malfunction of the libido! I can detect it! A classic paranoid schizophrenic! I knew it!"

"Doc, you're going to be a classic wreck if you don't beat it. Send in my lunch and we'll take this up someday when you're a little more sane."

"Hah! You believe you are being persecuted, don't you? You believe psychiatrists are after you, don't you? Answer me!"

"No, I don't!" said Jan, getting annoyed and feeling stronger.

"That's it, that's it!" said Dyhard. "All you patients think we psychiatrists are after you. You are plotting to kill me now, aren't you? All you patients get these plots!"

"I'm not so damned patient as you'd think!" said Jan, getting angry.

"Hah! Typical. You want to murder psychiatrists, don't you? You're all after us, you patients. But we've got your number! We know what you are plotting against us! It won't do you any good!" He wrote furiously on his pad.

"How old are you?" said Dyhard, looking intensely at Jan.

"Before I'm much older," said Jan, "I am going to enjoy kicking you the hell out of here, doc. Now git!"

"Hah! Persecution complex. A *classic* paranoid schizophrenic! Now tell me honestly, have you ever believed you were god?"

"Have you?" said Jan.

"Defensive and secretive," muttered Dyhard as he scribbled.

"Look, are you going to ring that bell for lunch and get out or am I going to have to—" he started to get up as he spoke.

Dyhard instantly leaped to the bars. "Guard! Guard! I'm caught! I'm trapped! Let me out of here, let me out! He's a maniac! Let me out!"

The guard instantly unlocked the door and Dyhard vanished.

"Calm down, buddy," said the guard at Jan.

"Calm down, sonny," said Jan, "and bring me some lunch. I'm three hours overdue."

But lunch did not come. Instead Dyhard arrived back with his friend Sharpington who, though not a psychiatrist, owned Balmy Springs.

"There he is," said Dyhard. "See that scowl? All classic paranoid schizophrenics have that scowl. All of them."

"Hmmm, yes," said Sharpington, hoping that Dyhard wouldn't kill this patient on the operating table. Patients were getting scarce since Dianetics. Only the electric shock and surgical failures of the yesterdays were taken to private and public institutions now and this Palmer was worth two hundred a week for the time he was here. Of course, on the brighter side, if whatever neurosurgery Dyhard tried came out with the usual lack of success, Palmer would be here for the rest of his life, a zombie without will or coordination, a drooling thing which would have to be fed like a baby and wear diapers.

"You see how he is crouched there to spring?" said Dyhard.

Sharpington watched Jan light a cigarette. "Indeed so," he said.

"Psst!" said Dyhard, wriggling his fingers through the bars at Jan. "How many fingers?"

"Go soak your skull," said Jan. "Where's my lunch?"

"Abnormal preoccupation with self," said Dyhard. "You notice that?"

"Hmm, yes," said Sharpington.

"Good, good, good," said Dyhard, dragging Sharpington away. "Then you can certify as to his irrational conduct."

"Well—" said Sharpington.

"For ten per cent, of course," said Dyhard.

"Naturally," said Sharpington.

"Good," said Dyhard, "we operate tomorrow."

At five they brought Jan his dinner, served without crockery, knives or forks. The guard shoved it under the door and took a second tray across the hall. There a man was leaping up and down, screaming and raving.

Jan ate as best he could and the guard presently came back for the tray.

"What's the matter with him?" said Jan, indicating his neighbor across the hall.

"Him?" grunted the guard. "He ain't got good sense *or* gratitude. They give him the best neurosurgery in the business, a first-rate prefrontal lobotomy and he starts raving as soon as he recovers. The ignorant boob's been screaming like that for two weeks now."

"Do they all scream when they get prefrontals?" said Jan.

"Naw. Usually they're quiet. They just sit and stare. But him, *he* ain't got good sense."

"Does anybody ever recover from a prefrontal lobotomy?" said Jan.

"Naw, but it's the best modern science can offer. That's what they say. But what the hell am I doin' talkin' to you?"

"You're talking to me," said Jan, "because you can make a thousand dollars." He had tried five hundred that morning.

"Whatcha think I am, dishonest? Get back there!"

"Taking five thousand dollars just to carry a message isn't dishonest," said Jan.

"What message?"

"Phone my wife and tell her to bring me the diamond I had."

The guard hesitated. "You loops! I'll do it for twenty dollars cash *if* you've got it on you."

Jan didn't have.

"All the same. Brother, I've collected a couple million in checks and notes that wouldn't pay off. I don't get sucked in again. Besides, you'll be operated on tomorrow and after that you won't never know what you're doin', not never."

He took himself off.

Jan sat down on the edge of the bed. For a while that afternoon he had felt brave. It had seemed as if he had contacted some part of him he had not before known existed. And yet somehow he knew that he had been more complete a short while ago.

A horrible thought hit him. Perhaps he had already had an electric shock! They gave them to people without their knowledge and with only a relative's consent. And they made the treatment look so attractive that relatives almost never disagreed. Perhaps he'd been treated. Perhaps that was why he was feeling so reduced.

The man across the hall was still screaming. Over and over he said, "I'm caught, I'm trapped! Let me out! Let me out! I'm caught, I'm trapped. They'll never believe me. My husband will kill me. I'm caught, I'm trapped. Let me out! Let me out!—"

Jan glanced across at him. The fellow had not been bad-looking. But now his eyes were red-shot and horrible and somehow dead. The screaming was not real. It was automatic, without feeling. It was as if a record had been turned on behind his mouth and was running, over and over.

Up to this instant Jan had not believed that such a thing could happen to a man in these United States. But now the evidence deluged him. By the mere statement that he was insane, made by one man, Jan had instantly been thrust outside the pale of all civil rights. A murderer stood a trial before a jury. Only when convicted was he subjected to physical punishment—and his death was quick; it was not the subtotal euthanasia of neurosurgery. The murderer was killed quickly and wholly in an electric chair or a gas chamber. His body was not left to live after his mind had been killed. And perhaps below the level of that zombyism, trapped somewhere inside but no longer in control, the "I" of the individual remained, shuddering with repugnance at the drooling shell it had once commanded.

Dyhard held authority beyond the authority of mere courts. Draped crazily and unfittingly with the mask of "science," Dyhard could and did execute sentences of subtotal death even when his shocks and operations were successful beyond the highest hopes of the originators of those barbaric techniques which disgraced the name of medicine and polluted the records of surgery.

Jan was beyond any hope of rescue, he suddenly understood. Before that, as a private citizen, he had read of the "marvelous techniques" of neurosurgery. He had read elaborate praises of methods which took out large sections of the brain or withered the neurones with raw shocks. Because the actual results had been masked by the title of "progressive science" and "medicine" he had not questioned figures which he now knew to be utterly fictitious and optimistic beyond madness itself. He understood dimly that these techniques derived from the dramatization of the hostilities of certain psychiatrists, themselves beyond the pale in their own professions.

What happened to the human soul in such an operation? What happened to the personality? Where was the gain, if after the most successful operation possible, a patient was incapable of affection, lost to initiative and adjusted on the order that one would adjust a marionette?

And that this could happen because his wife, ignorant and blindly trusting because medical doctors were trustworthy, had been convinced that it would be a wonderful thing, that he would be a better man, that he would return to society much more tractable and competent. On these assurances, as false as a Russian news release and quite as generally released, she had consented to leave all to Dr. Dyhard. Where was Jan's say? Jan, why, he had been branded with the indelible brand, the brand that none could erase—a psychiatrist had pronounced him insane!

What would happen to him now if he survived the dangerous operation? What would happen if luck decreed him to be one of the few who succeeded to the point of being only half unmanned?

The thought of it made his wits rock in earnest. Was this how unscrupulous psychiatrists made their diagnoses? Badgering a man to disgust and then using what he said to condemn him? He knew now that it was and he knew that if he did not come out of here before operation time tomorrow, he would be better off dead, much better off.

He grabbed the bars and began to examine the locks. But they were sound. And as he stood there a stretcher was wheeled by. On it was a young girl. Blood had spilled and caked from her swollen eyes. Her temples had been scorched by electrodes. Her mouth was slack and one arm dangled rigidly. A transorbital leukotomy, on its way to a cell, a woman, made a zombie forever, her analytical mind torn to shreds, ruined beyond repair.

Jan became sick at his stomach.

At about the time Dr. Dyhard was writing up his operation orders about Jan, that day, Alice sat with teacup balanced on her knee and talked about hats and other vital matters with her friends Julie Breen and Stephanie Gorse. The visitors had more or less exhausted general topics when Julie, desiring gossip for the dinner party she would later attend, led into a topic which should yield it.

"And your poor, dear husband. I understand he was victimized by some labor leaders and taken to a sanitarium," said Julie, all sympathy.

Stephanie delicately nibbled a biscuit. "Ah, what trouble we do have with these unions," said Stephanie sweetly. "Somebody ought to machine-gun such people, my husband says. Mere laborers, entirely lower class, and they cause so much trouble."

"Jan never had any trouble with unions," said Alice. "The unions were glad when he became head of Bering Steam. It's Communists, he says, who make the unions look bad. I always believed unions were an advance—"

But Julie wouldn't let her steer away from this tidbit. "No wonder your poor, dear husband had a nervous breakdown. What are they doing for him?"

"He's in excellent hands," said Alice crisply. "Dr. Dyhard called me a little while ago and said he was going to give him the best treatment available. It's a little operation. A minor thing, Dr. Dyhard said. A pre-fronted something. Really, they only give them to people they can trust, you know. It sometimes uninhibits people. But it makes them better adjusted, too. And Jan has been so badly adjusted lately. It has been quite a worry. He was actually quite rough to me."

"Oh, yes," said Stephanie. "I know the treatment. I read all about it in a medical magazine while I was waiting for my psychoanalyst one day. One has one done and then doesn't worry any more. It said so right in the magazine. I asked my analyst why *he* didn't do marvelous things like that and he wouldn't even talk about it with me."

"Oh, psychoanalysts are always fighting with the psychiatrists. They're not real doctors, you know, the psychoanalysts, I mean. The law wouldn't permit them to operate," said Julie as learnedly as could be expected from one who read *Woman's Day* exclusively.

"Did they try electric shock?" said Stephanie, hastily keeping her lead as the authority present. "My cousin went—had a nervous breakdown and they gave her twenty-one electric shocks. And really, she never knew a thing about it until she was all sane again. It made her well as can be, too. Wonderful, modern science. She used to quarrel with her husband incessantly about his drinking and now she rarely says a thing to anyone."

"I thought electric shocks didn't always work," said Julie, on the other side of the fence now, challenging authority.

"Oh, my dear. Of course they always work. All these operations they use today work or they wouldn't use them, of course," said Stephanie practically. "Of course, she does have trouble—my cousin, I mean—lying down now. Her heart races or something when she tries to sleep. But really she is so changed. She isn't a bit quarrelsome about anything. Tell me, Alice, dear, will your husband be home soon?"

"Oh, in a few days," said Alice. "Dr. Dyhard assured me that it was nothing very serious. Just exhaustion. Worry or something. This little minor operation will make everything right. Isn't modern science wonderful? Dr. Dyhard says he won't worry after the operation. Dear, dear, I almost wish I had one done on me. It's in all the magazines. Quite fashionable, I understand. And so expensive, too. Ten thousand dollars."

"My!" said Stephanie, impressed before she could stop herself. But she was saved the effort of asserting afterwards that she was unimpressed by the appearance of the Swede girl.

The Swede girl was desirous of seeing Mrs. Palmer alone. Alice excused herself, a little haughty as became a working girl who had married a millionaire, and demanded in the hall what the servant wanted.

It seemed that Chan Davies had found out that the chauffeur had quit and wanted the chauffeur's job. Chan Davies had a city license and he was an excellent driver.

Alice interviewed him briefly and hired him, the least she could do after the outrageous accusations her poor demented Jan had made against the fellow who, he was not slow to state, had lost an excellent job because the accusation had been printed in the paper.

Davies thanked her with a bobbing series of writhes which he thought were bows and as she turned to go said, "Oh, Mrs. Palmer. By the way, did they ever give back your husband's property? I have some connections, minor ones of course, but—"

"Why, yes," said Alice. "They did. Thank you for your interest, Davies." And she went back to her tea.

Davies shifted his eyes on and off the Swede girl's face. "I sure hope it's put away safe. I'd hate to be accused of stealing it again like both of us were."

"Yah, it vas safe all right," said the Swede girl, beaming at him and thinking how nice it would be with him working in the same house.

Adroitly he recovered the data that the diamond now rested in a wall safe behind a picture in the library. Despondently he learned that the wall safe had been holding Palmer documents and valuables for years and wouldn't surrender to anything short of dynamite.

He appeared reassured but he went out on the back step and gloomed. Then he brightened. There was just a chance that Stoky Joe was out of jail and might be found at the Social Hall. Just a chance—a very slim chance.

"I think," he told the Swede girl, "that I'll take a run downtown on an errand."

Followed by her fond smile, he sent Jan's roadster skittering down the drive.

Chapter 11

THROUGH FRYING PAN SHOALS

At eight bells in the morning, Tiger was yanked from a gloomy breakfast by the cry, "Tall sails nor'east by north, ten leagues!"

On deck he glanced at the lookout's post at the mizzen truck, and then, to confirm it with his own eyes, went hand over hand up a topping lift and swung his feet to rest on a yard. Hugging the mast he stared, keen-eyed, in a northerly direction and soon caught the white gleam of canvas there. Once his glance had picked that out from the tall cumulus on the far northern horizon above the land he saw another and then another skys'l. It was the fleet from Tarbutón! They were standing out for action. They would have Tombo aboard or in command. The strongest fleet was coming first!

Tiger looked down at the deck far below. The *Terror*, though much groomed, was a pitiful wreck of a ship at best. The others of the fleet, now five in number since fortunes of war had sent merchantmen into their hands, were still far, far less than twenty ships built and drilled for naval war. Pretty as they were, these buckaroon vessels from this height, white decked against blue water, ringed with their own spray and lifting in the swell, they were a mouthful for one broadside from the enemy.

Wrapping his headsilk around the lift, Tiger plumped back to the quarterdeck and brought up beside the helm. "Steer for a weather gauge," he told Ryan who had the watch. "You get below," he said to Wanna who, wind in her filmy raiment, had come bright-eyed up for the sight.

"I won't!" said Wanna. "I've a right—"

Tiger picked her up like a chip and sped down the ladder with her.

Sullenly, she permitted herself to be deposited on the bunk.

"See here," said Tiger. "There's going to be more than enough action for all hands. The deck may be swept by grape and chain. Splinters aren't particular who they hit and I want you whole if I'm to have you at all."

"I won't stay here and drown if we're sunk!" cried Wanna. And then she began to cry.

Tiger looked out through the stern ports. He took a stride and opened them. He thrust the heavy table into the gallery and lashed it there so that when the lashings were cut it would fall into the sea. He came back and gave her a knife.

"If we're lost, saw that table loose. You'll float until you're picked up. Use the knife on any survivors that try to haul you off to save themselves. Now—"

"You are abandoning me," she wept logically. "You mean me to be cast up adrift on some foreign shore, alone, friendless and hungry, prey to anyone who—"

"Stow that," said Tiger. He stood perplexed and then glanced around. Old Thunderguts had had booty aboard. Tiger had never been interested enough to look for it. But now he took in the iron chest against the wall, the ship's safe and with the keys which had come to him, opened it and reached in to grab some gems of value or a little gold she could tie into her girdle against need. He started to reach and then, open-mouthed, he stopped.

"What's the matter?" said Wanna, alarmed at his expression.

Tiger didn't answer her. Before his eyes lay the Two-World Diamond slowly materializing but already glittering brightly in the sunlight from the ports. He swallowed hard, so close had he felt his luck being crowded by the imminence of that powerful fleet. He grinned a grin of relief then and reached for the beckoning stone.

His hand closed.

But it closed on empty air!

The diamond, an instant before he touched it, had disappeared!

Tiger swore and made ineffectual snatches at the place it had been. But the diamond had thoroughly vanished. He sank back on his haunches and passed a trembling hand through his tawny locks. He collected his shattering thoughts. The diamond had not been there the instant he opened the chest. It had been *arriving* there for less than half of it had been visible and even that was somehow nebulous. Had his own reaching for it made it disappear? He thought not.

Vague, half-memories were stirring in him, memories of his life in another world, thin things like dreams. He seemed to be able to touch those memories up to the instant he looked at them, when they vanished as had this diamond. He harked back to the action of the *Graceful Jinnia*. In the boarding, a grizzled Ifrit had swiped at him with the butt of a pike, landing a blow which would have split the average skull. That injury had done him the service of laying him out long enough for the *Jinnia* to be taken without his being killed. He had revived when the Marid marines had picked him up to heave him over the side after the other dead and the conquering officers of Arif-Emir had grudgingly taken him prisoner.

As he thought back, things had shifted at that instant of the blow. Just before that he had been aware of something he could not now locate. It was as if he dwelt without sleeping, as if he lived in another existence. Something was missing from his personality. Legends and sailor hearsay stirred uneasily in him. Another world, a world where humans ruled and Jinns were not. The Two-World Diamond which bestowed immortality on Ifrits— He was Tiger, yes. But he was also an entity elsewhere, somehow.

The Two-World Diamond. Why was it called that? Did it dwell in another world and this? Did it pass from one to the other?

And had it been passing, almost in reach to save him by some miracle he knew it would possess, when somebody in another world snatched it back? Had it come to this chest before?

The thought that it might have been in this chest before made him angry. He got up and booted the chest. Then he remembered Wanna and, stopping, scooped up some of Old Thungerguts' loot, a few emeralds and rubies, and thrust them at Wanna. He slammed the lid.

"Put them out of sight and if we're sunk, do as I say," he commanded. "And stow the gab. I'm busy."

She nodded submissively and he swung back up to the deck. He was out of humor, a strange thing for Tiger, always so strong and sunny.

"Claw up to windward, you swab!" he snapped at the steersman. "Are you steerin' a washtub?"

"Lot of ships up there, Tiger," said Ryan, nodding to the north. "You really mean to attack?"

"We'll attack!" said Tiger. "We can't outrun them. We can at least take a few of them along to hell. I overplayed a hand, Ryan. I was counting on that diamond. It almost came back."

"What do you mean, almost?"

"Sir," said a youngster who served the cabin and whose eyes were sharp, "if you keep on this course, you'll hit Frying Pan Shoals. Beggin' pardon, sir. But I was just aloft."

Tiger looked at the child interestedly and suddenly smiled. The sight of the young face, the sound of such interest beyond his duties, brought Tiger to himself. "Well done, lad. You'll teach Ryan navigation yet. How's it you know so much about shoals?"

"My father was the sea artist for the buckaroons," said the serving lad. "They haven't another, you know, sir, since my father was killed in an attack. They don't know much about navigation, sir, the buckaroons; my father was the assistant astrologer once to Arif-Emir, sir, before he predicted something wrong. He run away with me and became the buckaroon sea artist and he never run aground." He added the last with great pride.

"And you're a cabin boy, aren't you?" said Tiger.

"I didn't mean impertinence, sir. Old Thunderguts, he said he'd kill me if my father ever run them aground and these be treacherous waters, sir. I'm still alive even if my father be dead—but not by shipwreck, sir."

"Enemy hull up and coming fast!" said the lookout far aloft.

"How old are you, lad?" said Tiger, unperturbed.

"Thirteen and I can write, sir, and read the charts and take pelorus sights and take meridian altitude shots and forecast coming events, sir."

"His nickname's Mister Luck," interjected the *Terror*'s bosun, unasked, passing with a work party which was padding the rails with hammocks against the flying of splinters. "And it ain't a complimentary name, skipper. He's been in bad ever since he read stars for Old Thunderguts and said he'd die by necromancy. Get along, sonny."

"Hold up," said Tiger. "I'm giving the orders here. Tend to your hammocks and boarding nets. Now there, Mister Luck, you say you know your charts?"

"All my father ever taught me was stars and charts, sir."

Tiger ran a big hand through the boy's blond hair. "How do you read the coming battle, Mister Luck?"

"How do you want it read, sir?"

"What's the width and breadth of Frying Pan Shoals, lad?" said Tiger. "And how much water in any channel through them?"

"Four channels through, sir. The deepest draws thirty-one feet. The shoals run thirty leagues east and west, sir, and five leagues north and south. Fine fishing grounds. My father could tell you more, sir. We fished there many a time. That was when we had a yacht, sir."

"And how did your father get in wrong with Arif-Emir?" said Tiger.

"Enemy on a broad reach, gun ports down!" cried the lookout high aloft.

"Why he read the stars to say, sir, that Arif-Emir would die in a fit without any soul, sir. And it got worded around the palace, sir. And you're damned near aground, sir."

"Lad," said Tiger, "scamper up to the crosstrees of the fore. Take this brass trumpet. You can call steering orders? Very good, sir. Take us through the main channel of Frying Pan Shoals and your head if we go aground!"

"They're called Allah's Revenge by the Ifrits, sir, and if the lunk on the wheel can steer, sir, we'll not go aground!"

"Wait!" said Ryan to Tiger but the boy was already gone.

"Well?" said Tiger, looking to port where the ships from Tarbutón had grown very tall and very splendid in the bright sunlight against the fleecy clouds.

"Thirty-one feet!" said Ryan. "That will take us through all right. But it'll take the men-o-war through as well. They don't draw more'n thirty, any one of them."

"Pass the signal astern," said Tiger to Walleye, "to follow close in line. We're going through the shoals."

"It's a tricky channel but they can follow!" said Ryan. "You'll get nothing out of it but fifteen miles of uneasy sailing and only six points off the wind in this old hooker at the turns. And that youngun! How'd you know he'll be able to?"

"Old Thunderguts died by necromancy," said Tiger. "And anyone with nerve to forecast that has nerve enough to tell the truth. Old cowards brag, laddie. Walleye, soon as we enter the channel have the ships up sprit to poop. The water's smooth in there if the wind is brisk. I want them *close*. I'm passing aft to the rearguard as soon as we're strung out."

The thin voice of the child in the fore crosstrees, made belllike by the brass trumpet through which he yelled, began to send his orders back. Ryan at first had been much discontented for it is hard to understand how a child may know anything so intricate. But Mister Luck had obviously been conning and charting since he was old enough to shed diapers, such was the confidence of his tones and the accuracy of his commands. Indeed, under the guiding of an indulgent father whom he dearly loved, Mister Luck had started spinning astrolabes when most boys start on tops, and if Mister Luck was short on everything but navigation, a master could have found no fault with his piloting that morning. He was up there looking down from an angle which made "Allah's Revenge" an undersea relief map to him, a chart in itself glassed over by the incredible blueness of the deeps and greenness of the shallows.

"Down a spoke!" came the piping voice up amongst the vast spread of tautened sail. "Ease her! Meet her! Steady as you go! Mr. Ryan, the main r'yal's luffing!"

"The upstart," growled Ryan. But it was true.

To port and starboard the breakers of the main channel were creaming white on reefs. The black ribs of a long-lost ship jutted from the niggerheads on the port bow, the carcass of another was combed by the swell.

The channel entrance was faced to the westward. Far to either side the seas were breaking and the *Terror* for some distance inside, still lifted in a swell. But soon the channel twisted into a southerly course and the swell was gone, broken by the expanses of shoals and shallows. The water became an absinthe green and flat but the wind was brisk and steady at fifteen knots. Ryan leaped about and bawled his commands to trim and brace, scared at the nearness of the fangs of rock at each twist and turn. All they needed, he swore to himself, was a shift of wind and they'd be gallows birds. Ryan allowed he could have run that channel himself but immediately shuddered over the next jagged shelf which came so close it seemed to graze their skin.

"Up, up!" came the bell-like voice from the crosstrees. "Up three spokes. Steady her. Up two more! Ease her. Meet her!"

The brown and mildewed sails slatted and spilled, too close to the wind. Another spoke and they'd be taken aback.

"Down! Down! Down! Down six spokes. Ease her. Ease her. Down another spoke. Ease her! Meet her. Steady as she goes!"

The *Terror* thrust around a channel bend, keeping near the windward bank of the channel. She was doing five knots, foul of bottom as she was, but Ryan and the crew, seeing the closeness of the menace in the murky green shallows and the sharpness of the outcrops lapping white, were absolutely certain she was doing thirty at the very least.

Ryan looked around for Tiger for permission to shorten sail. But Tiger was gone. By orders, four of the other vessels had drawn tightly into a line astern. Their various speeds and sailing and steering difficulties made them jockey and open and close their intervals, now almost overriding the next, now letting a wide gap appear which gave helmsmen an uneasy time in following the *Terror*'s precise wake. All of them on every ship had watched the maneuvers of the Tarbután fleet with stunned forebodings.

It had been very well to talk about actually fighting men-o-war but when they were there, tall mountains of canvas out of black hulls, studded with the brass of polished guns, alive with marine sharpshooters, the stouter hearts skipped a few beats. Twenty-seven ships in that fleet, eight of them first-raters, the rest of them frigates. And the buckaroons recognized the difference between fighting merchantmen and men-o-war with a shock. They were heavy and sluggish as men-o-war will be and the buckaroons at first hoped that they could outspeed them and get by these reefs and with a windward gauge show them clean heels. There had been a chance to do that and it was with dismay that the buckaroons had found Tiger headed into the long and twisting channel of Frying Pan Shoals for it was obvious that the Tarbután fleet could follow and just as obvious that at the far end, only three hours' sail, their position would be no better and probably worse than before entering. Further, a grounding would leave a ship to the mercy of the Ifrit might.

One vessel had not elected to obey Tiger's order. She had plunged out like a hare from the line as soon as her captain read the intent and, setting everything from stuns'ls to the cook's underwear, she had raced seaward, using her weather gauge. Her anxiety was much appreciated by the rest. They followed Tiger but their hopes inclined toward the escaping brig. They watched her staggering forward under her press of sail, they watched her draw ahead and almost cross the bows of the two frigates detached to take her. And then they saw her masts go by the boards like saplings, their rottenness unable to take the strain. The frigates swiftly came up to her and overran her and their gunports thundered white smoke and scarlet against the helpless brig. The acrid mist hid the action but the rolling broadsides told the fate. The Tarbutón fleet was murdering a ship already vanquished and the thin sharp barks of musketry might have been heard thereafter as her survivors one by one were picked off the jetsam to which they had clung. The temper of the Tarbutón fleet against the buckaroons sent a quiver of despair through the remaining five vessels and they threaded close and hot through the tortuous channel.

The Tarbutón fleet, not expecting this but supposing that the buckaroons would flee and trust to the weather gauge and lighter foot, were thrown badly out of formation when Tiger passed into the channel. The Tarbutón vessels, commanded by Ifrits were not bright, only batteringly stubborn and merciless. It took them long enough to recognize what had happened to lose any advantage of an early tack. The entire line of battle went on by well downwind of the entrance. Signal flags jumped high to their yards and fluttered there, commanding sparks of color. The van wore ship and passed the rearguard and came up on a port tack for the entrance. Like a coiling snake, the line of battle followed, the rearguard completing the ware just as the vanguard entered the channel mouth. This channel had no terrors for the Jinn. It was thirty-one feet minimum depth and in most places hundreds of yards wide, narrowing only at three turns where it would still admit a large vessel. A league, because of the overshoot, separated the vanguard of the Jinn from the last of the buckaroon vessels, the lugger Tiger and his mates had first stolen from Arif-Emir at Balou Bay.

Tiger, while Ryan acted as sailing master and the youth called Mister Luck conned from the *Terror*'s fore called for a gig to be lowered and towed astern. As it went under the counter he dropped into it and was paid off until he could swing aboard the vessel next astern. He landed on deck, glanced around and gave a volley of orders. Then he was dropped over again and passed to the third ship where he once more boarded and made his orders known. He visited the fourth and then the fifth and on the fifth he stayed. In the vessels ahead there was much activity. Tiger could look astern down the tortuous length of the passage to the vanguard of the Jinn. Gilded bows and gleaming sail, she rose tall and majestic, her bluff bows whitening the absinthe green of the water, her conning officer, brilliant in lace, insolent on her sprit. Behind her came the Tarbutón fleet, an orderly parade for whom this pass was routine since often, homeward bound, they used it when it served.

Tiger looked ahead. A long bend was coming, a bend which would put the wind on their starboard quarter for a distance of almost three miles. He saw the *Terror*, with much gathering of speed, square away for the run of it. The brigantine behind her entered that portion of the passage. Then a brig and the two luggers of which Tiger's was the last.

Tiger hand over handed into the rigging, a spyglass in his sash. He looked to the end of the downwind pass. After that the passage stretched for several miles, nearly all of it curved to make the run of it a starboard tack. But where the downwind passage turned there was a narrows not three ships' breadth wide.

The last lugger entered the run. The vanguard of the Jinn was a league and a half behind. Tiger swept them with his glass. The Ifrits stood out in their gold lace, the Marids in their green coats. The human crews, scampering to the pop of starters in the hands of Marids, trimmed smartly at each order or stood by their guns, their matches smoking in tubs. How well Tiger knew those ships! How bitter were their crews! But they would shoot on orders and fight on no other ethic than that of high command.

Sliding down the run at increased speed, the *Terror* was shortly through the narrows, tacking sharply to keep from slipping when she had turned. Then, behind her, the brigantine negotiated the turn but hastily furled and got an anchor into the bank about twenty yards beyond the extreme end of the curve. She steadied herself with a kedge and then dropped back toward the narrows with her capstan. A smart sailor that, thought Tiger. One buckaroon would get his due if it all came out all right.

The brig and the next to last lugger had no such difficult maneuver to perform. The brig, at the narrowest part of the passage, simply went hard right and ground into the reefs with a shock and lunge. The lugger went hard left, bounced off the stern of the brig and bludgeoned into the opposite bank.

Tiger glanced back at the Jinn. They were just entering the passage of the run and the vanguard was already picking up speed. At tight and proper battle interval behind them came the rest, twenty-six vessels besides the flag. They made, thought Tiger, a grand and beautiful sight.

With a swift drop down a halyard, Tiger reached the deck just before his own lugger struck. It pointed in toward a small gap which remained between the stern of the brig on the port and the side of the lugger on the starboard. The rendering and tortured squeal of wood and the snap of twisted pins was followed by the shuddering whisper of the masts as they began to fall.

"Stand clear!" barked Tiger. And the sticks went harmlessly down to drag their running rigging and canvas in the sea.

The three vessels, piled tight into the narrows, were unbothered by any swell. They settled gently, crowding and rending each other as the first two slid little by little off and crushed the third. Tiger's lugger was already decks awash. The crew, salvaging their belongings and treasure shares, sped over the settling decks of the brig.

The brigantine, aided by the wind, steadied by anchor and kedge, had eased back until she rested near the forepart of the brig. She was almost aground herself but the crews of the three wrecks could cross to her on hastily thrown gangways of planks and within fifteen minutes of the first grounding, all hands were on the brigantine, staring now at the oncoming men-o-war and at the settling wrecks which blocked, without opening, the narrows.

The Jinn must have seen the first grounding and then the second without suspecting that the way was entirely blocked for such was their angle of view that they would not have seen the complete state of the pass. The vanguard was halfway down the run before she realized it. Thick-wittedly she came on.

With a cool bravado her captain began to furl without haste. A gang of human sailors were driven forward, swarmed around the kedge and struggled aft with it under the stinging whips of the Marids. Signal flags snapped into view in the rigging of the flagship. The weigh began to come off the vanguard. Her kedge, properly hawsered, was dropped astern and she came to a steady, slow halt, still in channel, still intact. It must follow that she had to manage to turn herself with capstan and wait for a shift of wind or kedge herself up out of the pass. Behind her, with naval precision, the identical maneuver was carried out ship after ship.

Ten vessels, which had not yet entered the pass and could, by kedging, turn and reach back to sea the way they had come, were stopped by signals. All went smoothly with the eighteen remaining ships in the pass until a first-rater, the *El Zidan*, by some accident failed to grapple bottom. As eighth in line of battle, she had seven ships between herself and the blockade.

High-sided, sails still exposing great resistance to the freshened wind, the *El Zidan* crashed into the *Sapor* and tore out the *Sapor*'s kedge which, when it caught again and tried to hold two great ships, shattered the hawsers. With the wind pressing them, the *El Zidan* and the *Sapor* crushed into the *Ramus* and the three gathering weigh and pressed harder by the resistance they offered, swept rapidly down upon the remaining ships and smashed all into the narrows, a tangle of spars and rending hulls and falling rigging. Only two ships of the eight had held their own. The flagship, borne down upon by the mass was crushed into the barrier, her masts snapping into stumps.

A greedy and high-pitched fire chattered in the rigging of the brigantine. At a range of less than a hundred yards the buckaroons, freshly reminded of the activities of Ifrits by the fate of their shipmates who had sought to escape earlier, poured an accurate fire into the wreckage with every small arm to hand. Their targets were Ifrits and Marids, particularly Ifrits, and the targets, gleaming in gold and scarlet, could not well go unremarked. Many an Ifrit dragged himself from the water back into the tangle of wreckage only to fall dead with a buckaroon slug in him. Many another raised a sword to indicate the brigantine as a target to some Marid sharpshooter he had located and went into the sea before the command could be uttered, shot thoroughly and gleefully by a buckaroon.

The tangle of ships, the disorder of men and the clutter of entwined spars and hemp and canvas was so great that it was not possible to remove every officer by such execution and a small party was organized out of the wreckage to attempt to bridge the gaps and charge the brigantine. Marids and Ifrits and a handful of zealous humans were permitted to reach the coral just astern of the brigantine when a puff of grape wiped the coral clean.

And tangled up and confused in the wreckage was Admiral Tombo, rewarded by such command for his valor at Balou Bay. A dozen times death had whispered close to Tombo, a score of times he had sought to organize a means of attacking the brig which towered above the wrecks. And then death whispered closer.

Sliding an inch of sharp steel into Tombo's back as the admiral stood on a tilted quarterdeck, Tiger said, "Be quiet now, admiral dear. One word of alarm and you're dead." One word of alarm would have been lost in the screaming din and Tombo twisted around to see Tiger, water dripping from him after his swim, teeth set in a hopeful grin. Tombo succumbed.

Two hours later, in the cabin of the brigantine, Tiger received the complete and unconditional surrender of all ships and men in Admiral Tombo's command.

The haggard Ifrit, as thoroughly frightened of Tiger as if that gentleman were Sulayman himself, went passively into captivity. Tiger had gained some four thousand human sailors and considerable armament.

But the victory was short. The *Terror*, uninformed of the action until she had seen it happen so that if it failed the main buckaroon vessel and Wanna would escape, sent back a sailing cutter as soon as she was near the end of the channel through the shoals.

A pop-eyed Ryan was told what had happened and why all these strange sailors were cheering Tiger for their deliverance. The telling was done in the cabin of the brigantine and Tiger was anxious to start up to the deck and pass a signal to the intact men-o-war.

"You can spare that," said Ryan. "It's evening and the wind's shifted. Your birds have flown. You got six out of twenty-eight and that's wonderful but twenty-two sail are gathered up there on the north end of the passage."

"I've got their surrender right here!" said Tiger.

"You ain't got the surrender of Arif-Emir," said Ryan. "And he's right there with 'em with fifteen more men-o-war. They're peaceful. Go see for yourself from the truck."

Tiger knew Ryan. He didn't have to look. "Fish out all pulling boats from the wrecks. Cram them with men and weapons. We're making a run for Denaise and with luck we'll be there before two days are out."

"Where do you think those fleets will head?" said Ryan. "Denaise! And they may make it before us!"

"We've got to try," said Tiger. "Lively! Let's go!"

Chapter 12

TRAPPED!

Jan woke with a strange tension in him. For a moment he hung between slumber and wakefulness, a sound lingering in his ears, the combined sibilance of water rushing under a keel, the whistle of wind in the standing rigging, the slither of steering cables. He felt for an instant the rise and buck of a vessel striking urgently through the seas and then the sound and the feeling faded from him and he saw overhead the dirty white of the sanitarium ceiling. He tried to orient himself back to where he had been. He knew he had been elsewhere but a moment before and now he was here but he could not recall. He sat up rubbing his eyes and yawning.

A new sound was coming to him now. It was an automatic, emotionless screaming, "Let me out. Let me out. I'm caught, I'm trapped. Let me out." The prefrontal lobotomy case across the hall, the case which had not been a success, had begun his daily rote.

Jan shuddered. He recognized his whereabouts, he knew what day this was. By evening he might also be screaming some nonsense or, at best, sitting with a dead-man's stare, finished and done.

An optimism came to him. Alice might have gotten a writ of habeas corpus or some such thing. It was early—and then he saw the slanting rays of the sun and saw how little they slanted from the bars. It was almost noon. The institution had let him sleep, saving a breakfast.

He pulled on his clothes and while in the act he heard them coming up the hall. He looked around. There must be some weapon he could use, some way he could defend himself against this mockery of modern science. But the sanitarium was not in the habit of making things easy for a rebellion.

But they did not stop before his door. Instead they halted across the way where the prefrontal lobotomy case screamed monotonously. Dr. Dyhard and two student neurosurgeons looked interestedly at the case.

"If he had been a classic schizophrenic," Dyhard said, "the operation would have been more spectacular for he would have been far more insane."

"What was his psychosis?" said an interne.

"Why, as for that," said Dyhard clearing his throat, for the chant seemed to make him very nervous, "he demonstrated some very strange reactions. It was most difficult to classify him, most difficult. He was clearly mad, though. He saw two waiters in the ink blot test."

"Ah!" said both internes. "Two waiters!"

"Bowing!" said Dyhard for emphasis.

"Ah!" said the internes.

"What was his classification?" said an interne.

"Very difficult, very difficult. He came to us suffering from chronic alcoholism. Family very wealthy, very. And—"

"What psychosis?" persisted the interne.

"Very neurotic," said Dyhard wisely. "Drank."

"Ah," said the internes.

"And we gave him the best we could offer. Family very anxious to have it done swiftly. No time for Freudian treatment."

"No Freud?" said an interne.

"Would have been long and difficult and we're so pressed for time. Besides, he had been psychoanalyzed eight times. He came to us too late. And so we gave him the best we could offer—"

• • •

Two male nurses came, one of them carrying a straitjacket, the other carrying a stretcher. They brushed by the trio at the door, entered the cell and with expert twists soon had the madman prone, bound and ready to be taken away.

"You gentlemen," said Dyhard, "will be interested in this. The topectomy is very new. It was imported you know. From the very smartest clinics in Europe."

"That was the transorbital leukotomy," said an interne apologetically coughing behind his hand.

"Ah, yes. Of course," said Dyhard. "But you'll be interested in this topectomy. The instrument is not unlike an apple-corer. First one takes out a round section of skull about two centimeters or so in diameter. Then one selectively reaches into the brain and carves out a section."

They had begun to walk down the hall where the victim lay upon a wheeled table now.

"We've been able to do some wonderful research with topectomies," continued Dyhard. "One can take out the part of the brain which inverts images. He can take out the part which translates sound into thought. He can remove the portion which registers physical feelings. Very useful operation. I am sure that by removing a certain section from the patient here we can stop his screaming very easily."

"Ah," said the internes and the trio followed after the table and out of sight.

Jan had no thought of breakfast. He waited dismally, hopelessly. According to what he had been taught in school the prefrontal lobes were that portion of the brain which distinguished man from the lower animals. In elementary psychology, much stress had been placed on this by the instructor, a kindly old professor who held the remarkable tenet that much was yet to be learned about the mind, that psychology, if a science, was, in 1936 at least, a very inexact one at best and that someday someone might resolve the riddle of human behavior. He had laid considerable stress upon the fact that the two lobes behind the forehead, at the front of the brain, were much larger in man than any other animal and that they probably contained that ability to rationalize which made man a rational being. What would happen, Jan thought anxiously, when his prefrontals were sliced to ribbons by Dyhard? It seemed logical that insanity was irrationality. Why seek to cure it by damaging beyond hope the only part of the mind which made man rational. What strange insanity was this which stalked the society wherein the most elevated "healers of the mind" slashed and stabbed and withered with electricity the only portion of the mind where sanity lived? Could it be that some of those "healers" through long association with insanity were, themselves, no longer sane?

He shuddered as he waited through the hours. The sun slanted down into the west and his cell was but dimly lighted when they came again into the hall. The two nurses were wheeling a something on a table. They deposited it in the cell across the way and ran their cart to Jan's cell door.

Jan thought of resistance and then recalled the straitjacket. He was too slight to fight them. His wits racing wildly, thinking hard for the last time he might have the chance, he submitted in the hope of a future moment better suited to an all-out effort.

They saw he was docile and let him sit on the cart.

The thing they had brought back Jan had supposed to be still under an anesthetic. But as he passed the door he saw that the drugs had worn off. The thing would need no further drugs now, no alcohol, nothing. It was awake, staring vacantly at the ceiling. Tractable now, it obviously was, and it would so remain until the mercy of death came to it. The operation had been an entire success.

Jan clenched the edge of the table. The nurses were watchful but they had brawn and there was no place to run.

Evidently Dyhard, after the morning's operation, had gone about his affairs for he entered the hall now dressed in his street clothes. He saw Jan being wheeled by and Dyhard's eyes kindled with suspicion.

"It won't do you any good to plot," said Dyhard. "Watch him closely now," he admonished the nurses. And walking at a respectful distance behind the table, followed on into the operating room. He saw that Jan was laid out on the table and then started for the washroom to remove his street clothes.

The instant Dyhard was through the swinging doors, Jan measured the situation and executed the action.

"I can pay you twenty thousand dollars apiece if you will get me out of here!" he said urgently to the male nurses. "I'm Jan Palmer, head of Bering Steam—"

"Pleased to meetcha. I'm Rockefeller," said the shorter nurse.

"Lie down!" said the other.

Jan appeared to lie meekly back. But the moment the shorter one leaned over to fix the straps, Jan exploded. He chopped a short rabbit punch to the base of the man's skull and then, throwing himself forward, struck the other with both feet. That one sailed backwards. Jan reached the door and flung it open. He was about to dart through when the guard, approaching at that moment, enfolded him in a crushing grip and bore him struggling back. The nurses were on him in a moment and the three carried him to the table.

Swearing, the shorter nurse drew a straitjacket from a closet and they crammed Jan into it. They laced his arms around behind his back in a hugging position and then they tightened the laces so hard that it was all Jan could do to breathe. They slammed him to the table and brought up the web straps three inches wide and buckled their huge buckles tight. Jan looked at the ceiling light, dazed with lack of breath and numb from the tightness of the straps. The shorter nurse put his head in a vise-like set of prongs. The other seized a razor and shaved the hair off one side of Jan's head.

They were satisfied now, their hostilities properly abreacted. And the shorter one went about laying out the sterilized instruments. Jan could see and hear them as they were lined in a glittering row on a tray. There was a device like a brace and bit which was obviously used to drill a circle out of the skull. There were long wire loops. There was a long, sharp knife and another instrument like a buttonhook.

Dyhard came out putting on his rubber gloves. The shorter nurse tied a face mask on him and Dyhard looked with grim eyes at Jan. They were the kind of eyes one might expect in a Roman audience or in a father accustomed to beat his child or an executioner bent on doing his public duty.

An apparatus was wheeled to the head of the table and an oxygen valve was turned out.

"Please," begged Jan. "Please don't. Please don't. I—"

They slammed a cone over his face. He tried to hold his breath and could not. He heard the rattle of instruments on the tray and the click-click of the brace and bit affair being tested and extended to drill the proper-sized hole in the bone. There was a pass across the shaved portion of his head and it went cold with alcohol.

He was unable to hold his breath longer. He expelled it and, sucking back, took nitrous oxide into his lungs. The cone on his face seemed to spin. His reactive mind would record and remember all this and the last glimmer of his analytical mind told him that he was probably in his last moment of sanity. After this—

The point of the bit began to screw into his bone. His scalp jerked away from it. He tried to keep from taking another breath but he could not. The cone spun faster and faster before him. The bit was finding a hold in his skull and the worm was going deeper. The extension blade began to sweep a circle.

Suddenly Jan was not looking at the cone. He was staring at an overhead hurricane lamp and he heard a plunging ship. His skull hurt damnably and he felt wrath sweep through him. Suddenly there was the cone again and the agony of the biting bit. But as suddenly he flexed his arms.

There was the crack and pop of webbing, the rip of canvas jacketing and the snap of laces which went like thread.

Tiger, strong and mighty, snatched at the auger and twisted it out of his skull! He sent the instrument crashing into Dyhard's face. With a leap he came off the table, leaving the frayed straps behind and with a sudden snatch had in his hands the heads of the nurses. He smashed them together and with a vicious raise of his knees, now right, now left, he wrecked his assailants for days to come.

The guard at the door had leaped ahead to help. He tried now to leap back but Tiger-Jan caught him, whirled him into the air and sent him crashing through a steel-net reinforced window.

Whirling, Tiger grabbed Dyhard who, in a rush, had sought to escape.

"I'm caught! I'm trapped!" screamed Dyhard. "Let me go! Let me go!"

"I'll make sure you're caught, you bilge-bellied lunatic!" cried Tiger. And he lifted the lid of the steam sterilizer and shoved Dyhard's head into it. Tiger banged the lid down, nearly breaking Dyhard's neck. "You're caught now, you swab!"

Tiger did not wait to see if any rose from the shambles. He swung through the doors and beheld reinforcements coming, attracted by the noise. Like a bull in a doll shop, without a pause, he went through them and out the front door.

A car was on the drive, Dyhard's. Tiger paused for an instant, disoriented, blinking in the afternoon sunlight. Suddenly, from a dual nature, he became himself, a unity anew.

Jan the Tiger swung under the wheel and stabbed the car at the gates. The steel was locked but the bumper not only parted the gate but sent one half spinning from its hinges. Tires screamed and he was on his way to town. As he sped along the road which passed in their section for a highway, he gathered himself into himself. Thoughts of neurosurgery spun crazily with problems about Denaise. Dyhard's punishment thirst was shot through with the sadism of Arif-Emir, the Ifrit. Tall ships tangled with tall buildings and then he began to get himself straight.

Insensibly separated after the Curse had unified his two natures once before, Jan the Tiger was oriented well in two worlds. Half of his mind knew suddenly things the other half knew.

He knew, for instance, that when he had reached into the chest for the Two-World Diamond and almost grasped it, it must have been also in his wall safe at home, and, just as it was about to make passage between worlds, had been withdrawn from that safe and was now somewhere in Seattle. He knew that if he could not find that diamond he would probably be dead in both worlds for he could not guess whether or not he had killed anyone in that operating room and he was sure that Arif-Emir would seek to interpose his fleetest vessels between the buckaroons and Denaise. In the world of the humans and the world of the Jinns he could only be saved if he could find the diamond and if he could guess and use its powers, for powers it must possess.

The Tiger part of him would take long chances. The Jan part of him knew caution. He pulled up sharply in the suburbs, parked the car for which he knew there would be a search and took a taxi. He had ridden three dollars' worth before he recalled that he had no money or valuables of any kind. That meant he would have to go home. And there the police might swiftly come to see if he would do just that. He had no illusions about it—he was an escaped maniac and would be billed as such.

He had the taxi pull up at the servant's entrance and told the driver to wait. He swept into his study down the back stairs and scooped some bills from a drawer. He came back and threw ten at the driver and did not wait for change for off a few blocks a siren was moaning and the moan was getting nearer.

Alice was just sitting down to supper in the dining room. He went by without a nod. To her, aside from his determined stride and face, he looked just Jan.

He spun the dial on the wall safe in the library just to check. It was empty of the diamond. Alice, puzzled and concerned, had followed him in.

"Who took that diamond?" he said sharply.

"Isn't it there?" she said.

But he was already looking at the small drill holes in the steel. The safe had been looted. His wits were working at a furious pace. He recalled Chan Davies and the robbery and that the stone had been found in the other world on Muddy McCoy. There was only one conclusion to that. Muddy McCoy and Chan Davies were the same.

"Have you seen that Commie around here? The one who slugged me?"

Alice was very confused. "Jan, what are you doing home? You were to have one of these splendid new scientific operations that make everybody so well. Didn't you want to go through with it?"

A siren was sounding in the street.

"Have you seen that Commie?" snapped Jan.

"I— No. I hired him but he quit. I—"

Tires were grinding in the gravel of the walk. "Tell no one I'm here," said Jan. He sped down the back stairs into the servants quarters. He found the Swede girl sitting in a pool of tears.

"Where's your boyfriend?" said Jan.

"Oh, oh, oh, he vas so cruel," she moaned. But Jan wasn't interested as Tiger or as Jan about the disillusionment suffered by all minorities so led astray. He extracted the information that Chan Davies hung out in the Friends of Russia Social Hall.

The front doorbell was ringing but Jan didn't see any advantage in answering it. He went over a window sill and dropped into the garden. He opened the back garage door and took the car that was pointed down the drive, Alice's coupe. He could see the tail end of the prowler car. He supposed that it would start up in a moment, sent away by Alice. But he had not reckoned upon the propaganda which tells a public about the glories of neurosurgery. Two officers quickly came around the front corner of the house and started for the rear.

Jan decided he had waited long enough. He jammed down on the starter, raced the motor and shot the coupe forward. One of the officers leaped out into the gravel on the theory that he would not be knocked down. Jan threw his left wheels into a rose bed, careened back into the drive and rocketed out into the street. His tires screamed as he turned and screamed again at the corner. He could hear the siren starting to howl behind him as the police got going.

Weaving through traffic along Meridian Way, Jan outdistanced his pursuit. He plummeted off the express highway and shot along a side street toward the docks. He reached Alaskan Way and, playing it swift, picked up his lead by dodging in front of a freight engine. The squad car was paused by the freight and Jan hid the coupe behind boxcars and dodged through a parking lot to a line of shabby warehouses where the Friends of Russia held out.

Jan saw the inconspicuous sign ahead of him and started for the door. But just before he reached it, the squad car, evidently on radio directions received from Alice whose only thought was for her husband's "best interests," swerved in toward the curb.

With a rush Jan reached the door, a command to stop buffeting him. He went up the steps three at a time but as he neared the top he saw his quarry starting down.

Chan Davies was intent upon a sheaf of papers, the result of some days of work and worry, which included false passports and visas which would permit him to reach Mexico and jewel cutters. He saw Jan and screamed. He raced back across the hall, chattering with terror.

Jan bounded after him and saw that Davies would make a back staircase before he could be caught.

There was the crack of a pistol shot. Jan's leg buckled under him. He fell. There was a slam as Davies made the back door and vanished and then two police officers were standing over Jan, steel bracelets ready. There was a click and Jan's arms were cuffed behind his back.

Stunned by the shock of the bullet, it took an instant for Jan to collect himself. He struggled to rise but two strong officers held him down.

"Is he bleedin' much, Mike?" said one.

"Not bad. You better call that doc that was taking care of him."

"Poor guy. Screwy as a bedbug on the subject of Commies. Gosh, he sure wants to kill them on sight. Put some bracelets on his ankle. Got it? What'd his wife say the doc's name was?"

"Dyhard."

"Got him safe now? I'll go put in a call."

Chapter 13

THE CHASE

Tiger woke with the dawn pouring into the stern windows, spreading red light through the *Terror*'s cabin. The rush and plunge of the ship, driven before a freshening wind, resounded through her timbers.

Dazedly he looked at Wanna asleep on the far bunk. He had difficulty orienting himself for with these sounds seemed to mingle, in his half-awake state, the screams of a madman and the footsteps of a guard. Then he abruptly realized what had happened to him. He was complete, he was himself. He was Jan Palmer. He had another body in another world and that body was wounded and in danger.

Wanna started awake, looked dazedly around and began to weep. Tiger went to her.

"I had the most terrible dream," she said, weeping. "I dreamed you had gone mad."

He patted her shoulder, calming her. With reassuring words he pulled on his seaboots, stroked her hand and went up on deck.

The *Terror*'s people were swabbing her decks, hoisting frothy water from the sea. As they tossed it across the holystoned wood the sun caught it so that it appeared that they scrubbed with blood.

Tiger was no longer dazed. He was coldly competent. He strode forward through the work party and into the berthing where he thought he would find Muddy McCoy. There were blankets on the bunk but it was cold and Tiger came back instantly to the deck. He glanced swiftly over the side. The *Terror* had been towing several boats, the overflow of the stores of war which she

279

could not cram into her holds. A severed painter dangled there showing that one of the cutters was gone.

He took a short tour of search through the ship without finding Muddy. And then he raised himself into the rigging and gazed astern.

The vessels of Arif-Emir, reinforcing the remaining bulk of the Tarbutón fleet, had had to sail slightly to the north to round Frying Pan Shoals before they could set a straight course for Denaise. This had caused them to lose a considerable length of sea for, additionally, some islets had blanketed the wind on part of that voyage around. The *Terror* and the brigantine, though heavily laden and gunwales awash with men, could make almost as much speed as the fleet which, in keeping station on each other, was retarded. It was possible that the *Terror* and the brigantine might reach Denaise on the morrow before the fleet was within range of them.

But as Tiger looked aft he saw that during the night the two fastest frigates, either of them twice the tonnage and with four times the fire power of the buckaroons, had been sent ahead under all sail. These, Tiger saw with a shock, were within eleven miles of the *Terror*. And as he watched he saw that they made, little by little, a slow gain. They were sailing on their best course, they were being handled undoubtedly in a manner calculated to stretch any previous speed they had made. Such ships were capable of standing a lot of wind and, with a glance at the sky, Tiger saw that more wind was coming.

Tiger sung out to the quartermaster on watch and a moment later Mister Luck scampered up the ratlines, a brass telescope in his hands. Tiger trained it on the sea. Far to port, lifting and falling, now in sight and now out because of its size in relation to the waves, was a cutter. It was heading up toward a tangle of islands and reefs and it was obvious, with a swift guess at its speed and course, that it would escape into the shoals before the cutters could reach it. There, he knew, went Muddy McCoy.

He did a quick calculation. He made his decision. He bawled his orders to the quarterdeck and with a dismayed glance up at him, Walleye passed the commands to the steersman and the watch. The *Terror* jibed and put the wind on her port quarter. She was less easy to steer here because of the swell but it was a more favorable sailing angle for her. Tiger looked back at the frigates. Behind them, hulls down, came the vanguard of the combined fleets.

The brigantine sent up an anxious string of signal flags and Tiger replied to them with orders for her to keep her course for Denaise. That done he looked back at the frigates. They had also jibed. Their position was such that they had a shorter run to that cutter than had the *Terror*. It looked probable that they would be within range before the cutter was overhauled.

"Run out the stern chasers!" roared Tiger. "All hands stand to general quarters!"

The *Terror*, pressed almost beyond endurance by a wind which, as the dawn became clear day, rose to twenty-five knots and more. Blocks complained, spars stood from the masts, the mildewed canvas stretched. The silence of a ship under all strain settled upon her. Whitecaps began to pick up and race along with her. The sough and rush of the sea through which she tore and the creaming of churned water were loud in the quietness of her racing tension. She was doing thirteen knots, better than she had done in these later years of her life, but thirteen knots was her limit with her cargo in this wind.

"Cut away all boats!" commanded Tiger.

Knives slashed and the cutters drifted astern, turning to broach in the rushing sea. The *Terror* picked up half a knot. Thirteen and a half, according to the ship log cast by Ryan and Mister Luck.

Tiger mounted again into the ratlines. He was a little shocked to see how much larger the bow gun crews of the frigates looked. The bones in the teeth of that voracious pair rose up and as they

281

plunged, engulfed their manropes. They were doing fifteen and better and they had a shorter course to run to reach the cutter. They might not know the significance of that small vessel nor know what lay in the pocket of the thief aboard it. Indeed Tiger himself could not be sure the diamond was still there with Muddy McCoy, elsewhere Chan Davies. But Tiger knew he had to take that chance to save himself in two worlds if he could and to save these buckaroons and humankind as slaves to the Jinn. The frigates only saw that the *Terror* was rushing down upon a small boat in the sea and they strained to reach it before the *Terror* could, for there they would have a chance to blow the buckaroons to glory. It was a bit of luck, thought the frigates' commanders, a bit of luck they could use.

Straining and plunging, the *Terror* quartered the seas. Before it the cutter grew bigger. In the brass spy-glass Tiger could see Muddy's writhing back, for Muddy, seeing himself the goal for the *Terror* and frigates alike, was steering his own race, trying to gain the reefs over which only his small craft could make passage.

"Port batteries!" bawled Tiger. "Load chain shot!"

The frigates were nearer now, much nearer. Only a league of whitecapped sea separated them from the *Terror*. Only two miles remained between the *Terror* and the cutter. A puff of white smoke came from the nearer frigate. The dull concussion of it was faint in the strained faces of the buckaroons. The ball skipped across the crests of ten successive waves, sending geysers of white water up from the bright blue, falling short of the *Terror* by five hundred yards.

The buckaroons looked whitely at Tiger poised in the mizzen shrouds. They did not understand. They saw the cutter, but they also saw that the frigates made a steady gain on the same goal and would intercept them. Tiger seemed to know what he was doing. But fear was in them.

Another puff came from the Long Tom in the frigate's bow. The shot skipped within a hundred yards of the *Terror*.

"Load the starboard battery with chain!" bawled Tiger.

Though this was the off side of the action the ports were already down and gunners, late of the Tarbutón navy, stood ready to these guns. They hurriedly withdrew the wadding and shot and crammed the brazen mouths with chain shot, two iron balls connected together with a length of forged links and which, when fired, would spin around and around, a fine method of cleaning enemy decks or dismasting ships.

The frigates were lunging and pounding forward faster now, the freshening wind coming to them before it reached the *Terror*. They drew so far ahead in the race that it was obvious they would come up with the cutter well before the *Terror*.

"Stand by sheets and braces!" bawled Tiger. The seamen leaped to their stations, preparing to handle sail.

A report flatted from the nearer frigate. It was almost on the *Terror*'s port bow now, well within range. There was a splintering aloft and the fore-r'yal yard tipped crazily and came lunging down at the deck to crush a Long Tom's crew below. Bodies were swept aside. Axes sounded in the wreckage. The *Terror*'s bow gun was once more manned.

"Starboard your helm!" roared Tiger. "Bring her up. Brace and trim!"

The *Terror* swept broadside to the sea. Braces and sheets hummed, the sails trimming in ready hand for her new course, a reach. After an instant's slackening she began to pick up new speed.

Just as she turned, the whole side of the nearer frigate rolled white. From bow to stern in swift rotation, her starboard battery thundered out a broadside.

A solid shock crashed into the *Terror*'s bows in a fan of splinters. The sea on the *Terror*'s port, where she should have been had she not turned, churned high and white with thirty-seven battering shots which, had they landed, would have finished her. Tiger, watching the nearest ship's quarterdeck, had seen the order pass, had seen the gunner alert the frigate's maindeck crews.

The whipping wind fast cleared the smoke but it stayed long enough to permit the *Terror* a gain. Steering now for the stern of the nearer frigate, the buckaroons could read *Mount Kaf* across the gilding. Jockeying his ship in close, Tiger reached the *Terror* across the wake of the frigate.

"Guns one to eleven!" cried Tiger. "Train for her spars!"

The *Terror* came on range, the *Mount Kaf* was speeding directly away from them but not quite fast enough.

"Fire!" bawled Tiger.

There was a shuddering reel in the *Terror* and a momentary backing of her sails. The white smoke of half her starboard broadside went whipping after the *Mount Kaf*.

The second frigate had shortened sail to fall back behind her companion and have a chance at the game. She was on a starboard run, her crews busy with a temporary furl.

"Guns thirteen to twenty-one!" bawled Tiger, citing the remaining five guns in the starboard battery all of which were odd-numbered as was proper. "Stand by. Aim for her masts!"

The *Terror* was jockeyed closer to run perpendicularly across this second wake. The name of the second frigate the *Ras Faleen* became brightly visible on her stern, close aboard.

"Fire!" bawled Tiger.

The remainder of the broadside belched flame and smoke, the *Terror* reeled to port and white fumes raced after the shot to engulf the *Ras Faleen*.

Tiger whipped around to stare at the *Mount Kaf*. His naval gunners knew what they were doing. Like a great avalanche from the sky, the *Mount Kaf*'s mizzen and main were shedding sails. The masts themselves were teetering and then they crashed, borne forward by the pressure of wind. The foremast strained at the impact of the falling main, the foresail tilted crazily. Then suddenly all carried away.

A rush of air jerked his attention back to the *Ras Faleen*, now falling astern. The concussion of her stern chasers and the after guns of her port broadside struck at the *Terror*. Firing on the downroll, the *Ras Faleen* missed the decks of the retreating buckaroon. But the shots smashed greedily into her counter just as it lifted in the waves. The *Terror* reeled soggily. Then she carried beyond accurate range of the *Ras Faleen*.

A carpenter shouted to Tiger on the quarterdeck. "Three feet of water in the well! She's heavy damaged under the water aft!"

Tiger glanced over the starboard rail. He saw as she lifted that her hull was open to the sea. He looked ahead and saw the reefs and island toward which Muddy had been steering. He scanned the sea about for his quarry. He did not instantly see the cutter but he saw something else: they had cut the mizzen sail spar from the *Ras Faleen*, a thing which would not begin to cripple her. The rudder of the frigate had received a greater impact than the sails for the broadside had been too low. The *Ras Faleen*'s officers were hastening a jury rig already but for a little while she would not steer. Her sails were being furled for she was turning into the trough, out of control. But she would swiftly be in action again if the haste on her quarterdeck meant anything. Already she was dropping a cutter to capsize it and use it for a rudder.

Then he saw Muddy McCoy. In a frantic rush the thief was trying to put into effect something of the same trick Tiger had played on the Tarbutón fleet. Muddy was reaching swiftly for the reefs.

"Bring the helm down! Steer for that cutter!" shouted Tiger.

He turned, beckoned to two buckaroons and rushed below. Down there Tombo was in water up to his waist, locked solidly in the brig and certain of dying.

Tiger and the buckaroons half-waded, half-swam to the brig door. The roll and lunge of the ship, running now with the wind off the port quarter but soggy already in the sea, caused her interior water to rush and roar with a deafening din. The impact of it hurled Tiger and the mates about. They reached the door.

"You want to be saved?" shouted Tiger above the thunder of water.

Tombo, terrified, looked numbly at a man who could ask such an unnecessary question.

"Tell me the power of that diamond!" shouted Tiger.

"Let me out! Let me out! I'm caught, I'm trapped!" howled Tombo. "I'm caught! I'm trapped! Let me out!"

Tiger stared at him, stared at his fangs, stared at his claws. An Ifrit, yes. But in another world, all unknowing—

Gripping the Jinn's throat through the bars, Tiger yanked him close. "Tell me the power of that diamond! What can it do?"

"Let me out! I'm caught! I'm trapped!" screamed Tombo. "Anything, anything! But let me out! He's a maniac! I'm caught, I'm trapped!"

The phrase about the maniac completed the identification for Tiger. For a moment he had thought this might be the prefrontal case, but that was not so. Tombo was Dyhard in another world! A Jinn!

But there was greater urgency here. "Tell me the power of that diamond!" shouted Tiger, shaking the terrified Ifrit, battered by the rising water within the hold.

"Only the Jinn know it. I can't tell, I can't!"

"You're caught! You're trapped!" said Tiger, pushing his buttons.

That did it. Tombo clawed wildly at the bars, his great orbs of eyes staring in terror. He saw the water surging, he felt the ship staggering, ready to sink. The overhead was a crushing weight to him above.

"Used with the banishing sign, point down, it sends any of the Jinn anywhere! It accompanies only the human soul. Humans cannot move with it. It moves between the worlds only when it is in human hands! Save me!"

"More!" said Tiger. "Tell me more!"

"I'm betraying the Jinn!" wailed Tombo. But a wave in the hold surged over him and almost drowned him and he screamed, "With the point of the seal up it will invoke the spirit of Sulayman himself from the world of the dead! Spare me! I've told! That is why we stole it! So long as we have it our enslaver cannot return from the dead! I'm a traitor! I'm a traitor!" He was staggered off his feet by a stronger rush of black water. "I'm caught!" he screamed. "I'm caught! I'm trapped! There's no incantation. Just tell it what you want! Oh, let me out! Let me out! I'm caught!"

Tiger struck at the lock and the door swung wide. But as he started to fall back to the ladder there was a leaping crunch of keel on reef and the *Terror,* driven full aground only minutes before she sank, reeled crazily like a stricken horse, twisted down, rose and fell back, pierced in fifty places by the jagged coral fangs. She lunged drunkenly as the breaking waves struck her. She rose and fell back, driven further on, pierced anew. There was a crash on the stricken deck as a hail of yards and canvas came down.

Battered by the waves within the hold, Tiger fought through the black water and grasped the ladder. He reached back and yanked his shipmates up and then seized Tombo and thrust him on ahead.

Tiger sprang from the hold, sidestepped a late falling block and a tangle of running rigging and looked at a vista of breaking sea and ruined ship.

Cannon, loose from their tackles, bright-spotted with glistening spray were breaking away from the higher side and smashing across to splinter through the bulwarks on the other side of the deck. In the blazing sunlight and fresh wind, the *Terror* was dying and dying hard.

A new comber hit her, lifted her and thrust her further aground. She staggered and slipped, heeled the other way. The cannon on the side now high, loosened by the shocks, sprang away like things alive and carrying all before them raced and spun across the decks to crash through the down rail and overboard.

The ship's company was crowded on her forecastle and diving, one after another, into the lagoon which was quiet, guarded by the reef the *Terror* spanned.

Wanna stood holding hard to a belaying pin rail on the quarterdeck, supported by Mister Luck. They were being swept by the breaking combers. Tiger fought towards them. A larger wave lifted the wreck again and drove it further across the reef.

Ryan was suddenly at Tiger's side. They dodged a spinning cannon, sidestepped a falling spar and reached the quarterdeck. Tiger swept up Wanna. Ryan grabbed Mister Luck and they staggered across the crazily shuddering deck. There was a groan throughout the timbers and the sound of rending wood. The wreck was breaking in half.

They reached the lowering bows, almost in the water now, and stepped into the lagoon. Swimming the few yards which took them to shallower water, they staggered to their feet. Tiger set Wanna down in a depth which came only to her waist and stared about.

The wreck of the cutter drifted in the lagoon a few hundred yards away. A battered Muddy McCoy was seeking to make all speed away from there floundering to land. Tiger dived forward. Using a fast crawl stroke much swifter than walking, he had, in the space of minutes, the throat of McCoy in his aching hands.

But it was not Muddy McCoy's throat he wanted. It was the lump in Muddy's sash. With eager fingers Tiger took unto himself the Two-World Diamond.

Seaward, the *Ras Faleen* was standing in as close as she dared, gun ports open, the black mouth of grape-stuffed cannon hungry to cut down the *Terror*'s crew as it struggled toward the far beach.

Chapter 14

TOGETHER AGAIN

The diamond blazed in the sunlight, bluer than the deep, whiter than the spray which flew above the reef. In its depths lay the three-dimensional Seal of Sulayman, the monarch who had conquered once all the tribes of Jinn.

The fleets of Zongri and Arif-Emir stood high on the near horizon like clouds. The *Ras Faleen,* clumsily steered but adventuring revenge just the same, steadied on her course to give a maximum sweep of the luckless buckaroons. The captain on her quarterdeck raised his claws to command commence firing.

Tiger gazed into the depths of the stone and pointed the seal down in the banishing sign.

"Ifrits and Marids of the *Ras Faleen!* To the center of the Withered Desert all! Go!"

The *Ras Faleen* pursued her course. The din of the surf was such that no sounds reached the lagoon. But Tiger had eyes to see. And he saw a blur where her Ifrit officers had stood and the officers were not there anymore. And he saw where the green-coated Marids had stood in her shrouds. And those spots were empty. And he saw, like dolls at this distance, the human gunner's mates staring toward the quarterdeck, waiting for command and then start aft in an amazed walk.

For the *Ras Faleen* was without commander or officers or marines and had left but her human crew. And if one cared, that moment, to go to the Withered Desert he would have found a stunned group of Ifrits staring about, naval coats unfitting for that scenery of desolation and sand.

Tiger floundered into the shallows and reached the beach. Ahead there was an inlet where the reef broke and the surf, calmed by the constricted entrance, purred down upon the strand. He stopped there and thrust the diamond, still in his hand, beneath a flat but easily recognizable stone.

"By the Seal of Sulayman!" he said, "I wish I were the most commanding fellow on the *Ras Faleen!*"

He jerked back his hand, the diamond out of sight, but almost before the gesture was done—

Whirrr! Zzzzt!

He stood upon the quarterdeck of the *Ras Faleen*, finding himself to be a black-bearded, huge-chested human wearing a gunner's striped shirt.

The crew was still stunned but gathering aft with wondering looks, peering under things and into boats to find out what had happened to their enslavers, the Ifrits.

"Avast, you swabs!" roared Tiger in his new identity, discovering his voice to be somewhat more resounding than a bull's. "I'm taking command here and if there's argument, speak up so I can feed you to the sharks! Launch the cutter and the gig! Lively now. Shorten sail. Easy with that helm, you farmer."

"What the hell's got into you, Pete?" said a gunner's mate.

Tiger as Pete took one swipe at the gunner's mate and knocked him halfway the length of the waist. "Lively now!" he roared at the men.

They blinked, bewildered and because of that bewilderment, obeyed. The *Ras Faleen* fell off into the trough, giving them a lee in which to put over cutter and gig.

"Shove off," Tiger as Pete roared at the coxswain of the cutter. "Take her through that opening in the reef and load her with pirates. I'm following you!" He turned to a gunner's mate who seemed partial to him. "Take command while I'm gone. Obey him, you swabs!" he challenged the crew. "Stand off and on here and take the buckaroons aboard as they arrive. They're not prisoners. They're free men, naval seamen most, like yourselves."

They nodded at him dazedly and Tiger as Pete dropped down a line into the waiting rig. His oarsmen laid on with a will, making the light-pulling boat leap swiftly ahead at each stroke. They passed the cutter before they were in and Tiger was first on the sand.

Tiger as Pete raced up to a bewildered human being standing by a rock and watching first the ship and then the boats. Tiger was interested to see how well his body looked despite the sea stains. Tiger as Pete reached under the rock, grasped the diamond and said, "I wish I were you!"

Whirrr! Zzzzt!

Tiger, as himself, was looking at an even further dazed Pete.

"I'm Tiger," said Tiger. "You've heard of me. I'm taking command of the *Ras Faleen* from you as of now."

"But I don't command her. Sabud—"

"I'm taking command anyway," said Tiger. "We've a lot of Tarbutón navy men here mixed up with these buckaroons. We're going to save the lot. You understand?"

Pete didn't and scratched his black beard in an effort to think. And while he was doing that, Tiger hailed the first of the buckaroons and Tombo's men he had taken from the fleet and began a transport to the *Ras Faleen*.

Two hours later the frigate was crammed with men and the last of the *Terror*'s people were aboard. The main fleets were almost arriving now, the first of the men-o-war but two miles off.

Having made a clinical test with Tombo, Tiger had determined that Ifrits, when commanded by the diamond, sailed very nicely far away. Tombo was part of a bewildered group of naval men in the Withered Desert now.

Standing beside the signalman of the *Ras Faleen*, Tiger scanned the oncoming ships. "Hoist a signal," he ordered, "to the effect that all vessels are to proceed to Tarbutón harbor."

"What?" blinked the signalman. "But—"

"Sign it 'Tiger.' They'll understand soon enough."

The signalman grinned and Tiger sped below. In the privacy of the cabin he took out the diamond. He pointed the seal downward.

"By the Seal of Sulayman," he said, "all officers and Marids in all the nearby fleet to the Withered Desert, go!"

Two hours later, Tiger, cheered by the liberated human crews ship after ship as he passed, reached the *Magnificent* and to that mighty first-rater transferred his flag.

The naval vessels which had drifted aimlessly, merely avoiding each other when they came close to ram ever since their officers and naval police had so strangely vanished, gladly accepted Tiger's command. In the first place they knew or knew of Tiger. In the second place they had no other choice. Electing from their numbers officers of their own and expecting new and hopeful things, the human fleet took formation and made their way toward home.

The ships of the fleet cast anchor in a strangely quiet harbor. No shipping moved in the bay at Tarbutón. Instead the shore was lined with human beings in all conditions of misery but in a mood of uncertainty.

Yesterday their masters, the Ifrits, and the guards, the Marids, had vanished from the land in some strange fashion and there were tales going around that people had seen them fly away, though for what purpose none knew.

A dozen pulling boats filled with armed men approached the docks from the fleet. The crowd on the shore, increasing now by numbers from the white and scarlet minaretted town, expected Ifrits to land. Some were for mutiny against their masters. Others preached caution. Others were actually hauling up cannon in a feeble attempt to make a fight of it in a despairing effort to escape the slavery to which they had, it seemed, forever been condemned.

Then somebody with sharper eyes than the others saw no Ifrits in the boats. Then he saw something else.

"It's Tiger!" he shouted.

There was a murmur. Several cheered. Others were afraid. Tiger was a source of grief to Ifrits and the following of his banner might mean trouble.

The crowd parted as Tiger came up the quay. The humans watched him and said nothing.

The sailors landed, fully armed and burdened with boarding nets and chains. They had their instructions. They spread out the nets on the wharf and made ready the chains.

Tiger waved them all back. Sailors took hold of the corners of the nets. Tiger reached into his sash and touched and adjusted the diamond without showing it.

"I command," he cried, "that Zongri, the ruler of this land, that Arif-Emir, the ruler of Balou, and Tombo, admiral of the fleet, appear upon this netting! Come!"

There was a rush of air and a swirl. Dazed and staggering and much unkempt despite their gorgeous robes and jewels, the three named Ifrits came.

The sailors, with a seamanlike dexterity with hemp, lifted the boarding nets high and dropped them swiftly over the Ifrits. Other sailors ran in and wove the nets about with chains and straps.

"By Ahriman!" screamed Zongri, age-old enemy of Tiger, "I demand—"

"Pipe down!" said Tiger. "You demand nothing! By virtue of a power I hold and which you know, I give you your choice between exile and a swift voyage to hell. Before these witnesses assembled, Zongri, declare to me the lordship of your lands or else, by Ahriman, you'll roast!"

Arif-Emir, understanding suddenly, gave Zongri a hoarse caution. "The Two-World Diamond!" he said.

Zongri opened his fanged mouth to deny it but his eyes held upon the bulge in Tiger's sash. Zongri closed his mouth with a frightened snap. "I have no choice!"

"Choose!" and Tiger's hand in the sash moved a trifle.

"I declare you ruler of these lands!" cried Zongri anxiously.

"And you, Arif-Emir, am I the undisputed ruler of Balou? You have the same chance."

"Don't!" said Arif-Emir. "I'll say it. Don't! Before any witness you'll produce, before everyone, I declare you ruler of Balou and all my lands, successor without dispute to the kingdom!"

"Then by my authority," said Tiger before the bulging eyes of the multitude, "as soon as you are released, back with you to the Withered Desert, Zongri and Arif!"

The sailors let go the straps and chains and spread the nets and almost before the last fold was away, with a swish of air, Zongri and Arif were gone.

Tombo stood, shivering, alone upon the netting. "They'll kill me if they know! I pray you, Tiger, do not send me with them. Give me some lighter thing! I beg you!"

Tiger looked at him. He knew him for what he was, a Jinn that haunted in human form another world and wore the name of Dyhard.

"All I care to do to you," said Tiger, "is to curse you with eternal wakefulness and memory in another world of this! Except for that, you are free. Come lads, pass the word to the fleet to organize their ships and send me in a palace guard."

He pushed through the crush of madly cheering humans who knew at last they were free and made his way to the palaces of Ramus.

Alone in the great hall at length, he dared pull forth the diamond.

"Sulayman! Sulayman!" he said. "By virtue of this diamond hear me where you are in the world of the dead. The Ifrits who rebelled against you stand in the wastes of the Withered Desert. Bewitch them there so they can trouble man no more."

There was a rumbling sound above him as though the sky was laughing with pleasure at the deed.

Jan sat in a hospital bed, a strong and forthright Jan. He seemed bigger than he had and no wonder for he held as well the power of his other self in another world. He was much besieged by callers.

A pretty nurse adjusted his pillow. "Your leg is almost well, Mr. Palmer. You can go home tomorrow if you like."

She smiled and walked away. The detective lieutenant at the foot of the bed was so engrossed in what he had to say he did not even look at her legs. "I hope everything's all right, Mr. Palmer. No complaints or anything."

"No, no complaints," said Jan.

Alice, sitting in a chair at Jan's left, looked fondly at her husband. A definite change had taken place in her. She was her composite self, warm and interested, no longer coldly businesslike, the artistic part of her restored and shining in her glance. She patted Jan's hand.

"Funny about that Commie," said the lieutenant. "Davies, I mean. The California cops that picked him up said he was in a state of nervous collapse. Scared stiff about something. He confessed to the two robberies and he had a stack of forged papers on him that would convict a saint. No hard feelings?"

"I'm sure he hasn't," said an unctious member of the Bering Steam board of directors, the ringleader of the failed rebellion, very anxious now to gain Jan's good will. "And if you'll pardon us, lieutenant, I'd like to tell Mr. Palmer about the highway that we voted to endorse to Alaska. I—"

"Well," said the lieutenant, twisting his hat, "I just wanted Mr. Palmer to know all about it. That was a bum deal he had. That Lucar that swore out the complaint was a Commie too, part of the same ring. These Commies always try to gang up but they're such a bunch of worms they sell each other out any time it's worth anything to one."

"I am sure," said the Bering Steam director, "that Mr. Palmer has quite forgiven the whole thing. Now, if I could go over these papers to change the name of the new ship to the *Greg Palmer*, Jan—"

"Well, I just wanted him to know he got a bum steer, that's all," said the lieutenant, "and we're sorry we had any part of it. We put the cop that shot you out in the suburbs. We kind of feel to blame, too, about lettin' that psychiatrist take you away. But how was we to know he'd turn out like he did."

"I'm sure I can forget about it," said Jan with a smile. "Thanks for coming to tell me."

The lieutenant breathed relief and left. The director got his papers signed and he, with many bows and ingratiating smiles, left.

Jan sighed happily, Alice's hand on his arm. He unfolded the evening papers, looking for the comics.

"What did he mean about the psychiatrist?" said Alice. "Is that Dyhard?"

Jan looked up from reading his favorite strip. "Huh? Oh, Dyhard. Yeah, poor guy. Started telling people he was from another world."

"Oh? Why, there it is on the back page!"

Jan read it disinterestedly.

PSYCHIATRIST SAVED BY OPERATION

Dr. Felix Dyhard, local psychiatrist, who suffered a nervous breakdown last Tuesday was operated on yesterday, according to his colleague, Dr. Steining. The operation, the most modern technique of neurosurgery, is called a prefrontal lobotomy which places the patient completely beyond worry. Dyhard, Steining said, was in excellent condition after the operation and can be expected to experience an uneventful recovery after which he will be transferred to the state institution until such time as some routine employment which requires little thought can be found for him.

"Poor Tombo!" said Alice.

Jan went back to reading the comics.

Full-Rigged Sailing Ship

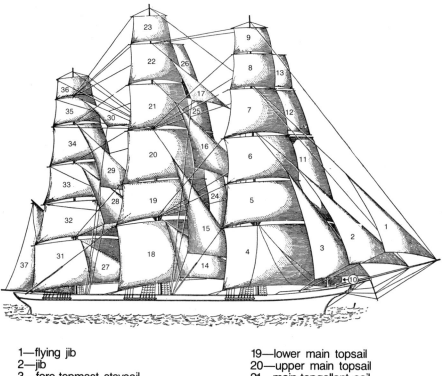

1—flying jib
2—jib
3—fore-topmast staysail
4—foresail
5—lower fore-topsail
6—upper fore-topsail
7—fore topgallant sail
8—fore-royal
9—fore-skysail
10—lower studding sail
   (never on the main)
11—fore-topmast studding sail
12—fore-topgallant studding sail
13—fore-royal studding sail
14—main staysail
15—main-topmast staysail
16—main-topgallant staysail
17—main-royal staysail
18—mainsail

19—lower main topsail
20—upper main topsail
21—main-topgallant sail
22—main royal
23—main skysail
24—main-topmast studding sail
25—main-topgallant studding sail
26—main-royal studding sail
27—mizzen staysail
28—mizzen-topmast staysail
29—mizzen-topgallant staysail
30—mizzen-royal staysail
31—mizzen sail (crossjack)
32—lower mizzen topsail
33—upper mizzen topsail
34—mizzen-topgallant sail
35—mizzen royal
36—mizzen skysail
37—spanker

By permission. From Webster's Third New International Dictionary © 1986 by Merriam-Webster Inc., publisher of the Merriam-Webster® dictionaries.

Glossary of Nautical Terms

aft: (*adv.*) at or toward the stern or end of a ship. *The mate, likewise an Ifrit, started to pass him on his way aft and then recognized him.*

amidships: in or toward the middle part of a ship or aircraft; midway between the ends. *Fearfully they aided the port captain to his seat of state amidships.*

batteries: (*n. pl.*) **a.** (on a warship) a group of guns of the same size or used for the same purpose; **b.** the whole armament of a warship. *There came the groan of shifting yards and the pop of fluttering canvas as the seventy-four came about to bring her port batteries to bear.*

beat to quarters: (*v.i.*) a drumbeat calling all hands to their battle stations. *"Mr. Malek," he said to his waiting lieutenant. "Beat to quarters!"*

bilges: (*n. pl.*) **a.** the part of the underwater body of a ship between the flat of the bottom and the vertical topsides; **b.** the lower part of a ship's inner hull. *There is nothing worse than a dark hold when a battle rages, listening to the broadsides thunder and feeling the seventy-four trip and wallow as round shot took its count, hearing the wounded scream and weep, sensing the rising levels in the bilges and having no idea whatever of how the battle goes.*

binnacle: (*n.*) a stand or enclosure of wood or nonmagnetic metal for supporting or housing a compass. *Jan had scarcely lifted his head and felt the spokes of a helm under his fingers and then he was jarred fully awake and almost into sleep again by the most tremendous blow which rocketed him all the way across the quarterdeck, from binnacle to scupper.*

bitt: (*n.*) a strong post of wood or iron projecting, usually in pairs, above the deck of a ship, used for securing cables, lines for towing, etc. *Jan blinked in the blazing sunlight which glanced hurtfully back from polished bitts and scoured deck and from the wide harbor.*

boom: (*n.*) a long spar used to extend the foot of a sail. *He dropped over the rail, balanced his eight feet of bulk on the boat boom and then slid down into his gig.*

bosun: (*n.*) [variant **boatswain,** representing the common pronunciation] an officer on a ship who has charge of all the sails, rigging, anchors, and other gear. Also **bo's'n**. *Staggering forward, his head roaring and spinning, Jan almost collided with a bosun.*

bow: (*n.*) the forward end of a vessel or airship; (*adj.*) of or pertaining to the bow of a ship. *The flagship, probably with Arif-Emir on her quarterdeck, was opposite Gallows Point already and her bow was beginning to lift to the chop sea which extended just within the harbor mouth.*

bow-chaser: (*n.*) a gun mounted at the bow of a ship. *Two bow-chasers loomed on the fo'c's'le head.*

bowsprit: (*n.*) a pole projecting from the bow of a ship. *A sprits'l was furled under the bowsprit, and long abandoned had such "water sails" been in modern usage.*

brig (1): (*n.*) the compartment of a ship where prisoners are confined. *The brig door was shattered on its hinges.*

brig (2): (*n.*) short for **brigantine,** a two-masted sailing ship that is square-rigged, except for a fore-and-aft mainsail. *Then a brig and the two luggers of which Tiger's was the last.*

brigantine: (*n.*) a two-masted sailing ship that is square-rigged, except for a fore-and-aft mainsail. *The brigantine behind her entered that portion of the passage.*

Glossary of Nautical Terms

broadside: (*n.*) 1. the whole side of a ship above the water line. *The* Terror *swept broadside to the sea.* 2. a simultaneous discharge of all the guns on one side of a warship. *A broadside of their own was instantly answered by the roar of another close by.*

capstan: (*n.*) a machine for moving or raising heavy weights that consists of a vertical drum which can be rotated and around which cable is turned. *She steadied herself with a kedge and then dropped back toward the narrows with her capstan.*

cat: (*n.*) a cat-o'-nine-tails (a whip, usually having nine knotted lines or cords fastened to a handle, used for flogging.) *"Go get the cat, d'ya hear me? Get it and bring it to me!"*

chain shot: (*n.*) cannon shot consisting of two balls or half balls connected by a short chain, formerly used in naval artillery to destroy the masts and sails of enemy ships. *"Port batteries!" bawled Tiger. "Load chain shot!"*

cleat: (*n.*) a piece of wood or metal, often wedge-shaped, fastened to a surface as a support or to prevent slipping. *A guttering lamp showed him bracketed muskets, hung in orderly racks, and glittering cutlasses held fanwise in cleats.*

coaming: (*n.*) a raised border around an opening in a deck, roof, or floor, designed to prevent water from running below. *He sat down on the coaming and put his face in his palms.*

companionway: (*n.*) a stair or ladder within the hull of a vessel, or the space occupied by this stair or ladder. *The mate came out of a companionway.*

corbita: (*n.*) a vessel used for carrying cargo, dating back to the Roman Empire. *In the harbor about them lay hundreds of* *other vessels, both large and small, ranging in style from a Greek corbita to a seventy-four.*

counter: (*n.*) the curved part of the back of a ship. *Manned by humans, the cutter was soon under the counter of the lugger which, slopping off, now lay in the trough; booms trembled as the canvas thundered.*

cromster: (*n.*) a small vessel, usually employed in carrying passengers and goods, particularly in small distances on the sea coast. *Wonderingly he looked about at the ship itself to find that it was not unlike a cromster of the Middle Ages though considerably larger.*

crosstrees: (*n. pl.*) two horizontal crosspieces of timber at a mast-head that spread the ropes leading to the top, in order to support the mast. *"Lad," said Tiger, "scamper up to the cross-trees of the fore."*

cutter: (*n.*) a small, swift boat; a single-masted sail boat. *The human in the red shirt played an eye over the lugger, discovered that it did lack a boat and so, with a volley of orders, got a cutter into the sea.*

demi-cannon: (*n.*) a large cannon of the 16th century. *And all along each side, evidently manned from the deck below, were the muzzles of thirty demi-cannon.*

dhow: (*n.*) a sailing vessel used by Arabs on the east African, Arabian and Indian coasts. It has a lateen-rigged sail. *It is that model of the Arab dhow.*

flattie: (*n.*) flat-boat; a broad, flat-bottomed boat used for transport, especially in shallow water. *Jan was half-minded to put the flattie about and scud back across the wind-patterned Puget Sound; but he had already luffed up into the wind to* *carry in to the dock and Thompson had unbent enough to reach for the painter—more as an effort to detain Jan than to help him land.*

flotsam: (*n.*) the part of the wreckage of a ship and its cargo found floating on the water. *The Palmers, until now, had voyaged the world and the flotsam culled from many a strange beach had at last been cast up in these rooms.*

fo'c's'le: (*n.*) forecastle. A structure at or immediately behind the bow of a vessel, used as a shelter for stores, machinery, etc., or as quarters for sailors. *The captain's roars seconding the still braying lookout, the crew spilled helter-skelter from the fo'c's'le, rubbing their eyes, scarcely knowing what they were doing but automatically taking their stations.*

frigate: (*n.*) a fast, heavily armed naval vessel of the late 18th and early 19th centuries. *Like ants they crawled along the polished floor of a hall which could have berthed a frigate with ease.*

galley: (*n.*) a seagoing vessel propelled mainly by oars, used in ancient and medieval times, sometimes with the aid of sails. *"Now I'll get the galleys."*

gangway: (*n.*) an opening in the ship's side or railing, or the bridge which goes into this opening, leading to the shore or another ship. *The captain made a motion toward the port gangway and the file halted there, tightly ringing Jan.*

gig: (*n.*) a light boat rowed with four, six, or eight long oars. *He dropped over the rail, balanced his eight feet of bulk on the boat boom and then slid down into his gig.*

grape: (*n.*) grapeshot. A cluster of small, cast-iron balls formerly used to shoot from a cannon. *Screaming grape slapped like giant hailstones in the rigging and he flinched.*

grapnel: (*n.*) a small anchor with four or five flukes or claws used for grappling or dragging or for anchoring a small boat. *We're on fire and that means we'll have to come to grips with another ship and the toss of grapnels aboard.*

gunwale: (*n.*) the upper edge of the side of a vessel. *It was crammed from gunwale to gunwale with armed men, but they were port sailors and rather given to fat and softness.*

halyards: (*n. pl.*) rope or tackle for hoisting and lowering something (as sails). *Jan let go his jib and main halyards and guided the sail down into a restive bundle.*

hawsepipe: (*n.*) an iron or steel pipe which an anchor chain runs through. *He went down into the abyss of sleep, awakened instantly by the howl of winches and the cannonading of sails and then the grinding roar of chain racing through a hawsepipe.*

helm: (*n.*) a wheel controlling the rudder of a ship for steering. *Jan had scarcely lifted his head and felt the spokes of a helm under his fingers and then he was jarred fully awake and almost into sleep again by the most tremendous blow which rocketed him all the way across the quarterdeck, from binnacle to scupper.*

helmsman: (*n.*) a person who steers a ship. *"Now! Where's the helmsman?"*

hooker: (*n.*) *Slang.* Any old-fashioned or clumsy vessel. *"Steer small, Walleye, we want what speed this hooker'll make."*

house: (*n.*) any enclosed shelter on the upper deck of a vessel: bridge house; deck house. *Jan sprawled against the handrail of the sterncastle house.*

Jacob's ladder: (*n.*) a hanging ladder having ropes or chains supporting wooden or metal rungs or steps. *They swarmed* *up the Jacob's ladder and stood in the waist, giving a hand while the cutter was swung aboard, all but Tombo and Malek who stood apart, disdainful.*

jib: (*n.*) a triangular sail set on the forward part of a vessel. *Jan let go his jib and main halyards and guided the sail down into a restive bundle.*

jibe: (*v.i.*) to change a vessel's course when sailing with the wind so that as the stern passes through the eye of the wind, the boom swings to the opposite side. *The* Terror *jibed and put the wind on her port quarter.*

kedge: 1. (*vt.*) to move (a ship) along by hauling on a rope fastened to an anchor dropped at some distance. *It must follow that she had to manage to turn herself with capstan and wait for a shift of wind or kedge herself up out of the pass.* 2. (*n.*) a small anchor used to pull a ship along. *She steadied herself with a kedge and then dropped back toward the narrows with her capstan.*

keel: (*n.*) a timber or steel piece along the entire length of the bottom of a ship or boat. *One instant it was a normal enough boat, full of sleek and flawlessly uniformed sailors and the next the only thing which could be seen was the keel, all dripping and bobbing on the waves.*

knot: (*n.*) a unit of speed of one nautical mile (6,076.12 feet) an hour. *It was a brisk morning and a chop sea was running in a fifteen-knot wind.*

lateen: (*n.*) a triangular sail set on a long sloping pole. *A conglomerate rig it was, with a lateen on the mizzen, fore and aft on the main, the peaks held up with sprits, with a large square topsail and a t'g'l'nt above that and with three huge staysails forward.*

Glossary of Nautical Terms

Long Tom: (*n.*) a long, heavy cannon formerly carried by small naval vessels. *Another puff came from the Long Tom in the frigate's bow.*

luff: (*v.i.*) to bring the front of a sailing ship closer to or directly into the wind, with sails shaking; (of a sail) to shake from being set too close to the wind. *Jan was half-minded to put the flattie about and scud back across the wind-patterned Puget Sound; but he had already luffed up into the wind to carry in to the dock and Thompson had unbent enough to reach for the painter—more as an effort to detain Jan than to help him land.*

lugger: (*n.*) a small ship with oblong sails. *"He is gone and a swift lugger is missing in the harbor!"*

man-o-war: (*n.*) man-of-war; a warship. *At the time our story opens, Tiger had managed promotion up to the rank of gunner's mate in a man-o-war in the world of the Jinn.*

meridian altitude: (*n.*) the angular distance between horizon and the sun at noon. Used for navigating. *"Thirteen and I can write, sir, and read the charts and take pelorus sights and take meridian altitude shots and forecast coming events, sir."*

mizzen: (*n.*) the lowest sail on the mast or the mast aft, or next aft of the main mast in a ship (see diagram on page 298). *A conglomerate rig it was, with a lateen on the mizzen, fore and aft on the main, the peaks held up with sprits, with a large square topsail and a t'g'l'nt above that and with three huge staysails forward.*

packet: (*n.*) a small vessel that carries mail, passengers, and goods regularly on a fixed route, esp. on rivers or along coasts. *He knew rightly enough what a cat was, but where he could find one aboard this packet he certainly could not tell.*

painter: (*n.*) a rope, usually at the bow, for fastening a boat to a dock, etc. *Jan was half-minded to put the flattie about and scud back across the wind-patterned Puget Sound; but he had already luffed up into the wind to carry in to the dock and Thompson had unbent enough to reach for the painter—more as an effort to detain Jan than to help him land.*

peaks: (*n. pl.*) the upper outer corner of a sail extended by a spar. *A conglomerate rig it was, with a lateen on the mizzen, fore and aft on the main, the peaks held up with sprits, with a large square topsail and a t'g'l'nt above that and with three huge staysails forward.*

pelorus: (*n.*) a navigational instrument resembling a mariner's compass without magnetic needles and having two sight vanes by which bearings are taken. *"Thirteen and I can write, sir, and read the charts and take pelorus sights and take meridian altitude shots and forecast coming events, sir."*

pins: (*n. pl.*) any of various pegs or rods used to secure ropes. *He seized the halyards and, braking them on the pins, swiftly slacked them off.*

poop: (*n.*) a structure at the stern (after end) of a vessel. *He had been a trifle confused by the fact that all four men on the poop were wearing white djellabas, cloaks used by merchant seamen in these parts to keep off the sun.*

port: (*n.*) the left-hand side of or direction from a vessel or aircraft, facing forward. *"Let go the port sheets!" bellowed the captain.*

quarterdeck: (*n.*) the after part of the upper deck of a sailing ship, usually reserved for officers. *Jan had scarcely lifted his head and felt the spokes of a helm under his fingers and then he was jarred fully awake and almost into sleep again* *by the most tremendous blow which rocketed him all the way across the quarterdeck, from binnacle to scupper.*

rail: (*n.*) a narrow, horizontal piece forming the top of a ship's side. *He brought up against the rail and lifted himself cautiously.*

ratline: (*n.*) small ropes or lines that run horizontal to the ropes supporting a ship's masts and serve as steps for going aloft. *He went up over the beast's back like it was a ratline and before two roars had gone shatteringly down the hall he was astride the brute's head and twisting his tender ears until they creaked like cabbage leaves.*

reaching: (*v.i.*) to sail with the wind coming in, more or less, from the side of the vessel. *From where they stood, reaching idly back and forth, the r'yals of any ship putting out from Tarbutón would be visible.*

rigging: (*n.*) the ropes, chains, etc., employed to support and work the masts, sails, etc., on a ship. *Personally he had rather liked that little dhow with its strangely indestructible rigging.*

roads: (*n. pl.*) a partly sheltered area of water near a shore in which vessels may lie at anchor. *In truth, the condition was very ordinary, seeing that there had to be some manner of swell about a vessel anchored in the roads, but Boli had had one or two in the captain's cabin and he well knew that his reputation only wanted a ridiculous incident to throw down much of his carefully built authority.*

r'yals: (*n. pl.*) royals; the highest or second highest sails on a full-rigged sailing ship (see diagram on page 298). *From where they stood, reaching idly back and forth, the r'yals of any ship putting out from Tarbutón would be visible.*

sampans: (*n. pl.*) a flat-bottomed Chinese boat propelled by two short oars. *Small shore boats, not unlike sampans, scudded back and forth on a brisk breeze, carrying all sorts of passengers.*

scupper: (*n.*) an opening in a ship's side to allow water to run off the deck. *Jan had scarcely lifted his head and felt the spokes of a helm under his fingers and then he was jarred fully awake and almost into sleep again by the most tremendous blow which rocketed him all the way across the quarterdeck, from binnacle to scupper.*

serpentine: (*n.*) a cannon used from the 15th to the 17th century. *Almost against his head a serpentine thundered.*

seventy-four: (*n.*) a ship designed to carry seventy-four guns. *In the harbor about them lay hundreds of other vessels, both large and small, ranging in style from a Greek corbita to a seventy-four.*

sheet: (*n.*) a rope or chain that regulates the angle at which a sail is set in relation to the wind. *"Let go the port sheets!" bellowed the captain.*

shroud: (*n.*) taut ropes or wires used to support a mast. *The list was so bad that no man could have climbed the down side of the shrouds.*

skys'l: (*n.*) skysail; a light, square sail at the top of the highest mast of a ship. *Once his glance had picked that out from the tall cumulus on the far northern horizon above the land he saw another and then another skys'l.*

slat: (*v.i.*) to flap violently, as sails. *He and Ryan slacked off the sheets and the lugger, thus headed, was soon slatting her way to a halt.*

sloop: (*n.*) a single-masted sailing vessel, with two or three sails. *Next time he would take his cabin sloop and enough food to last a day or two—but at the same time, realizing the wrath this would bring down upon him, he knew that he would never do so.*

spar: (*n.*) any pole used for supporting the sails on a ship. *He twitched as spars crashed down over them, one end protruding through the gun deck.*

spitkit: (*n.*) an insulting, scornful term for a small, unseaworthy vessel. *She was a seagoing spitkit and would have been a disgrace to an army transport service.*

sprit: (*n.*) a small pole crossing a sail diagonally, serving to extend the sail. *A conglomerate rig it was, with a lateen on the mizzen, fore and aft on the main, the peaks held up with sprits, with a large square topsail and a t'g'l'nt above that and with three huge staysails forward.*

sprits'l: (*n.*) spritsail; a sail extended by a sprit. *A sprits'l was furled under the bowsprit, and long abandoned had such "water sails" been in modern usage.*

stand (stood off and on): (*v.i.*) to take or hold a particular course at sea. *"You never stood off and on in the ship here listening to Admiral Tyronin's flagship people burn up every one."*

sta'b'd: (*n.*) starboard; the right-hand side of or direction from a vessel or aircraft, facing forward. *"Breakers two points off the sta'b'd b-o-o-o-o-w!"*

staysail: (*n.*) a triangular sail set between two masts. *A conglomerate rig it was, with a lateen on the mizzen, fore and aft on the main, the peaks held up with sprits, with a large square topsail and a t'g'l'nt above that and with three huge staysails forward.*

stem: (*n.*) the forward part of a vessel. *At dawn the sound of ten thousand kettle drums struck violently at once shook the seventy-four from stem to taff!*

sterncastle: (*n.*) the stern is the after part of a vessel. By extension, the *sterncastle* would be a superstructure at or immediately forward of the stern of a vessel, used as a shelter for stores, machinery, etc., or as quarters for sailors. *Jan sprawled against the handrail of the sterncastle house.*

sternsheets: (*n. pl.*) the after part of an open boat, occupied by the person in command or by passengers. *Nervously they prodded Tiger into the sternsheets.*

tack: (*v.t.*) to change a course of (a ship) by turning its bow into the wind. *The van wore ship and passed the rear guard and came up on a port tack for the entrance.*

taff: (*n.*) taffrail; the upper part of the stern of a ship. *At dawn the sound of ten thousand kettle drums struck violently at once shook the seventy-four from stem to taff!*

thwarts: (*n. pl.*) seats across a boat, especially one used by a rower. *The two moved hastily, getting up on thwarts to reach for Boli's hands and steady him.*

t'g'l'nt: (*n.*) topgallant sail: the second or third highest sails on a full-rigged sailing ship. (See diagram at page 298.) *A conglomerate rig it was, with a lateen on the mizzen, fore and aft on the main, the peaks held up with sprits, with a large square topsail and a t'g'l'nt above that and with three huge staysails forward.*

topping lift: (*n.*) a line for raising and supporting a pole. *He put the trumpet in its clips, swung over the side of the basket, wrapped his cap around the topping lift which led down to the*

311

quarterdeck and, with this to protect his hands, swung his heels into space and swooped down like a meteorite to the quarterdeck.

tumblehome: (*n.*) an inward and upward slope of the middle body of a vessel. *From tumblehome to tumblehome, the boat displayed its bottom.*

waist: (*n.*) the central part of a ship. *"Lively now," cried a mate somewhere in the waist.*

weigh: (*n.*) [same as "way", used in the phrase "under weigh"] Motion or speed of a ship or boat through the water. *"Get him down, I say, before that canvas catches air and puts weigh on us!"*

wheel: (*n.*) a circular frame with projecting handles for controlling the rudder of a ship, for steering (see *helm* in this glossary). *When all was in order, the captain turned the wheel over to another man and gave him a course and then, with both hands on his hips, he planted his feet solidly on the deck and glared about him.*

wore (ship): (*pt* of **wear** *v.t.*) to cause (a ship) to go about with the stern presented to the wind. *The van wore ship and passed the rear guard and came up on a port tack for the entrance. Like a coiling snake, the line of battle followed, the rear guard completing the ware just as the vanguard entered the channel mouth.*

yard: (*n.*) a long pole, fastened to a mast, to which a sail is fastened. *And the barrel of that musket was pointed up in the general direction of the cantankerous Lacy, balanced precariously upon the whippy lateen yard.*

About the Author

Born in 1911, the son of a U.S. Naval officer, L. Ron Hubbard was raised in the state of Montana when it was still part of the great American frontier. He was early acquainted with a rugged outdoor life and as a boy earned the trust of the Blackfeet Indians who initiated him as a blood brother. He became the nation's youngest Eagle Scout at the age of thirteen.

During his teens, L. Ron Hubbard made several trips to Asia, carefully recording his observations and experiences in a series of diaries, as well as noting down story ideas resulting from his many adventures. His travels were extensive, including Malaysia, Indonesia, the ports of India and the Western Hills of China. By the time he was 19, he had logged over a quarter of a million miles on land and sea in an era well before commercial air travel.

Returning to the United States, he enrolled at George Washington University where he studied engineering and participated in the first classes on atomic and molecular phenomena. He was also an award-winning contributor to the University's literary magazine.

While still a student, he took up "barnstorming." He quickly gained a reputation as a daring and skilled pilot of both gliders and motorized planes and became a frequent correspondent for *The Sportsman Pilot*.

His intense interest in understanding the nature of man and the different races and cultures of the world took him once again to the high seas in 1933. This time he led two expeditions through the Caribbean. He was subsequently awarded membership in the prestigious Explorers' Club and would carry their flag on three more expeditions.

Drawing from his travels and first-hand adventures, L. Ron Hubbard began his professional writing career in 1933. He went on to create an amazing wealth of stories in a variety of genres which included adventure, mystery, detective and western. Ron produced a broad catalog of entertainment which attracted a huge readership, and in 1935, at age 25, he was elected president of the New York Chapter of the American Fiction Guild. During his tenure as president, the Fiction Guild membership included many renowned authors such as Raymond Chandler, Dashiell Hammett, Edgar Rice Burroughs and other notables who were the life-blood of the American literary marketplace.

Ron was invited to Hollywood in 1937, where he wrote the story and scripted fifteen screenplays for Columbia's box office serial hit "The Secret of Treasure Island." While in Hollywood, he also worked on screenplays and story plots for other wide-screen productions.

In 1938, fully established and recognized as one of the country's top-selling authors, he was approached by the publishers of *Astounding Science Fiction* magazine to write for them. They believed that in order to significantly increase the circulation of their speculative fiction magazines, they would need to feature real people in their stories. L. Ron Hubbard was the one writer they knew who could deliver this better than any other. The upshot was a wealth of celebrated science fiction and fantasy stories, which not only expanded the scope of these genres, but established Ron as one of the founding fathers of the great "Golden Age of Science Fiction."

Slaves of Sleep was published in Astounding's sister magazine *Unknown* in July, 1939, to the enthusiastic delight of its readers.

During this period, Ron also wrote the classic tale *Final Blackout*, a gripping novel of unending war. "Not half a dozen stories in the history of science-fiction can equal the grim power of this novel..." stated Astounding's editor, John W. Campbell, Jr. A short time later, Hubbard's story *Fear* appeared, setting a whole new standard for horror fiction and influencing generations of writers. Stephen King calls *Fear* a true classic of "creeping, surreal menace and horror."

With the advent of World War II, L. Ron Hubbard was called to active duty as an officer in the U.S. Navy. The course of this brutal war effectively interrupted his writing career and it was not until 1947 that he was once again turning out exciting stories for his many fans. These included the benchmark novel *To the Stars*—a powerful work centering on the impact of space travel at light-speed—and his critically acclaimed story, *The End Is Not Yet*. It was during this same period that Ron wrote the ever-popular *Ole Doc Methuselah* stories. Published under the pen name René Lafayette, a byline which Ron reserved for the captivating series, the adventures of Ole Doc and his companion Hippocrates quickly became a reader favorite.

In 1950, with the culmination of years of research on the subject of the mind resulting in the publication of *Dianetics: The Modern Science of Mental Health*, L. Ron Hubbard left the field of fiction and for the next three decades, he dedicated his life to writing and publishing millions of words of nonfiction concerning the nature of man and the betterment of the human condition.

However, in 1982, to celebrate his 50th anniversary as a professional author, L. Ron Hubbard returned to science fiction and released his giant blockbuster, *Battlefield Earth,* the biggest science fiction book ever written. *Battlefield Earth* became an international bestseller with millions of copies sold in over 60 countries. In the U.S. alone, it appeared on national bestseller lists for over 32 weeks.

Ron followed this singular feat with an even more spectacular achievement, his magnum opus—the ten-volume *Mission Earth* series, every one of which became a New York Times bestseller. *Mission Earth* is not only a grand science fiction adventure in itself, but in the best tradition of Jonathan Swift and Lewis Carroll, is a rollicking, satirical romp through the foibles and fallacies of our civilization.

L. Ron Hubbard departed this life on January 24, 1986. His prodigious and creative output over more than half a century as a professional author is a true publishing phenomenon. To date, his books have been published in 90 countries and 31 languages, resulting in over 105 million copies of his works sold around the world. This vast library includes over 260 popular fiction novels, novelettes and short stories (all of which are planned to be republished in the years to come) as well as hundreds of nonfiction publications, establishing L. Ron Hubbard as one of the most acclaimed and widely read authors of all time.

"I am always happy to hear from my readers."

L. Ron Hubbard

These were the words of L. Ron Hubbard, who was always very interested in hearing from his friends and readers. He made a point of staying in communication with everyone he came in contact with over his fifty-year career as a professional writer, and he had thousands of fans and friends that he corresponded with all over the world.

The publishers of L. Ron Hubbard's literary works wish to continue this tradition and would very much welcome letters and comments from you, his readers, both old and new.

Any message addressed to the Author's Affairs Director at Bridge Publications will be given prompt and full attention.

BRIDGE PUBLICATIONS, INC.
4751 Fountain Avenue
Los Angeles, California 90029